Sheila O'Flanagan is the author of many bestselling novels, including *All For You, Stand By Me, The Perfect M___ ___eone Special, Bad Behaviour, You___ ___ ___ow?* and *Anyone But Him,* a___ ___ ___ions *Destinations, Connections* ___ *___ ___ Remember.*

Sheila O'Flanagan has always loved telling stories. After working in banking and finance for a number of years, she decided it was time to fulfil a dream and give writing her own book a go. She is now the author of more than fifteen bestselling titles, and lives in Dublin with her partner.

Praise for Sheila O'Flanagan's bestsellers:

'Romantic and charming, a real must-read'   *Closer*

'Her lightness of touch and gentle characterisations have produced another fine read'   *Sunday Express*

'A great read and the perfect escape from those dreary winter evenings'   *Sun*

'Sheila O'Flanagan is one of the blinding talents on the female fiction scene'   *Daily Record*

'A big, comfortable, absorbing book . . . bound to delight fans and guaranteed to put O'Flanagan on the bestsellers list – yet again'   *Irish Independent Review*

'Hugely enjoyable'   *Best*

By Sheila O'Flanagan and available from Headline Review

Sheila O'Flanagan
Better Together

headline
review

First published in 2012
by HEADLINE REVIEW
An imprint of HEADLINE PUBLISHING GROUP

First published in paperback in 2013
by HEADLINE REVIEW

2

ISBN 978 0 7553 7841 8 (B-format)
ISBN 978 1 4722 0661 9 (B-format)
ISBN 978 0 7553 9869 0 (A-format)

Typeset in ITC Galliard by Palimpsest Book Production Limited, Falkirk, Stirlingshire
Printed and bound in Great Britain by Clays Ltd, St Ives plc

Headline's policy is to use papers that are natural, renewable and recyclable products and made from wood grown in sustainable forests. The logging and manufacturing processes are expected to conform to the environmental regulations of the country of origin.

HEADLINE PUBLISHING GROUP
An Hachette UK Company
338 Euston Road
London NW1 3BH

www.headline.co.uk
www.hachette.co.uk

Acknowledgements

When it comes to turning the idea in my head into a book that people can read, things are always better together! I'm very fortunate in having some really wonderful people who work with me on the way. And so many, many thanks to:

My agent, Carole Blake
My editor, Marion Donaldson
The fantastic people at Hachette/Headline
All of my publishers and translators around the world.

My family and friends have been a constant support and I can't thank them enough.

Special thanks to Colm, for everything.

A big thank you to Andrea Smith for the entertaining and informative chat about freelance journalism, though sadly the gossipy bits couldn't be used . . .

Thanks to the booksellers and librarians who do such a great job in bringing the joy of reading to so many people.

And, of course, enormous thanks to all my readers, both of the printed books and the digital versions. I feel as though I know many of you personally now, through my website, Facebook and Twitter. It's always a joy to meet you virtually and in real life too. Happy reading!

Prologue

Sheridan Gray knew that the piece she had written, full of tragedy, drama and long-kept secrets, was one of the strongest she'd ever done. It was a compelling story and she'd got the balance just right. She'd been sympathetic where sympathy would be expected, and critical where it was important to criticise. It was everything she'd been asked for and more. It would change the lives of the people concerned for ever.

And it would change hers too. At least that was what she hoped. That was why she'd written it. To change everything. Back to the way it was before. Back to when she'd had everything she'd ever wanted.

Well, almost.

She stared unblinkingly at the computer. Was it ever possible to go back? And would she ever be able to forget the people about whom she'd just written? People who had become part of her life.

She had to. Because that was the only way to be a winner. She'd always wanted to be a winner, and with this story, she was.

1

The only problem, she realised, as she saved the document and closed her laptop, was that she didn't know if the prize was worth it. Or even if it was the prize she truly wanted any more.

Chapter 1

Sheridan was so engrossed in the newspaper report she was writing that she dismissed the notification about a new email in her inbox without even thinking. Her fingers continued to fly over the keyboard as she described the carnival atmosphere in Dublin the previous night, where an unprecedented crowd had turned up to watch the Brazil women's national soccer team play a friendly match in the city. It had been a fun evening, full of colour and good humour, helped by the unexpectedly balmy weather which, as Sheridan now wrote, the Brazilian women had brought with them – along with their footballing skills, cheerful personalities and undoubted good looks. A large portion of the sizeable crowd had been teenage boys following the footballers' every move, and every time the glamorous striker got the ball, the stadium had been illuminated by thousands of flashlights as they took yet another photo of her. After the match the ladies had posed for more photos on the pitch, much to the delight of the supporters.

From Sheridan's point of view it had been a lovely assignment, in sharp contrast to the times when she was sent to the back of beyond to watch dour men's matches in torrential rain. She wanted the readers of the *City Scope* – Dublin's biggest newspaper – to absorb the atmosphere too and, she admitted to herself, she wanted to present women excelling in what was generally seen as a men's sport in the most positive light she could.

So she was taking special care about the piece, making sure she got the balance exactly right. It wasn't until Martyn Powell, the sports editor, pushed a pile of papers out of the way and sat on the edge of her desk that she glanced up from the screen in front of her.

'Looks like D-Day.' Martyn's naturally long face was even gloomier than usual, his drooping moustache adding to his hangdog expression. 'It's from the top.'

Sheridan felt her heart beat faster as she opened the email, which was headed 'The Future of the *City Scope*', and scanned its contents.

Rumours about the paper where she'd worked for the past five years had been circulating for weeks. The staff had listened to every one of them and come up with some ideas of their own too, but nobody really knew what the fate of the thirty-year-old newspaper would be. Changes would have to be made, they all acknowledged that. The newspaper industry was in a precarious state and the *City Scope* had been haemorrhaging money over the past year. Everyone knew that something had to give sooner or later. The reporters had been gossiping for weeks. Now it looked like the time had come.

'What d'you think?' asked Martyn.

'I haven't a clue.' Sheridan pulled her flame-red curls back from her face and secured them with a lurid green bobble, which she took from her desk drawer. 'I suppose they can try some more cutbacks.'

The paper had introduced a raft of cost-cutting initiatives a few months earlier, most of which had irritated the journalists without delivering the required savings.

'I hope it's only cutbacks,' said Martyn. 'And not anything worse.'

'Well yes. So do I.' Sheridan tightened the bobble. 'But we're an institution, Marty, they have to come up with something.'

'Huh. So far all they've come up with is reducing expenses. Ours, not theirs, of course.'

Sheridan grinned. Martyn was a man who liked to take full advantage of his expense account.

'How's the piece going?' Martyn nodded at the open document on her computer screen.

'Nearly finished.' She glanced at it herself. 'It was good fun and nice to see the ladies on the pitch for a change.'

'There were some real crackers there all right.' Martyn had been looking at the photos earlier.

'Skilful athletes,' Sheridan reminded him, and he nodded even though she knew he only paid lip service to women's sporting abilities. 'And not a diva among them.'

'I wonder will we all still be here to report on the European Cup qualifiers?' asked Martyn, who enjoyed talking football with the paper's only female sports reporter.

'I hope so.' Sheridan looked worried. 'Ireland has a great chance this time. I want to get the *Scope* totally behind the team.'

'You're supposed to be impartial.'

'Get lost, Powell.' She roared with laughter. 'When was the *City Scope* ever impartial about football?'

Martyn's smile still wasn't enough to rid him of his gloomy

expression, but the conversation had temporarily taken their minds off the contents of the email. Which had said that there would be a meeting of all staff in the boardroom at noon. Everyone was expected to attend.

The boardroom of the *City Scope* wasn't really big enough to accommodate all of the newspaper's staff, so they stood shoulder to shoulder in the limited space as they waited for the arrival of the management team. There was a buzz of chatter as people speculated on the news that Ernie Johnson, the managing director, might bring. But Sheridan wasn't talking. She was considering all the possible outcomes and not liking any of them.

The worst, of course, was that the newspaper might close down. But that was utterly unthinkable. The *City Scope*, with its extensive sports coverage, had been in existence all of her life. Even before she'd joined the paper, reading it had been a major part of her week. When she'd finally landed a job there, she hadn't quite been able to believe it. And it had turned out to be the best job in the world. Even though she'd originally studied journalism to get away from sport. Even though she'd wanted to carve a very different career for herself.

Sheridan Gray had grown up in a sports-mad family. Sitting down in front of *Match of the Day*, *Sportsnight* and *Grandstand* was practically mandatory in the Gray household (as had been the daily purchase of the *City Scope*, widely regarded as the paper with the most authoritative sports section in the country). Sheridan's father and her two older brothers played both soccer and Gaelic football, and her mum was a PE teacher. But Sheridan wasn't obsessed in the same way as her parents and her brothers, and (being perfectly honest about it, although she wouldn't dream of saying so out loud) she disliked competing against other people. This was in contrast to everyone else in the family, who didn't believe that it was the taking part and not the winning that counted; as far as they were concerned, winning was the most important thing of all.

Sheridan didn't know why the competitive gene that ran so strongly through her parents and her brothers had passed her by, but the truth was that her favourite sporting activity was simply running by herself, not trying to beat anyone, not even the clock. She enjoyed jogging, which she found relaxing, and she needed relaxation because the Gray household, caught up as it always was with matches that the others were involved in, was rarely a relaxing place to be.

For most of her childhood it had been a given that she would spend weekends with her mother, Alice, on the sidelines of a pitch, wrapped up in a quilted anorak, warm gloves and knitted hat against the biting cold, while shouting encouragement at the men in her family. Afterwards there would be endless, sometimes heated, discussions about the match. The coach's selections were analysed, as was the team's performance, the opposition's tactics and even the level of support that both teams received. Sheridan would listen to the conversation without taking part. As far as she was concerned she'd done her bit by screaming until her throat was sore.

Matt and Con, her brothers, were picked to play for the Dublin Gaelic football team when they were old enough, which was the pinnacle of success as far as everyone in the family was concerned. They threw a huge party the day the announcement was made and Alice (not normally known for her baking skills) produced an enormous rectangular cake, which she'd decorated to look like a football pitch. Plastic figures wearing green shirts were placed in each goal mouth to represent Matt and Con, while a referee in the middle took the place of their father, Pat.

It was unfortunate, Sheridan thought, that her brothers' time with the Dublin team had also coincided with a slump in its fortunes, otherwise there would have been even bigger and better parties to celebrate more success. However, the Gray boys, as they were known, were always given high praise by the media for their unstinting efforts on behalf of their county, and indeed for their local club too, which regularly won the league, more often than not due to a spectacular shot from one or other of the boys.

It was when these reports (always from the *City Scope*) were being solemnly read out that Sheridan felt both proud of and yet disconnected from the rest of her family. She couldn't understand why being beaten totally devastated Matt and Con, and left them stomping around the house, slamming doors and impossible to talk to. Both Alice and Pat seemed to think that this was perfectly normal behaviour, but Sheridan asked herself why on earth they didn't just get over it. She was used to hearing people say 'it's only a game', but as far as the Grays were concerned, it seemed to be so much more than that.

As she grew older, she became impatient with their obsessions. She wished that she lived in a house where she didn't fall over football boots as soon as she walked in the door, and wasn't greeted by a forest of drying sports shirts in the kitchen every day. She longed to have discussions on hair and make-up from time to time (something she knew woefully little about) instead of listening to constant arguments about disallowed penalties and professional fouls. But there was nobody to have these discussions with. Alice wasn't the sort of person who devoted much time to hair and beauty. She was a tall, trim woman who kept her greying hair short and whose main beauty product was an industrial-sized jar of Pond's moisturiser which she kept on the bathroom shelf, between the cans of Lynx and tubs of Brylcreem. And the truth was that Sheridan couldn't categorise herself as the kind of girl who knew a lot about beauty either. Despite her weekly jogs, she didn't have the lean, wiry build of a runner. She was as sturdy as her brothers, broad shouldered and statuesque rather than thin and elegant, and infinitely more comfortable in jeans and jumpers than dresses and high heels. From time to time she went on a blitz of fashion shopping with some of her friends, but more often than not the micro miniskirts or tight boots that had seemed like a good idea at the time ended up unworn in the back of her wardrobe, a testament to the fact that her thighs were the body feature she disliked the most.

Her relationship with the opposite sex was, in many ways, as comfortable as the clothes she preferred to wear. Unlike many of her female friends, she didn't get tongue-tied in the presence of a boy she'd never met before, because she was accustomed to a constant stream of beefy soccer and GAA players traipsing in and out of the house, and she was perfectly at ease talking to any of them – especially as their conversation was generally about their matches, and she'd been to most of them. She knew that men weren't mysterious creatures who would magically change your life. She knew that they could get anxious and worried just like girls – although, in fairness, usually about different things. Matt and Con were rarely anxious about their dates; they were more concerned about their matches. Nevertheless, when Con was stressing about where to bring the lovely Bevanne Dickinson the first time they were going out together, Sheridan was the one to suggest that taking her to see *Jerry Maguire* in the warmth of the cinema would probably be better fun for her than standing on the terraces in the rain watching a League of Ireland match; and when Matt was at a loss to know what to get for his girlfriend's eighteenth birthday, she told him firmly that Melissa would prefer a dainty watch to the bulky thing with multiple functions and two different timers he was considering. The boys were always surprised when she came up with girlie tips but always grateful for what was generally the right advice. In turn, they steered her away from men they regarded as messers and not good enough for her (even though she didn't always agree with them and didn't solely judge prospective boyfriends on their footballing prowess).

In the end, most of the guys she eventually dated were people she'd met at one sporting fixture or another. They generally knew her parents and her brothers, and seemed to regard her as more of a friend than a girlfriend. They usually brought her to rugby matches (which she enjoyed) or to dark and gloomy bars (which she didn't quite as much – she preferred the trend for bright, modern gastro-pubs that was beginning to hit the country). Most of them, at some point or another, would tell her that it was great to go out with someone like her, a decent sort who liked a laugh, could talk soccer, rugby and GAA and could get ready for a date in less than ten minutes.

Sheridan wasn't insulted by being regarded as a decent sort rather than a sex symbol. After all, she didn't think her body could ever be regarded as sexy, and her interest in make-up and clothes was fairly minimal. She didn't mind a dash of lip gloss before she went out, but the idea of spending absolutely hours in front of the mirror, like some of the girls she knew, bored her beyond belief. Besides, she couldn't help thinking that it was far better to be someone that men felt comfortable talking to, and who got on with them all (even if most of her relationships petered out after a couple of months), rather than one of the group of air-headed, giggling women who seemed to regard them as creatures that they would never understand and who were a prize to be won if they only knew how. Sheridan felt that she had a lot to be thankful for in that respect and was glad that the opposite sex wasn't a mystery to her; in fact there were times she felt that she knew far too much about them and their interests. However, there were also times when she felt a bit of an outsider among her friends because she was never at ease participating in breathless conversations about fanciable guys. She wondered if she'd ever meet someone who would fill her every waking thought, or turn her legs to jelly, or make her think that an evening spent waxing her legs and plucking her eyebrows was worth the pain. Somehow she doubted it.

That feeling of being an outsider extended to her home life too, although the reasons were different. But she couldn't help feeling distant from the rest of her family whenever she looked at Matt and Con's trophies, the symbols of their success, which were proudly displayed in the huge walnut cabinet in the corner of the room, and totally dwarfed the only award she'd ever won. This was a plastic medal for the under-10s girls' five-a-side football tournament (which wasn't a proper tournament at all but was designed to give the girls the chance to kick the ball around and wear themselves out, while their mothers sat in the clubhouse for a cup of tea and a chat, and for which all of the young participants had received a medal).

She didn't want to be an airhead but she didn't always want to be the fallback girl that men dated when they couldn't get anyone else either. (Matt's friends in particular used her as a last-minute date whenever they needed someone, knowing that she'd enter into the spirit of whatever the occasion was.) She didn't need to be a winner but nor did she want to be the perennial loser in her testosterone-filled family home. Most of the time she was comfortable in her own skin, but occasionally it was hard to be the one who simply didn't match up, no matter how hard she tried.

Matt and Con both went to college after school, choosing to study business while hoping to get jobs that would allow them plenty of time to devote to playing for their football club. Sheridan knew that she didn't have a business brain and wanted a job that could become a career. Alice suggested that she follow in her footsteps and become a PE teacher (you mightn't be all that good at competing yourself, she told Sheridan, but you know how it should be done). Sheridan had scotched that idea immediately. She wanted to do something dramatically different from the rest of the family. She needed to break out on her own.

She decided to study journalism on a whim, mainly because one of her teachers complimented her on a report she'd done on the school fashion show. Miss Kavanagh said that it had been a vivid piece of writing that had brought the show to life for anyone who read the piece. Was Sheridan very interested in fashion? she asked.

It was a question that reduced Sheridan to fits of laughter, and Miss Kavanagh, realising that designer dresses were intended for women who looked like a half-decent puff of wind would blow them over rather than well-built girls like Sheridan, looked suitably embarrassed. Sheridan told her not to worry, that she'd enjoyed writing the piece because it was about something so alien to her, which led Miss Kavanagh to sigh with relief; although then Sheridan remarked that nobody would take seriously as a fashion journalist a woman who liked her food and had never been on a crash diet. Miss Kavanagh tried to convince her otherwise but Sheridan knew that she was wasting her time. All the same, she thought, maybe she could become an investigative reporter and one day have her name in big print beneath a story that could be added to the enormous file of cuttings that Alice kept documenting Con and Matt's successes on the playing field. And maybe then she'd finally feel like a success in her own right too.

By the time she qualified, however, the economy was sluggish and jobs were hard to come by. Instead of going straight on to a busy news desk as she'd hoped, she'd ended up in the classifieds section of a daily newspaper, looking after the personal notices that covered births, marriages and deaths. She didn't need a college qualification to take down funeral details, but she did always wonder about the person concerned, the life they'd led and the people they'd left behind. She liked the birth notices best, amusing herself by guessing what kind of life the baby would have based on the name chosen by its parents. Samanthas, she decided, would be blonde and beautiful, and marry for money. Kates had to be groomed, businesslike and destined for success. Jackies would be sporty. If Pat and Alice had called her Jackie, then she might have fulfilled whatever sporting dream they had for her.

In fact they'd chosen to name her after Martin Sheridan, a five-time Olympic gold-medallist. Born Bohola, County Mayo, in 1881, Martin had also won three silvers and a bronze representing the USA in the discus, shot putt, high jump and long jump. Pat and Alice had clearly believed that he'd be someone for Sheridan to live up to, but all that had happened was that she'd been teased mercilessly for having two surnames (she'd once suggested that simply tacking on an 'a' to his first name would have saved her a lot of grief, but Alice had shaken her head and told her that Sheridans were tougher than Martinas).

When she'd seen the ad for a junior reporter for the *City Scope* sports desk she almost hadn't bothered replying. She wanted to do hard news, to report on politics and crime, not football matches. But she was going steadily crazy in classifieds and she thought that getting any reporter's job would be better than nothing.

It surprised her, when she was offered it, at how pleased she was. It surprised her even more how much she enjoyed it.

She'd never thought that all the times she'd spent cheering on Con and Matt would be good for anything. Or that she'd learned so much from the after-match debates at home. Or that she knew as much as she did about the winners and runners-up in so many different events. It was her encyclopaedic knowledge of All-Ireland football winners that had stunned Martyn Powell when he interviewed her. But it was her analysis of a recent Republic of Ireland soccer match that had convinced him that she was the best person for the job.

'I never met anyone as knowledgeable as you,' he'd said. 'You can even explain the offside rule in a single sentence.'

'The offside rule is usually overly complicated by men who like to make it mysterious,' she'd told him cheerfully. 'As is most stuff about sport.'

'If you write as clearly as you talk, I think you could have a good future at this paper,' Martyn remarked.

Sheridan couldn't help smiling at his words. She'd been told that she was pretty when she smiled (Decco Grainger, three dates and a lot of kissing practice, had been the one to offer the compliment), but Martyn often said that when Sheridan smiled she reminded him of a happy cocker spaniel, with her glossy hair framing her generous face, and her big golden-brown eyes alight with enthusiasm. Sheridan herself wasn't quite convinced that being likened to a cocker spaniel was a compliment, but she supposed it was better than being compared to a Jack Russell. She'd suckered him at the interview with her smile, Martyn told her, even though she lacked the experience that other candidates had. But there was something about her that made him think he'd found the perfect addition to the team.

And Sheridan definitely was.

At first she was sent to cover local events that nobody else wanted to bother with. She never minded, even when she got lost looking for a small club in the middle of nowhere.

15

She drove her two-year-old VW Beetle all over the country and found herself once again on the sidelines of windswept pitches, although this time, instead of cheering herself hoarse, she was making notes on the game.

Afterwards, though, it was her opinion that counted, her words that people read and sometimes reacted to, by emailing the newspaper and sharing their own views.

'I always knew you'd find your niche one day,' Alice told her one evening as she read the piece Sheridan had written about a League of Ireland football match between rival clubs Shamrock Rovers and Shelbourne. 'This is a great report.'

'Thanks.'

'You see – all those times we took you to the football were worth it.'

'Yes.'

'I'm sure the goalie was sick when he gave away the penalty.'

'So were the supporters.'

'Did you enjoy the match?'

'Of course. It's kind of nice to watch and not care who wins.'

Alice looked horrified. 'You always have to care who wins.'

'I'd be exhausted if that was the case,' Sheridan told her. 'You can't pick a side every time. People don't want to know who I want to win, they want to know what the game was like.'

'Hmm.' Alice didn't sound convinced.

'If you were a Hoops supporter, you wouldn't want to think I was writing from a Rovers point of view, would you?'

'No,' conceded Alice.

'Anyway, Martyn Powell is very happy with me,' said Sheridan.

'Good.' Alice sounded pleased. Then she took a pair of scissors from the kitchen drawer.

'What are you doing?' asked Sheridan.

'Cutting out the report,' replied Alice. 'It's the first one they've put your name on.'

'I know.' Sheridan hadn't wanted to make a big deal of having her byline in the paper, but the truth was she was very excited about it. And the fact that her mother was too wrapped her in a warm glow of self-satisfaction.

Over the following years at the paper there had been more and more pieces with her byline. So many that Alice stopped cutting them all out. Sheridan didn't mind. She'd found her place. And finally she felt like a winner in the family too.

She stopped reminiscing when Ernie Johnson walked into the room. From the look on his face she could see that he didn't have unqualified good news to share. The rest of the staff could see it too, and a quiet murmur of anxiety rippled through them before he held up his hand for silence.

He spoke about the newspaper's iconic status over the past thirty years and about the great stories it had broken. Then he went on to remind them that times were tough, that the print media in particular was suffering, that competition was fierce and that they couldn't go on losing money.

The journalists were expecting the worst. The picture Ernie had painted was so bleak that they couldn't see how the paper could possibly last another day. But then Ernie smiled.

'Up to last week it was looking very much like the *City Scope* would fold,' he said. 'But I'm pleased to say that we've had a cash injection from an investor who has taken a stake in our business.'

The ripple broke through the journalists again. Of course there had been talk of new investors, but they'd been doubtful that anyone would be interested in the ailing newspaper.

'That's the good news,' said Ernie. 'The bad news is that costs are still an issue. I'm sorry to say that even with a cash injection there will be some redundancies.'

The ripple had become a buzz now as people turned to each other, each immediately worried about his or her own future, but equally worried about the ability of the newspaper to live up to its ideals with a further decrease in the number of reporters.

'I've already had numerous consultations with our investor,' said Ernie. 'We'll be in touch with you all before the end of the week about the redundancy packages.'

'So what d'you think of all that?' asked Talia Brehon as they walked back to their desks. Talia was every inch a fashion editor, with shoulder-length, honey-blond hair, a tall, slender body, impeccably made-up face, and a size zero capsule wardrobe.

Sheridan knew it often surprised people that as well as working together on the *City Scope*, she and Talia also shared an apartment in Kilmainham, a few kilometres from the newspaper offices. Talia had been looking for someone to share with her at around the same time as Sheridan had needed somewhere to live. Pat had retired and was keeping his promise to Alice to move back to Kerry, where she was originally from. By that stage, all of their children were working and self-sufficient, so they'd decided to sell their house in Dublin. When Sheridan had seen the email Talia sent round the paper looking for a flatmate, she'd replied straight away, although at that time she hadn't known the fashion editor very well.

They'd met for coffee to talk it over. In her small-ad days, Sheridan would've put Talia in the same category as the Samanthas, and she would certainly have been right as far as her glamour was concerned. But although Talia shared her looks with the models she so frequently wrote about, she was also one of the most down-to-earth people Sheridan had ever met. Nevertheless, she couldn't help thinking that sharing an apartment with someone as feminine as Talia would be the ultimate in life-changing experiences.

It hadn't entirely been like that, because at home Talia liked sloping around in comfortable tracksuits and trainers rather than designer clothes (although her sports gear of choice was Stella McCartney for Adidas), and the apartment was cool and chic rather than pink and girlie; but she did introduce Sheridan to the joys of concealers and pore mini-misers, while Sheridan reciprocated by demonstrating how to change the filter in the washing machine and mend the leaky shower. Both girls enjoyed each other's company and the flat-share worked out better than either of them had anticipated.

'I wonder who the investor is?' mused Sheridan.

'Paudie O'Malley,' replied Talia promptly. 'I've just been talking to our esteemed business editor, who has the inside scoop. Apparently Paudie expressed an interest a while back but they rebuffed him. Now he's in on better terms.'

'God Almighty.' Sheridan felt slightly sick. 'Slash-and-Burn O'Malley's finally got his claws into us. We're toast.'

'He has a hard nose when it comes to business all right,' acknowledged Talia.

'He makes Scrooge look like Santa Claus!' wailed Sheridan. 'Our first story will have a picture of him cracking the austerity whip.'

Talia laughed. 'According to Alo, he's only taken a twenty-five per cent stake. His influence will be limited. And he's reclusive. I don't think there's been a picture of him in the papers for years.'

'Just 'cos people don't see him much doesn't mean he can't be ruthless.' Sheridan nibbled anxiously at her thumbnail. 'What d'you think about our jobs?'

'Ah, you'll be fine, the *Scope* is famed for its sports coverage.'

'Hmm. I'm not sure that sport is an O'Malley priority. He's into business and politics, isn't he?'

'He'll still need good sports reporters, and you got that great interview with our latest Italian manager, didn't you?'

Sheridan grinned. 'I was lucky. Con was going out with an Italian girl who knew his interpreter at the time.'

'You make your own luck,' said Talia.

'True. Oh well, I'll just keep my fingers crossed.'

'Me too,' Talia told her. 'Whatever Paudie feels about sport, I'm pretty certain he's not that interested in fashion.'

'He won't be able to resist you,' Sheridan told her friend. 'You can twist men around your little finger. C'mon. Let's go for a drink. We could do with something to take the edge off today.'

'Aren't you meeting love's young dream?' asked Talia.

'Nope. Griff is at his mother's house tonight. It's her birthday, so they're having a family dinner.'

'And you weren't invited?' Talia arched an eyebrow.

'Quite frankly, even if I had been, I wouldn't have wanted

to go. I'm scared of that woman! And as for his sisters – five of them – they're just too much for me. It's like being on the set of *Pride and Prejudice* when they start yammering on like excitable sparrows.'

'While you're the intellectual Elizabeth and Griff is the irresistible Mr Darcy?'

'Not entirely,' said Sheridan. 'I'm not exactly famed for my intellect, and thankfully Griff isn't all brooding and sulky – I did think Darcy could've done with a good slap myself. But I'm lucky to have a boyfriend who's so great and who remembers things like birthdays and anniversaries and all that stuff.'

'You guys must be coming up to an anniversary soon,' said Talia.

'One year next week.' Sheridan sounded smug. 'I never would've thought that I'd land myself someone like him, to be honest. He's so good looking and I'm so . . . so . . .'

'Sheridan Gray! What have I told you before? You're a very attractive woman and he's lucky to have you for a girlfriend!'

Sheridan smiled at her friend. 'And you say the nicest things. But I've got to be honest. I can scrub up OK when I make a big effort, but I can't do the whole slinky-dress routine or wear high heels. You know that.'

'High heels are overrated,' said Talia darkly. 'I nearly broke my ankle wearing the Manolos I brought back from Milan.'

'I love having a friend who talks about Manolos and Milan,' said Sheridan. 'It makes me feel very cosmopolitan.'

'Well I love having a friend who can get me freebies to the footie and the rugby,' said Talia. 'It makes me feel part of the sporty set.'

'You're such a fool, Brehon.'

'So are you. Right. Let's get to the pub before the news department does. You know what they're like. They'll have it drunk dry in an hour.'

Chapter 2

When Sheridan went in to work the following day, Martyn immediately asked her to see him in the conference room. Her heart was beating wildly in her chest as she followed him; his face was even gloomier than usual and he sounded dispirited. She wondered how hard the axe had fallen on the sports department, and she wondered even more how it would affect her.

Ten minutes later she was sitting in the chair opposite him trying hard not to cry. Martyn had been as sympathetic as she'd ever known him to be; he'd told her over and over how sorry he was that Paudie O'Malley had insisted on the redundancy programme in return for his investment. The businessman was looking to cut the overall staff on the paper by thirty, and every department would have to let someone go. The sports desk would lose two people, and Sheridan was one of them. Martyn said that it was a sad day for the *City Scope* and that even though the paper had been saved, the cost was catastrophic.

Catastrophic was a word Sheridan never used in her reports. Nothing about sport was catastrophic. A great loss was still just a loss in a game, after all. She always tried to keep that in mind even as she acknowledged that for many people sport was more than just a game.

But today's news was a catastrophe for her. From the moment Martyn had told her he was sorry but that there wasn't a job for her any more, she'd felt as though someone had punched her in the stomach. She couldn't believe that she was being let go. She was a good member of the team. She worked hard. She pulled her weight. Hell, she even more than pulled her weight sometimes. Hadn't her vast knowledge of winners and losers in All-Ireland finals stopped Martyn from giving the OK on a report in which he'd reversed the result of the 1987 match, giving the win to Cork instead of to Meath? Something that would have made the paper look very stupid. He'd been relieved when she'd pointed it out to him, and stunned too – surely, he'd said, she was too young to remember it?

'I was four,' she'd told him. 'And I don't remember the game, but we had a big wall chart at home with the draw on it, that's how I know.'

All the wall charts in the world were irrelevant now. The department was being downsized and she was being let go.

'Is it because I'm a woman?' she asked.

'Don't be silly,' said Martyn. 'Legally that'd be a minefield! Besides, we've never treated you like a girl here. You know that.'

That was true. She'd fitted in with them because she was relaxed around men and the sort of person who could hold her own in a sporting conversation. She also had the ability to drink a pint of beer as quickly as any of them. (Not something she did very often these days, because it usually went to her head, but it had been very effective in getting her accepted into the macho fold.) They hadn't made any concessions to her femininity. She wouldn't have expected them to either.

'It was on seniority.' Martyn sighed. 'I'm sorry, Sheridan, I really am.'

'Who else is going from sports?'

'Ronan Kearney.'

She nodded. Ronan had joined around the same time as her.

'I hate all this,' said Martyn. 'It'll change the paper completely. We're going to take more stuff from agencies. Paudie O'Malley has media interests in the UK as well as Ireland. He's an investor in a couple of local papers and radio stations, and I believe he's diversifying into telecoms too.'

Sheridan couldn't have cared less about Paudie O'Malley's business empire. All she cared about was that he'd put her out of work, the capitalist bastard!

'I'm sure you'll get something else,' said Martyn. 'You're a good reporter, Sheridan.'

'Not good enough, obviously.'

'Look on this as an opportunity,' he said. 'Maybe you'll get something even better. And you can always freelance. I'm sure any editor would love to get stuff from you.'

'The *City Scope* is one of the best newspapers there is!' cried Sheridan. 'Working here *was* my great opportunity. I don't want to be a freelancer. I want to work for a decent newspaper.'

'I'm sorry,' said Martyn again.

Sheridan had never cried in front of anyone on the paper before, but she knew she was about to now. So she got up from the chair and hurried quickly to the Ladies', where she locked herself in a cubicle and only came out when Talia eventually banged on the door asking if she was all right.

'How can I be all right?' Sheridan asked later that evening when they were (once again) in the pub closest to the *Scope*'s offices. 'How can I be all right when I know that I'm better than Martyn bloody Powell but I'm the one who's been given the boot? How d'you think that makes me feel?'

'It's not fair,' said Talia, as she'd already said more than a dozen times since Sheridan had emerged, blotchy faced, from the cubicle.

Sheridan emptied her bottle of beer into the glass in front of her. It was her fourth since they'd arrived and she was beginning to feel its effects.

'I know it's not just me,' she said. 'I know other people have lost their jobs too. I realise that.' She sniffed. 'It's just that I loved it. OK, it wasn't what I'd started out thinking about, but I worked my way into it. And I did well. Now it's been whipped away from me and I can't believe it.'

'I'm so sorry.' Talia had said this more than a dozen times too. 'I feel terrible about it.'

'You're not to feel guilty because they're keeping you on,' Sheridan told her. 'I'm glad for you, honestly.'

'I know.'

'I'm the one who should apologise, for being so self-absorbed.' She scrabbled in her bag for a tissue and blew her nose loudly.

'Hey, you've had terrible news. You're entitled to feel self-absorbed.'

'It's just . . .' Sheridan stared unseeingly across the pub.

'How am I going to tell them this at home? They'll be so disappointed in me.'

Talia was startled. 'They'll be disappointed *for* you, not *in* you,' she corrected her.

'No,' said Sheridan. 'They'll think it's my own fault. That there's a reason I was picked. They'll assume it's because I was the weakest person at the paper, or at least in the sports department. That's how they think. It'll be like the time I was dropped from the basketball team at school. They reckoned it was because I wasn't trying hard enough. Mam said I needed to make my presence felt a bit more, and I told her I was trying, and she said if I wasn't good enough I deserved to be dropped even if I *was* doing the best I could against girls who were way faster than me.'

'Wow,' said Talia. 'That's a bit harsh.'

'It's not that she's harsh.' Sheridan defended her mother. 'She doesn't sugar-coat things, that's all. She sees life through the eyes of a coach. Like my dad. They look at the bigger picture all the time, and I wasn't good enough for the bigger picture.'

'Well I don't know what the *Scope*'s big picture is, but you were certainly good enough for it.'

'Sometimes a coach benches good players anyway.' Sheridan's voice was glum. 'Oh Talia, I can't believe this. It's so unfair.' Then she looked anxiously at her friend. 'I'm good for the rent this month,' she said. 'I can pay my way for a while from my savings. And I'll have my statutory redundancy plus another couple of months that they're giving us too. Hopefully I'll get another job before that runs out and everything'll be fine.'

'I wasn't even thinking about that,' said Talia truthfully.

'Don't get into a state about it, Sher. I'm sure it'll all work out in the end.'

It was about an hour later that the door of the pub was pushed open and Griff Gibson walked inside. Everyone turned to look at him because Griff was a striking figure – a tall man with corn-coloured hair, wearing a black leather jacket, black jeans and black boots.

He sat down beside Sheridan and hugged her.

'How's my honey?' he asked.

'Not good,' said Talia over Sheridan's head. 'She switched from Bud to Jemmies half an hour ago.'

'Whiskey!' exclaimed Griff. 'She doesn't drink whiskey.'

'Only on shitty days,' mumbled Sheridan. 'And this has been a shitty day.'

'I know,' said Griff. 'But you'll get over it. They don't deserve you anyway.'

'Stop with the trying-to-be-nice-to-me stuff,' she said. 'They made some kind of commercial decision that I wasn't good enough. That I'm a loser.'

'That's nonsense,' said Griff. 'You're not a loser to me.'

'But I am to them,' said Sheridan.

'She keeps talking like this,' Talia told him. 'Obsessing about winners and losers. Blaming it on herself.'

'For crying out loud, Sher, you've done a cracking job,' Griff said.

'Still not good enough.' Sheridan straightened up and rubbed her eyes. 'Stop talking about me as though I'm not here.' She sniffed and looked blearily at them. 'Sorry. I know I'm being an arse. I don't mean to be. I just can't help it.'

'It's perfectly understandable,' said Griff. 'C'mon. Let's go back to my place. You'll feel a lot better there.'

Talia looked at him gratefully.

'I need to phone my parents first,' said Sheridan. 'I have to tell them.'

'Leave it till the morning,' advised Talia. 'I know how your mum feels about drink. If she hears you now, she'll know you've been hitting the bottle. Probably best not.'

Sheridan's sigh came from the very depths of her being. 'Probably. Thanks, Talia. You're a lifesaver.'

'Yes, you are,' said Griff. 'I'll see you tomorrow, Talia. Meantime, I'll get her home.'

'Thanks,' said Talia again. She stood up and so did Sheridan. Talia put her arms around her and hugged her. 'It's going to be fine,' she told her friend. '*You're* going to be fine.'

'Maybe,' said Sheridan as she sniffed again. 'I know it should be an opportunity. I just don't know what kind of opportunity it could possibly be.'

Chapter 3

Nina Fallon worried at night. She didn't have time for worrying during the day because she was far too busy with running the guesthouse (even though that brought its own regular panic attacks, which sometimes left her frantically gulping for air); but in the dark, when everything was silent and she was alone in her bed, all the things that worried her most crowded her mind and kept her awake long after she wanted to be in a dreamless sleep.

She usually worried about the same things but not necessarily in the same order. The guest house, naturally. Her children, always. Her husband . . . she didn't want to worry about Sean any more, but she did. Although the truth was she couldn't be sure if she was actually worried about him, or whether her real worry was about herself.

She rolled over in the bed and let out a little yelp of pain. Tonight it wasn't worry that was keeping her awake but the pain in her back caused by the fact that she'd stupidly tried to move a heavy dresser in one of the guest bedrooms and had jarred her back doing it. That was the trouble about trying to do everything on your own. Sometimes something had to give.

But, she reminded herself, she was coping despite everything. The guesthouse was holding its own in the toughest times she'd ever experienced. She had a good relationship with her two children, although they were currently far from home. Alan was on a peacekeeping mission with the Defence Forces (thankfully not in the front line, though she still said a prayer for him first thing in the morning and before she got into bed each night); while Chrissie was backpacking in Australia. However, they were sensible people and kept in touch with her. In fact they probably kept in touch more with her when they were away than they ever did when they were in Ardbawn. So she always knew what they were up to.

But Sean. She felt her entire body tense up as she thought of Sean. Sean was another matter altogether. She could talk to her children and she could fix things in the guesthouse but she didn't know what the hell to do about Sean. She didn't know if she'd acted out of hurt or rage or bloody-mindedness, or even because she had no other course of action, but she still didn't know if she'd done the right thing. She occasionally wished there was someone she could turn to for advice, but Nina had always kept her problems to herself, even though she had plenty of friends who would be only too happy to discuss the state of her marriage with her. People in Ardbawn loved to dissect each other's relationships. Nina had never been like that. She wasn't interested in gossip and she certainly wasn't interested in being a topic of gossip either.

So, despite the concerned phone calls from people like Peggy Merchant (who ran the local riding school) and Hayley Goodwin (who'd phoned and said that she felt it was all her fault), she'd simply said that they were working their way through their issues and that hopefully things would be resolved in the best way possible. She knew she was talking bullshit, because they weren't working their way through anything and she truly didn't know what a good resolution would be, but she had to say something to keep them off her back. Rather embarrassingly, and entirely out of character for her, she'd turned to the horoscope column in the local paper for the comfort she wasn't able to accept from her friends. The last few weeks for Cancerians had all been about embracing change, but the honest truth was (as she allowed herself to admit during the night) that she hadn't wanted anything to change at all.

It was almost impossible to believe that a few months ago she would have been able to turn to Sean himself for comfort and he'd have sleepily rubbed her aching back, which would have relaxed her and helped her to drift off. Now, thinking of him sent a white rod of rage right through her, followed by the sweeping desolation that brought her, as always, to the brink of tears. She should be all cried out by now, she told herself, but she was nowhere near that state. She didn't know if her tears were because she'd been devastated by what Sean had done, or because she felt so foolish. She felt it was important to know, but she simply couldn't decide. So she worried about that too.

Yet it had all started out so innocuously, with no reason to worry at all. That was what was gut-wrenching about it. Plus the fact that she'd encouraged him, not realising what she was about to allow to happen. Not realising how it would all end.

She hadn't imagined that an unstoppable chain of events would be set in motion the day Hayley, the bubbly chairwoman of the local amateur dramatic society – and someone Nina regularly met for coffee in the Blue Rose café – called to the guesthouse to ask Sean if he'd be interested in putting an ad in the programme for their upcoming production of *Pygmalion*. Nina had continued preparing the evening meal while Hayley sat at the kitchen table and tried to persuade Sean to hand over some cash.

'I wish we could.' Sean looked up from the laptop on which he'd been balancing the bank statement. 'But the truth is that we don't have a red cent to spare this year. Do we, Nina?'

She paused at her peeling of potatoes for a moment, slightly irritated that he was putting her in the position of having to make the actual refusal, and shook her head. 'Afraid not,' she'd said. 'People are leaving it later and later to decide about holidays or short breaks. Our bookings have fallen to a trickle; sure, we haven't even got any guests here right now.'

'It's a tough time for everyone,' Hayley agreed. 'The hotel's quiet too.'

The Riverview Hotel was on the other side of the town (and the river) to the Bawnee River Guesthouse. It had been built during the last property boom and had an impressive spa and leisure centre as well as an over-the-top nightclub. At the time of its construction there had been much amusement at the thought of a nightclub in Ardbawn, but it had proved to be surprisingly popular, with people coming from the neighbouring towns every weekend. At first Sean and Nina had been worried about a possible loss of business to the hotel, but the people who came to the guesthouse (usually for fishing and horse-riding, with some occasional golfers) weren't the sort of people who wanted to stay in an ultra-modern hotel. And, as it turned out, the hotel drew more people to the town anyway, so the reality was it had been a bonus.

'Ah, well, times have been tough before and we've got through them,' Sean said brightly. 'We'll get through this too as long as we don't spend money on things we can't afford. Like the ad in your programme, Hayley. Sorry.'

'The hotel is taking an ad,' she told him.

'I wish we could.' He sounded truly regretful. 'But I never do anything without Nina's say-so. If it's any use, we can do a special deal for anyone who stays over in the town for the nights of the production.'

'That doesn't help the drama society,' Hayley pointed out.

'You might get people coming who otherwise wouldn't.' Sean's dark eyes twinkled at her.

'I doubt it,' she said.

'All the same, it's something to offer.'

'Hmm.' She looked doubtful.

'If you've got leaflets and stuff, we'll keep them here, of course,' said Sean, 'and we'll hand them out to our guests. You never know, some of them might return for the show.'

'You think?' Hayley was sceptical.

'The amateur dramatic group is very accomplished,' Sean assured her. 'Why shouldn't people travel to see them?' He allowed his eyes to twinkle at her again. 'Are you playing Eliza?'

Nina, whose back was to them, couldn't help smiling. Sean was turning on the charm. And he could be very, very charming.

'I'm not good enough,' Hayley told him. 'Lesley Chapman's got that role.'

'It's a great play,' Sean said. 'I'll definitely be along to watch.'

'You'd have made a good Henry Higgins yourself.' Hayley was blushing slightly. 'You've got a certain arrogance. And charisma . . .'

Nina glanced over her shoulder.

'I was a bit of an actor myself back in the day,' Sean said. 'In fact I did once star as Henry Higgins.'

'Really?' asked Hayley. 'When? And how come you've never joined us, in that case?'

'Oh, I don't have time for it these days. It was in my college years,' replied Sean. 'For one week only, but it was a great performance, according to the critics. Who were students too, so perhaps they were a bit biased, although they fancied themselves as harsh reviewers. After that I trod the boards for a time, but then . . .'

'. . . he met me and his priorities changed,' Nina finished for him.

'I just didn't get the breaks,' said Sean. 'I would've given George Clooney a run for his money.'

This time Nina guffawed. But Hayley looked at Sean appraisingly.

'You know,' she said. 'I absolutely think you would.'

After Hayley had gone, Nina sat down at the kitchen table.

'You were flirting with her,' she told her husband in amusement.

'Bringing a little glamour into her life,' Sean said. 'It must be dreary enough having nothing better to do than run a crummy amateur dramatics show with a bunch of losers.'

'You said they were very accomplished,' protested Nina.

'I was being polite,' said Sean. 'One or two of them are OK. Most of them are hopeless. And naturally the good parts go to the people who are the pushiest, not the ones who're best. There's no way Lesley Chapman's good enough for Eliza Doolittle.'

'How would you know?' asked Nina.

'Didn't she do a reading at that literary night you dragged me along to last month?' demanded Sean.

'That's true.'

'It was torture,' Sean said. 'Both the night and her damn reading.'

'It was important to be seen at it,' Nina told him. 'It's nice to be part of the community.'

'How can we be anything but part of this community?' he asked her. 'Haven't we lived here all our damn lives?'

It was hard to believe that she'd lived in the same town for ever. And yet Nina had always been a home-bird, someone who loved Ardbawn even though for most of her youth it had been a backwater, small and dreary and lacking in excitement. But then Nina wasn't much for excitement herself; she liked a quiet life, although, when she was older, she sometimes went up to Dublin with her mother or her older sister for a bout of shopping (the fashion business in Ardbawn providing particularly slim pickings). However, she wasn't as interested in the shops as her sister Bridie; she thought the capital was dirty and crowded and she always longed to be back in Ardbawn and their rambling house beside the river.

It had been a guesthouse for as long as she could remember. Dolores and John, her parents, had opened it the year she was born; at first as a sideline because John's paying job was in a creamery. But after he suffered a severe leg injury following an accident, he started to work in the guesthouse too. John had died a few years after the accident, leaving Dolores as the linchpin of the family. She was a stern matriarch who took no nonsense from her children – or from her guests. Nina's sister and two older brothers had moved out as soon as they possibly could, before, Bridie once said, Dolores's mean-spiritedness could wear them down. All of them had emigrated – Bridie to the States, Tom to New Zealand and Peadar to London. By the time Nina left school, all three of her siblings were married with families and had settled in their new homelands.

'You know enough about the guesthouse to be useful on a full-time basis,' Dolores Doherty told her daughter one day when she was loading an armful of bedlinen into the washing machine. 'It's a good asset in this family. And it can be yours. Anyhow, you're the only one who gives a damn about it.'

It wasn't entirely true that Nina cared about the guesthouse. She knew that it was hard work and she sometimes questioned its viability. But her whole life had been spent helping Dolores and so she was familiar with every aspect of how to run it.

She was twenty-five when Dolores died and left it to her. Her siblings sounded her out about selling the house and, indeed, she seriously thought about it herself, but after talking to the local auctioneer, she realised that there would be very limited interest in a difficult-to-heat, in-need-of-refurbishment, damp and rambling building near the river. He advised her to modernise it and think about selling when the market picked up. Her brothers and sisters agreed. Anyway, they said, they had no interest in returning to Ardbawn and they didn't need whatever money selling it might bring. She was welcome to it. Nina felt that they were just grateful that she'd been the one left at home to look after both the guesthouse and their mother. Not wanting money was a way of purging their guilt. The solicitor made sure that there couldn't be any comeback in the future (in case, he said merrily, property prices rose and the other Dohertys changed their minds), and so Nina was secure in her ownership. Peadar, the day he left, told her that it was more trouble than it was worth. It had been a drain on them all their lives.

Peadar wasn't entirely correct. Although its upkeep and maintenance was costly, the Bawnee River Guesthouse had a steady stream of visitors, mainly those who came for the fishing and who didn't mind Dolores's strict meals timetable, or sharing two draughty bathrooms between eight equally draughty rooms. But Nina knew that people now wanted warmth, en-suite bathrooms and better facilities. If she was to keep the guesthouse profitable, she would take the estate agent's advice and do some upgrading. There were possibilities for attracting more visitors too. In addition to the already excellent fishing opportunities, a new golf course was being developed a few miles outside the town, and there was a riding school which, she was sure, could offer lessons to guests. The way Nina looked at it, she'd been handed a potentially profitable business, but if she didn't modernise it she'd be left with a millstone round her neck. However, she wasn't at all sure that she knew how to go about changing things. Dolores had been a strong, domineering woman who was respected if not particularly liked in the community. Nina was considered a pale imitation, the girl who'd stayed at home to be with her mother, who hadn't had the guts to leave home like Bridie, Tom and Peadar. It didn't matter that this wasn't true, that Nina was happy to stay in Ardbawn and that (despite Dolores's testiness and difficult nature) she loved her mother. She was considered to be the loser in the family, regardless of the fact that she was now the owner of one of the biggest houses in the town.

It took her nearly two weeks to pluck up the courage to meet with the bank manager. It was a difficult encounter. Dominic Bradley patronised her throughout, remarking that she was a bit young to think about running the place single-handed and that she hardly had her mother's brain for business. Dolores was unique, Dominic told her. A special sort of woman. Nina was glad she'd spent so much time the night before going through the figures, so that, despite her nervousness, she was able to answer every question the bank manager put to her. She thought he was rather disappointed that he hadn't managed to trip her up, but in the end he said he'd let her know about the loan, although he doubted they'd be able to give her everything she wanted. Even though she felt deflated after talking to Dominic, she then went to see Peggy Merchant in the riding school about a joint venture offering B&B and riding lessons for an all-inclusive price. Peggy, surprised by the younger girl's visit, nevertheless agreed that it might be a bit of a money-spinner and she gave her some leaflets to put in the guesthouse. While she waited to hear from Dominic Bradley about the loan, Nina started to experiment with more exciting evening-meal choices than her mother's – substituting lasagnes and pastas for the stodgier fry-ups and chops that had been the usual offering. (Her success in changing the menu was rather limited. Most of the fishermen had loved Dolores's fry-ups.)

She'd hoped she'd have the renovations done by the beginning of the summer season, but the day she met Sean Fallon she was in a foul mood, frustrated by the lack of a positive response from the bank and thinking that her sister and brothers had been right and that her mother had left her a poisoned chalice. She'd come off the phone from Dominic Bradley, who'd told her that there was no point in her throwing a hissy fit, there were procedures to be followed before any loans could be authorised, and she was stomping angrily down the main street when she bumped into Sean. Literally.

'Hey, careful,' he said as he steadied himself. And his eyes narrowed as he looked at her. 'Bernadine, isn't it?'

'Nina,' she said. Only some of the older women in the town still called her Bernadine. She'd switched to Nina in her teens, although it was a switch Dolores had ignored.

'Suits you better all right,' said Sean. 'That dark hair. Those smouldering eyes. You're a definite Nina.'

That was what she'd always thought. Although she'd never considered her eyes to be smouldering. She liked the idea. She smiled at him.

'And those lips.' He winked. 'Pure Nina.'

She blushed. She wasn't very experienced when it came to handsome men (there was a distinct lack of eligible bachelors in Ardbawn, handsome or otherwise), and Sean Fallon was one of the best looking of them all. His father was the town's most respected GP, and the Fallon family had always been considered a cut above everyone else.

'So, Nina Doherty, how come I haven't seen much of you lately?'

40

'I rather think it's because you live in Dublin now,' she told him.

'Splitting hairs.' He grinned. 'I do have a place there. But I come home a lot of weekends.'

'Do you?' She was surprised. She couldn't imagine Sean would find anything to interest him in Ardbawn.

'My mother hasn't been well,' he told her. 'She likes me to visit.'

'Ah, I see.'

'But now I might have another reason.' He grinned again.

'You might?'

'Doing anything tonight?'

She looked at him in surprise. Was he asking her out? Sean Fallon? Surely not. She wasn't in his league at all. Despite his flattering comments about her hair and eyes, Nina doubted that her overall package – average height, carrying a few too many pounds, old jeans and even older jacket – would be Sean Fallon's cup of tea. In their schooldays (at four years her senior already way beyond her) Sean had always been seen with the popular and attractive girls in the town. Sometimes he even went out with girls a year or two older than him, who were nevertheless happy to be seen in his company because Sean Fallon was self-assured, attractive and mature for his age. Any time she'd spotted him since he'd gone to college, he'd had someone glossy and groomed by his side.

'Well?' He looked at her enquiringly.

'I'm sorry. I'm working,' she replied. It was better surely not to accept any invitation from Sean Fallon than to go out with him for a night simply because he hadn't got anything better to do. Nina wasn't stupid. She had no intention of being his stopgap.

41

'On a Saturday?' He sounded disappointed.

'Saturday's are busy days for guesthouse owners.'

Sean looked at her curiously. 'You own the guesthouse now?'

'Ever since my mother died.'

He hadn't been at the funeral, but she wouldn't have expected that. His parents had, though. Anthony Fallon had been Dolores's doctor.

'I'm sorry. I didn't know. At least,' he checked himself, 'I'm sure my parents told me, but I forgot.'

'That's OK.'

'So . . . when do you get time off?'

'Afternoons sometimes,' she told him. 'It depends on the guests.'

'Tomorrow?'

There was no point in going out with him. He broke women's hearts. He always had. It had been rumoured that Ellie Slater had tried to throw herself in the Bawnee River when Sean had ended their six-month relationship. Flora Morgan had lost a stone in weight when she and Sean split, causing her mother (who'd been friendly with Dolores) to spend hours at the guesthouse worrying about her daughter. And Aidie Keogh had failed her finals because she'd been devastated when Sean had dumped her. Admittedly they'd all eventually got over him (all three were married with children now), but Nina wasn't going to allow him to mess with her heart. She had a business to run; she couldn't afford to be dumped and spend a few weeks or months pining after a man. But maybe if she knew that already, there was no harm in one date. She was twenty-five, after all. Not young and silly like Ellie, Flora and Aidie had been.

Although she was a quiet-living home-bird, Nina also longed for a semblance of a social life. Practically all of her friends had left both Ardbawn and Ireland because they'd found it so difficult to get work. There weren't many people of her age around to party with, and the guesthouse had been both a blessing and a burden as far as socialising was concerned.

'I suppose I could take a bit of time tomorrow,' she said slowly.

'I'll pick you up at two.'

'You will?'

'Absolutely.'

'OK.'

'See you then.'

She couldn't quite believe she was going out with Sean Fallon.

She'd had three boyfriends in her whole life and none of them could match him for wit, or humour, or sheer good looks. He was handsome in a matinée-idol sort of way with his black hair, square jaw and deep blue eyes, and she couldn't help catching her breath every time she saw him. She didn't know what he saw in her; why, even after his mother had recovered from her illness, he went on coming to Ardbawn to see her. She continued to remind herself that Sean was a heartbreaker and that she didn't have time to have hers broken. She told herself that he was a pleasant diversion for her and she was an equally pleasant diversion for him. It wasn't love, she knew. Sean didn't love her. And she couldn't possibly love him. She said the second part out loud every night but she didn't really believe it. Because she'd utterly fallen for his easy charm, his casual nature and those dark good looks. She hadn't been able to help herself. And how could she? Every woman she knew was a little bit in love with Sean Fallon. But she wanted to keep a part of her heart intact so that she had something for herself on the inevitable day when he'd dump her, just as he'd dumped so many women in the past.

Besides, she was sure that he had a far more exciting life in Dublin, where he was a part-time actor, a job that sounded exciting and exotic to someone whose only experiences of theatre had been the pantomimes she'd occasionally been brought to as a child. Sean's acting career was far more authentic than panto. He'd been in a number of plays and had one or two walk-on parts in TV shows, but the work was sporadic and not well paid, so he also had a job as a van driver for a delivery company. Nina thought it sounded a glamorous sort of life (although she accepted that spending your days in a delivery van probably wasn't all that glamorous), but when she went to Dublin to see him in a walk-on part in the theatre and then to a party afterwards, she asked herself why on earth he still visited Ardbawn when there were so many exciting things to do in the city instead.

'Although I probably don't get the most out of Dublin,' she told him that night as they lay side by side in his single bed – Sean shared a flat with another part-time actor. 'I'm a country girl at heart.'

'You could make me into a country man again,' he murmured as he slid his hand between her legs. 'Because you're far more exciting than anything that this city has to offer.'

Nina laughed at that but Sean wasn't entirely wrong about her, because, although she had initially been tentative about sleeping with him, he discovered that she was surprisingly enterprising between the sheets, even if she did have a tendency to suddenly sit up in the bed after making love and scribble in the notebook she always carried around with her. When he asked her, the first time, what she was doing, she said that she'd just thought of something else that needed looking after in the guesthouse. If, she added, she ever got the damn loan from the bank. It was nearly three months since she'd asked for it and Dominic Bradley told her that they were still discussing it.

'What do they need to talk about for three months?' he asked.

She shrugged. 'I think they believe that I'm a silly young girl who doesn't know what she's doing. They're right up to a point. I'm terrified I'll make a mess of it. But I've got to try. If I don't get the money, though, I'm not sure what I'll do.'

She'd been astonished the week after that conversation when Dominic had phoned her up and told her that her loan had been approved. She'd jumped up and down with joy and had phoned Sean, who was back in Dublin again, to tell him.

'Great,' he said. 'I'm glad it worked.'

'What worked?' she asked.

Sean told her that he had asked his father to talk to the bank manager on her behalf.

'And because your dad did this they're giving me the loan?' Nina was shocked.

'Hey, why not? Dad plays golf with Bradley. Knows him well.'

Nina was delighted to get the loan but not entirely happy with Anthony Fallon's involvement. After signing the agreement at the bank, she went around to the doctor's house. Anthony told her that Sean had been very enthusiastic about her plans for the guesthouse and that he had persuaded him that it could be very profitable.

'. . . and so I went and talked to Dominic, and of course you do have a lot of work to do, but the house itself is an excellent asset and good security for the loan,' said Anthony. 'I reckoned that it was worth the risk.'

'Well, thank you very much,' said Nina, who was still taken aback at the notion that the two men had been discussing her financial situation.

'You're welcome,' said Anthony. 'If my wayward son is sleeping with someone, I'm comforted by the fact that she's a woman of independent means. And a lot more intelligent than the airheads he normally associates with.'

'Wayward?' asked Nina to cover her embarrassment over the fact that Anthony knew she was sleeping with Sean and didn't seem perturbed about it.

'He's wasting his time with that acting lark.' Anthony snorted. 'He's not good enough, I've told him that over and over. He's nearly thirty. He needs to settle down, get a proper job. Fooling around with fringe theatre while working for a delivery company is a waste of his time.'

'He's a great actor,' said Nina loyally.

'Great doesn't always mean lucky,' Anthony told her. 'He should know that by now. Oh, and speaking of luck, I hope you're not relying on that to avoid getting pregnant. If you need a prescription for the pill, let me know.'

At that time in Ireland, the pill was prescribed for medical, not family-planning reasons, and it was hard to come by in small towns. But Nina wasn't stupid. She'd gone to the Well Woman clinic in Dublin. She tried not to look embarrassed as she told Anthony this, but he nodded approvingly.

'I knew you were a sensible girl,' he said. 'That's what I told Sean, too.'

A few months later, Sean asked Nina to marry him. He proposed to her on the banks of the Bawnee River, where the sunlight dappled through the trees and sparkled on the water. It was a favourite place of theirs, peaceful, secluded and quietly romantic. He told her that he knew she was the one for him and he hoped that he was the one for her. He traced his finger along the curve of her jawline as he spoke and Nina knew that she was going to say yes. But first she wanted to know why he loved her.

'Because you're a sexy little minx underneath that quiet exterior.' He winked as he spoke, which made her laugh.

'It can't only be sex,' she said. 'I'm sure you've had plenty of women who are better than me in bed.'

'Not plenty,' said Sean. 'And not better, either. Of course I've had other girlfriends, you know that already. But you suit me the best, Nina Doherty.'

'Why?'

'You're my anchor,' he told her. 'You keep me sane.'

'I do?' She wasn't sure that being an anchor was a great reason for him wanting to marry her.

'You're the sensible side I don't have. You're good for me. You don't pander to me.'

Not in the way his actor friends did, but whenever he called, she came running. She couldn't help it.

'I'm fed up with Dublin,' he said. 'It's a rat race. And I've got to realise that I'm never going to make it as a serious actor there.'

'Is this because of what your father thinks?'

'My father has a point,' Sean said. 'It's time for me to face facts. I auditioned for a part going on *Chandler's Park* last week. They said I was too attractive. The last audition I did, I was told I didn't have enough character in my face. I'm fed up with their bullshit.'

Nina was sympathetic. Sean was a good-looking man, but his face was smooth and line-free and didn't fit in with the gritty times the country was going through. It would have been great for him to have landed a part on *Chandler's Park*, which was a new soap opera set on a suburban housing estate in Dublin and was getting high ratings.

'So you want to come back to Ardbawn?'

'I want to come back to you,' he said. 'Besides, I think I'll be a much better guesthouse owner than actor. I'm hoping you'll think so too.'

'Are you sure you love me?'

'I couldn't be more certain.'

'You'll be happy in Ardbawn?'

'I already am.'

'You won't think you're settling for second best? After all—'

'Absolutely not,' he interrupted her. Then he put his arms around her and kissed her, and she allowed herself to melt into his embrace.

It was a big wedding, paid for by the Fallons. Bridie and Peadar returned for it (it was too far and too expensive a journey for Tom), and they were amazed by the difference to the guesthouse since they'd been there for Dolores's funeral. Peadar remarked that it must be worth a fair few bob now and that Sean Fallon was doing well marrying a woman with bricks and mortar behind her. Bridie said that her sister had done well for herself in marrying the doctor's son; didn't everyone know that old man Fallon had a stash of cash, and hadn't he pushed the boat out for the wedding? She also muttered that she'd never seen Nina look so well, that her dress was stunning and that it must have cost a fortune. The two of them asked themselves if they shouldn't have badgered Nina into selling the house when their mother had died, because it seemed to them suddenly that their younger sister had got the better end of the deal, and wasn't she the sharp one making sure that everything to do with her ownership of the house had been legally dealt with? Not as thick as we supposed, said Peadar darkly. A shrewd little cookie after all.

But the only thing Nina thought was that she was the happiest girl in the world, and that she and Sean would live happily ever after together in their lovely house by the river.

Chapter 4

When Sheridan finally woke up, she thought her head was going to explode. She wished fervently that Talia, who in fairness had looked after her so well the night before, had nevertheless saved her from herself and refused to allow her the two glasses of whiskey she'd drunk on top of the bottles of Bud. Whiskey wasn't her drink. She'd allowed herself to acquire a bit of a taste for it when she went out with some of the other sports writers, because there was a breed of them (the older ones in particular) who liked hard drink. Those times she took it well watered down and slowly. Just so that she didn't look different. Last night she'd chugged the damn stuff back as though it was lemonade.

She opened one eye and closed it again as the light from the half-opened curtains stabbed through her brain. And then she opened both of her eyes, more gingerly this time, and realised that she was in Griff's bed. But he wasn't there. She vaguely remembered him collecting her from the pub the night before, and a taxi drive to the townhouse in Donnybrook that he shared with two of his five sisters, but she didn't remember anything else.

She rolled over and looked at the alarm clock. It took a

few minutes before the red numbers, which seemed to dance in front of her, settled down again and she could see that it was nearly ten.

She groaned softly. She couldn't remember a time in her whole life when she'd stayed in bed past nine. At home with the rest of the family half-eight was considered a lie-in. Her dad and the boys were up and out for an early run every single morning. Alice would have come in from her own run by the time they were leaving so that she could have breakfast ready for their return. Occasionally Sheridan ran with Alice, and sometimes she even went out with her father and brothers, but regardless, she was still usually up by eight for breakfast. When she'd moved in with Talia, she hadn't been able to break the habit of early rising, even on her days off. She'd stretched the lie-in to nine o'clock after a late night, but she always felt that half the day was wasted if she wasn't out of the house by ten.

It occurred to her, as she stared at the ceiling, that it wouldn't much matter what time she got up at in future. There was no reason for her to leap out of bed at all.

'Stop dramatising,' she told herself. 'Get your act together. Remember that this is an opportunity, not a tragedy.'

She sat up and the room did a dizzying 360-degree spin in front of her. She waited for a minute or two to allow it to settle, before sitting up a little more gingerly and reaching out for the bottle of water Griff kept on the bedside table. He'd left a note propped up beside it too. She had to blink a few times before she could make out the words: *Hope you're feeling better this morning. Didn't want to wake you. Call me later. Stay in the house as long as you like. Gemma and Marianne are out.*

OK, she said to herself. Time to take stock of the good things. I can take my time about getting up. I have a great boyfriend. I have a great girlfriend. I'm twenty-nine years old and I can change my life. I'll get another job and I'll work my way back to where I was before. And I can freelance. Even though I don't want to. I just need to think positive thoughts.

Think Positive Thoughts was one of Pat's mantras. He said it to the boys before they went off to play their matches. He said it to himself too. Both he and Alice were great believers in the power of positive thinking and not letting negativity hold you back. I wonder, thought Sheridan, as she eased herself out of bed, if they win so much because they think positively, or whether it's because they're all winners that they don't understand what it's like to feel down?

Every bone in her body ached. She pulled Griff's bathrobe from the back of the bedroom door and wrapped it around her. Then she walked slowly downstairs to the kitchen and made herself a cup of the strong black coffee she needed.

It was early afternoon by the time she headed back to the apartment she shared with Talia in Kilmainham. Kilmainham had been very convenient for getting to the *City Scope*, a half-hour's walk at most for Sheridan, who normally set a brisk pace. She usually walked to and from Griff's place in Donnybrook too, which took about an hour, but although she started off today with good intentions, she was feeling so shaky by the time she got to Ranelagh that she flagged down a cab for the rest of the journey.

Not that I can afford to be jumping into cabs now, she thought gloomily. I'm unemployed. I have to economise.

She hadn't quite got to grips with that concept yet, but

when she said the words in her mind she felt herself shiver. She told herself not to panic. There were bound to be opportunities out there. She just had to find out what they were.

She was surprised to find Talia sitting at the table by the window when she opened the door to the apartment.

'Decided to work from home today,' said her friend as she closed the laptop in front of her. 'How're you feeling?'

'I've got the hangover from hell,' confessed Sheridan. 'My head has an army of hobnailed boots marching through it and my mouth feels like the Gobi Desert after a particularly dry spell. Otherwise I'm fine.'

Talia grinned. 'That's my girl.'

'Yeah, right.' Sheridan slumped into an armchair and put a cushion behind her neck. 'Did I make a total arse of myself last night?'

'You were grand,' Talia assured her. 'Once you'd knocked back the Jemmies, you were out of it.'

'Sorry.'

'No need to be.' Talia stood up. 'Cup of tea?'

'I'm not sure I can hold it down,' said Sheridan. 'I had coffee at Griff's and threw it up.'

'Oh dear. I'll make you some green tea. That'll fix you.' Talia was a great believer in its therapeutic qualities, especially for rehydrating hung-over flatmates. 'I've a bit of a confession to make,' she said as she handed Sheridan the tea and sat down beside her. Sheridan could hear a certain nervousness in her friend's voice, and she looked at her curiously from her bloodshot eyes.

'Oh?'

'Remember the interview I did about a month ago?'

53

Sheridan rubbed her temple. Talia's job involved her interviewing lots of people, and there was no way she could remember all of them.

'For the fashion mag in Belfast. *They* interviewed *me*. For the job.'

'Oh, of course. You said you weren't all that interested.' Sheridan's eyes widened. 'Has what happened changed your mind? Are you going to call them?'

'The thing is, I got a phone call from them an hour ago.'

'And?'

'They've offered me the job.'

'Wow.' Sheridan put the mug down. She was stunned by Talia's news and, she realised, a little jealous too. Not only had her friend been kept on by the *City Scope*, but she also had the offer of another job. That didn't seem fair somehow. 'Are you going to accept?' she asked.

'I have to, don't I?' replied Talia. 'Even with Paudie O'Malley's investment, I'm not sure about the future of the *Scope*. Besides, with all that's happened, it's not the same paper any more. I'm not sure I want to keep working there, and the salary at the magazine is better than I expected.'

'Even though you'll have to move to Belfast? Even though you said you didn't want to? Won't you be bored out of your head there?'

'Well, it's not Dublin, but there's a good vibe about the place these days. Besides, things have changed, I have to go where the work is.'

'I guess so,' said Sheridan.

'It might be good for me,' added Talia. 'I'm in my comfort zone right now. It's not a bad idea to step out of it from time to time.'

Pat and Alice were big into getting out of comfort zones. Stretch yourself, they used to say to their children. Do things you don't like doing. Try harder. That was what Sheridan was going to have to do now.

'When do you start?'

'Next month,' said Talia. 'But I've loads of holidays to take, so I'll finish up at the *Scope* next week.'

'I'm delighted for you,' said Sheridan. On one level she was. On another, she was gutted.

'My plan is to head off for a week somewhere warm, then get to Belfast to find a place to live and all that sort of stuff before I start at the mag. Fancy coming to the Canaries? They'll be warm enough even at this time of year.'

'Tempting,' admitted Sheridan, 'but my finances . . .'

'You'll have your redundancy money,' Talia reminded her.

'Yes, but . . .'

'But what?'

'I'm going to have to do some flat-hunting. I can't afford to keep this place without you, it's too expensive. I don't have much savings . . .'

'Would you stop worrying,' said Talia. 'You'll get something else, no problem.'

'It might take a bit of time,' Sheridan said.

'You deserve a break after what's happened. Treat yourself.'

'I've never been unemployed and on the scrapheap before,' said Sheridan. 'It makes you worried.'

'You're not on the scrapheap,' Talia assured her. 'And I have an idea about the flat.'

'You do?'

'Why don't you ask Griff to move in with you?'

Sheridan took a sip of her tea and said nothing.

'It must have crossed your mind at some point over the past few months,' said Talia. 'In fact I'm surprised you haven't dumped me for him already.'

'I've thought about it,' conceded Sheridan. 'But I like sharing with you. It's the best of both worlds. Sharing with Griff – that's a whole different ball game. It's making a bit of a statement, isn't it?'

'I thought you loved him!'

'Of course I love him.' Sheridan smiled and closed her eyes. 'He's one in a million in so many ways.'

'So what's holding you back?'

'Well . . . I kind of feel he should be the one asking me to move in with him. I know that sounds sort of girlie and unfeminist of me, but still – me asking him seems somewhat desperate, don't you think? As though I want to tie him down. Get married, even . . .' Her voice trailed off.

'Have you talked about it?'

'Only in a vague sort of way. To be honest, I wasn't looking for someone to marry when I met him. I wanted to have my big journalistic career first.' She grimaced. 'Not that it's going entirely to plan now. All the same, I wanted to make a name for myself before I got married.'

'Your byline is on every second sports piece in the *Scope*—'

'*Was* on every second piece,' Sheridan corrected her.

'You did make a name for yourself.'

'Yeah, but I wanted to land a big interview. With someone controversial. I wanted to make people proud of me.'

'People? Like who?'

Sheridan shrugged. 'Well . . . everyone. My mum and dad, I suppose.'

'I'm sure they're proud of you already! How many people

get to read their daughter's analysis of an Ireland match in the most influential sports section there is?'

'I know, I know. It's just . . .'

'What?'

'They aren't proud of me in the same way they are of Matt and Con,' she confessed. 'I know my mam reads all my stuff, but pieces in the paper aren't as good as trophies in the cabinet.'

'You're joking, aren't you?'

'Why would I be joking?'

'Because you're a very successful journo in a male-dominated area. So quit with the "I'm not a winner" stuff. That's ridiculous.'

'To you, maybe. But winning is everything to my parents. While I was at the *Scope*, I felt as though I had some credibility in their eyes. I reckoned that if I could get a really important interview they'd be so impressed they'd forget I was the one who always came last in the races at home.'

'You need therapy if you're thinking like that,' said Talia.

'If you'd grown up in my household you'd need therapy too.'

'Forget your parents and your muscle-bound brothers for a minute and think about yourself. You've done well. You've had a successful career and you can continue to have a successful career. You have a brilliant boyfriend who'll probably jump at the idea of moving in with you. So go for it. Ask him.'

'What if he says no?'

'He won't say no,' Talia told her. 'You'll only barely have the question out of your mouth when he'll be saying yes.'

* * *

Sheridan was a little nervous about asking Griff to move in with her, but deep down she was fairly confident that her boyfriend would be excited by the idea. He stayed over often enough (her stays in his house were less frequent because of the fact that his two sisters shared it with him – she didn't feel comfortable sleeping with him knowing that they were the other side of the wall), he liked lounging on the sofa in front of the TV with her, sometimes commenting that they were becoming a boring couple. But he always said that with a laugh.

Griff was different to any of her previous boyfriends because he didn't treat her like a friend who just happened to be a girl. When she was with him she felt like a proper girlfriend. Someone who was cherished and looked after. Griff was romantic. He complimented her on her body (he liked curves, he said); he took her to rom-com movies as well as thrillers (she enjoyed thrillers but it was nice not to have explosions in every film she saw) and he generally made her feel wanted and special. Talia thought he was a gem of a boyfriend and that his understanding of women came from the fact that he'd been raised in an all-female household. Sheridan agreed, though on the one occasion when she'd been with Griff's entire family she'd felt overwhelmed by the femininity of it all.

It was ironic, she sometimes thought, that her first meeting with her perfect boyfriend had, in fact, been because of sport. She'd been conducting a vox pop outside the Aviva Stadium one day and she'd collared him to talk about the candidates being touted for the role of manager of the rugby team. Griff had come up with the name of a little-known Australian coach, to which Sheridan had responded that the coach was linked to a move to Fiji and so it was probably unlikely. Griff had stared at her in amazement, confessed that he'd brought up the name just to confuse her, and apologised for being a sexist pig for assuming that she knew nothing about the game. Then he'd asked her out.

Sheridan had surprised herself by accepting. She'd thought he was a bit of a sexist pig too. She was happy to realise that she was wrong, and very happy to have finally found someone she really cared for. And someone who seemed to care for her just as much too.

I'll ask him tonight, she said to herself, as she lay on her bed mulling over Talia's news. Her friend had gone out for a while, knowing that Sheridan needed some solitude to recover from her hangover. It'll be nice living with him. And maybe . . . who knows, maybe we'll think about the whole marriage thing. It wasn't something that had ever bothered Sheridan before. But she couldn't help thinking about it now.

After half an hour she got up from the bed and went back into the empty living room. She knew that she'd have to ring her parents and tell them about her redundancy soon. But she wanted to feel a bit better before she did. At the same time, she also had to call them before Talia got back, because it wasn't a conversation she wanted to have in front of her friend.

But she didn't have time to wait, because within five minutes her mobile rang and she recognised Alice's number. She took a deep breath before answering.

'Hi,' she said.

'What's all this about jobs going at the *City Scope*?'

demanded Alice. 'It was on the news today. Why didn't you tell me?'

'I was busy,' said Sheridan.

'Well that's a good sign.' There was relief in Alice's voice. 'I thought maybe yours might have been one of the ones to go.'

'Um . . .' Sheridan gripped her phone tightly, 'the sports department has lost two of us.'

'Two of you? Don't tell me you're one of them!'

'Afraid so.' Sheridan kept her voice as light as she possibly could. 'But it's not all bad news. I get a redundancy package and hopefully I'll find something else soon, so I could end up doing quite well out of it in the end.'

'You've. Lost. Your. Job.' Alice said each word distinctly. 'How can that be a good thing?'

'I didn't say it was. I just said that I could end up doing OK.'

'It was a great job,' said Alice. 'You wrote good stories. What did you do to make them fire you?'

'I wasn't fired,' Sheridan reminded her. 'It was a redundancy issue. And I didn't do anything. It's all about costs.'

'You must have fluffed something,' said Alice.

'I bloody didn't!' Sheridan was getting annoyed. 'Redundancy happens. They don't always have to have a reason to choose you.'

'No. I know.' Alice's voice suddenly softened. 'I'm sorry, Sheridan. I was just angry on your behalf. I remember when Con was dropped from the team and there was no reason for it other than the manager wanted to try a different formation. They brought him back, of course, it was a disaster without him.'

'I remember.' There had been utter consternation in the Gray house that day. Nobody could believe that the manager had left Con off the team sheet. He was one of the star players. Afterwards he'd confided in Sheridan that he'd had a row with the manager and that was why. He'd never told Alice that. She didn't believe in players arguing with managers.

'Well, I'm sure you're right and they'll come crawling back looking for you,' said Alice. 'In the meantime, though, would you like to come to Kerry for a few days?'

'I was thinking of going on holiday with Talia.'

'I'm not sure you should be going off gallivanting when you need to be around looking for a job,' said Alice.

'Talia said it would be good for me to have a break.'

'Perhaps,' conceded Alice. 'But it would be cheaper for you to have a break in Kerry.'

'I want to go somewhere warm. Get a bit of sun into my bones. That'll energise me.'

'Hmm.' Alice didn't sound convinced. 'Do whatever you think is best. But we're here if you need us.'

'Thanks, Mam. Maybe I'll drop down for a day or two. But I need to be in Dublin to look for jobs.'

'We do have the internet down here, you know,' Alice remarked. 'We're not entirely behind the times.'

'I know. I know.'

'I worry about you,' said Alice abruptly 'You're not like the boys.'

'I never made the Dublin team, no,' agreed Sheridan.

'You're not as tough,' said her mother. 'You don't have the hard edge.'

'I'm hard enough,' Sheridan told her.

'I hope so.'

'I'll be fine.'

'OK. Take care. Keep in touch.'

'I will.'

Sheridan ended the call. There was a lump in her throat. She'd expected Alice's initial reaction, blaming her for losing her job. She'd even expected her to be a bit snippy about her deciding to go on holiday. But she hadn't expected her concern. Somehow that had been harder to take than the blame.

Chapter 5

Griff texted Sheridan shortly after she finished her phone conversation with Alice, and they agreed to meet up that evening in his favourite Mediterranean restaurant, off Georges Street. She arrived before him and was already sitting at a table when he arrived. He apologised for being late and she said that she was a bit early and they both ordered without looking at the menu because they ate there so often they didn't need it any more.

'How's the head?' asked Griff.

'Not great,' she admitted. 'Talia should've stopped me.'

'I don't think you were in the mood to listen.'

'Probably not,' she conceded, and then reached for the water that the waiter had placed on the table. 'Thanks for looking after me and bringing me back to your place. And for letting me sleep on this morning. I've been chugging back isotonic drinks all day but I know I'll be wrecked until tomorrow.'

'Poor darling.' He smiled at her and rested his hand on hers.

'Ah, I'll be fine.' Much as she loved the sympathy, she didn't like the use of endearments or pet names. They always seemed fake to her. She slid her hand from beneath his and pushed back her hair. She'd left it loose today because tying it back would only worsen her headache, and it fell in a cloud of vivid red around her still-pale face.

'Of course you will,' he said. He repeated Talia's assertion that she was a great reporter and that she'd get another job and that this was probably an opportunity. Sheridan was already getting tired of the word 'opportunity', even though she'd used it herself. She wondered if other people who'd been made redundant got fed up with well-meaning friends telling them it could be an opportunity too. She told Griff about Talia's job offer and that she was going to take it. He looked surprised.

'I thought she was committed to the *City Scope*.'

'Yeah, well, so was I and look what happened.' Sheridan ground some black pepper over the fish she'd ordered. 'She's right to take the chance while she can.'

'Absolutely. Smart girl, keeping her irons in the fire like that. I wonder, did she know what was going to happen at the *Scope*?'

'There've been rumours for ages,' Sheridan reminded him. 'If I'd been less of a fool myself I'd've started looking for something else before now.'

'So when she's moving out?' asked Griff.

Sheridan told him, and added that they were planning to go to the Canaries first.

'Excellent idea,' he said. 'That'll get your spirits up.'

'And afterwards I'll have to knuckle down to getting a job. And,' she added hesitantly, 'a new flatmate.'

Griff added some extra garlic potatoes to his plate.

'Any thoughts?' he asked as he sliced his steak.

'Well . . .' Sheridan looked at him through lowered eyes. 'I did have an idea, yes. Well, it was Talia's idea actually, but I think it's a good one . . .'

Griff waited for her to speak.

'We thought that maybe you'd like to move in with me.' The words came in a rush, and she noticed the suspicion of a frown cross his face. 'Of course it's just a suggestion,' she added quickly. 'It's not like you have to do it. I'm not trying to pressurise you into something you . . . you're not ready for.'

She wished she hadn't said anything. Griff was scratching his chin thoughtfully, as though working out how best to reply to her. But it was clear that he wasn't exactly thrilled with the idea. She felt a hot flush scorch her cheeks.

'It was just that with her moving out, I need someone, and you spend a lot of time there already, so she thought and I thought too I suppose that it would be a good idea.' She realised that she was blathering. And that he was still scratching his chin.

'I suppose it was a question that would come up eventually.' He finally left his chin alone and looked at her.

'If you're uncomfortable about it . . .'

'No. No. It's something we probably needed to talk about.'

We might be going to talk about it, she thought, but I can't believe it's going to be in a good way. She took a gulp from her glass of wine, thinking that redundancy was turning her into a total lush. Griff took a measured sip from his own glass and then put it carefully on the table.

'It's not that I don't want to be with you a lot,' said Griff slowly. 'I'm really fond of you, Sher. We've had some great times together.'

This was a sentence that was definitely going to include a 'but', Sheridan realised. She waited for it.

'But I like living with Gemma and Marianne. It's relaxing.'

'Living with me wouldn't be?' Sheridan waited a moment before she spoke, unable to keep the hurt out of her voice.

'It's not that,' said Griff. 'Living with you would be . . . well, living with my girlfriend. And that would kinda make you more than just a girlfriend, wouldn't it?'

'I guess . . .'

'And what I'm saying is that I love you and want you to be my girlfriend, but not a girlfriend I live with. Not right now.'

Sheridan thought about this for a moment.

'So what you're really saying is that we have a good relationship now but you don't want to mess it up by making it more than it is? Which would happen if you moved in with me.'

'Exactly.' He looked relieved. 'You know, the thing I love best about you, Sher, is that you think like a man. You don't get messy and emotional and cry at stupid things. You don't think that I have to be with you twenty-four/seven for me to care about you.'

'No, I don't think that.' Sheridan was picking at the corner of her paper napkin.

'You're one of the best women I've ever gone out with. There's no bullshit with you.'

'Thanks.' She injected the word with as much irony as she could manage.

'Honestly,' said Griff. 'I absolutely love the way things are with us. But moving in with you – that's taking things to a whole new level, isn't it?'

66

'And that bothers you?'

'It's a lot to think about right away,' said Griff. Suddenly his eyes lit up. 'I know you're under pressure to get someone, though. What about Eithne? Last time we spoke, she said something about the landlord needing vacant possession of her flat soon. Hey, don't you think that'd be perfect?'

Sheridan scrunched the napkin into a ball. Eithne was the eldest of Griff's five sisters. And the gabbiest.

'I'm not so sure that would work out,' she said.

'It was just a thought,' he told her. 'Etty is great company, very easy to get on with.'

The idea of having Griff's sisters in both his house and her apartment, keeping an eye on them, was too freaky for her to even contemplate. It should have been freaky for him too.

'OK, so not Eithne,' he said when she remained silent. 'We'll think of someone.'

'But not you.'

'No. That doesn't matter, though, does it?' He covered her hand with his again. 'We're still grand the way we are, aren't we?'

Would she be turning into a stereotypical girl if she yelled at him that she'd asked him to move in with her and he'd said no, and so by no stretch of the imagination could she possibly think things were all right? After all, he'd told her that she thought like a man. He wasn't the only person to have ever said that to her, although it was the first time for him. There was no reason to get emotional over something that he was regarding as practical. Was there?

'I think we're fine as friends,' she told him finally.

'I knew you'd see it like that.'

67

'It's just . . .'

'What?'

'Well, if we're going out together on dates, not just as friends, but we don't want to be in a relationship – well, where's it all leading?'

'Does it have to be leading anywhere?'

She hadn't thought so before. At least, not consciously. But she was thinking about it now. He loved her, he liked sleeping with her, but he didn't want to move in with her. That sounded like a problem to her, even if he imagined it was a perfect arrangement. She was obviously less like a man than he thought. Damn it, she thought, if it hadn't been for the trouble at the *Scope*, we wouldn't be having this conversation. And I'd be perfectly happy to think that he might come back to Kilmainham tonight but go home in the morning. As it is . . .

'Hey, you're just a bit upset because of your job. I understand that.'

'It's more than my job,' she told him.

'Why?'

'Why d'you think?' She felt herself suddenly losing her composure. 'You don't want to live with me. You don't love me enough. But you're OK sleeping with me whenever you feel like it. You're happy with things the way they are, but you know what, Griff, it makes me feel a bit like . . . like your plaything.'

'You know that's not true.' He looked bewildered. 'I wouldn't dream of regarding you as a plaything. Besides, I thought you liked how things between us were too. You did until yesterday.'

'I lost my job yesterday and I had to do a bit of thinking,

68

and I thought that maybe we were in the sort of place that you'd *want* to live with me. I know it's Talia's suggestion, but it matters to me too. I wanted you to move in with me because we've being going out for ages and it seems to me, that being the case, that moving in might be a next step. But I was wrong.'

'You sound just like Gemma when she's having a row with Jerry. All kind of incoherent and emotional and . . . and . . . like a girl.'

'Because I *am* a girl! And I'm not incoherent. I'm making a valid point.'

'What do you want from me?'

She sat back in her seat. She hadn't thought it through. But she did now. The logical consequence of them living together was, perhaps, to eventually get married. Or have children. Children weren't on her radar yet. But one day they might be. Marriage hadn't been. Now it was.

'I think I want a future,' she said, after all these things had filtered through her mind. 'A long-term future.'

Griff exhaled sharply. 'With me?'

'That's the way my mind was going, obviously. But not yours,' she added as she observed the hunted expression in his eyes.

'It's not that I mightn't,' he told her. 'But I'm not ready yet. C'mon, Sher. With us it's all about having a good time and great sex.' He grinned at her. 'Don't tell me you don't think the sex isn't great.'

'Of course it's great,' she said.

'So we don't need the other stuff. The dull stuff. The making-plans-and-settling-down stuff. It's way too much responsibility for me right now.'

He was thirty-one years old. Sheridan's father had been married with kids by then. She wondered when it had happened that men in their early thirties decided they were too young for responsibility. Then she reminded herself that, until yesterday, she hadn't been thinking much about responsibilities herself. And that her mother had had three children by the time she was twenty-nine.

'We've had some great times,' she agreed. 'I suppose they won't last for ever. Obviously they won't,' she added, 'if we're not interested in . . . in taking things further.'

'This is the best relationship I've ever had,' he told her. 'You're one of the most brilliant girlfriends in the world. There's no reason to mess it up by making it into something else. Not yet.'

'I know. But . . .' She sighed. 'I shouldn't have listened to Talia. I shouldn't have thought about the whole living-together thing. The problem is, now that I have . . .'

'You've changed everything,' finished Griff.

'I'm sorry.'

Griff took his credit card out of his wallet and handed it to the waiter, who'd arrived with the bill. 'My treat tonight, seeing as you're one of the recently unemployed.'

They normally split the bill. Sheridan preferred it that way. But tonight she let Griff pay.

'So what now?' asked Griff as they stood on the pavement outside the restaurant. 'Do you want to come back to the house?'

'I don't think so.'

'D'you want me to come back to your place?'

'No.'

'Do you want ever to see me again?'

Of course she wanted to see him again. She still loved him. But she couldn't unsay what had been said and she couldn't get past the fact that he didn't want to live with her.

'I'll call you,' he said when she didn't speak.

'OK.'

'Well, good night so.' He hesitated for a moment, then put his arms around her and drew her towards him.

'No.' She swallowed hard. 'No, Griff, don't.'

'Come on, Sher.' His expression was pained. 'You'll be fine. We'll be fine.'

'I don't think we will,' she said. 'And . . . and . . . maybe it's better if you don't call me after all.'

'Are you sure about that?' he asked. 'You've had a rough time. I'm sorry I didn't say what you wanted tonight, but maybe you'll see that ultimately it's the right thing.'

'If it's the right thing, then we're wasting our time together.'

'How can enjoying somebody's company be wasting your time?' he asked.

She'd once asked the same question herself. Talia had been nagging her about her habit of going out on Saturday nights with different male friends to watch the match in a pub. Her friend had asked if there wasn't one guy that she wanted to go out with more than others. When Sheridan said no, Talia had questioned her as to why she was wasting her time with so many men if none of them mattered to her. Sheridan had responded that she enjoyed being with them. That they were friends. And, she'd asked Talia, how could having fun with people you liked be wasting your time? She'd spoken the truth then. What had happened to make her change her mind?

71

'But if you think that's what we've been doing . . .' His voice was harder than she'd ever heard it before. 'No point in hanging around. No point in long goodbyes.'

'No point at all.'

She watched him raise his arm and hail a taxi, and then he was gone. She turned up Georges Street and began walking. She couldn't quite believe that in the space of two days she'd managed to lose her job, her flatmate and her boyfriend. A hat-trick of losses. She felt sick. As a parrot.

Chapter 6

Nina had once felt that God was looking out for her the day she married Sean Fallon. She was totally and utterly in love with her husband and, to her astonishment, because he could have had anyone he chose, he seemed to be totally in love with her too. She reckoned that she was the kind of woman he needed, someone calm and sensible who could rein in some of his madder ideas and be a bulwark against his occasionally emotional outbursts. She sometimes still felt inadequate in the glamour stakes in comparison to his previous girlfriends (because no matter how hard she tried, she simply didn't have that extra something that all truly glamorous women do), but she knew that Sean hadn't married her for glamour. He'd married her because he loved the down-to-earth practicality of her and her ability to abandon that side of her nature when they were beneath the sheets together.

'You're my perfect match,' he whispered on their wedding night. 'My dad was right about you.'

Nina, despite her initial reservations, got on well with Anthony Fallon, although his wife was cooler towards her. But she didn't care about her in-laws any more. All that mattered was that she was the one who'd tamed Sean, and that she was the one who had him by her side.

Over time, Sean took over the front-of-house running of the guesthouse. Nina didn't mind that he was the one who was greeting the guests and making them feel welcome, even though that was the part of owning the Bawnee River Guesthouse that she'd always enjoyed the most. But Sean was even better at it than her, charming the guests with his broad smile, making them feel instantly at home, allowing them to believe that they were treasured friends instead of paying customers. He also took over the finances. Nina didn't mind that at all – she never wanted to talk to Dominic Bradley again if she could help it. So she was happy to look after the cooking and the cleaning and allow Sean to be the kind of host who ensured that everyone who stayed with them had a good time. The result of which meant that their level of repeat bookings rose steadily higher every year.

The success of the guesthouse allowed them to have a comfortable, if busy, life. After the children were born, they hired a succession of young women to help with the cleaning, while Sean brought them into the digital age by ensuring that there was Wi-Fi access for the guests, who increasingly booked through the well-laid-out website with its enticing videos of the surrounding countryside. And although the last few years had been difficult as a result of recessionary times, Nina always felt that with Sean at her side she could weather any storm. They were a couple whose marriage worked. There had been a time when the children were small when there had been a rip in the fabric of their lives together. It had shaken Nina to the core. But they'd overcome it. They'd set boundaries for each other. It had all been, if not exactly worthwhile, constructive in the end. She was quite certain that there was nothing in the world that could drive them apart.

At least, she thought, that was what she'd believed until Hayley bloody Goodwin had turned up a week before the production of *Pygmalion* and sobbed that Brian Carton, who was playing the role of Henry Higgins, and Stephen Lyons, his understudy, had both broken a limb (an arm in Brian's case, a leg in Stephen's) trying to rescue a stupid sheep that had got stranded on the riverbank. The two men had lost their footing when loose earth had given way, and fallen down an embankment.

'Why were they so bloody stupid!' cried Hayley.

'Because they're men.'

It was Nina who answered, because Sean had taken out the SUV to pick up a guest from the riding stables and wasn't there to hear Hayley's anguished wails.

'Stupid sheep, stupid men,' said Hayley morosely. 'Didn't either of them stop to think about the play at all?'

'I doubt it,' Nina replied. 'After all, sheep are far more important to farmers.'

'Well, I'm in a total mess,' said Hayley. 'And the only person I could think of to help me out is Sean. He knows the role, doesn't he? He said so.'

'Hayley, it's more than twenty years since Sean even stood on a stage. He wouldn't remember the part, or how to play it, for that matter.'

'He's my only hope,' said Hayley. 'The guesthouse isn't that busy – you said yourself that bookings are down. You can spare him, surely.'

Nina looked at the other woman helplessly. 'There's a lot of work to be done here no matter how many guests we do or don't have.'

'But you'll ask him if he can help, won't you? Otherwise we'll have to cancel the show. And that would be an absolute disaster.'

Hayley had gone by the time Sean returned and Nina gave him her message. She laughed and told Sean that she couldn't imagine him on stage with the amateurs at all and that she was sure he wanted to refuse but that she hadn't liked to give Hayley the brush-off. She'd expected Sean to be equally dismissive, but instead he looked thoughtful.

'It might be a bit of fun,' he said.

'You've got to be kidding me.'

'It was once my dream.'

'You've always been scathing about the dramatic society. You never wanted to be involved.'

'Because they're so unprofessional.'

'That's because they're not professionals,' said Nina. 'You used to say you weren't a professional either.'

Sean had always told Nina that unless he could make a living from acting, it was better to consider himself an amateur rather than a professional. But he had always tried to be professional in how he approached his work. He reminded her of this now.

'Do you regret giving it up?' She'd picked up on the tone of his voice. 'Do you think you could've made a proper go of it? You were good enough,' she added loyally. 'I always thought so.'

'You know you have to be more than good, you have to be lucky. Back then you didn't have the chance of instant

TV or internet fame either. It was hard graft. And I didn't have the right look – or luck – remember.'

Nina doubted that anyone would be considered too good looking for acting these days. She felt a sudden pang of sympathy for her husband.

'You could've made a go of it, I'm sure.'

'Not married to you and living in Ardbawn, which, let's face it, isn't exactly a teeming thespian metropolis.'

Marrying her had been the decision he'd wanted to make. The grown-up choice, he'd said. And Ardbawn was the place for him to be.

'Do you want to act in the play to regain your lost youth?'

'Less of the lost youth,' said Sean. 'I've grown better with age.'

'That's true.'

He kissed her. 'I want to help them out. The show must go on and all that sort of thing. D'you mind?'

'Of course not. It'll be fun. You deserve a bit of fun.'

'I do, don't I?' And he went to phone Hayley to give her the good news.

Nina couldn't go to any of the performances of *Pygmalion* because – happily – the guesthouse was almost full that week, and every night at least some of the guests wanted evening meals. But over the course of the week-long run of the show, everyone staying with them saw it, and they all agreed that Sean had been brilliant as Henry Higgins.

'Got the accent right, got the character right – just fantastic,' said Mona Bartholomew, a woman who'd been coming to Ardbawn at the same time for the past five years. 'And he looked the part too. Very distinguished.'

Nina smiled. Sean had been right when he'd said he'd grown better with age, because he certainly was more attractive now than he'd been in his thirties. He'd lost the smooth look and become more rugged. And he had a faint scar too, which ran from the corner of his eye across his cheek. (So not fair, she often thought, wrinkles and grey hair suited him, while she had to lash out on ever more expensive creams and colour foams to try to keep the lines at bay and retain the dark hair that had attracted him in the first place.)

She knew that he was relishing being the centre of attention. Sean always liked being in the limelight; it was why he was so good with the guests. He joked with them, pandered to them and generally made them feel as though he was working for each one of them individually. But the truth was that he enjoyed being the one they turned to and the one they asked for advice on where to go and what to do in Ardbawn.

For the week of the show she was the one doing all these things, but Sean was still the person everyone was talking about. The guests who went to see the play congratulated her on having such a talented husband. The local paper ran a piece on him, calling his performance a 'tour de force', which Nina thought was possibly exaggerating, but then again the *Central News* liked to big up the townspeople as much as possible. So she cut out the report, had it framed and hung it in the hallway where all the guests could see it.

After the run, the society held a big party for the cast and their families. She'd heard nothing but good things about her husband's performance. Hayley Goodwin had been euphoric, saying that she hadn't realised what a talent had been hidden in Ardbawn. She was already talking about Sean in a leading role for their next production, although they hadn't yet decided what it would be. Nina thought that other members of the society might resent him, but they didn't. They embraced him. Though none as enthusiastically as Hayley.

He could have had an affair with Hayley Goodwin. After all, she'd been one of the many girls to write Sean Fallon's initials on her schoolbag over twenty years ago in the hope that he'd notice her. She'd admitted this to Nina with a laugh at Nina and Sean's wedding reception. But Sean didn't have an affair with Hayley. Sometimes Nina thought it would have been easier to deal with if he had.

A few weeks after the end of the show, Sean received a phone call. It was from Kieran Keating, one of the guests who'd gone to see it. Nina heard her husband speaking to him and she hoped Kieran was making another booking. He'd been a model guest, no trouble and a pleasant person to deal with.

When Sean finished the call, he came into the kitchen, a stunned expression on his face.

'He's a TV producer,' he told Nina. 'He saw me in *Pygmalion*. He's interested in me for a part in *Chandler's Park*.'

'You're kidding me.' She looked at him in utter astonishment.

'I know, isn't it amazing? I told them they'd passed me over years ago and he couldn't believe it. Said that I had great presence – and rugged good looks.'

Nina looked at the scar on his face, which hadn't been there the first time he'd auditioned for *Chandler's Park*. The scar that elevated him from being boyishly attractive to having a certain edge. She dug her nails into her palms and then relaxed.

'Just goes to show, doesn't it?' she said calmly. 'What role are they thinking of?'

'Apparently Kathryn's estranged brother returns and Fiona gets a bit of a crush on him. They want someone "rakish" to be the brother.'

Nina couldn't help laughing, and Sean grinned. 'Rakish enough for Fiona, anyway.'

'Isn't she a bit young for you?'

Kathryn was one of the soap's main characters, and Fiona, her daughter, was a rebellious teenager who'd had addiction problems but was trying to clean up her act. She was played by Lulu Adams, a rising star who – despite being in her early twenties – looked every inch a stroppy seventeen year old on the soap.

'Yes. But I'm not interested in her, of course. I think it's just so's her character gets even more drama in her life. I don't know where the storyline is going and I might not even get the part. Kieran wants me to come and do a screen test.'

'A screen test.' Nina's eyes opened wide. 'Sounds like Hollywood.'

'I never thought I'd get this sort of chance again,' he told her. 'I thought that maybe I was being punished.'

'Oh, Sean . . .'

'This is real acting,' he said fiercely. 'With real actors. And I know I mightn't even get the part, but I want to try.'

'I'm sure you will,' said Nina. 'I'm sure you're exactly right for them.'

*   *   *

She was right. He got the part. And the feedback was so good that they extended his time on the show. A few weeks after the role had finished, he got another call from Kieran. Audiences had liked him so much they were thinking of bringing the character back for a longer run. Would he be interested?

It was something Nina and Sean had to discuss. His few weeks on *Chandler's Park* had been fun but stressful, because they involved twelve-hour days, which meant that he was out of the guesthouse the whole time. It didn't matter too much as it was a slow period, with very few guests, so Nina could easily manage on her own, but the idea of Sean having a full-time job outside the guesthouse was something they'd never had to consider before.

'I managed before I married you; I guess I could manage again,' said Nina, although the prospect seemed daunting now.

'It wouldn't be for ever,' said Sean. 'I'm sure they'll write me out of it sooner or later.'

'You know how it is with some of those soaps. Once you're in, they only kill you off to get rid of you! There are actors who spend their whole lives in a part.'

Sean laughed. 'I'm a bit long in the tooth to be considered a whole-lifer,' he said. 'I'm fifty-one, after all.'

'Maybe they'll keep you till you're eighty.'

'I don't think so. I'm supposed to be a kind of devil-may-care, heartbreaker type. Wouldn't quite work with a Zimmer frame.'

'With you it probably would.' Nina had enjoyed her husband's role in the soap, even though it also made her a little bit nervous. He'd loaded on the charm as Kathryn's devil-may-care brother, and the word was that middle-aged women everywhere had fallen for him. If she hadn't already been married to him she would have fallen for him herself.

'So what do you think?'

'I think you're going to do it anyway.'

'Not without us talking it through first.'

'So talk.'

'It's a huge opportunity. For me personally and for us as a family. The money will make up for the last couple of seasons and help get things back on to an even keel.'

'Sounds like a good enough reason.'

'And I deserve it.' There was a glitter in his eye. 'I've paid my dues and I deserve it.'

Nina nodded slowly. 'I guess you have.'

'If it all becomes too much I'll get them to write me out. They can have Fiona run me over in that new cabriolet she's somehow managed to buy.' The intensity had gone out of Sean's voice and he smiled.

'Maybe they'll have a big accident,' said Nina. 'Like in *Corrie* with the runaway tram. Wipe out half the cast.'

Sean looked cheerful. 'If I go, I take them with me.'

Nina chuckled.

'I don't think I can turn it down,' he told her. 'The money's too good.'

'It's still quiet here,' Nina conceded. 'I can easily cope for a few more months.'

'That's my girl.' Sean picked her up and whirled her around. 'I knew we'd agree it was a good move in the end.'

And it could have been a good move, Nina thought over and over again. It nearly was. But it had turned into a complete

82

disaster. It was extraordinary, she muttered to herself, how things that should have ruined your life didn't. And things that should have been wonderful did.

Sean had to stay in Dublin for the shooting of the soap. The production company put him up in a small apartment near the studios, which, he told Nina, was a damn sight better than the poky flat he'd shared when he was working for the delivery company.

She knew he was enjoying his time on the show and she didn't begrudge it. It was time for him to live his dream. Running the guesthouse had been hers. A small dream by most people's standards, but it had come true for her. It had never been Sean's, though, despite all the effort he'd put into it. There had been times when she thought the whole thing had been a mistake, that marrying Sean and running a guesthouse with him had been the wrong thing to do. She'd wondered if his whole life with her was one long act. But he always said that it was a life that had been good for him in the end. Once he'd added, with a self-deprecating smile, that he rather liked being a big fish in a small pond, which was what he was in Ardbawn. In Dublin he'd been nobody.

But he was somebody in Dublin now. His face started to appear in the gossip pages of the newspapers, usually coming out of a bar or restaurant (and very occasionally a nightclub) with other members of the *Chandler's Park* cast. Sean told Nina that all of these photos were staged with the aim of upping his profile and making people interested in him and the soap. They helped the profile of the guesthouse too. Nina had noticed a big increase in the number of hits on the website, and almost everyone who'd visited since Sean started working on the show had asked about him. So his presence on screen was helping in more ways than one. She told him to keep getting noticed and keep mentioning Ardbawn. That way, she said, both of us will be happy.

And then she found out about Lulu Adams.

And everything changed.

Like so much of her husband's life over the last few months, Nina had discovered the truth about him and Lulu through the newspapers. This time, though, it was because a member of the showbiz team on the *City Scope* newspaper (it was supposed to be a decent paper, she thought afterwards, not a gossip rag) rang her and asked her for her comments about the fact that Sean had been pictured kissing Lulu at a birthday party in one of the lesser-known city nightclubs.

'Sean is very fond of Lulu,' Nina told the reporter. 'He thinks of her like his daughter.'

She was wrong, though. Sean wasn't thinking of Lulu (who was, after all, only a few years older than their own daughter Chrissie) like a daughter at all. He was thinking of her as the undeniably hot and sexy woman that she was. And Lulu (when asked for a quote by the same reporter) said that Sean Fallon was the most passionate actor she'd ever worked with and she was very glad he was only her fictional uncle.

When Sean had come home at the weekend after Nina had been contacted by the paper, she'd asked him about Lulu and he'd replied dismissively that she was a lovely young girl and that the kiss had been a friendly peck on the cheek. But after she read the story in the *City Scope*, along with Lulu's quote and a grainy picture of Sean and the actress with their heads almost touching, Nina knew, with a blinding certainty, that it was something more. She stared at a second photograph of Lulu, noting her shiny blond hair falling around her face in careless curls, and she felt her stomach spasm. She knew why Sean was with her. Although he'd married a woman with dark hair and allegedly smouldering eyes, Sean's preference had always been for blondes. And in particular, graceful, ethereal blondes like Lulu Adams. Nina exhaled sharply as she looked at the photo. This girl was trouble. She could feel it. And it scared her.

She wanted to confront her husband but she didn't know what to say. The wrong words now could reopen old wounds and recall a part of their life that she thought they'd put behind them for ever. She knew she wasn't wrong about Sean and Lulu but she didn't know exactly how right she was either. Sean had told her it was nothing. Maybe, in his mind, he was right. She would wait and see. She wouldn't rock the boat.

The following week, the *City Scope* (which had evidently hired a photographer to follow the man who'd been dubbed Ireland's sexiest soap star) snapped Lulu coming out of Sean's apartment at five o'clock in the morning.

Nina thought for a long time about what she was going to say to him, but when he walked in the door, all she did was sob that he was a fool and a liar and that he'd finally broken her heart. Then she grabbed the framed review of his performance from the wall and flung it at him. Fortunately (as he told her afterwards, it wouldn't have helped to have her arrested for assault) he ducked and it had hit the wall behind him, the glass front smashing into hundreds of pieces.

'I hope you're happy now,' he had said. 'And I hope the guests didn't hear it.'

Nina had totally forgotten that they didn't have a private life in the guesthouse. The thought of the guests hearing their row stopped her in her tracks. But the following week there was another snippet in the *City Scope*, this time saying that the new star's home life was 'stormy'.

When Sean returned after the next week's shooting, Nina, who'd spent the previous days assuring Chrissie, home from college for the weekend, that the papers were printing rubbish, told him that they had to talk.

'I won't be made a fool of,' she said, trying hard to keep the quaver out of her voice. 'I'm not young and green any more.'

'I swear to you it's nothing,' he said. 'Those idiots at the *City Scope* are blowing it up out of all proportion.'

'You were looking at her as though it was everything,' said Nina.

'I wasn't. It was just the camera . . .'

'Don't lie to me.' Her voice was grating. 'Don't. How much of an idiot do you think I am?'

'I don't think you're an idiot at all,' he said. 'God knows, Nina, you've never been that.'

'So why do you constantly treat me as if I am?' she demanded. 'Why?'

'I don't,' he said. 'Lulu and I—'

'Lulu and you what? What?' She choked back tears. 'I can't believe it, Sean. Not after everything we've gone through.'

'This is different.'

'Different!' She brushed the back of her hand across her eyes. 'I should bloody well hope so. When I think . . .' And then she starting crying properly, the tears streaming down her face. 'I was an imbecile to trust you, Sean Fallon. An utter imbecile.'

'No you weren't.' He went to put his arm around her but she shook it away. 'There's nobody in Ardbawn who's been a better husband than me these last years. Nobody.'

'Years of doing what you're supposed to do doesn't make up for even one night of . . . of . . .'

'OK, OK. I admit I fooled around with Lulu. But it was just a bit of fun, Nina. There was never anything serious in it. Nothing at all for you to worry about. I swear it.'

'Nothing to worry about! You're having an affair, Sean. And we had a deal.' She was suddenly angry.

'Oh, come on . . .'

'Don't "come on" me.' Nina blinked furiously. 'What are you doing with her, Sean? What are you trying to prove? You're more than twice her age, for heaven's sake. You can't possibly . . .' She'd stopped then, not sure what she either needed or wanted to say.

Sean had walked out of the room and neither of them had spoken. Later that evening he got a call on his mobile. Nina heard him say that he couldn't talk now, things were a bit fraught, then she grabbed the phone out of his hands.

'Don't be stupid,' Sean called as she raced up the stairs with it, ran into the bathroom and locked the door. 'Nina – for God's sake . . .'

There was no name assigned to the last call received. She rang it back and immediately recognised the distinctive girlish voice of Lulu Adams.

'Stop chasing after my husband,' she hissed through clenched teeth. 'You don't know what you're doing.'

'Oh, get over yourself,' said Lulu Adams, her tone much harsher than Nina had ever heard on TV. 'He works hard, he's entitled to a bit of fun. Which he doesn't get with you.'

Nina had ended the call and crumpled on to the floor. Suddenly all the fight had left her. Everything she'd wanted from Sean had gone. When she eventually unlocked the bathroom door and returned downstairs, he was sitting in front of the TV.

'I want you to leave,' she said.

'For heaven's sake, Nina . . .'

'That was our deal. You cheat, you leave.'

'But I never—'

'You fooled around. That's that. And I won't be told I'm no fun by some chit of a girl either.'

'She's a kid. She knows nothing.'

'A kid you're . . .' Nina clenched her fists. 'I don't care, Sean. I want you to go.'

'Nina, if you kick me out now, it'll rebound on you, not me.'

'You think?'

'People will think you're crazy.'

'No they won't.'

'Who knows what digging the papers'll do?'

She flinched.

'Please.' His eyes were soft and cajoling. 'We need each other, you and me.'

'You should've thought of that sooner.'

'We've been together a long time. We've made it work, Nina. You've said it yourself.'

'We made it work because *I* made it work,' she told him. 'Now you've destroyed it. On a whim.'

'It wasn't a whim.' He sounded desolate. 'I didn't mean—'

'I don't care what you meant or didn't mean.'

'I love you.'

'I don't think you do.' Nina could hear her own voice break. 'I don't think you do and I don't think you ever did, and I was an idiot to think that you might.'

'You're making a big mistake,' said Sean.

Nina shook her head. 'I made that a long time ago.'

It was like a *Chandler's Park* plot, she thought later that night as he threw some things into a bag and left. Their entire lives had been like a bloody *Chandler's Park* plot. Only in *Chandler's Park* people seemed to be able to deal with the consequences of their actions a lot better than in real life. They moved on quickly. Other things happened to them. The men got their comeuppance and the women ended up being stronger. Usually the put-upon female characters found someone else and were happy they'd stood up for themselves.

In real life it was very, very different. She knew that she'd been so angry with Sean that she couldn't bear to have him near her, and she knew she'd been the one to tell him to leave, but she'd never thought about what her life would be like after he'd gone. And it was miserable. She missed him terribly and she couldn't help thinking that she'd rushed into a course of action that she'd felt forced into but was too stubborn to change.

She kept going because of the guesthouse, although at night she couldn't sleep. She cried into the pillow that still smelled very faintly of him and asked herself why she'd been so determined to make him go. She knew the answer to that already – it had been the ultimatum she'd given him years ago – but she couldn't help thinking she'd allowed herself to be suckered into making a terrible mistake, mainly because she'd been so very angry at Lulu Adams. It was the younger girl's remark that she was no fun that incensed her. How dare Sean allow her to think that?

And yet . . . maybe it was true. Because she was the one who'd wanted to live her life in Ardbawn, working all the time, even when Sean said that maybe they should sell the house (which had eventually soared in value, making it a very desirable property) and leave. Perhaps if she'd listened to him, things would've been very different. And that was why she couldn't sleep at night and why she worried incessantly and why these days she felt, as Lulu Adams had put it, no fun at all.

Chapter 7

Talia was watching the TV when Sheridan arrived home from her date with Griff, and she could see straight away that things hadn't gone according to plan.

'What happened?' she asked.

'I guess I've broken up with him,' Sheridan replied. 'My life is officially in the toilet.'

'Oh, Sher.' Talia put her arms around her. 'Tell me.'

Sheridan related her conversation with her now ex-boyfriend word for word while Talia's mouth tightened.

'The shit,' she said.

'Not really.' Sheridan shook her head. 'I can understand it from his point of view. He's having a great time with a mate who happens to be female, which means he can shag her as well as play pool with her. Why should he exchange that for being with a proper girlfriend twenty-four/seven? For putting up with PMT and requests to empty the bins or unblock the drains or whatever.'

'I'm sure he has to do bin-emptying and drain-unblocking now.'

'It's different with his sisters, though, isn't it?'

'I guess so.' Talia gave her a sympathetic smile.

'I'm such a fool,' said Sheridan. 'I was so damn smug. About my job, my boyfriend, my life. Now I've got nothing.'

'You've got the Canaries to look forward to,' Talia reminded her. 'We'll have a great time there. Maybe you'll find a gorgeous Spanish hunk who'll take you away from all this so that you can live a life of luxury in the sun.'

'I peel in the sun.'

'And I shouldn't be flippant,' said Talia. 'Break-ups are shit. But you're being sort of composed, aren't you? I always end up in floods of tears and my face like a strawberry when I break up with someone.'

'I'm not composed at all but I don't do crying much,' said Sheridan. 'It wasn't the done thing in our house. We were supposed to learn from our mistakes and move on. Only sometimes it's not that easy, is it?'

'I do think that your upbringing was a bit emotionally underdone,' said Talia.

Sheridan laughed, although her voice cracked a little. 'We didn't waste our tears,' she said. 'And I'm not going to waste them on Griff Gibson. But I wish I hadn't asked him to move in. That way I'd still be in a relationship, even if it was headed nowhere fast.'

She was still feeling emotionally shaky by the time she left for the week's holiday with Talia. And although she tried to enjoy the cloudless skies and the cheap booze, she was thinking too much about the past and the future to be able to relax into the present. She tried hard not to be a wet blanket for Talia, who was being a great friend and not hooking up with any of the handsome men who asked her to join them for a drink or come to dinner with them. Talia said that she hadn't come on holiday to have a romance, she'd come to recharge her batteries before starting her new job. Sheridan wished that she felt her batteries were recharged too. But after the week she still felt as flat as a pancake. And as sick as a parrot.

After they returned to Ireland, and as soon as Talia moved to Belfast, Sheridan decided that she'd bite the bullet and visit her parents. She was finding it difficult to sit in the apartment on her own, despite the fact that as soon as she'd come back she'd reminded herself once again that her redundancy should be taken as an opportunity and had set about updating her CV and sending it out. Her key target was the *Irish Journal*, the *City Scope*'s biggest rival, but she tried everywhere else she could possibly think of. However, the net result so far was one request for a colour piece about women who followed football, for a fee that was derisory. The lack of other assignments was scaring her. She hadn't really expected to be totally without work. She wasn't sure what to do next. She needed to keep busy, not only so that she felt she was doing something useful with her time, but also so that she didn't brood about Griff. She was missing him badly and part of her wished she hadn't told him not to call. She couldn't help feeling that if he'd ignored her request and phoned, she would've come running, because she was feeling desperately lonely without him, especially as Talia wasn't there to distract her.

Although she wasn't entirely sure she wanted to hear her mother's advice on job-hunting (Alice was very good at dishing out advice although not quite so good at following it herself – headstrong, Pat would say affectionately, but rightly so), she couldn't bear the thought of sitting on her own in the empty flat any longer. She rang Alice and asked if it would be all right to stay for a few days. Alice told her that they'd be delighted to see her.

She threw some clothes into an overnight bag and put it into the boot of her Beetle. Normally she'd think that a four-and-a-half-hour drive was a desperate waste of her time, but time was now something she had plenty of. She got into the car, started the engine and selected her downloaded podcasts of *Fighting Talk*, the BBC sports comedy programme, which she loved and which, until now, she didn't always have time to listen to.

She stopped off for a coffee near Cashel and spent half an hour reading the *Journal*, mentally editing the sports reports herself though acknowledging that the coverage was good. She was glad to see that a young sprinter she'd tipped as a potential star had set a new personal best at a recent event and been voted Young Athlete of the Month. I'm good at what I do, she told herself. I know I am. A job will happen for me. I just have to stay positive. I just need to keep the winning mentality.

She maintained her positive mood for the rest of the journey and arrived in Doonlara at just after four o'clock. She turned off the town's main street and continued along the small side road where her parents' house was located. (Town was, of course, overstating things, she reminded herself. Doonlara was just a jumble of houses, a few small shops, three pubs and a petrol station.) Pat and Alice's house, about five kilometres past the garage, was a picture-perfect bungalow. It nestled in the shelter of low hills, backed by purple mountains and with views towards a navy-blue lake that glittered under the afternoon sun. Brightly coloured flowers, in both carefully tended flower beds and glazed ceramic pots, were a striking contrast to the whitewashed walls and slate roof. The front door, beneath an arched porch, was pillar-box red.

Sheridan could hear the barking of the dogs before she rapped on the enormous brass knocker in the shape of a lion's head. When her mother opened the door, Sheridan had to pat and greet Cannon and Ball, the two excited terriers, before she could even say hello to the trim woman standing in front of her.

Country life suited Alice, who was wearing a pair of fawn jodhpurs and an emerald-green polo-neck jumper. The vibrancy of the curly red hair, which Sheridan had inherited, had faded over the years, but Alice's eyes were as clear and sharp as ever and she looked far more energetic than Sheridan herself currently felt. She hugged her mother, then patted the dogs again as she followed Alice into the kitchen at the back of the house.

The sun slanted through the Velux windows in the kitchen roof and gave natural warmth to a room that was surprisingly modern. The floor was tiled in ivory marble and the units were high-gloss gunmetal grey. The table was dark wood, with brushed metal surrounds. Sheridan sat on one of the high-backed chairs and looked through the floor-to-ceiling windows at the garden beyond. Like the front of the house, it was a patchwork of colour against the darker mountains. She could still see the lake too. It was, she thought, spectacularly beautiful. But the space made her feel almost agoraphobic. She was used to being surrounded by buildings and roads. Wide-open country unnerved her.

Alice opened the patio doors and shooed the dogs outside, where they barked in protest but then settled down in a pool of sunlight to gnaw at a couple of ham bones.

'Your dad's up at the golf club,' she told Sheridan as she brought a pot of tea to the table. 'He'll be back this afternoon.'

'Are you still working there?' Sheridan took a Jaffa Cake from the tin that was already on the table.

'Of course. It's a handy number for me, three days a week.'

'Does it mean you can fiddle his handicap?' asked Sheridan.

Alice looked shocked and her daughter laughed.

'Only joking,' she said.

'You don't joke about things like that,' said Alice sternly. 'Now, come on, tell me how you're getting on. Have you sent your CV to everyone who matters?'

'Of course I have,' said Sheridan. 'I'm not stupid, you know.'

'I never said you were,' Alice told her. 'But sometimes people don't think outside the box about things like this.'

'Mam, I'm so far outside the box I'm catching pneumonia,' said Sheridan. 'There isn't anyone in the media who hasn't seen my CV by now. But all the newspapers are struggling because so many people want their news over the internet for free. Even though I've also sent my CV to loads of radio stations, I'm useless at broadcasting. Remember when I did that match report for the radio station? The stuff of nightmares!'

Sheridan had been covering a League of Ireland soccer match in Limerick and had been asked to do a report on air for a local station. But she'd stumbled her way through it, uncomfortable with speaking instead of writing, thinking that her words sounded stupid and contrived.

96

'It was your first attempt,' said Alice.

'And last,' observed Sheridan. 'They never asked me again.'

'Well that doesn't mean you won't be asked in the future.'

'Maybe not, but broadcasting is under the cosh a bit too,' she told her mother. 'It's an industry in a state of flux.'

'Perhaps you should think of something else.' Alice got up and took an ironing board from a built-in cupboard. She set it up and plugged in an iron. Then she brought in a basket of dried clothes from the utility room beside the kitchen. 'That's what I mean by outside the box.'

'I've been racking my brain,' said Sheridan. 'But I'm not sure what else I'm good at.'

'You're talking like a loser.' Alice banged the iron on to a jersey. 'I can't believe a daughter of mine is talking like a loser.'

'Not like a loser,' protested Sheridan. 'God knows, I haven't been brought up that way. But I've got to be a realist.'

'Listen, if I was a realist I wouldn't have put money on the Doonlara team to beat Killorglin last week,' said Alice. 'I wouldn't have backed Ireland against France in the World Cup qualifiers. I wouldn't have bought tickets for the All-Ireland final because I'd've been afraid Kerry wouldn't make it.'

'Ma – I hate to break it to you, but Kerry didn't win that final. And Ireland lost against France.'

'But Doonlara beat Killorglin,' said Alice in satisfaction. 'And a great game it was too.'

'One out of three isn't exactly a storming result,' remarked Sheridan.

'The Ireland–France was from the heart, not the head. But I put the money on Kerry before the season even started.

So they had to win a lot of matches to get to Croke Park in the first place. Losing the final was irrelevant in the end.'

'It's not the same thing,' said Sheridan.

'It's a winning mentality,' Alice told her. 'I have it. Your dad does too. So does Con. And Matt. But you – you're afraid of losing, and that's why you don't always win.'

'For crying out loud!' Sheridan looked at her mother in exasperation. 'Everyone else in the whole world thinks I'm a winner, except you.'

'Listen to me,' said Alice fiercely. 'You're in competition with everyone else who's unemployed and you're trying to win a job and you can't take any prisoners. You've got to go out there and beat off the competition and not be afraid of losing.'

'I'm not afraid of losing.'

'Of course you are. You always were.'

'That's nonsense.'

'It's the truth.' Alice folded the jersey and started on another.

'It's bullshit.' Sheridan found, to her horror, that her lip was trembling. She certainly wasn't going to cry in front of her mother. That would mark her as a loser for sure.

'Watch your language, Sheridan Gray.' Then Alice's tone softened. 'I just want what's best for you, that's all. I don't want you to undersell yourself.'

'I don't,' Sheridan told her. 'But I can't work miracles either.'

She brought her bag into the guest room and sat on the bed, staring out of the window at the dark mountains. She knew her mother was trying to be helpful, but sometimes, she thought wearily, helpful mothers gave you nothing but grief.

When she went back to the kitchen again, Alice had finished the ironing and was sitting at the table, a laptop open in front of her.

'I'm working on some stuff for the golf club,' she told Sheridan. 'I'm nearly finished.'

Sheridan had brought her laptop with her and she opened it too. 'Take your time,' she said. 'I'll check my emails.' She was hoping that someone would have contacted her about a job so that she could prove her winning status to her mother, but her inbox contained the usual amount of spam, chain mails and jokes. She busied herself with clearing it out in an effort to look like she was doing something useful.

'Any job offers?' asked Alice.

'Not this time.'

'We have to come up with a plan,' Alice told her.

Sheridan said nothing. It wasn't as though she didn't have a plan of her own. It wasn't as though she'd given up trying. She kept her eyes fixed on the screen as her fingers flew over the keyboard. But she was simply hitting random keys and not doing anything useful at all.

Alice made fish pie for dinner and it was ready when Pat finally came home. He left his golf gear at the back of the house and walked into the kitchen in his stockinged feet.

'Your ma loves her tiles,' he told Sheridan as he gave her a hug. 'It's more than my life's worth to walk on them with my golf shoes. She never worried about stuff like that in Dublin.'

'These tiles were very expensive,' Alice told him, her eyes twinkling. 'And you'd have them ruined if I didn't keep an eye on you.'

Pat and Alice joked with each other while Sheridan watched them. There was no doubt that they were still as much in love with each other now as they'd been when they'd married over thirty-five years earlier. She asked herself if it was possible these days to love the same person for such a long time. If she and Griff had married, would they have stuck together for thirty years or more? Of course, she would have gone into it expecting it to last for ever, but how realistic was that? She shivered suddenly. Until that moment she'd been feeling as miserable about losing Griff as she'd felt about losing her job, but now she was relieved. She'd loved him, sure. But did she have ten years' worth of love for him? Twenty? Thirty? Was breaking up with Griff the first blessing in disguise of her unemployed state?

'So how's the job-hunting going?' asked Pat as Alice served up the fish pie.

Sheridan told him the same as she'd told her mother, and Pat, too, started talking about plans and how to make herself stand out among everyone else who was looking for a job.

'I do know all this, Dad,' she said.

'Yes but you've got to put it into practice,' he told her. 'Fail to prepare . . .'

'. . . prepare to fail,' Sheridan finished. She knew the phrase well. It was one that both her parents had used incessantly when she and her brothers were smaller. The idea had been drilled into them.

'Success isn't everything . . .' Alice continued.

'. . . you can learn from failure.' Sheridan completed

another of her mother's favourite sayings. 'But you know what, Mam, there was nothing I needed to learn from being made redundant.'

'You're having to learn how to fall back on your own resources,' said Alice.

'Hum. And that's good, why?'

'It's always good to learn how to fend for yourself,' Alice said. 'Your team might let you down but you have to keep going. You have to have a fallback plan. Your flatmate, Talia, did. She was out of the stalls quickly. Smart girl. You should've had your eye on the ball like her.'

'I thought I had.'

'That won't happen to you again. And so you'll know to grab whatever opportunity you get in the future and use it to make a name for yourself again.'

'I was sure I *had* made myself a name,' said Sheridan. 'The problem is that it clearly wasn't good enough.'

Pat looked thoughtful. 'You did well at the *City Scope* but you didn't build on it. If it had been Matt or Con, they'd probably have moved on after landing a few exclusive interviews.'

'Dad! It was a good job. It was a good paper. It still *is* a good paper. There was no need to move on.'

'Y'see, you want to get ahead, you want to do well but you're always a little behind the game,' said Pat. 'I don't know why that is.'

'Everyone at the *Scope* thought I was competitive and hard hitting,' Sheridan told her. 'It's only in this family that I'm considered soft and useless.'

Neither of her parents rushed to correct her, which made her sigh in exasperation.

'I'll get a job,' she told them. 'I know I will. When I first went into journalism, I wanted to be a crime reporter. I need to look at those possibilities again. And other areas too. I was concentrating too much on sport, but there's much more to journalism than that.'

'That's the spirit,' said Pat. 'That's a Gray speaking. And I bet you'll find a great story to catapult you to the top.'

'I'll do my best. Now, can we stop talking about me and my lack of work and concentrate on something else instead?'

'Of course,' agreed Alice. 'But just one more thing – what does Griff have to say about your situation?'

Sheridan kept her voice as even as possible as she told her parents about her split with him. Alice frowned and Pat's eyes darkened.

'Well, I know things are different these days, but I'm glad he didn't move in with you if he'd no intention of marrying you,' said her mother. 'Girls are so foolish now. They let men have what they want and then the man gets bored with them and moves on. The rules of the game have never changed as far as fellas are concerned.'

'Mam!' Sheridan felt herself blush. Alice was outspoken and didn't care what she said in front of Pat. But Sheridan really didn't want her dissecting her love life as well as her career in front of her father.

'It has to be said.' Alice ignored her daughter's pained expression. 'Eventually most women want to settle down with a decent guy. But all this moving in together, drifting along doesn't help things. Because there's always a time when he gets itchy feet, and unless there's something to fight for, he can just walk away.'

'Did you get itchy feet, Dad?' Sheridan turned to Pat, sudden amusement in her eyes.

'In fairness, I was very lucky with your father,' Alice conceded, while her husband grinned. 'But men can be foolish, and there were always potential opportunities for him to make a holy show of himself. Fortunately for him, I was at his back. His team manager, keeping him on the straight and narrow.'

Pat guffawed and Sheridan couldn't help laughing.

'Is she right?' she asked her father.

'Ah, look, I like to let her think so,' Pat replied. 'The manager likes to think she's in charge. But she'd be nothing without the talent.'

Alice threw a cushion at her husband, who ducked so that it bounced harmlessly on to the floor. Alice was smiling as she picked it up. And Sheridan knew that her parents had a unique relationship. She doubted hers and Griff's would ever have been as strong. But, dammit, she would've liked him to have wanted to try.

Chapter 8

The apartment seemed very empty when she got back from Kerry. Other times when she'd been away and returned, she'd have come back to the lingering aroma of the Indian food that Talia loved but she didn't, and which her friend always had when she wasn't around. Talia would've left clothes or papers or various bits and pieces around the place, which would have given the apartment the feeling of being lived in. But now, as Sheridan stood in the living room and thought about the possibility of becoming a crime reporter, she felt very alone.

The next few days were difficult. She tried to tell herself to make the most of her days of freedom, but she was worried that her career was over and that people considered her a has-been. The *Irish Journal* had contacted her to say that they had nothing at the moment but that they'd keep her information on file. She'd got a similar response from other places to which she'd sent her CV (although most of them hadn't bothered to reply at all, which was very disheartening). She constantly reminded herself that it was important to be motivated and enthusiastic and to scan the newswires and the internet for possible stories to chase down, yet she was finding it difficult even to wake up. There didn't seem to be any urgency to her life any more. She wanted to be out there and doing something. But couldn't summon up the energy. And there was nobody to pester her about it either.

She was running out of money and allowing herself to fall apart, and she had to do something about it, she thought as she lay in bed a few mornings later. Her mother would be right in thinking that she was a loser. She was allowing the loser mentality to catch hold of her. Just because things weren't going to plan right now didn't mean that they wouldn't in the future.

Today, she told herself as she pulled on a T-shirt and jogging pants, today will be the day that something brilliant comes up. Or something quite good. Or even something adequate. Or, she thought, as she tugged a brush through her wiry hair, anything at all that would make her feel like a useful human being again.

It had been a while since she'd gone for a run, and the exercise calmed her. When she got back to the apartment she sat down and edited her CV, making herself sound like the sports-writing equivalent of Carl Bernstein. By the time she'd finished, she reckoned that only a fool wouldn't employ her. For the first time since she'd been made redundant, she felt as though she'd done something useful with her day. She saved all her files as PDFs and then sent them as emails to the sports editors of every newspaper she could think of. Then she sat back and waited for the phone to ring.

She was playing World Cup football on her Wii when finally it did. Her heart jumped with excitement, and then she realised it was Talia. She took a deep breath and switched on her bright, optimistic voice.

'How's it going?' asked her friend.

'Grand. How are you?'

'Och, fine.' Talia had already developed a bit of a northern twang to her voice. 'It's very different, but I like it. Miss the *Scope* – and Dublin, of course – but it's not too bad here.'

'I'm glad to hear it. We miss you in the big smoke too.'

'How's the job-hunting coming along?'

'Still looking,' Sheridan said lightly. 'I'm putting together some new material and I'm going to pitch some possible stories to editors. I think I'll end up freelancing, it's the way the whole industry is going. Nobody seems to be hiring right now.'

'That's partly what I was calling about.'

'Oh?' Sheridan tried to keep calm, but already she was hoping that Talia had got her something on the magazine. She pictured living in Belfast with her friend, working and socialising together like they'd done before. It was very comforting.

'It's a bit weird,' warned Talia. 'In fact, I don't know if . . . but the thing is, it's a job, even though it's only for a few months and even if . . . Well, you can judge for yourself, but it seems to me that you'd be better doing something than sitting around on your arse all day.'

'I'm not sitting on my arse all day,' protested Sheridan with a glance at the TV screen. 'What's the job?'

'It's with a regional paper,' Talia told her. 'They need maternity cover. I thought perhaps that if you were working, then it would be easier to get accepted somewhere else.'

Sheridan knew her friend was right. Potential employers

were much more likely to hire someone who already had a job.

'Which paper?' she asked.

'The *Central News*,' Talia replied.

'The what?'

'*Central News*,' repeated Talia.

'Is it a Belfast paper? I've never even heard of it.'

'It's a weekly paper and it covers the South Leinster area. Not huge, but not tiny either.'

Sheridan said nothing. Although she knew many regional papers, she couldn't remember ever hearing about the *Central News* before. So despite Talia's comments, it couldn't be that big.

'The thing is,' continued Talia, 'it's owned by Paudie O'Malley.'

'Paudie O'Malley? The shit who made me redundant? You've got to be kidding me!'

'Look, I know you probably don't think much of him right now, but—'

'It's his fault I'm out of work!' cried Sheridan. 'Him and his so-called investment in the *Scope*. D'you really think he's going to employ me on his crappy local paper when he wouldn't keep me there?'

'I'm quite sure Paudie didn't personally choose you for the chop,' said Talia.

'Did you see the quote attributed to him in the *Journal*?'

'What quote?'

Sheridan gritted her teeth. She still couldn't think of it without getting angry. 'He said that the *City Scope* had been carrying passengers for too long and it was time to cut the dead wood. Dead wood! How dare he! I'm not dead wood.' Then her voice faltered. 'At least I wasn't until he got his hands on me. Imagine, he stays out of the limelight for years and then his first pronouncement is one that insults me.'

'Sher, it wasn't aimed at you personally.'

'Maybe not.' Sheridan cleared her throat. 'Maybe not, but it felt like it.'

'He's insensitive, I'll admit,' conceded Talia. 'But you can't let that hold you back.'

'Given that he considers me to be a dead wood passenger, he'll hardly welcome me on board his provincial paper, will he?'

'He's not the editor of the *Central News*, just the owner. He has nothing to do with hiring and firing.'

'How d'you know all this?' demanded Sheridan.

'My aunt lives in Ardbawn, where the paper is produced. I was talking to her about the changes at the *Scope* and my new job and she told me about this. From what she says, I think it's a bit of a vanity project for O'Malley, because I doubt very much it makes any money, although its website is quite good. The paper itself carries a lot of ads for his businesses – you know he started out in print and packaging before moving to media stuff. He still has big interests there. Apparently the main admin person, who also writes some of the local news, is going on maternity leave and they're looking for a person to take her place.'

'Are you really suggesting that I go for a temp admin job on something that sounds like a freebie newsheet?'

'Aunt Hayley says it's very popular in the town. And in Carlow and Kilkenny as well. There are plenty of local-interest stories.'

'Like what – "Parking ticket issued to overdue shopper"?'

Sheridan snorted derisively. 'Talia, I truly appreciate you telling me about this, but you're talking about a temporary position at a paper that undoubtedly pays the bare minimum – and I'd have to move to a one-horse town in the middle of nowhere to do it.'

'Have you got someone to share the flat with you?' asked Talia.

'Not yet.'

'So you were thinking of moving out anyway?'

'Clearly I've been looking for somewhere smaller . . .'

'I understand if you don't want this job,' Talia said. 'I know it's a bit of a stopgap. I know you probably feel terrible because you haven't been snapped up by the competition. I know you! I bet you're sitting in playing video games and feeling crap. That's what you do when you're frustrated.'

'I'm not frustrated. I'll get something!' Sheridan turned her back on the TV monitor, where her Wii World Cup squad was still waiting for her next instruction.

'You're impatient, though,' said Talia. 'If something doesn't work straight away, you don't give it a chance. And you're probably feeling lonely and down.'

'Give me a break! You're making me sound like a total basket case.'

'You said it yourself before I left – you've lost your job and your boyfriend and your flatmate. I'd be feeling a bit shell shocked if I was you. So all I'm doing is giving you the opportunity to cut loose for a few months, get your head together.'

'On a rubbish paper owned by Paudie O'Malley!'

'Hey, come on, think of the irony. He'll be paying your salary again despite everything.'

'I'm not big into irony.'

'I know this isn't what you wanted, but it's better than nothing.'

'I'm sure they'd rather give the job to a local person,' said Sheridan. 'They probably don't want someone like me anyhow.'

'Why not?' demanded Talia.

'I'd be a blow-in. They'd resent me.'

'They should be grateful to get you. Give them a call. Set up an interview at least.'

'I'll think about it,' said Sheridan.

'The editor's name is DJ Hart. According to Aunt Hayley, he's a sweetheart.'

'I've never yet met an editor who was a sweetheart.'

'Call him.'

'All right, all right, I will.'

'Attagirl! Bring a touch of the Sheridan Gray magic to the sleepy local rag.'

'Rag?'

'You know what I mean.'

'Yes, I do. And . . . well, thanks, Talia, for thinking about me.'

'What are friends for?'

'You're a good friend,' said Sheridan. 'I hope it's going brilliantly for you in Belfast.'

'Ah, it's not the *Scope*. But it's grand. I'm grand. And you will be too.'

'Sure I will,' said Sheridan. 'I'll keep in touch.'

They chatted for a few more minutes and then finished the call. Sheridan picked up the Wii remote and pointed it at the television. She wasn't sure if she'd bother to ring this

DJ Hart guy. The idea of working with anything associated with Paudie O'Malley set her teeth on edge. No matter what Talia said, his remark about dead wood had hurt. Besides, she truly did believe that someone local would get the job. She'd be putting herself through the mill for nothing. She waved the remote at the screen. Fernando Torres made a searing run up the wing and scored a goal. The crowd went wild with excitement.

Sheridan started another game and then threw the remote to one side. She opened her laptop and googled Paudie O'Malley. Not surprisingly, there were a lot of hits, many referring to his recent stake in the *City Scope* and his demand to the management team that it radically cut costs. An article quoted him as saying that people were a necessary part of doing business, but a very unreliable part because they mixed up emotion and business sense far too much. Typical, she thought, of a man who considered decent journalists to be nothing but dead wood!

As she dug a bit deeper and delved further into his past, she learned that Paudie's business success had taken off after the death of his wife sixteen years previously. It seemed that he'd immersed himself in his work after Elva had been found dead at the family home in Ardbawn. Sheridan surfed through the hits, her curiosity piqued. She'd known that Paudie was a widower, but she hadn't realised that his wife had died after apparently falling from an upstairs window at what was described as their 'gracious period home'. Paudie had been interviewed by the police after the body had been discovered, but her death had been eventually described as 'a tragic accident'. While some reports said that Paudie was 'devastated', others seemed to insinuate that the O'Malley marriage

111

wasn't happy and that Elva's death had been something of a release for him. One, in particular, noted that he hadn't shed any tears at his wife's funeral. Another (from a now defunct newspaper) seemed to imply that he had been treated by the police as a prime suspect in Elva's death and that there was a distinct possibility that he'd tried to cover up what had happened.

Sheridan's eyes widened as she read. She tried googling Paudie O'Malley+wife+murder, but there were no links that specifically accused him of pushing Elva out of the window. Nevertheless, it was an intriguing thought. What if his marriage had been totally miserable and he'd decided to end it; not by divorcing his wife (Sheridan frowned, thinking that sixteen years previously he wouldn't have been able to anyway), but by finding a more permanent solution. After all, she thought, if a man believed – as Paudie did – that people were generally unreliable, perhaps getting rid of his wife for good was a better option for him than separating from her and knowing she was in the background all the time. It wouldn't be out of character for someone with his ruthless reputation. Would it?

She exhaled slowly as she closed the laptop and told herself that she was probably letting her imagination run away with her. After all, there had been a proper garda investigation and Paudie hadn't been charged with anything. But what if it hadn't been as thorough as it could've been? What if there was another story there? What if Paudie, at the start of his business success, had somehow managed to influence the gardai? Finding out could be the opportunity she'd been looking for. It would give her the chance to submit something radically different to the editors who'd already told her that they didn't need sports journalists. She could make a name for herself as a fearless investigator instead. And she'd show Mr Slash-and-Burn that, whatever else she was, she certainly wasn't dead wood!

The investigative task would be a lot easier if she was based in Ardbawn, a mole in his nearly freebie newspaper.

She picked up the phone and dialled DJ Hart's number.

Chapter 9

Nina tried to maintain a determined front when Sean left, even though she was no longer determined inside. She told herself that this wasn't the time to forgive and forget, and that she'd behaved like a strong, independent woman. The only problem was that she didn't feel strong at all.

She felt even less strong when the children called, as they did regularly, although she tried to sound positive and upbeat for their sakes. Chrissie had considered putting off her backpacking trip to be with her, but Nina had insisted on her not changing her plans, promising that she'd be perfectly fine on her own. So she absolutely had to sound cheerful whenever her daughter called. When she'd told Alan about it, her son had muttered something about punching his father's lights out. Nina reminded him that he was on a peacekeeping mission and that he shouldn't be thinking about reacting with violence. Alan retorted that sometimes violence was a solution, no matter what people thought.

Nina was comforted by the fact that her children were supportive, even though she didn't want them to feel that they had to take sides. It was probably a good thing that both of them were out of the country for an extended period.

She didn't think she could cope with listening to their opinions as well as spending nights debating with herself.

Sean's affair with Lulu Adams was a hot topic of conversation in Ardbawn too. Although most people believed that Nina had been right to show him the door, there were a certain number who thought that the affair had been almost inevitable and that Nina should have accepted it for what it was, forgiven him and moved on. As it was, though, speculation continued about whether Sean and Lulu were still an item. They hadn't been seen in any further paparazzi-style photos, but they were together on *Chandler's Park* every single night. The programme's ratings were higher than ever, and a current subplot was indicating that Sean's character, Christopher, wasn't actually Fiona's natural uncle at all – that he'd been taken in as a child by the family, who'd kept his origins secret. The lack of a genetic bond between them (only in a bloody soap, thought Nina despairingly) meant that the way would be cleared for a sizzling affair, if that was what the producers thought would keep the ratings high. All the indications so far were that it would. Such an affair would be par for the course for Fiona anyhow, most people said. Sure, there was no one in Chandler's Park that she hadn't gone to bed with.

The blurring of the characters and the real people hurt Nina more than she could have imagined. She would open the paper and see a story about the soap talking about the searing chemistry between Fiona and Christopher, and she would think about the relationship between Lulu and Sean and wonder where it was heading. Her initial response of anger and betrayal was now being replaced by sadness and nagging worry that she was handling things the wrong way.

She'd made a decision to ignore his phone calls and delete his emails without opening them, even though it was very hard. She knew that he was able to manipulate her and she didn't want it to happen this time. But as time went on and the phone calls and emails stopped, she felt alone and adrift and uncertain about her future.

She checked her horoscope on a regular basis to see if it could give her any pointers. She felt that the astrologer, Phaedra, was talking directly to her, because almost every week forgiveness and understanding were mentioned. Yet she didn't want to forgive Sean, no matter how much she understood him. However, with every passing day her anger was abating and her loneliness was increasing, and she became more and more unsure of herself and the decisions she'd made.

It seemed to Nina that her life was a succession of choices, none of which were necessarily working out the way she'd expected. She kept asking herself how things would have turned out if she'd made different choices in the past. Would she still be in Ardbawn now? Would her life with Sean have taken a very different path? Would she still be happy with him? Or would she be much, much happier without him? Would he have ended up on a TV show anyway? Or would his life have been just as humdrum as he apparently thought it was?

And then she got the solicitor's letter and almost fell to pieces.

Sean wanted a reconciliation. He wanted to meet her to work things out, either at home or at a neutral venue. He was prepared, according to the letter, to consider counselling. But if Nina refused what was a perfectly reasonable request and continued to bar him from the family home, then he would have no option but to consider a formal separation and divorce. In that case they would have to look at their joint assets, the biggest of which was the guesthouse. The solicitor's letter reminded Nina of how much work Sean had put in to bring it up to its present level of business. And how it was his livelihood as much as hers. His time on *Chandler's Park* was limited. He had reasonable expectations that his role in the guesthouse would have been for life. The entire letter seemed like blackmail to Nina, whose hands shook as she read it. If she didn't take Sean back, he'd take her home from her. She realised that he had rights too, but the way she looked at it, he was the one who'd messed things up. She didn't see why she should have to suffer for it. Especially when she was suffering already.

She was completely wiped out by the letter. She felt that she'd used up all of her emotional strength in telling Sean to leave and she didn't know how to cope with reconciliation talks. She knew she missed him more than she'd ever imagined and she couldn't help thinking that if she saw him she'd simply cave in and take him back, but if she did that, she'd lose the outer shell she was building up around herself. He'd be able to hurt her again. And she couldn't cope with being hurt. Not any more. But, she would tell herself as she tossed and turned and tried to figure out what was best, she wasn't coping very well being without him either. He was part of the fabric of her life. They were bound together more tightly than anyone else she knew. Maybe that was why he wanted to come home. Maybe that was why, deep down, she wanted him home too.

She was disgusted by her own neediness. She reminded herself of the promises he'd made, the ones he'd now broken.

He'd known what would happen. He'd walked into it with his eyes wide open. And her problem, she thought, was that she'd kept her own eyes shut. She'd ignored the signs. She was good at that. She always had been.

She didn't know what to do. She wished someone else could tell her. That someone else would make the decision for her. These days she was finding it hard to decide on whether to wear a black or a white T-shirt under her jumper each day. So how could she possibly be clear about what she wanted for the rest of her life?

Despite the teeming rain outside the window, she needed to go for a walk. Walking had always helped to clear her mind and order her thoughts. Being out in the elements, she thought, as she pulled on a coat and her practical but very unstylish wellington boots, was exhilarating. She would walk as far as Ardbawn and back, and perhaps by then she would know how to react to Sean's letter. It was better not to rush into anything stupid; she should reflect on what she wanted, on what was important to her. She'd made decisions in the past on impulse, with a desire to protect herself and her family, and now she wondered how right they'd been. For sure, she murmured to herself as she opened her umbrella and set off down the road, her life would have turned out differently. She certainly wouldn't have been walking in the Ardbawn rain, worrying about Sean.

That was the thing, though. You made decisions you hoped were the right ones and you had to live with the consequences. But sometimes it wasn't until a very long time afterwards that you realised what those consequences actually were.

Chapter 10

Even with her satnav, Sheridan nearly missed the turn-off for Ardbawn because of the relentless rain beating against the windscreen of her car and defeating the frantic swishing of the Beetle's windscreen wipers. It was only as she was at the turn itself that she saw it, and spun the steering wheel so sharply that she almost ended up in a ditch. Which would be a great start to my rural life, she muttered to herself, as she proceeded slowly along the secondary road, keeping an eye out for waterlogged potholes. If I have a potential rural life at all.

Much to her dismay, DJ Hart hadn't sounded all that enthusiastic about interviewing her. When she told him she'd worked on the *City Scope*, he'd asked why on earth she'd want to come to a place like Ardbawn.

'It would be a challenge,' she told him, given that the whole idea of moving out of the city *was* a major challenge as far as she was concerned, and that unearthing the truth about Paudie O'Malley would probably be an even greater one.

'It wouldn't be what you're used to,' he said.

'I'd like to discuss it with you all the same.'

'Oh, all right. Thursday at twelve.'

His lack of enthusiasm was off-putting, but Sheridan felt better than she had in weeks. She was finally going to an interview. And she was very definitely regarding it as an opportunity and not as a chance to languish in total boredom for the next few months.

The road ahead of her widened suddenly and she realised she'd reached the town. She drove slowly past the stone-clad church into a diamond-shaped plaza paved with granite stones and dotted with flower planters, although the flowers were now battered thanks to the incessant pounding of the rain. The wooden benches in the plaza were, naturally, empty.

There was a traffic jam on the main street, which Sheridan supposed was a result of the weather. The crawl through the town allowed her to see that the façades of the various shops and businesses were traditionally styled and painted in pretty pastel colours that looked cheerful even on such a wet day. When she reached the narrow bridge that crossed the river, she realised that it was this, and not the rain, that was the main cause of the slow traffic. After the bridge the road widened out again, and she started looking for the offices of the newspaper.

In the new commercial centre, DJ had told her. She'd been wondering about that, because despite its obviously recently renovated plaza, Ardbawn didn't seem to be a hotbed of commerce, but as she rounded another bend the satnav told her she'd reached her destination, and she saw a two-storey yellow-painted building to her left with a sign announcing that it was the Ardbawn Commercial Centre.

She pulled into the only available space in its small car park and turned off the engine. Commercial Centre was far too grand a name for it, she thought. The ground floor consisted of a deli, an estate agent and a veterinary practice. As she looked through the rain-spattered windscreen, she could see the offices of a dentist and a solicitor as well as those of the *Central News* on the first floor. Further along the road, on the opposite side, she spotted the distinctive blue and yellow sign of a Lidl supermarket.

What the hell am I doing? she asked herself as she got out of the car and grabbed her laptop bag. This is so not me.

She pressed the button marked 'Central News' on the red door in front of her. She was beginning to think that she'd got the wrong day or time when eventually a disembodied voice said, 'First floor,' and it buzzed open.

The internal door for the *Central News* was immediately in front of her at the top of the stairs. There was no bell, so she rapped on it, and after another pause it was eventually opened by a giant of a man wearing faded denims and a check shirt open at the neck. (Open at the neck because it would be impossible to close, thought Sheridan, as she looked at him. He was bigger and more powerful than many of the rugby players she'd met in her life. She reckoned he was anywhere between thirty-five and fifty.)

'Sheridan Gray.'

'How're ya? DJ Hart. Editor, *Central News*.' He took her extended hand and almost crushed it in his own

'Thanks for seeing me,' she said.

'No bother.' He waved her towards a white melamine desk covered with papers, filing trays and the remnants of an early lunch, which had clearly been a burger and chips. (She'd noticed a takeaway burger bar as she'd rounded the bend.)

There were two more desks in the room. One was occupied

by a tall, thin man in a black T-shirt and jeans, who didn't look up from the computer monitor in front of him. The other was vacant, although, like DJ's, it was covered in papers and files.

'Well, now.' DJ sat behind the desk and cleared a space with a wave of his enormous hand. 'Sheridan Gray. Here in Ardbawn. We're honoured.'

She couldn't be sure if he was being sarcastic or not.

'Thanks for giving me the chance to come,' she said. She glanced towards the desk where the thin man was still engrossed in his work and ignoring them.

'It's not often we get high-profile reporters looking to fill in with us,' said DJ.

Sheridan gave him a rueful smile. 'I guess the local papers are doing better than the high-profile ones at the moment,' she said. 'And Paudie O'Malley owns a hundred per cent of the *Central News*, not just twenty-five per cent.'

DJ laughed. It was a deep, belly laugh that made his entire frame shake.

'You're not so bad after all,' he said. 'I was thinking that you'd come here with notions about yourself.'

'How can I have notions?' asked Sheridan. 'I'm the one who's looking for a job.'

DJ laughed his belly laugh again, and Sheridan felt herself relax a little.

'So, lookit,' he said. 'I've read your stuff. I liked the piece you did about the All-Ireland last year. Very good. And your soccer coverage is excellent. Even the article you did about the Brazil girls' football was interesting. But the thing is, sweetheart, I don't need a sports reporter. I have one of those.'

122

Sheridan glanced towards the man working at the other desk again.

'Not Seamus,' he said. 'Shimmy – as he's known to his nearest and dearest, which we are of course – is our ads man. That means he's the most important person here. He sells space in the paper. He doubles up as our IT person, which makes him practically indispensable. He keeps our website up and running. We couldn't function without him.'

Seamus looked up and grinned so that he no longer looked stern, forbidding and just a little scary. 'I'll remind you of that next time you're trying to cut my wages,' he observed.

'Don't mind him,' said DJ. 'He loves a joke. So, OK, Shimmy is the powerhouse, I'm the managing editor and Myra is the admin person.'

'Who does the sports?' asked Sheridan.

'Des Browne,' replied DJ. 'He's been with us for years. Freelance, that's all we need, because most of our sports stuff is local. We get the big reports from syndicates.'

'Right.'

'Which means we don't honestly need your particular talents.'

'I can do more than sports journalism,' she told him. 'That happens to be what I've concentrated on for the past few years, but it's not the only writing I'm able to do.'

'Maybe. All the same, you're probably too specialised for us.'

'Why did you ask me here then?'

'Because you were pushy on the phone,' he said. 'I liked that.'

'If you're not going to treat me as a serious candidate for the job, you've wasted my time in getting me to come here on a pig of a day,' said Sheridan.

'Feisty, which I like as well.'

'Look, I'm not here for you to like me,' she told him. 'I'm here to interview for the job of . . . well . . . some kind of reporter, I thought. But if Myra only does admin, and she's the person you're replacing . . .' Her voice faltered. She wasn't great on admin. But she still wanted the job. She wanted the chance to prove herself. And, she reminded herself, the chance to investigate Paudie O'Malley.

'Myra does everything,' DJ said. 'She writes stuff, she edits the bits we get in from the locals – a lot of our reporting is stuff sent in from the locals; we just tidy it up. She makes sure we have our regular features and the girlie things like hair and beauty and recipes and horoscopes and all that blather. Which is why I'm not sure you'd be good at it.' He looked at her appraisingly and Sheridan felt her cheeks redden. She wished she'd thought more about her appearance for the interview. She was perfectly neat and presentable, with her hair drawn back and wearing a white shirt and black trousers, but perhaps she didn't look like the sort of person who would be good with horoscopes and beauty treatments. Or recipes. Not that they were things she was traditionally good at, or even interested in. But she had to make DJ believe that she was.

'I know absolutely loads about beauty and fashion,' she told him firmly. 'I'm totally up to speed on it. I shared an apartment with the *City Scope*'s fashion editor and I've been to loads of fashion shows. I've even been to Milan.' She didn't say that this was for a girls' weekend with Talia and some of her mates, and not for Fashion Week. The way she looked at it, it was impossible not to soak up fashion in Milan anyway.

124

'Really?'

She stayed calm even with the astonished expression on DJ's face.

'I'm completely clued into the latest looks and . . . and face creams and . . . stuff like that,' she finished.

'It's not just about the writing.' DJ had regained his equilibrium. 'Myra gets all the womany stuff together from different sources but she also goes out and meets people. We do reports on local school events and the amateur dramatic society and the various social groups and committees . . .'

'No trouble at all to me,' said Sheridan.

She wanted this job now. Not because it was an opportunity for her to add to her CV, or because it might give her the chance to do a bit of quiet snooping on the man who'd made her redundant, but because she couldn't bear the idea of being turned down. The competitive gene that she always thought had passed her by had suddenly flared into life inside her. She wanted to be able to phone her mother and say that she'd got the first job she'd interviewed for. Besides, she thought, she deserved it. There was nobody better than her at getting copy together, and she'd often had to edit reports sent in by various sporting groups about their events. Cutting a piece about the local flower show down to size would be child's play to her.

'We're a small organisation and the job is temporary,' said DJ. 'Myra hasn't finalised her plans yet. Obviously she could take up to a year off, but she's very keen on coming back well before then, perhaps even after three or four months. That being the case, I'm not sure it's what you really want.'

'What I really want is to be a sports writer on a major newspaper again.' Sheridan decided to be completely candid with him. 'I can't lie about that. But working here will give me a great deal of experience that I wouldn't otherwise get, and hopefully you'll find that my experience is helpful to you too.'

'I have someone else to interview,' said DJ as he stood up. 'So I'll let you know.'

'You haven't interviewed me yet.' Sheridan remained in her seat.

'Ah, I only had to hear you talk,' DJ told her. 'I've read your stuff.'

Sheridan couldn't help feeling that she was being short-changed. It had taken her an hour and a half to get to Ardbawn and she was being dismissed after less than ten minutes.

'We're a close-knit bunch here,' added DJ. 'Everybody gets on with everybody else.'

She wasn't sure if he meant the town or the newspaper. She stood up too.

'Thanks for seeing me,' she said.

'You're sure you could do fashion and beauty?' He scratched the back of his head as he looked at her appraisingly.

'Absolutely,' she assured him. 'And the horoscopes and recipes too. No bother at all.'

'Right so. I'll be in touch.'

'Thanks.' She smiled at him and stretched out her hand. As he crushed it again, she rather wished she hadn't.

It was still raining when she got into the car and edged back on to the main road. Heavier if anything now, and once again the wipers swiped across the windscreen in a mild frenzy. She was driving cautiously over the bridge when the bright red umbrella of a woman who'd been crossing the road ahead of her was jerked out of her hand by the wind and whirled into the air towards the car. The woman stopped in the middle of the road. Sheridan jammed on the brakes and aquaplaned to a halt, narrowly avoiding both the pedestrain and a signpost saying 'Bawnee River', where the umbrella had ended up.

Her hands were shaking as the woman finished crossing the road. When she reached the pavement she shrugged apologetically before hurrying along the main street. All Sheridan had time to see was her huge dark eyes in her paper-white face. The driver of the car behind honked his horn, because the Beetle was now blocking the road. Sheridan restarted the engine with trembling fingers and drove as far as the plaza, where, spotting a vacant space, she parked the car and released a relieved sigh.

When the car had skidded on the wet surface, she'd been terrified that she wouldn't be able to avoid the woman in front of her. It wouldn't have been her fault – if the woman hadn't stopped so suddenly in the middle of the road there wouldn't have been any chance of hitting her – but she reckoned that it wouldn't have done her chances of a job with the *Central News* any good if on her first visit to Ardbawn she'd killed one of the locals.

She was feeling too shaky to drive, so she got out of the car and sprinted across the plaza (which she could now see was called The Square – a name she felt could have done with some editorial input) to a small café with a blue facade and bedraggled flower baskets handing outside.

The café was warm and steamy and three of the eight

tables were occupied by women chatting. A lone man sat at the fourth, reading a magazine with a picture of a large green tractor on the cover. Sheridan ordered a cappuccino and a doughnut and picked up a copy of the *Central News* that had been left on the table.

Before coming for her so-called interview, she'd checked the paper's website (a professional-looking job she'd had to admit, so Shimmy was clearly good at what he did) and had eventually managed to get hold of the previous week's print edition. Now she browsed through the most recent paper, noting that – as with the one she'd seen – almost all of the stories had a bias towards Carlow, Kilkenny and Ardbawn, with most of them being about issues affecting Ardbawn itself. This week the paper focused on the preparations for the town's Spring Festival, the issue of unfinished houses on the estate near the Dublin road, a medal for local girl Jacinta Halpin in an Irish dancing competition and the designation of new no-parking areas near St Raphaela's school. The sports pages were almost exclusively about Ardbawn events, while the fashion and beauty section was bland: a new miracle diet (Sheridan loved her food too much to ever last more than two days on any diet), the latest raincoats (timely, she reckoned), the top six waterproof mascaras (equally timely) and a foolproof way of doing your own French manicure.

Horoscopes were near the back and written by someone called Phaedra. Hers told her that it was time to take the plunge. She glanced out of the window at the rain-sodden streets and wondered if the astrologer was talking practically or metaphorically.

The remainder of the paper was devoted to advertisements, with a double-page spread for O'Malley's print works and more for other O'Malley companies. Sheridan had done some additional digging on Paudie O'Malley's business empire over the last few days and discovered that it was more extensive than she'd realised. It was amazing to think that someone like him was holed up in a backwater like Ardbawn. But maybe he had his reasons. And perhaps she could blow the lid on them. She suddenly felt as enthusiastic and empowered as she had at the beginning of her redundancy, optimistic about possibilities instead of broken by realities.

She'd just got back into her car when her mobile rang.

'Is that Sheridan?'

'Yes.'

'DJ Hart here.'

'Hi, DJ.'

'Listen to me, love, I've talked to the other candidate.'

She glanced at her watch. It was nearly one thirty. 'That was quick.'

'Yeah, well, it was all set up and I knew it wasn't going to take much time. So here's the thing . . .'

She didn't care that she wasn't going to get a job in Ardbawn. It was a pity, but it didn't matter. She felt good about herself again. She'd get something, somewhere. She wouldn't mind what it was.

'I want you to come and work for us, pet. You're by far the most suitable person.'

It took her a second to realise he was offering her the job.

'Are you sure?'

'Of course I'm sure. For God's sake, none of the other feckers who applied have a qualification at all. They're just looking for a bit of work experience. And the thing is that I need someone who knows what they're doing. You mightn't have thought so because you're used to a big organisation, but we're a busy office. There's lots going on. At least you know how it works. And sure, we need the woman's touch anyway.'

Sheridan was pretty certain that any employment tribunal would be horrified at the idea that DJ wanted her to work for them to bring a woman's touch.

'Myra keeps the whole show on the road,' said DJ. 'I know you can do that too.'

'You hardly spoke to me,' Sheridan pointed out.

'You said enough.'

'I'm still in Ardbawn,' she said. 'Should I come back and talk some more?'

'Sure. We can get it all done and dusted today.'

'I'll be there in a few minutes,' she said.

Taking the plunge, she said to herself as she switched on the wipers and headed back towards the commercial centre. Fulfilling my destiny. Getting a job, at last.

Chapter 11

Having her umbrella ripped out of her hand by the wind and almost freezing with terror in front of a moving car hadn't done Nina's nerves much good. Her mind had been totally fixed on the letter from Sean's solicitor when she'd stepped out on to the main street, her view of the oncoming traffic partly obscured by the umbrella that was now being carried downstream by the fast-running river. She'd been lucky that the driver of the car had reacted so quickly. Nina felt a wave of sympathy for the woman, who, she was sure, had received just as much of a fright as she'd done herself. She'd walked home quickly, alert for oncoming traffic, although the road to the guesthouse was relatively quiet. As a method for sorting out her jumbled thoughts, the walk hadn't been very successful, but at least her tiredness was now of the physical rather than the mental kind.

She removed her coat and hung it on the rack inside the kitchen door, pulled off her boots and then made herself a cup of tea before sitting down at the table and opening the most recent copy of the *Central News*. Nina always bought the local paper, because she liked to know what was going on in the town, even though she didn't always bother to read it.

She flicked through the paper and stopped at the home page. She read the latest recipe for barm brack (something she was famed for: she added a touch of ginger to it which anyone who tasted it loved) and scoffed mentally at a tip for chopping onions so that your eyes didn't water. She'd never been able to do that, and as for Sean . . . he used to wear a snorkelling mask whenever it was his turn to chop them. She couldn't help smiling at the memory, even though she wanted to cry too.

Her horoscope was mildly encouraging, telling her that a new arrival would have a positive impact on her life. She wondered which new arrival that might be. Although bookings were slow, she had a fisherman coming early the following week and a couple of overnighters for Friday. The overnighters would be in the main house but the fisherman was staying in one of the studios. The studios, two self-contained apartments separate from the rest of the house, had been Sean's idea and were very popular with the fishermen because there was plenty of room for their gear.

She turned to the crossword page and began filling in the answers. It was restful, she thought, to have the house to herself today, even if the battering rain and howling wind was making the atmosphere eerily like a horror movie in which the lone woman is terrorised by—

The sudden shrill of the front-door bell startled her so much she knocked her teacup on to the floor.

The woman standing on the step seemed vaguely familiar. And she was looking at Nina as though she knew her too. Both of them remembered at exactly the same time.

'You were in the road . . .'

'You were driving the car . . .'

'I'm so sorry I made you stop like that,' said Nina. 'I was just so taken aback when my umbrella flew out of my hand, I didn't think of where I was.'

'It's OK,' Sheridan told her. 'I got a terrible fright, though.'

'Sorry,' said Nina again.

'No harm done. Um . . . are you Nina Fallon? Can I come in and talk to you?'

The first thought that came into Nina's head when she realised that the woman wasn't here to harangue her for stopping in the middle of a main road was that she was a reporter from one of the national newspapers. They'd camped outside the guesthouse for a while, wanting to get a photo-graph of the woman that Sean Fallon had left. (None of the papers had printed the truth. That she'd told him to go. So much for checking the facts, she'd thought grimly.) They'd abandoned their stakeout after she hadn't emerged for a few days and when they realised that she was getting all her supplies delivered. Apparently they'd also tried to get some information from the local shops about her, but the Ardbawn people had clammed up, which she appreciated very much.

'It's about a room,' Sheridan added.

Nina nodded and beckoned her into the residents' lounge. It was bright and airy, with spectacular views over the Bawnee River, although those views were obscured by the day's driving rain.

'We have eight guest rooms,' she told Sheridan. 'How long did you want to stay?'

'Actually, I'm coming to town for a while,' said Sheridan. 'I was wondering about a studio room. For three months to start with?'

When she'd gone back to see DJ Hart again, she'd agreed to join the *Central News* at a salary significantly less than she'd been paid by the *City Scope*. She realised that the money didn't matter to her. Having the job and being able to tell her parents that she'd succeeded was far more important. DJ had shaken her hand in delight (she hoped there'd be no more need for him to do that; she was pretty sure that eventually he'd break every bone in it) and told her that she could start the following week. Work with Myra before she leaves, he said. Get a feel for what she does.

Sheridan had nodded her agreement, and then broached the subject of where she might stay.

'Somewhere not too expensive,' she said, and DJ nodded thoughtfully before suggesting the Bawnee River Guesthouse.

'I can't afford to live in a guesthouse!' Sheridan was aghast, but DJ had told her about Nina's studio rooms and said that he was sure she'd be interested in a long-term rental in the low season. And staying with Nina for a few months would give her the opportunity to look around the town for something else, depending on how long Myra decided to take for her maternity leave. He'd shown her a picture of one of the studios from an ad Nina had placed in the paper the previous year, telling her that it would ideal for her. Sheridan agreed with him.

She explained this to Nina, who looked thoughtful.

'It's quiet enough now all right,' she agreed. 'I'm sure we could work out something until the busy season starts.'

'DJ reckoned you might do a decent price for me,' Sheridan told her.

Nina smiled. 'That's DJ for you. Always looking for solutions to problems his way.'

'Does that mean you're not interested?' Sheridan was worried. The studio had sounded ideal to her.

'It's just something I've never thought of before, but I don't see why it wouldn't be possible.'

'I'll be working,' said Sheridan. 'I won't be in your way if you have other guests.'

'I wasn't thinking that,' Nina said. 'And to be honest . . . well, it would be nice to know that there was someone around.' She was surprised to hear herself say that. She hadn't really wanted anyone to be around since Sean had left and she'd been secretly relieved when the flow of bookings had eased up, even though it impacted on her cash flow.

'Excellent.'

'D'you want to have a look at a studio before you make your mind up?' asked Nina. 'They're not exactly huge, you know.'

'Can we get to them from the house? DJ said they were totally separate.'

Nina shook her head. 'They're both independent of the main house. But they're very comfortable,' she added quickly. 'Just not big.'

'Oh, look, I don't want to drag you out in the rain again. The photo DJ showed me looked absolutely fine,' Sheridan said. 'If the price is OK, then I'm not going to worry.'

'All right then.' Nina thought for a moment, and then named a price that was a third of what Sheridan was paying for the apartment in Kilmainham. Given that her salary had been downsized too, it needed to be. However, she was relieved that she could afford to pay Nina and keep on the Beetle for the time being, and so she agreed to the deal.

'DJ wants me to start work next week,' she said. 'Does that fit in with the availability of the studio?'

Nina nodded. 'It's perfect. There'll be one free from next Monday.'

'Great,' Sheridan said. 'In that case – I look forward to seeing you.'

Nina shook the other girl's outstretched hand. It suddenly occurred to her that the horoscope in the *Central News* had been spot on for today. She wondered who they got to do them. A local psychic, maybe? Now that she had an inside track to the local paper, Nina thought that she might be able to find out. Maybe get something more personalised done for her. She'd often thought about visiting a psychic, especially since Sean had left. But she'd never had the nerve to try.

Chapter 12

It was ridiculous, Sheridan told herself, to be so excited about the job in Ardbawn, but knowing that she had something to do again filled her with a sense of purpose. Over the weekend, after she'd phoned her parents, who told her it was a good start and to seize the moment, she'd abandoned Wii soccer in the pursuit of her quest to find out more about Paudie O'Malley. After surfing the net without discovering any more than she already knew, she rang Alo Brady at the *City Scope* to ask him about the businessman.

'Why?' Alo's antennae were finely tuned. He knew it wasn't a casual enquiry about the paper's biggest shareholder.

Sheridan told him about her job offer at the *Central News*. She could hear Alo's muffled splutter of astonishment that she'd fallen so low, but she ignored it. She wanted to know more about her new boss, she told him calmly. She was interested.

Alo didn't have very much more for her, but he pointed her in the direction of further information she could access.

'Thanks,' said Sheridan. 'Have you seen anything of him at the paper?'

'He dropped in to give a bit of a pep talk,' admitted Alo.

'Did he say that it was going to be great now that all the dead wood is gone?' she asked.

'He apologised for that comment,' said Alo.

'Oh really?' Sheridan was unimpressed. 'He didn't apologise to the people he got rid of, though, did he?'

'Ah, Sheridan, you know that was Ernie and the team. They picked who went, not Paudie.'

'Don't tell me he's managed to charm you, of all people!' Sheridan knew that Alo was as hard nosed as they came.

'He was polite. Respectful.'

'Huh.' She snorted.

'I'm really sorry you were let go,' said Alo.

'Thanks. I'm using the *Central News* as a backstop,' she added. 'I'll be working on a few other stories in the meantime. Freelancing.'

'Good idea,' said Alo. 'Sports stuff?'

'All sorts.'

'Well, if you hear anything juicy in the business world, don't forget to call me.'

'Right.'

They said goodbye and she hung up. *Don't forget to call me*: she repeated Alo's words under her breath. Not a chance, she thought. Any good stories, no matter where they come from, I'm keeping for myself!

She checked out the information Alo had given her, and then trawled through some the articles she'd downloaded. Despite Paudie's fearsome reputation, he certainly kept a much lower profile than many lesser businessmen. The Slash-and-Burn moniker had been given to him after he'd acquired an ailing printworks, laid off most of the staff and sold off some subsidiary businesses. The redundant staff had picketed the plant and their placards had urged him not to slash and burn the company, but it had been futile. Sheridan knew how they felt, although the piece about Paudie noted that the print-works had returned to profitability two years later, which meant that his strategy had paid off. Nevertheless, the name stuck, and he was known as a ruthless businessman who didn't suffer fools gladly. The word 'abrupt' appeared a lot of times when describing his personality.

She'd gone through half a dozen more business stories before she found the one she was really interested in: 'Millionaire's Wife in Death Plunge'.

Quite suddenly she remembered the incident herself. It had been a long time ago, but she was surprised it hadn't come to her straight away. She'd read about it when she was living at home. Alice had walked into the room and tut-tutted about it saying that it was a terrible thing and that the man must be devastated. And then, later, there was a report on the investigation into how Elva O'Malley, the wife of busi-nessman Paudie O'Malley, had fallen to her death (from a window according to one report; from a balcony according to another). There were some pictures of Paudie and his family at the graveside that had been taken from a distance, along with a statement he'd made saying that their hearts were broken and appealing for privacy.

The acquisition of the printing works had happened before Elva's death, but almost all of his aggressive takeovers and restructuring had happened afterwards. There were few pictures of Paudie in these reports, which never referred back to the family tragedy. A story some time later showed a picture of the businessman with another woman on his arm, but she seemed to have faded from the scene, as did the increasingly rare photographs of Paudie himself. The business stories grew drier and drier too, simply noting that he'd bought a company or sold a different one, although each time saying that he'd made money from the deal. They spoke about his diversification from print and packaging into more media enterprises. It seemed that everything Paudie O'Malley touched turned to gold although nothing, Sheridan assumed, could possibly take the place of someone you loved who'd fallen out of a window.

Unless it was life assurance. There were references in the early reports to the policy that had paid out a large sum on Elva's death, along with further speculative comments about the state of their marriage. But the stories petered out and Sheridan didn't know if this was because there was no real substance to them or because Paudie O'Malley was influential enough to suppress them.

There was no question that he was a man of influence. His companies donated funds both to political parties and to popular charities. But as more and more was written about his various business ventures, there was less and less information about the man himself. There was also very little information about his family, although Sheridan found a brief story and photograph of his elder daughter, Sinead, on her wedding day, with Paudie standing behind her and her new husband, Michael. Paudie looked pleased and proud, while Sinead was smiling at her husband.

Eventually she learned that Paudie's elder son, JJ (what was it with people in Ardbawn and initials? she asked herself. Could they not have proper names like everyone else?), had followed his father into the business and managed one of the subsidiary printing companies, while the other son, Peter, raced motorbikes in the UK – although she had to assume he wasn't very successful, because she'd never heard of him. There was nothing at all about the youngest child, Cushla.

Was there a proper story in Paudie, she asked herself, or was it simply wishful thinking on her part because she blamed him (however irrationally) for losing her her job? After all, if she'd been kept on at the *City Scope*, she'd probably be thinking of him as a saviour. Nevertheless, it was worth questioning if everything about the businessman was totally above board. Why was he bankrolling the *Central News* when everyone knew that it could be a licence to lose money? Why had he invested in the *City Scope*? Was he a benign businessman or a Machiavellian monster?

Lots of questions, she thought. It would be interesting to get the answers. And at least it would give her a focus for her time in Ardbawn. Because, despite her delight at getting the job, she wasn't entirely looking forward to spending her days writing about beauty, horoscopes and recipes. She needed something more exciting to keep her interested.

She didn't have a lot of stuff to bring with her. She was surprised at that because she thought she was a hoarder, but then she realised that most of the things she hoarded were newspaper articles, and those she kept on her laptop – either downloaded from the internet or scanned to the hard drive. She didn't have folders of files with her own stories or cuttings; they, too, were all stored on the laptop.

As for non-work-related items, they were mostly clothes, and Sheridan's wardrobe was patchy in that regard. She had plenty of fleeces, tracksuits and jeans and more T-shirts and trainers than she could possibly need, but there wasn't much by way of dresses, skirts or smart outfits. All her clothes fitted into her suitcase, while the contents of the bathroom cabinet, as well as the rest of her make-up, were easily contained in the elegant Estée Lauder bag that Talia had given her the previous Christmas. There wasn't much else – her *City Scope* mug, some family photos in click frames, a small selection of books (mainly sporting biographies and autobiographies) and a shocking-pink teddy bear that Griff had presented to her on her last birthday.

She was going to leave the bear behind – after all, she'd split with Griff, and pink wasn't her favourite colour – but she'd got used to it on the chair in her bedroom, and abandoning it suddenly seemed like a heartless thing to do. She couldn't quite believe she was feeling emotional about a pink teddy bear she hadn't even bothered to name. When Griff had given it to her (thankfully also with a box of her favourite chocolates) he'd remarked that she didn't seem to have many cute things in her bedroom, which was why he'd thought it was appropriate.

Sheridan had nothing against soft fluffy toys, but even when she'd first moved out of the family home and had resolved to have a few more feminine things around the place, she couldn't bring herself to load up with stuffed animals and fairy lights. She didn't understand why grown women would find the need to festoon their bedrooms with them; even though she agreed that Talia's arrangement of pink lights trailing around both her mirror and her bedposts was kind of cute, she knew it was a feminine step too far for her.

She hadn't said any of this to Griff, but simply thanked

him for the chocs (telling herself that she'd ration herself strictly to one a day, something she utterly failed to do) and plonked the teddy on the bedroom chair, where it had remained ever since.

When she'd finished packing her clothes and make-up and put the rest of her stuff into a few brown boxes cadged from the Spar around the corner, Sheridan carried them to the Beetle. She went back to the apartment and looked around her. Even though she hadn't had much to remove, it now looked bare and desolate. She felt tears welling up in her eyes, but she didn't know whether they were from sadness at leaving a place where she'd enjoyed living, or frustration at the way she was being forced to move to somewhere she didn't want to go, no matter how much of an opportunity she told herself it could be.

She sniffed loudly, told herself not to be a fool, left the keys on the kitchen table and walked away.

The drive to Ardbawn was far more pleasant than on the previous occasion, because this time the air was warm and the sun was shining in a milky-blue sky. She had no problem seeing the turn-off from the main road and stopped outside the guesthouse earlier than she'd expected.

Nina answered her ring at the bell and smiled in welcome.

'Would you like a cup of tea before I show you to the studio?' she asked.

'That'd be lovely,' replied Sheridan, following Nina into the lounge and settling once again into one of the comfortable armchairs.

'It's not so much of a drive from Dublin these days,' Nina remarked when she returned with a tray and poured tea for both herself and Sheridan. 'People find it much easier to visit us than before.'

'I feel bad about thinking that Ardbawn was in the middle of nowhere,' confessed Sheridan. 'When I first heard about the job I was sort of horrified at the idea of moving out of Dublin. Well, it's still a bit of a stretch for me, to be honest. But at least here I have a job. Since the *Scope* laid me off I've felt like a total waster and I'm not really. I have plans for while I'm here.'

'The *Scope*?' Nina looked puzzled.

'*City Scope*,' said Sheridan. 'I was a reporter there.' She'd been going to say that she was a sports reporter but changed her mind. She didn't want to pigeon hole herself here in Ardbawn.

'On the *City Scope*?' Two pink spots appeared on Nina's cheeks.

'It was a great paper to work on,' said Sheridan. 'Everyone pulled together and we were a good team.'

Nina remembered the innuendo-laden article written by one of the *City Scope*'s feature writers about Sean and Lulu and she felt her jaw tighten.

'To be frank, I was hoping to get a . . . a bigger job than the one with the *Central News*,' continued Sheridan. 'But it's tough out there at the moment and anything's better than nothing. DJ seems a nice enough guy and hopefully we'll get on together. Are you all right?' She'd noticed that Nina was staring straight ahead of her, her eyes fixed on the wall, and didn't seem to be listening to a word she was saying. 'Are you all right?' she repeated.

Nina blinked, exhaled sharply and gave Sheridan a small smile.

'Of course,' she said. 'Sorry, I lost track of things there for a moment.' She stood up. 'If you're ready, I'll bring you to the studio now.'

'Right. Great.' Sheridan put her half-empty cup on the coffee table.

Nina led the way out of the house and across the gravelled space in front of it to a small building. It was grey stoned, and had a similar slate roof to her parents' house in Doonlara. There was an identical building a few metres away.

'They were both originally garages,' said Nina. 'It made more sense to convert them, and because you can directly access the river from the studios, the fishermen love them.'

Sheridan couldn't help noticing that the other woman's voice was clipped and tight. She wondered if Nina was regretting agreeing to the longer-term stay, thinking that perhaps she might have done a better deal with fishermen instead.

'The one on the left is yours,' said Nina.

She took a key from her pocket and inserted it into the lock of the honey-coloured wooden door. She pushed the door open and motioned Sheridan to step inside.

Despite the photo DJ had shown her, Sheridan's expectations for the studio had been low, almost entirely based on the fact that she'd imagined being greeted by a lingering smell of old fish, and not the distinctive scent of the orange lilies in the vase on the round table in the centre of the room. She'd also expected something spartan and utilitarian, dedicated to men with angling gear. But the studio was pretty in a chintzy sort of way, with delicate mauve curtains that matched the plump cushions on the cream sofa. The paintings on the walls were soft-focus scenes of anglers standing on riverbanks. It was also more generously sized than she'd

145

anticipated, with a small kitchen area containing an impressive array of cooking utensils set to one side of the living area, and a double bed hidden behind a bamboo screen. There was a compact bathroom too, cleverly tucked away off the sleeping area.

'It's very pretty.' And totally suitable for my pink teddy, she added to herself, just as well I brought it.

'The sofa can be turned into a bed,' Nina told her. 'Let me know if you've got anyone coming to visit, and I'll make it up for you.'

It was highly unlikely that anyone would want to visit her in Ardbawn, Sheridan thought as she continued to look around her. There was a small TV on a low sideboard, an iPod docking station beside it.

'There's plenty of storage space.' Nina indicated a tall pine cupboard as well as giving a general wave in the direction of the sleeping area, where there was a wardrobe and dresser.

'Excellent,' said Sheridan. 'I'm glad DJ put me in touch with you.'

'Hopefully it will work out for both of us.' Nina cleared her throat. 'Obviously it's self-catering, but if you want to eat at the house that's fine, once you let me know in advance. There's more information on the guesthouse and the town in the welcome booklet. You might find your phone signal is a bit weak here. It's usually OK for calls but not if you want to download information. We have Wi-Fi in the house, which you're welcome to use.'

'Thank you,' said Sheridan. It would be a pity if she couldn't access her emails and the net from the studio. She wasn't exactly sure how welcome she'd be in the guesthouse itself. Nina had definitely seemed friendlier the last time they'd met.

146

'I'll leave you to settle in,' said Nina. 'There's milk in the fridge as well as tea and coffee in the kitchen.'

'OK, thanks.'

'Right then.' Nina let herself out of the door. 'I hope you have a pleasant stay in Ardbawn.'

I hope you have a pleasant stay in Ardbawn. A ridiculous thing to say, thought Nina as she strode back to the main house. The girl is here to work, not to have a pleasant stay. And not that I'd be letting her stay here at all if I'd realised she'd been involved with that rag, the *City Scope*. Nina gritted her teeth. What if Sheridan had been one of those reporters who'd followed Sean and Lulu around? What if she'd been instrumental in exposing his infidelity? What if she was an undercover reporter, here to try to find out more about Sean's former life and the woman he'd left?

She told herself not to be so bloody silly. The woman had lost her job at the *City Scope*. She was working for DJ Hart. DJ would never let her write anything horrible about Nina. DJ was a decent person and he'd printed as little as possible about Sean and Lulu's relationship. The local paper had always been circumspect in writing about the private life of any local person, no matter how shamelessly it might trumpet a public success.

Would it have made a difference, Nina asked herself, if the *City Scope* had never reported it in the first place? Would his affair with the young actress have petered out when he realised that she was just a flighty airhead? (Nina didn't know if Lulu was an airhead or not, but she was convinced that she must be.) And if she'd never found out about it, would their lives have gone serenely on? Or would there inevitably have been someone else? Someone as beautiful as Lulu Adams? Someone who would have taken a greater hold of his heart?

Lulu had doubtless appealed to his ego. What man wouldn't like a gorgeous twenty-one year old lusting after him, reminding him that he was strong and handsome and virile, instead of a forty-eight-year-old wife reminding him to unload the dishwasher? Sean enjoyed making a fuss over women and women making a fuss over him. Nina understood his need to feel as though he could still attract the opposite sex. That was why he flirted with all the female guests. That was undoubtedly why he'd flirted with Lulu, too. But she couldn't help thinking that it wouldn't have gone much further if it hadn't been splashed all over the damn papers, making him feel like someone important.

All of Ireland wouldn't have known either. And no one would have taken a picture of Nina looking like Lulu's grandmother as she stood in the grounds of the guesthouse one day, her hair unwashed and wearing her faded three-year-old parka.

In some ways, running the guesthouse then had been a blessing, because she couldn't go to seed entirely. Even after her most sleepless, sobbing nights she'd had to get up and dressed and make a bit of effort for the guests. She'd got through more tubes of concealer and tinted moisturiser and blusher in the weeks immediately after his departure than in all of the years of their marriage put together. Sean had never cared about her wearing much make-up. He'd always told her that she didn't need it. Now, she thought, without the aid of Touche Éclat and Max Factor she simply looked haggard.

She went into the kitchen and put the kettle on again. It

freaked her out that she was becoming the sort of woman who made a cup of tea every time she felt upset. It had been something her mother had done and Nina had always associated constant tea-making with an older generation of people. Now she'd turned into a tea-maker herself.

And, of course, she *was* that older generation. The fact that her husband had run to the arms of a woman less than half her age only went to prove it.

After Nina left, Sheridan unpacked her case and hung her clothes in the pine wardrobe. Then she arranged her bits and pieces around the studio so that it resembled, at least slightly, the flat in Kilmainham, albeit a softer, gentler version. Finally she boiled the kettle and made herself a cup of extra-strong coffee.

She was standing at the window sipping it when her mobile rang and she saw that it was her ex-flatmate calling.

'How's it going?' Talia asked when she answered. 'Have you taken to country life yet?'

'I've only just arrived,' Sheridan told her. 'It's a bit weird, to be honest, because I'm here in my little studio and all I can hear is the rustle of trees outside.'

Talia laughed. 'You'll get used to it.'

'Hopefully. Ah well, I guess I'll just spend a lot of time watching TV.'

'Aren't you going to be a fearsome investigative journalist?'

'Of course.' Sheridan didn't allow even a trace of irony into her voice. 'But I guess I'll also be investigating the best way to bake bread or help a sheep give birth. God, what's that called? Lambing, of course! Jeez, I'll be a laughing stock if I have to write some agricultural sort of piece and haven't a clue what I'm talking about.'

'I'm sure your landlady will bring you up to speed on the appropriate terms,' Talia assured her.

'I'm not sure landlady is exactly the right word for her,' said Sheridan. 'I think I'm somewhere between a guest and a tenant.'

'Huh?'

'Well the studio is part of a guesthouse,' she explained.

'You didn't say that when you rang me last week,' said Talia. 'You said you'd got a studio apartment and I told you that Ardbawn couldn't be that backward if it had apartments.'

'Every last town in Ireland has apartments these days,' Sheridan reminded her. 'Even if half of them are empty. I hadn't seen it myself then. It's a converted garage in the grounds of a guesthouse. It's not bad, to be honest.'

'Sounds different.'

'It's lovely if you like the whole back-to-nature sort of thing,' said Sheridan. 'Though the owner is a bit weird. She was very friendly when I enquired about it first, but she was a bit stand-offish today.'

'Probably suddenly worrying about having the fearless journalist snooping around her guests.'

Sheridan chuckled. 'You never know what goes on in these guesthouses. I could crack a cow-smuggling ring or something and the next thing Nina Fallon will be headline news.'

'Nina Fallon!' exclaimed Talia. 'You're staying in her guesthouse?'

'Well, like I said, in a studio—'

'Yeah, yeah, I know. Sheridan Gray, do you not read your own newspaper?'

'Which one? Given that I'm now the ace at the *Central News*.'

'The *Scope*, you eejit.' Talia went on to remind Sheridan of the previous year's exposure of Sean Fallon as a cheating husband.

'Oh my God!' Sheridan couldn't believe she'd forgotten (although, she thought, tracking soap stars and their lives wasn't really her thing and she didn't watch *Chandler's Park* so she couldn't really blame herself). 'Nina's his wife?'

'Yes, you clot!'

'Poor woman,' said Sheridan. 'It must be horrible to have your husband's stupidity plastered all over the paper. Who broke that story? Elise?' Elise had been one of the *Scope*'s lifestyle journalists.

'Of course it was Elise,' replied Talia. 'You know what she's like. Loves digging the dirt. She's got a job now, by the way.'

'Has she?'

'With one of the tabloids.'

'Bloody hell.' Sheridan couldn't help the dart of envy that went through her. She'd been in touch with the tabloids and they'd told her they weren't hiring. She'd been gutted by that. Sport was as big a deal to most of them as cheating husbands. Of course sometimes they were the same story . . .

'You didn't want to work on a red-top, did you?' asked Talia.

'They would've paid better than the *Central News*,' said Sheridan. 'And I'm not snobby about it. OK, so they're light on actual writing, but they do have their fingers on the pulse.

151

Whereas here . . .' she picked up the copy of the *Central News* that she'd taken from the café when she'd come for her interview, and looked at the story about new stalls being available for the weekly farmers' market, 'here the pulse is pretty slow.'

'You'll speed it up,' promised Talia. 'I know you will.'

Sheridan wasn't so sure about that. As far as she could tell, the pace of life was going to be glacial. Just like, it seemed, the owner of the Bawnee River Guesthouse.

Chapter 13

Sheridan woke early the next morning and was at the offices of the *Central News* before nine. She wasn't sure there'd be anyone in before her. There had always been someone in the *Scope*'s offices no matter what time of day it was, but she assumed that the *Central News* had a more laid-back sort of approach to punctuality and sniffing out important stories. So she bought herself a coffee in the deli before ringing the bell at the commercial centre. Almost at once the buzzer on the door sounded and she pushed it open. In the shadows at the top of the stairs she saw a figure leaning over the rail

'Sheridan Gray?'

She nodded.

'Myra Clarke,' said the figure. 'Delighted you're here.'

Sheridan had already built up a mental picture of Myra Clarke. In her mid-thirties, she'd imagined. A bit bossy, because she was an admin person and they were always bossy. The ones at the *City Scope* had driven the journalists mad asking for receipts and time sheets and holiday rosters and all sorts of rubbish and getting narky when they didn't hand over what they wanted straight away. Myra was probably the same, she'd decided, and possibly looking a bit tired given that she was so far advanced in her pregnancy.

Her mental image bore absolutely no relation to the person she was looking at now. Myra was a tiny woman who appeared barely out of her teens – although that might have been something to do with the fact that her hair, in a feathery pixie cut, was shocking pink and she had the smoothest, clearest skin Sheridan had ever seen in an adult. She was dressed in a black silk smock that came down to her knees. She was also wearing black leggings and black biker boots. Her pregnancy bump was enormous.

'Come on in,' said Myra. 'We've loads to talk about before I head off and Genevieve gets a move on.'

'Genevieve?' said Sheridan uncertainly.

'My baby.' Myra sat down behind her desk. 'I can't wait for her to come along. I feel like a flipping rhino at the moment. I mean, you can see for yourself.'

Sheridan nodded, not really knowing the appropriate response.

'And those feckers DJ and Shimmy, well, they spend their time laughing at me because I waddle around the place. I tell them that I'll sue their sorry arses for discrimination and harassment, but sure they're nothing but big lumps of eejits themselves.'

'Right,' said Sheridan.

'I'm the one that keeps the show on the road,' said Myra cheerfully. 'They'll natter on about their editing skills and their IT skills and their sales skills and whatever, but they'd be nowhere without me to keep an eye on them.'

'I see.'

'So you have to be on the ball the whole time with them

154

or they'll run rings around you and nothing will get done. Now to be fair to Shimmy, he's great at the aul' website stuff and he's an absolute demon of a salesman, but pure useless at getting the money in, which is the most important job you have in the whole place.' Myra's big blue eyes looked earnestly at Sheridan. 'Paudie – Mr O'Malley – has a minimum amount of revenue he expects us to bring in, and if we don't, well, we're up the creek without a paddle 'cos he could close us down in an instant. You have to balance his ads against the proper paying ones. Not that he needs to advertise and not that he couldn't afford to keep the *Central* running anyway, but he says everything has to have a commercial bias and so that's important.' Myra paused for breath and then began talking again. 'So, the way it is, Sheridan, no matter what you think, it's vital to get that ad money in. I have a system set up on the computer and I'll show it to you. After that, it's the pieces from our contributors. Naturally we need to keep them coming, but it's not a crisis if one of them makes a total mess of it because we can always write something ourselves. DJ is great at it, but sure you're a proper journalist so you'll be able to do it no bother at all.'

'Right,' said Sheridan in Myra's next pause for breath.

'I've a list of people who send us contributions – household tips, beauty advice, recipes, that sort of stuff. You've got to make sure that Des sends in the sports reports, and keep at him to go to the girls' and ladies' matches – he's a sexist bollix and wouldn't bother otherwise, no matter that the girls all love seeing their names in the paper and their mammies buy multiple copies when there's a report on their games. You have to write some articles – DJ will tell you about them. Sometimes he starts them and you have to finish them; to be honest I was pure shite at that, it would've been quicker for him to write it all himself but I think he thought I should sort of try to be a journalist person even though I'm not . . .' She beamed at Sheridan. 'He was very concerned that I'd be worried about a real one with experience taking over my job, but it's not a worry at all because it's not like you'd want to stay in Ardbawn for ever; you're practically famous, you've had your byline in a proper paper.'

By now Sheridan was almost dizzy listening to Myra, but the younger girl had more to say.

'The stuff you have to do yourself, absolutely have to, is the agony-aunt column and the horoscopes. We don't get the horoscopes on syndicate – Paudie thinks it's nice for them to have a kind of local flavour – and people *do* write in with problems, God love them, so we have to do the replies ourselves.'

'Agony aunt!' Sheridan looked horrified. 'DJ never said anything about being an agony aunt. I can't possibly do that.'

'Of course you can,' said Myra. 'It's just common sense.'

'Well, yes, but . . .'

'Just imagine you're talking to your best friend who wants to do something stupid,' Myra said. 'Easy-peasy. The horoscopes are harder, I think. You have to make up stuff and I'm desperate at it.'

'I told DJ I could do horoscopes, but to be honest I was spoofing,' admitted Sheridan. 'I don't believe in them at all.'

'You don't have to.' Myra grinned at her. 'All you have to do is write them.'

By the time DJ and Seamus (Shimmy, Sheridan reminded herself) arrived about fifteen minutes later, Myra had

156

introduced Sheridan to the accounting system that she used. Sheridan had never had to worry about accounts before, and she wasn't entirely sure she'd be any good at it now – maths had never been her strong point.

'How're ya, sweetheart!' DJ held out his hand and Sheridan did her best not to wince. 'Welcome to our little hive of activity.'

'What activity?' demanded Myra. 'You pair of slackers should've been here ages ago. Though I suppose it's letting Sheridan know how things really are – she'll be doing all the work and you'll be taking all the credit.'

DJ chuckled. 'Ah, get that bee out of your bonnet, Myra, and make us a nice cup of tea.'

'Make it yourself,' said Myra. 'Last time I looked you had hands of your own.'

Sheridan's eyes darted anxiously between the two of them, but then she realised that this was routine banter. There was no malice in their words, and when both of them guffawed, she allowed herself to relax.

'Have you told her everything that needs doing?' asked DJ.

'Well we had to do something while we were waiting for you,' said Myra. 'We've gone through the accounts stuff, because the rest of it will be like falling off a log for her.'

'I'm not all that familiar with accounts,' said Sheridan apologetically.

'Get yourself up to speed as quick as you can,' DJ said. 'We send in monthly reports to Paudie. He expects us to keep the finances under control.'

'That's what I told her,' said Myra.

'Does everything depend on Paudie O'Malley?' My first investigative question, Sheridan told herself.

'Not entirely,' DJ replied. 'But he's the owner, and you know what it's like, the owner is the boss.'

'Like a football club,' said Myra helpfully. 'They might know jack-all, but they're still paying the bills.'

Sheridan laughed. And so did Myra. As DJ and Shimmy joined in too, she started to think that maybe a few months with the *Central News* might not be the worst way of spending her time. Especially if she came out of it as a winner in the end.

By five o'clock she was utterly exhausted. She'd never worked as hard in her life. There had been plenty of times with the *City Scope* when she'd had to churn out a few thousand words in a single sitting, but they had always been her own words and she'd always been in control. Now she realised that at the *Central News*, everything was about teamwork. She was expected to be able to answer the phone, do some filing, make tea (everyone takes turns, Myra assured her; this isn't the last bastion of male chauvinism, I promise you, no matter how much they'd like it to be), edit pieces sent in by local contributors (or possibly rewrite them, she realised as she looked at an almost incomprehensible account of a fund-raising book sale, still not sure at the end of it what it was actually raising money for) and then read the emails and letters sent in for the Ask Sarah advice column.

'I always thought the problems in local papers were made up,' said Sheridan as she leafed through them.

'No, we get loads of them,' said Myra. 'The thing is, everyone thinks their problem is unique, but it's not. So you've buckets of advice to fall back on. Look – I have a whole folder of stuff here you can go through.' She double-clicked on an icon on the computer screen and a window opened with a series of folders marked 'cheating husband', 'jealous boyfriend', 'affairs', 'mother-in-laws', 'difficult children' and a variety of other headings.

'Wow,' said Sheridan. 'All these problems exist in Ardbawn?'

Myra chuckled. 'Well they probably do, and maybe we need one big psychiatrist's couch,' she said. 'But our letters come from all over – Kilkenny, Carlow, in fact anywhere in the whole world, because people who grew up in the area and moved away still look at the *Central News* website or the digital version. They have to subscribe to get full access,' she added, 'but you'd be surprised at how many do. Loads of them still log on from places like the States and Australia.'

'No place like home,' said Sheridan.

'Exactly.' Myra beamed at her. 'And we do our best to reach out to those readers and give them what they want, which is news from the town and the surrounding area, information on how things are changing and all that sort of stuff.'

'What if you discover that someone from Ardbawn has become famous or something?'

'Oh, we give them lots of coverage,' said Myra confidently. 'We love to see people doing well.'

'What about Sean Fallon?'

The office was suddenly silent. Sheridan could feel three pairs of eyes looking at her.

'I'm staying with his ex-wife,' she reminded them.

'She's still his wife.' Myra corrected her. 'They're not divorced.'

'Sean's an idiot,' DJ said. 'Everybody in Ardbawn supported

him and then he makes fool of himself by his carry-on with that tramp. You'd imagine he'd have more sense.'

'How did you run the story?' asked Sheridan, mentally filing away the thought that if her investigations into Paudie didn't come to anything, perhaps Sean would be a good alternative.

'We put up something about it,' acknowledged DJ. 'But we didn't sensationalise it. Not like the *City Scope* did.'

Sheridan paused before speaking. 'I don't think it was particularly sensationalised,' she told them. 'It was a human-interest story. Sean is a well-known personality.'

'And I wouldn't give a shit about him,' said DJ. 'But it was horrible for poor Nina. She still hasn't got over it.'

'Is it true that after he left her she flung all his stuff out of their bedroom window?' That story had been run by one of the tabloids, much to the disgust of the *Scope* staffers.

'Not that I know of,' said DJ.

'Or that she siphoned petrol out of his car to make him stay?' asked Sheridan. 'Having met Nina, I can't help thinking that she's not the sort of woman who'd do that type of thing. She's very quiet and gentle.'

DJ grinned. 'Don't let that fool you. Or the fact that she's been knocked back a bit by this business with Sean. Nina's a strong woman. She built up that guesthouse herself. Plus she's a contributor to the paper. She sends in recipes for Cook's Corner.'

'Ah.' Now Sheridan understood why the *Central News* had gone easy on her.

'She's a great woman,' DJ said. 'Hopefully now that Paudie's involved with the *City Scope* it'll stop those intrusive stories about her life with Sean.'

160

Sheridan wished DJ had told her all this before she'd turned up on Nina's doorstep. It would've been helpful to know in advance that her ex-paper had apparently made the woman's life a misery. But the big lump probably hadn't even thought about it. Or maybe he had and didn't care.

'You've got to print the truth,' she reminded him, thinking that she sounded a bit sanctimonious.

'Yeah, we did.' It was Shimmy who spoke this time. 'We said that there were rumours about Sean and Lulu Adams, and then when he left Nina we printed that too. But we didn't splash it all across the front page with a picture of him making a grab for Lulu's assets.'

Shimmy's words had heightened the atmosphere and Sheridan could feel herself growing tense. She didn't want to argue with everyone on her very first day.

'Ah, now, none of that was Sheridan's fault,' said DJ, giving Shimmy a warning look. 'She was a sports reporter on the *City Scope*, after all. The day they printed that stuff about Sean, she was writing about Arsenal v Chelsea.'

'Really?' She looked at him quizzically.

'Probably.' He grinned at her. 'You always did good reports on the footie. And since I'm an Arsenal fan and young Shimmy here supports Chelsea, we always read them with great interest.'

Sheridan smiled. 'Thanks.'

'So what d'you think about the Gunners' chances in our next Champions League match?' DJ asked. 'Any chance of us finally showing our worth and leaving the rest of them eating dust?'

Sheridan happily talked football with DJ for a while, and then Myra reminded them both that working at the *Central*

News wasn't all about jabbering on and that they had a paper to get out by the end of the week and it was time to get cracking.

'The real boss has spoken,' said DJ. 'We'd better do as she says.'

He turned back to his computer and Sheridan returned to her desk. She wondered if she'd manage to gain the same sort of respect Myra clearly had. She certainly hoped so.

Chapter 14

Nina was sitting in the residents' lounge. When there was nobody else in the house she often sat there instead of in her own private living room because of its stunning views towards the river. Sean had occasionally joined the guests there in the evenings but she only sat in it when it was empty. It had been a family room when she was a child, but when the renovations were being done, Sean had decided that it would be more suitable for the guests. He'd been right, but she still liked to sit in it and remember how it once was. She wasn't trawling through her memories right now, though, simply revelling in the stillness of the house. Two couples who'd come down for a wedding were now at the reception in the Riverside Hotel and the fisherman who was staying in the studio was in Ardbawn town. She wasn't sure where Sheridan Gray was tonight; she didn't know what she did in the evenings because since the journalist's arrival a week earlier she simply hadn't seen her.

She'd gone into Sheridan's studio that morning with fresh bedlinen, and had been surprised at how impersonal it looked. Given that the girl was staying for an extended period, she'd expected to see more of her possessions there, but apart from cosmetics in the bathroom, a few books in the living area and a pink teddy bear on the bed there was very little to show that someone was staying there at all. (By contrast the other studio was a mess of angling gear, magazines and clothes. Paul Proctor, the fisherman, was only staying for a week, but, unlike Sheridan, he'd made the place his own.)

Nina was taken aback at the neatness of Sheridan's studio. She'd always imagined that journalists were untidy creatures, who'd have papers and overflowing ashtrays all over the place. She realised that her expectations had been based solely on a few movies she'd seen, but the fact that Sheridan specialised in sports had coloured her views too. Nina had never met a tidy sportsperson in her entire life. Her son, Alan, who'd played soccer when he was younger, had always driven her crazy whenever he marched into the house with muddy boots and then proceeded to leave shin pads and the rest of his gear in the middle of his bedroom floor. Chrissie, who didn't play any sport competitively but who liked to swim, was notorious for leaving her wet things in her bag so that Nina would often be confronted by damp, mouldy towels and togs. But Sheridan didn't leave anything around. Of course writing about sport didn't have to mean she participated herself, but the array of trainers lined up beside the chest of drawers had led Nina to assume that she was a fitness freak. Though clearly a tidy fitness freak.

Anyway, she thought now as she watched the large TV from the comfort of one of the wide armchairs, if the rest of Sheridan's stay turned out like the first week, she wouldn't regret having her here. In fact she was feeling a little guilty at having been somewhat distant towards the younger woman when she'd first arrived. She'd been totally taken aback by

Sheridan's disclosure that she'd worked for that awful rag the *City Scope* and had been utterly unable to look the girl in the eye because of it.

She'd googled Sheridan's name afterwards and realised that she'd only reported on sporting stories and not on Sean's affair. She wondered if Sheridan knew Elise Comerford, whose name had appeared under most of the stories about him. She was the entertainment correspondent, apparently. Nina supposed she'd been well entertained by Sean and Lulu's behaviour.

She pressed the button on the TV's remote control. *Chandler's Park* was just starting. She hadn't watched it in weeks. When Sean had first got the part she watched it every single day, even though seeing him in the soap was like looking at a different person. Sean was able to do that, Nina realised, become someone else completely. He spoke differently, walked differently, everything about him screamed that he was someone else. It was only occasionally, in the way he turned his head or shrugged his shoulders, that she could see her Sean.

Is he still my Sean? she asked herself now. Was he ever? Didn't I learn before that he was good at acting a part? So what does this reconciliation request mean? That he really wants to come home? Or is it all about his share in the guesthouse? The guesthouse that his father helped me to modernise because I was going out with his son. Does Sean think I owe him? Doesn't he know that I already paid him back a hundredfold?

She didn't want to think that Sean could be so mercenary about the house. He'd never been, in the past. In that respect he was very unlike his father, who'd been known as a shrewd money-manager. But the solicitor's letter had made it clear. If he wasn't going to get his marriage back, he felt entitled to something from his life with her.

She could understand his motives but she found it hard to accept them. He'd been the one to mess it up, after all. She was the one picking up the pieces. All over again. She closed her eyes and tried not to think of how loving Sean made her want to forgive him. How she was always so ready to forgive him, no matter what the situation.

She opened her eyes again. Sean, as Christopher Hart, was currently dating a glamorous businesswoman. Nina watched him put his arm around her and draw her close to him for a kiss. She picked up the paper to consult the summary of the plot. He was kissing Melanie Blake, the actress playing Carmella Boyd, the businesswoman.

It must be difficult to live like that, thought Nina. Being more than one person at a time. Blurring the lines between reality and make-believe. But he was good at it. Just as he was good at being a fool. 'A damn stupid cheating fool!' she shouted at the character in front of her. 'And I hate you!'

She felt better for having shouted. She'd kept herself too quiet, too tight for too long. Shouting was a release. 'Fool!' she yelled again, and then whirled around as she heard the sound of someone shifting uncomfortably in the doorway behind her.

'Sorry if I'm disturbing you.' Sheridan looked apologetically at Nina. 'The front door was open. I wanted to use my laptop so I had to come to the house to get the Wi-Fi connection.'

'Of course, that's fine.' Nina tried to sound composed, but she knew her voice was shaky.

'If you're sure . . .'

'Absolutely.'

'Great.' Sheridan hesitated, then sat down in the armchair nearest the screen.

'How was your first week?' asked Nina while Sheridan waited for her laptop to connect to the network.

'Not bad,' she replied, still looking at the computer. 'More to learn than I expected, but they seem like a nice bunch.'

'Better than the *City Scope*?' asked Nina.

'Different.'

'I suppose it seems very tame by comparison.'

'To be honest, I think I'm going to be run off my feet.' Although she was now logged on to the guesthouse network, Sheridan wanted to break the ice with Nina, so she didn't open her email program. She looked up at the other woman. 'Myra seems to do everything! She's an expert multitasker and I'm woefully underskilled in terms of replacing her.'

Nina smiled slightly. 'I doubt that.'

'It's true,' said Sheridan. 'I took the job thinking I could do it in my sleep and that I'd have plenty of time to do other things for myself, but when I see all the stuff she does, I start to panic. There's heaps of admin as well as the writing and the editing of the pieces that people send in. You wouldn't believe how . . .' She broke off, not wanting Nina to think that she was criticising the way she presented her recipes. Not that anyone could go too far wrong with a list of instructions anyway, but Nina's were very clear and precise. 'How much work is involved,' she amended.

'It's a good paper, the *Central News*,' said Nina. 'Ethical.'

'The *City Scope* was ethical too,' said Sheridan, wondering why she was springing to the defence of her former employer when she was still hurt and angry about what they'd done to her.

'Hmm.'

'I realise that we – it – broke the story of your husband's affair,' Sheridan said, deciding that they needed to clear the air about it. 'But it was a reasonable human-interest story.' She knew that was what Elise would have said, although she herself thought that there was a fine line between public interest and private lives.

'I don't agree.' Nina's eyes were bright and her voice sounded forced. 'I can't believe it's ethical to poke around in other people's private lives just because they're also in the public eye. It's none of the public's damn business. Besides, it's not as though Sean was someone with moral authority who was telling other people how to behave and not sticking to it himself.'

'That's true.'

'So you could've left well enough alone.'

'I'm really sorry if something my old employers did messed up your life.'

Nina sighed in sudden resignation. 'I guess it wasn't anything they did that messed up my life,' she conceded. 'It was something Sean did. They just told me about it. The only thing is . . .' she shook her head slowly. 'I can't help feeling that if it hadn't all come out into the open it probably would've blown over.'

Was Nina right? Sheridan wondered. Had Elise's story actually wrecked the other woman's marriage? But Sean had left her, hadn't he? That had nothing to do with the *City Scope*.

'I threw him out,' Nina replied when Sheridan put the question tentatively to her.

168

'Hey, good for you!' Sheridan was truly pleased that Nina had given Sean his marching orders. It was better than her being the woman who had been left.

Nina gave her the ghost of a smile. 'I don't know if it's good for me or not.'

Sheridan was dying to ask her why, but she didn't want to appear to be interviewing her.

'I find it hard by myself,' added Nina.

'Well of course,' Sheridan agreed. 'You're running a business and everything. While he's living the high life. Sorry,' she added. 'I don't know what kind of life he's living. I don't keep track of that sort of stuff.'

'The *City Scope* keeps me in touch,' said Nina wryly. 'I don't suppose it's the high life exactly, but it's probably better fun than being here with me.'

Sheridan looked embarrassed.

'It's both good and bad to hear about your husband's activities through the paper,' Nina said. 'I know what he's doing but I'm not sure if I want to know.'

'I can understand that.'

'It's weird seeing stories about someone you know,' Nina told her. 'I don't know how properly high-profile people don't crack up.'

'Is it making you crack up?' asked Sheridan sympathetically.

'To be fair, it's not the paper's fault that Sean couldn't keep it in his pants,' said Nina. 'So, no, the *City Scope* isn't making me crack up. But my damn husband is.'

'I hope it all works out.' Sheridan knew that her words were trite. But she meant it.

This time Nina's smile was more substantial. 'Thank you.

I'm trying to figure out what having it work out actually means. Divorce or . . .'

'Would you take him back?' There was a hint of incredulity in Sheridan's voice. 'After making him leave?'

'I don't know,' admitted Nina. 'You think things are cut and dried, but they're not.' It was a comfort to say the words out loud, to share her feelings with someone else, even if that someone was a person she hardly knew. Maybe, she thought, it was easier to talk to a stranger about Sean than the people closest to her.

'I've never properly done the break-up and make-up thing,' confessed Sheridan. 'None of my ex-boyfriends ever asked me to make up.'

'Would you have gone back if they had?'

'Depends on the boyfriend, I guess.'

'And even if you go back, things wouldn't necessarily be the same. Well, they can't be, can they?'

Sheridan nodded. She realised that she was having the kind of conversation with Nina that she sometimes wished she could have with her own mother. Talking about feelings, which Alice simply didn't do. Not, she added to herself mentally, that Nina was a mother figure. She was an attractive woman who, while clearly older than Sheridan herself, was still of a younger generation than Alice. Besides, whenever Sheridan had thought about mother–daughter conversations, she'd assumed she'd be the one getting advice, not giving it.

'Men are always difficult,' added Nina. 'We spend far too much time worrying about them and they don't worry half enough about us in return.'

'I guess you're right,' agreed Sheridan. 'In reality, my relationships with men have been pretty straightforward. We go out, it's good for a while and then it's over. The only one I felt bad about was my last boyfriend. I thought there might have been more to it, but . . . I was wrong.'

'You're better off without him,' said Nina.

'We always say that, don't we?' Sheridan said. 'When a couple split up. We always say you're better off, but what if you're not?'

What indeed? thought Nina. If someone asked her now was she better off without Sean, she'd have a hard job answering that she was. Because she wasn't. Telling him to go had been the strong thing to do. It was just that she couldn't help feeling it had also been the wrong thing to do.

She picked up the newspaper so that she didn't have to continue the conversation. Sheridan, seeing that the older woman had said all she was going to say, turned her attention back to her laptop. Interesting though Nina and Sean's lives were, they were none of her business. Paudie O'Malley and his media empire, on the other hand, definitely were.

Nina didn't want to get up and walk out of the lounge straight away. Sheridan might think she was scurrying away to sob, and she didn't want her to think that. She was pretty sure that the younger woman already thought of her as a flake for shouting at the TV and then for being uncertain about whether or not she'd take her husband back. She felt a bit of a flake herself. She couldn't understand why she'd shifted from being furious with Sean to wishing that he was with her again. She tried to tell herself that it was simply because she was used to having him around, but she was afraid it might be because of the solicitor's letter. But if that was the case, she wanted Sean home to protect the guesthouse. Not because she truly wanted him back. After all, she'd been brave enough to make him leave. She couldn't go back on that choice now, could she?

She glanced across at Sheridan, who was apparently engrossed in her computer. A single woman, Nina thought, and therefore someone with idealised notions of love and marriage and how things should be. It wasn't Sheridan's fault that the *City Scope* had blown a hole in Nina's life. And it had been wrong of her to allow her anger to influence the way she felt towards the reporter. It was also wrong of her to start confiding in her. The girl was a paying guest, for heaven's sake. She needed to treat her that way.

'Would you like a tea or coffee?' she asked.

Sheridan looked at her in surprise. 'Coffee would be lovely. But there's no need . . .'

'I'll bring some in.' Nina got up and went into the kitchen. While she waited for the kettle to boil, she glanced through the copy of the *Central News* that had been on the kitchen table all week. At least the local paper hadn't printed awful things about Sean when the news broke. The *Central News* wasn't sensationalist. She hoped that wouldn't change with the arrival of Sheridan Gray.

When she'd read her emails (from Talia, hoping things were going well, and from Alice, telling her to work hard and take no prisoners), and had finished surfing the net and updating her social networking pages, Sheridan closed her laptop. Nina hadn't stayed in the lounge after she'd brought the coffee but had told Sheridan that she'd things to do and disappeared into another part of the house. Sheridan walked into the hallway and called out that she was leaving, but there was no reply. She shrugged and let herself out of the front door.

The gravel crunched beneath her feet as she walked back to the studio. Even though it was only ten thirty, she was tired. She'd told Nina the truth when she'd said she was run off her feet. The *Central News* was far busier and less homely than she'd expected, and trying to remember everything that Myra told her had left her feeling overwhelmed. DJ seemed to think that it should be a walk in the park for her, but everything was new and different and she was scared of getting things wrong. She was particularly worried about living up to the other girl's standards when it came to the paper's financial controls, about which she knew nothing. At the same time she couldn't wait to get her editorial hands on some of the stuff the contributors were sending in. Even if the *Central News* was a backwater paper, she thought, there was no reason for the writing to be rubbish. If there was nothing else she could do well during her time here, at least she could up the quality of the writing. Although she also wondered how DJ would react if she managed to dig up a sensational warts-and-all story about Slash-and-Burn O'Malley. Would he react like a proper journalist and have the balls to run it? Or would he feel he had no option but to cave in to the man who paid their wages?

Chapter 15

On Saturday morning Sheridan left her car outside the newspaper offices and walked into the town. It was the first opportunity she'd had to wander around Ardbawn – during the week she'd been too busy, because every time she'd had a spare moment, she spent it studying Myra's financial spreadsheets, trying to clamp down on her feelings of hopeless inadequacy. It seemed to her that everything she'd done the previous week had been littered with mistakes or slip-ups. In tackling the admin, she'd somehow managed to delete a spreadsheet of advertising income, which had left Myra totally panic-stricken (fortunately Shimmy had been able to retrieve it eventually from some hidden location on the hard drive); she'd edited a local-interest article to make it more readable, but DJ had undone every single change, telling her that Perry Andrews was a historian who wrote for his fellow history buffs and they never altered a word; finally, she'd been utterly unable to come up with any horoscope predictions, even though Myra had left her alone to do them for an entire afternoon before taking pity on her and rattling them off in less than half an hour.

It had been a traumatic week and she didn't expect the

following one, when she'd be dealing with things entirely on her own, to be any better. She told herself that this was a challenge to be overcome, but the fear of making a complete fool of herself threatened to overwhelm her. However, on her day off, she shoved her doubts and fears to one side and told herself to embrace the life of the town. Which today was buzzing with activity.

This was mainly because of the farmers' market, which was set up in the plaza and from where an aroma of freshly baked bread and hot food wafted down the main street. Sheridan spent time browsing the stalls, where some of the townspeople introduced themselves and wished her luck in her new job, something that utterly astonished her until she realised that Myra was at the market too, and had pointed her out to them.

'They need to know you,' said Myra, who was wearing a pink woollen hat and a pillar-box-red coat that didn't quite close over her pregnancy bump. 'And you need to know them too. Everyone will be on your side, I promise. And listen to me, don't let DJ take advantage of you and run you off your feet. You're a better writer than him, you know.'

'Not really.'

'Absolutely,' Myra told her. 'I read your stuff. Especially what you did to Pompous Perry's local history article. It was the first time I was ever able to understand a word he wrote.'

Sheridan looked rueful. 'But DJ changed it all back again.'

'Ah, don't mind him. He likes to have a bit of incomprehensible culture in the paper. Makes him feel upmarket.'

This time Sheridan laughed.

'All the same, I don't know how you do it,' she told Myra.

'You're completely on top of everything, whereas I'm totally terrified the whole time.'

'Don't be,' she said. 'You're great, and DJ's a big aul' softie.'

'I'm not afraid of DJ,' said Sheridan. 'Just of messing up.'

'You won't,' said Myra confidently.

'I'm glad you have faith in me.'

'You're Sheridan Gray,' said Myra. 'You're a top-notch proper reporter. You're great. But if you need anything, just call me.'

She sounds just like my mother, thought Sheridan. Totally positive.

'Hopefully I won't need to,' she told her. 'I want you to be able to put your feet up and enjoy the last few weeks of your pregnancy.'

'I'm not sure that enjoy is the right word. I feel like I'm carting around a mule at this point.'

'You *will* be coming back after she's born, won't you?'

'Are you afraid that I will or I won't?' asked Myra in amusement.

'That you won't.' Sheridan's tone was heartfelt.

'You might like that spot after a few weeks, all the same.'

'No. Honestly.'

Myra grinned. 'Don't you worry, I'll be back as soon as I can. But listen to me, now, I meant it when I said call me if there's anything that's completely stumping you.'

'Thank you.'

'No bother,' said Myra. 'You don't think I'd throw you to the wolves, d'you?'

'I thought DJ was a softie.'

'Even so.'

176

'Thanks,' repeated Sheridan.

'While you're here . . .' Myra turned and waved at a tall, thin girl. 'This is Jennifer Boyle. She works on the local council. She keeps me in touch with anything that might affect Ardbawn. Jenny – meet Sheridan. She's a dote.'

'Everyone's a dote as far as you're concerned,' said Jenny as she extended her hand. 'Nice to meet you, Sheridan.'

'You too.'

'I don't give out confidential information,' said Jenny. 'But you're welcome to call me any time if you need something clarified.'

'And Jenny will ring you if there's anything you should know,' said Myra.

'Sometimes,' added Jenny.

'You'll get on fine,' said Myra. 'Oh, and Sheridan . . .' She waved at someone else, this time a man wearing an old-fashioned cap. 'This is Bill Rutherford. He's the captain of the golf club.'

Bill shook her hand, as did more people that Myra knew – the local florist (takes ads, lovely person), a garage owner (another great source of advertising revenue), a couple of pub owners and a dressmaker. By the time Myra was leaving the market, Sheridan's head was in a whirl.

Left to her own devices again, she wandered round a bit more and emerged with a couple of warm blueberry muffins, home-made fudge and a russet scarf that she wound loosely around her neck. Then she went into the newsagent's and picked up the *Central News*. She'd restrained herself from rushing in before doing anything else, not wanting to seem too eager (even if only to herself) to see how the final product looked on the shelves. Once she had it in her hand, she had to buy it, even though she already knew almost every word of every story.

She'd intended to read it over elevenses in the Blue Rose café, but when she opened the door she could see that there were no free tables. A woman she'd met a couple of times in the deli said hello, while one of the solicitors whose offices were in the commercial centre nodded to her in acknowledgement. It astounded her that she was already becoming someone people in the town knew and greeted. She smiled at them, murmured something about the place being incredibly busy, and left again. As the day was bright and sunny she decided to walk to the playing fields outside the town (and not far from the troublesome housing estate). It was better for her in any event, she reminded herself, to be walking briskly along the road than sitting down drinking coffee and eating cream buns – especially when she had freshly baked muffins too! She was getting incredibly lazy; she hadn't been for a run since she'd come to Ardbawn. She picked up her pace as she strode towards the playing fields, though because she was hungry she nibbled at a piece of fudge as she went, her hair blowing around her face in the breeze, her neck warm thanks to the new scarf.

She heard the shouts of encouragement long before she reached the Gaelic football pitch, where, she realised, the players were schoolboys. When she finally arrived she stood to one side and listened to the roars of the parents as they exhorted their sons to do even better. Almost immediately she was transported back to the days when she stood between Pat and Alice cheering on either Matt or Con, wanting them to win while wondering if she'd ever find anything her parents would cheer her on for too.

178

'Tackle him!' roared an angelic-looking woman on the sidelines. 'Give him a kick! Take him out!'

Sheridan knew why the woman was screeching: a boy from the Ardbawn team was racing up the pitch with the ball, leaving the away players stranded in his wake. Just as it looked as though he was bound to score, he tripped and fell and the ball rolled harmlessly out of play. The boy – Sheridan guessed he was about seven or eight – looked for a moment as though he was about to cry. But as the game had moved on without him, he simply hitched up his shorts and pounded back up the pitch again.

Sheridan couldn't help laughing. Boys had so much energy, she thought. And they were so damn competitive!

The game ended in a win for Ardbawn, which led to a great cheer from the home supporters and a lot of high-fives on the pitch. Then the boys ran to the sidelines, where they were congratulated by their proud parents. The boy who'd tripped was patted on the head by a tall, dark-haired man wearing a sweatshirt emblazoned with the club's logo. He had an athletic build and Sheridan thought he might be a coach too.

'Never mind, Josh. Anyone could trip.' His tone was sympathetic but not patronising, and Josh's face brightened.

'It was my own fault,' he admitted. 'I was looking at the goal and I forgot that the pitch can be bobbly.'

The man patted him on the shoulder. 'You made a great run. Next time you'll keep your concentration.'

'As long as Mr Reid doesn't drop me.'

'I'm sure he won't.' The man glanced down the pitch to where the coach was chatting to the referee. 'You played well and the team won.'

'I s'pose so.'

'You were very good.' Sheridan, standing close to them, couldn't help adding some praise of her own. 'I haven't seen anyone as fast as you in a long time.'

'I do lots of running.' He looked pleased.

'And jumping and screaming and shouting,' the man with him said benevolently, and then turned to Sheridan. 'Josh is a demon in disguise. It's just as well he can get rid of some of his energy on the pitch.'

The boy chortled and punched him gently. The two of them wrestled for a bit while Sheridan thought about a possible piece about junior football in the town. Maybe linked to a story about pushy parents. Not that Josh's father seemed to be a pushy parent, quite the opposite, but Sheridan knew they existed, and the screeches of the angelic-looking woman seemed to put her in that category. She'd once covered an under-13 rugby game in which an enraged father had punched the coach when his son had been substituted. She'd been astounded by the man's actions but Martyn Powell had told her that assaults on referees in all sorts of team sports were more common than anyone would believe.

'But it's only a kids' game,' she'd said in total disbelief, and Martyn had said darkly that the kids' games were the worst.

She supposed she'd better check the paper's archives before she wrote a story, see if Des had already beaten her to it. She glanced around her, wondering if he was at this match, but she didn't see anyone who looked like a reporter.

'I'm starving.' Josh abandoned the wrestling. 'Are we going home? Will lunch be ready?'

'I'm sure your mum has something lovely waiting for you. Doesn't she always feed you up after a match?'

'Yes.' Josh looked pleased. 'I think she's doing burgers today.'

'Excellent. Well, say goodbye to the nice lady who thinks you're a fast runner, and let's go.'

'She's just telling the truth,' said Josh complacently. 'I am fast. Everyone says so.'

'Yes, but it's polite to say thank you when someone says something nice about you.'

'Thank you.' Josh's tone was serious, and Sheridan had to bite back a smile.

'You're welcome,' she said.

'We'd better head off.' The man put his arm around the boy's shoulder, and to her utter astonishment, Sheridan felt a lump in her throat. She couldn't believe that she was getting sentimental about the camaraderie between a father and son at a football match, but there was something about the gesture, so warm and so easy, that touched her.

Then Josh's father looked up and smiled at her. And this time she felt more than a lump in her throat. This time she felt a surge of electricity race through her, like a physical force. She'd never felt anything like it before. Her heart began to beat faster, her mouth was dry and there was a pleasurable, yet nerve-racking fluttering in the pit of her stomach. On a subliminal level she knew that around her people were talking and laughing about other things, but she didn't know what those things could be. She couldn't imagine that there was anything more important than standing here, looking into the eyes of the man in front of her. No man in her life had ever had this effect on her. No one had ever made her feel as if they'd reached into her body and grabbed hold of her heart and soul. She wanted to stay opposite him for the rest

181

of her life. For time to stand still so that she could be here with him, feeling this way for ever. She was utterly spellbound.

And then the spell was broken.

'Goodbye.' His voice was normal and friendly and seemed to come from a million miles away.

'See ya.' Josh was already hurrying away.

'Goodbye. Nice to meet you both.' She was surprised that she could speak and that the words were sensible.

He turned away from her and hurried after Josh. She stood looking after them, unable to move. She wanted to call out, to make him stop. She wanted to put her arms around him and bury her head in his chest. She was horrified that she felt like this and yet overcome with a desire to do it anyway.

But, of course, she didn't.

The man and his son were going home to a woman who would have their lunch waiting for them. He had a life of his own in a world of his own, and she could never be a part of it. Her feelings were irrational and irrelevant. She wasn't the sort of person who was overcome with lust or desire or whatever it was that had so unexpectedly engulfed her.

Besides, she would never have been the right person for him or for Josh. She wasn't the cooking sort. If they'd been coming home to her expecting food on the table, they would have been sorely disappointed.

She knew it was ridiculous but she couldn't stop thinking about him. All during the day, as she drove back to the guest-house and flopped onto the sofa in her studio, as she flicked through the channels of the TV or just stared into space, the man's face continued to hover in her consciousness. His wide smile as Josh came off the pitch. The way his black hair stood up in spikes. His dark blue eyes, which had softened whenever he looked at the boy . . . Sheridan didn't know why she was thinking about him so much and why she was envying fiercely the woman who'd been left at home to do the cooking. But she was.

There was no Sky Sports on the TV, so she couldn't watch the football, and she didn't want to go up to the guesthouse itself and ask if it was available there. So she connected up her Wii and began to play World Cup soccer on the tiny TV in the studio. But for the first time in ages she couldn't get into the game. After a while she abandoned it and flicked through the channels. RTÉ was showing a repeat of *Lost in Translation* with Bill Murray and Scarlett Johansson. Sheridan had never seen it before. She sympathised with Scarlett's character, adrift in Japan, looking for someone and something to make her feel at home. Despite the friendliness of the people she'd met, she was feeling that way herself. Even if she hadn't had to leave the country for it to happen.

There were no guests booked in for the week ahead. This was normal for a time of the year when bookings were sporadic, but Nina was feeling anxious all the same. Although she had enough money in the bank to weather the quiet times, she wished that the guesthouse was full. It wasn't just about the money. It was about being alone for the first time in over twenty years. Living on her own hadn't bothered her after Dolores died. Back then she hadn't been the sort of person who allowed her imagination to run riot, and she'd never felt that the spirit of her mother (or indeed her father) was watching over her. Not that Dolores would actually have watched over her, of course; her mother would've been a lot more likely to have sent criticism from the grave, telling her that she didn't need to renovate the house or change the fry-ups to lasagnes or any of the things that Nina had so enjoyed doing. But the point was that she'd been too busy and too optimistic to feel alone. Besides, such an occurrence had been rare. There had been fishermen staying in the house two weeks after Dolores's death because they'd already booked and there was no way she was going to let them down. Sean had come along shortly afterwards. Her solitary moments had been few and she'd been able to savour them.

Not any more. Being on her own now just ratcheted up her stress levels. And it was another reason why she questioned her motives whenever she considered taking Sean back. Would it be because she still loved him or because she was afraid of being alone?

She went into the kitchen. It was the place where she felt most comfortable, most secure. It had been part of her original renovations so was now a bit dated, with its huge pine cupboards and dressers, although the Belfast sink and the Aga were back in vogue again. But it was warm and welcoming and Nina felt safer there than anywhere else in the house. From the wide window behind the sink she could see the entire length of the garden as it sloped down to the river. She could also see the yellow light in the window of the studio room occupied by Sheridan Gray.

Did the young reporter like being on her own? Did she think it was wonderfully peaceful after a day out and about interviewing people to sit alone in silence? Though Nina couldn't imagine her having to do much interviewing in Ardbawn – it was hardly a bustling metropolis. Nevertheless, the *Central News* did do profiles of local people and businesses from time to time, and they covered council meetings and stuff too, so perhaps that was what Sheridan was doing now. And maybe getting involved with the sports coverage, which Sean had always said was risible. 'How Des Browne can make an exciting hurling match sound like a sedate game of croquet is beyond me,' he'd once raged after reading a report of a game he'd gone to see. 'Honestly, the man is a plonker.' Nina, who wasn't in the slightest bit interested in sports, had dismissed Sean's rant, but she wondered if there would be a noticeable difference in the reports as a result of Sheridan's arrival at the paper.

She sat down at the table and picked up the latest edition. She'd already skimmed through it, but she saw that Des was still doing the sports reports and that so far, at any rate, Sheridan didn't seem to have written anything at all. She stopped at the problem page. She always read Ask Sarah, up to recently with a sense of superiority that she didn't have the kind of problems that necessitated writing to a perfect stranger, and with a certain self-satisfaction that she had always managed to overcome things on her own. The issue that Sarah was dealing with this week was a woman who wanted to leave her husband but who didn't know how she would cope afterwards.

The future is always a blank slate, she had written in conclusion to her supportive reply. *We are all stronger than we think. We have more support than we think too.*

'I wish,' muttered Nina to herself.

She glanced up from the paper and looked out of the

window again. The light in Sheridan's studio had gone out. She looked at her watch. It was only ten thirty. It seemed awfully early for Sheridan to have gone to bed, but she would have heard a car starting up if her guest tenant had gone out.

Maybe Sheridan was lonely too. Maybe it would be a nice gesture to ask her to come to the house for dinner. She'd seemed a pleasant enough sort of person, despite her allegiance to the *City Scope* and her views about journalistic ethics. And Nina supposed she couldn't blame her for those.

Perhaps we could have coffee together from time to time, she thought. It doesn't make sense that the two of us should be sitting in on our own when we could at least share some time together. I'll ask her tomorrow. And if she doesn't want to come, at least I'll have tried.

Sheridan decided to go for a jog the following day. Both her acknowledgement that she was getting lazy and seeing the boys running around on the sports pitch had reignited her desire to do something active again. Besides, she tended to put on the pounds when she was sedentary, and she couldn't really afford to let that happen.

She was a little nervous as she started out, being more used to city streets than country roads, but eventually she got into the rhythm of it and enjoyed the sound of birdsong as her feet covered the easy eight-kilometre distance she'd set herself. She'd just arrived back when the internal phone rang, startling her so much she nearly knocked it from the table. It had never rung before – anyone who wanted to contact her had her mobile number; she doubted she'd even given a landline one to Alice.

'Hello,' she said tentatively, and then realised that of course Nina Fallon would use it to ring her and she was particularly stupid not to have guessed that. She listened in surprise as Nina extended an invitation to the house – nothing exciting, just a bite to eat, she said. Sheridan was uncertain at first about accepting, but then, thinking that the other woman was clearly trying to be friendly after the awkwardness of the other night, she said she'd be delighted.

A few hours later she was sitting in Nina's aroma-filled kitchen and removing her fleece because the heat from the Aga made it totally unnecessary.

'It's just roast chicken,' said Nina, who'd decided that it would be nicer to invite Sheridan for food rather than just a cup of coffee. 'Not very challenging, but Brian, the butcher, was doing a great deal on them this week and so I thought it would be nice. Then I realised I'd be eating it alone.'

'No better woman than me to make a dent in food,' Sheridan told her, which made Nina laugh.

She set to work on the chicken with enthusiasm, hungry from her run earlier, rueing the fact that her own limited skills in the kitchen were being sadly exposed by the cooking facilities of the studio, and also thinking that if she didn't want to gain weight, she shouldn't take up Nina's offers of food too often, because the guesthouse owner was a very good cook indeed. She'd also uncorked a bottle of Sauvignon Blanc, from which she'd poured them both a generous glass.

'I wanted to apologise to you for the night you were here before,' she said quickly to Sheridan. 'I offloaded on you about my marital troubles, which was very unprofessional of me.'

187

'Not if you were blaming them on me,' said Sheridan.

'Not you personally,' Nina assured her. 'Your paper, ex-paper, to some extent. But,' she added, 'that was displacement activity, wasn't it? I wanted to blame the paper because that way I didn't have to blame Sean.'

'Do you blame him now?' asked Sheridan. It occurred to her that listening to Nina was a good way of learning more about being Sarah, the agony aunt, although she told herself that as far as the other woman was concerned she should simply listen, not offer unasked-for advice.

Nina sighed. 'I should blame him. But there's a part of me that thinks he was just caught up in living his dream.'

'Doesn't mean he had to cheat on you.' Sheridan was firm about this.

'Men are weak about things like that.'

'Well they shouldn't be.'

'Sometimes they can't help falling for a pretty girl.'

Sheridan stared at Nina. 'You've got to be kidding me.'

'Excuse me?'

'Just because a girl is pretty and just because the opportunity is there doesn't mean a man should take it. Would you?'

'Me?'

'If you'd been living away from the guesthouse and a gorgeous guy came on to you – would you have cheated on Sean?'

'It wouldn't happen,' said Nina. 'Sean has a kind of magnetism, he really does. Women like him.'

Sheridan bit back a retort that Sean sounded like a sleazeball to her and that Nina was better off without him. It was a comment she might have made as an agony aunt, but she certainly wasn't going to come out with it face to face. She was afraid she'd antagonise Nina if she continued talking about Sean, and so she abruptly changed the subject and asked Nina to tell her about the guesthouse.

'Do your brothers and sister come back often?' asked Sheridan after Nina had given her a potted history.

'Hardly ever,' said Nina. 'Bridie's on her third marriage and doesn't have time for flitting back here. She's lived in New York, Boston and Chicago. She'd be a total fish out of water in Ardbawn now. Peadar comes back from time to time because it's only a short hop from London, but his life is very different to mine. He works for an airline so he travels a lot. And Tom has only been back twice. We keep in touch a bit through Facebook and emails, but we were never all that close to begin with.'

'My brothers both work for local government and coach Gaelic football,' said Sheridan. 'They've turned out just like my dad. We're close but not in a meeting-up-very-often kind of way. They're always madly busy.'

'How are you liking Ardbawn?'

'Adjusting,' said Sheridan carefully.

Nina smiled. 'I'm sure it seems as dull as ditchwater to you.'

'No. But I'm having to get used to the whole small-town thing, and people saying hello all the time.'

'Knowing people can be nice,' Nina said. 'There are loads of community initiatives; many of them are sporting ones, so that might keep you busy. There are reading groups, a musical society and a drama society too.' Mentioning the drama society made her wince, though Sheridan didn't notice;

she was too busy finishing up the floury roast potatoes that accompanied the chicken.

'I don't think I'll be staying long enough to get involved in much other than work,' she told Nina. 'But it's nice to be here tonight, thanks for asking me.'

'Drop up any evening. You're always welcome to use the Wi-Fi or watch the TV. The ones in the studios aren't great for movies, the screens are too small.'

'I'm not a big TV watcher at the best of times,' said Sheridan. 'Unless it's a football match or something.'

Nina reached for her copy of the *Central News* with the TV listings. Sheridan saw that it had been left open on the horoscopes page. After she'd taken over the task the previous week, Myra had given her a tip on how to come up with them.

'I allocate each sign to a person I know,' Myra told her. 'I try to think of what would be good in their lives and I make up the prediction based on that. For example, my mother-in-law is a Gemini. She's a bit of a fusspot and tries to meddle far too much, so I generally tell her to keep her distance and not to get too close to things.'

Sheridan had burst into laughter at that, while Myra beamed and told her it was a foolproof system.

'What's your birth sign?' she asked Nina suddenly.

'Cancer,' said Nina. 'Why?' She caught sight of the horoscopes. 'Are you superstitious?' she asked.

'Only about sports,' replied Sheridan. 'When my brothers used to play competitively, I always used to bring my lucky scarf to their matches. Whenever I wore it, one or the other of them scored. I knew that realistically it was nothing to do with the scarf, but I did it all the same. I'm not one for horoscopes, though.' She couldn't remember what had been predicted for Cancerians. She herself was a Leo. Myra had suggested that it was time for Leos to grab the tiger by the tail, which had amused Sheridan.

'I like the *Central News* horoscopes,' said Nina. 'They can be uncannily accurate sometimes. My latest says that painful events should be coming to a conclusion.'

'That's nice to know.' Sheridan wondered who Myra's Cancerian subject was, and what painful events were in her life. 'We have a great psychic,' she added, crossing her fingers at the blatant lie.

'Do you really?' Nina's eyes grew larger. 'Who is she?'

'I can't possibly tell you that,' Sheridan said. 'They'd kill me.'

'You've a good agony aunt, too,' added Nina. 'Sarah's very down-to-earth.'

'I know,' said Sheridan. 'I don't know how she keeps on top of the troubles people have.'

'I felt like writing to her myself,' said Nina. 'After Sean went. But everyone would've known it was me. There can't be too many people in Ardbawn who'd be saying that their husband was shacking up with a TV star.'

'Can you guess who sends in the problems?' asked Sheridan.

'I try sometimes,' Nina admitted. 'Though maybe I'm completely wrong.'

'At first I thought they were made up,' confessed Sheridan. 'But they're not. They come from lots of places, though, not just Ardbawn.' She repeated what Myra had told her about readers from all over the country and beyond.

'Amazing how so many of us have things we need help with and nobody we can turn to,' said Nina.

'Didn't you have anyone to talk to when the whole thing with Sean broke?'

'Of course. I have plenty of friends in Ardbawn,' said Nina. 'But I'm not much good at having that type of conversation. Besides, I always felt Sean and I seemed to have it worked out. We've had our ups and downs and come through them OK.'

'I'm sure your friends would have been supportive,' said Sheridan. 'It's always nice to know that you can rely on people.'

'Oh, I know. And they *are* very supportive. But I still feel so let down by him. Humiliated. Embarrassed, too.'

'I was embarrassed about being made redundant,' said Sheridan. 'And when my friend who hadn't lost her job was offered another one, I felt even worse. I was jealous of her. I hate having to say that, but I was. Getting the job here and coming to Ardbawn was kind of humiliating for me.'

'But the *Central News* is great,' protested Nina. 'DJ is a lovely man.'

'He's a character,' agreed Sheridan.

'He does a lot of good work in the community,' said Nina. 'The *Central News* supports local businesses.'

'Mostly Paudie O'Malley's.' Sheridan thought this would be an excellent opportunity to gossip about him. Gossip was, after all, far more interesting than hard news, and a good way to get the sort of information that wasn't currently public.

'That's because he has so many businesses in the area. He employs people locally as well as nationally. He's very well respected in the town.' Nina's voice was suddenly clipped.

192

'Hard to believe that anyone can be as successful as him and not walk on a few toes,' Sheridan said.

'Of course.'

'D'you know him?' asked Sheridan.

'I've met him.'

'Is he as abrasive as everyone says? Or is he simply reclusive?'

'I haven't seen or talked to him in a long time,' replied Nina.

'There was that incident with his wife . . .'

'Such a terrible tragedy.' Nina started to clear away the dishes and stack them in the dishwasher. 'But it was years ago.'

'She fell out of a window? Or off a balcony or something?'

'Out of a full-length upstairs window,' Nina clarified as she took an apple tart from the Aga and began to slice it.

'And there was an investigation.'

'Yes. It was inevitable under the circumstances.'

'But it was all just a tragic accident?'

Nina turned around to Sheridan, the knife still in her hand.

'Of course it was an accident. What are you implying?'

'Nothing.' Sheridan was surprised by the sudden tension in Nina's voice. She couldn't help thinking that nice as the guesthouse owner was being tonight, she was a very volatile character. She wished Nina would put down the knife. It was disconcerting to have her holding it like that when she seemed upset.

'The police investigated it thoroughly.' Nina spoke calmly again as she slid the slices of apple tart on to plates. 'There was no reason to suspect anything of anybody. Elva fell.'

'Did some people think she was pushed?' asked Sheridan. 'I read something . . .'

'Such rubbish!' exclaimed Nina. 'Of course she wasn't pushed.'

'Anyway, Paudie seems to have moved on,' said Sheridan, startled by the vehemence in Nina's voice. 'He's done amazingly well.'

'Yes, he has,' Nina told her. 'He's a strong man.'

'Behind every strong man there's a woman,' said Sheridan. 'Is there a woman in Paudie's life?'

'Not that I know of.'

'So he lives all alone?'

'More or less,' said Nina. 'His children stay with him from time to time, but they're adults now. They all have their own lives and their own homes.'

'There were three – no, four children?'

'Have you researched him?' Nina looked curiously at Sheridan.

'A bit.' Sheridan shrugged slightly. 'He's Ardbawn's claim to fame, after all, as well as my employer.'

Nina didn't say anything.

'It must have been hard for him, bringing up the children on his own after Elva died,' added Sheridan.

'Yes.' Nina's eyes darkened. 'Yes, it must have been. Of course JJ was sixteen or seventeen when the accident happened, not exactly a child any more, and he was always old for his years. The youngest is Cushla. She was about ten at the time. I remember her in the graveyard, all dressed in black with a red rose pinned to her coat, God love her.' Nina's voice cracked and then she recovered. 'Still, she's doing well now, she's an auctioneer – art and jewellery and

194

stuff like that. Peter – the boy who was closest to her in age – is a motorbike racer.'

'I read that.'

'I supposed you must have, it's a sport, isn't it? I don't think he's won any races, but he's happy and so are we because better he's racing on a track over there than speeding through the town here, which is what he used to do. A total tearaway, particularly after his mother died. But a good boy behind it all.'

'There was another daughter, wasn't there? Married? And JJ works in the family business, doesn't he?'

'JJ's the sensible one, always has been,' said Nina. 'Paudie wanted his kids to be involved, but JJ is the only one who was interested. He spends a lot of his time in Dublin, though. Sinead's the only one still in Ardbawn. Mike, her husband, is a nice guy, but I'm sure things aren't always easy for her.'

'Oh, why not?' Sheridan was interested in what sounded like a decent bit of gossip at last.

'Mike's an engineer. He works on oil pipelines, which often keeps him away for weeks at a time. That's difficult when you've got a small kid. Also, he's a real outdoor-adventure sort of guy. Loves mountaineering and rock-climbing, all that sort of thing. Last year he was injured when some rocks fell on him. Broke an arm, concussed, had to be airlifted off the mountain. It was touch and go for a while.'

'I'm surprised that wasn't in the papers too,' said Sheridan.

'Paudie does his best to keep his family private,' Nina said. 'He struggled after Elva's death to keep some of the more ghoulish stories away from the kids' eyes. Bloody newspapers, you really are vultures.'

195

'You can't have it both ways, Nina,' said Sheridan. 'The *Central News* is a paper too. You can't say DJ treats everyone sensitively and then call all the others vultures.'

'I think it was because of some of the more sensationalist coverage all those years ago that Paudie developed an interest in the media himself,' said Nina. 'He couldn't bear the way tragedy was turned into sales.'

Sheridan nodded. She couldn't deny that some newspapers did very well out of other people's grief and suffering.

'Anyway, he's doing incredibly well now.' Nina sounded relieved. 'Everyone in Ardbawn thinks he deserves his success.'

'And how about his personal life?' asked Sheridan. 'It seems odd that he hasn't met someone else.'

'Elva was the love of his life. He dated a few times after the accident. But nobody will ever replace Elva for him. Ever.'

Sheridan wondered how well Nina Fallon knew Paudie O'Malley. Would she be able to swing an interview for her? If she swore to Nina that her motives were pure and that she only wanted to write a quality piece about the town's most famous businessman, would she agree to ask him? Although that's not strictly true, she acknowledged to herself. *I want to write something controversial about him. Because I don't believe he's all sweetness and light like Nina wants to make out, and because I'm sure that the tragedy with his wife changed his attitude too.*

'Where does he live?' she asked Nina. 'He's not a tax exile only dropping in from time to time, is he?'

'His house is another few kilometres up the road,' Nina told her. 'He lives there, although he's got a place overseas too. I can't remember where. March Manor is the most gorgeous house. He did a big renovation job on it a few years ago. Invited everyone in the town along to a party afterwards.'

'Nice of him.'

'It was a great evening, I believe. The *Central News* said it was like something out of the movies. He picked a summer's night and there were lights all over the garden and along the driveway.'

'Didn't you go yourself?' asked Sheridan.

'I . . . no.'

'Why not?'

'It was the summer,' said Nina. 'We were very busy with the guesthouse.'

Sheridan's eyes narrowed as she looked at her. 'But surely . . .'

'I didn't feel the need to go and look at the house,' said Nina. 'I knew it well before. I've lived here all my life.'

'Are you friends with Paudie?' asked Sheridan.

'He's twelve years older than me,' said Nina. 'I know him but I was never close friends with him. He didn't own the house when I was younger. The Farrellys did. Tina Farrelly was in school with me, that's how I knew it. He bought it from them after he got married, even though it needed some work done to it.'

'Right.'

'He was always ambitious, but he wasn't a rich man then. He couldn't afford to do the house up until much later.'

'Was that the reason his wife fell out of the window?' asked Sheridan. 'Because it was rotting away or something.'

'Of course not,' said Nina. 'They'd long since made it habitable.'

'I'd love to see it.'

'You can drive by,' said Nina. 'It's hidden by trees, but you can make out the chimney stacks.'

'Not very interesting.' Sheridan laughed. 'What I'd want is to see the window his wife fell out of.'

'Why?' Nina looked annoyed. 'Why would you want to?'

'It's the reporter in me,' admitted Sheridan.

'You don't want to go raking all that up again.' Nina looked anxious. 'We leave Paudie alone here. He deserves it.'

'What was his wife like?' asked Sheridan.

Nina didn't reply straight away. Sheridan could see that she was back in the past, remembering.

'She was beautiful,' she said eventually. 'She was easily the loveliest woman in Ardbawn.'

'Did you know her?' asked Sheridan.

'Yes.'

'Friends?'

'Not really. She was older than me too. Not as old as Paudie, but out of my circle. They came to the guesthouse a few times, though. Sean and I did Sunday lunches for a while. Elva and Paudie used to come.'

'It must have been a real shock to everyone when it happened.'

'Yes.'

'You don't like talking about it.'

'It's a private matter,' said Nina. 'It was a sad time for the town. For Paudie.' She swallowed. 'For everyone.'

'Was she popular?' asked Sheridan.

'She was Ardbawn born and bred,' said Nina.

'Did you like her?'

'I hardly knew her.'

But, thought Sheridan, as Nina got up and put the kettle

198

on, there's something about her that bothers you. That you envied. Or disliked. Because whenever you talk about her, there's a hesitation in your voice. And I'd really like to know why.

She watched Nina as she took tea bags out of a cupboard. I've upset her, thought Sheridan. Though that's probably because of her own marital troubles, not because of anything to do with Paudie O'Malley and his dead wife. Maybe it's because she's afraid I'll go nosing around and upset Mr Slash-and-Burn. It's clear that everyone in Ardbawn thinks the sun shines out of his arse. But I'm not so certain. And I'm not entirely convinced that his wife's death was the accident everyone says it was either.

She smiled to herself. She knew she had a vivid imagination and she knew she was letting it run away with her. But she still wanted to know more about the ambitious Paudie and the beautiful Elva.

Nina put the teapot on the table.

'I'm sorry if I was asking too much,' Sheridan said. 'My friend Talia tells me I'm missing the sensitive gene. Comes with having been raised in a testosterone-filled household.'

'There wasn't a whole heap of sensitivity in my upbringing either,' Nina told her. 'My mother was a "you've made your bed now lie in it" sort of woman and she didn't have much time for tears or tantrums.'

'She'd have got on well with mine, so.' Sheridan grinned. 'Mum was sympathetic about me losing my job, but she wants me to look on it as an opportunity.'

'It is.' Nina gave her a slight smile. 'It's an opportunity to leave the rat race for a while and find a gentler way here in Ardbawn.'

'I don't think life is gentle no matter where you live,' said Sheridan. 'It has an unending capacity to bite you on the bum when you're least expecting it.'

'You're right,' agreed Nina. 'And I suppose that, after a period of feeling sorry for yourself, you just have to get on with things.'

'Exactly.'

'It's hard sometimes.'

'I know,' said Sheridan. 'But Nina, you're running the guesthouse on your own and you're coping. Maybe you need to get out more, but I understand why you want to keep to yourself for a while. When my boyfriend split with me just after I was made redundant, it totally shattered my confidence.'

'We're a pair of right old losers, so,' said Nina.

'Never!' Sheridan spoke fiercely. 'You're not a loser, and neither am I.'

Nina looked surprised.

'I'm not allowed to be,' explained Sheridan. 'It's practically mandatory in my family not to give in to anything.'

'So are you and I going to be cheerleaders for positivity?' asked Nina.

'Absolutely.'

'Fair enough, so.' Nina nodded. 'I'll try to keep that in mind.'

After they'd had another glass of wine, and kept the conversation well away from Ardbawn, Sean Fallon and the O'Malleys, Sheridan left the guesthouse and walked a little unsteadily back to the studio. She was glad that she and Nina had talked and that they'd forged some kind of friendship.

She liked the older woman even if she was a mercurial character. She seemed to know everyone in Ardbawn, which could be useful in the future. Sheridan wondered if she was acquainted with the handsome stranger and his tousle-headed footballing son. She wanted to know more about him. Even though she already knew the only thing that mattered.

He wasn't available.

Chapter 16

She arrived before DJ and Shimmy on Monday morning, but because she didn't have any keys to the office she waited in the deli, sipping her freshly brewed coffee, until DJ turned up, swinging his Range Rover into the space directly in front of the door. She hurried outside and stood beside him as he opened up the office.

'It's going to be weird without Myra,' he said.

'I'll do my best so's you don't miss her too much,' Sheridan told him.

'I'm sure you will,' said DJ as they went upstairs. 'It's just that she's been with us a long time. And she's good at looking after us.'

'You're grown men,' said Sheridan. 'You can look after yourselves.'

DJ grinned and filled the kettle.

'I take it you don't want a cup,' he said, 'seeing as you've already shelled out a ridiculous amount of money on that muck they make next door.'

'It's nice coffee,' she said defensively. 'And I had to buy something while I was waiting for you to turn up.'

'I'll give you keys,' said DJ.

'Thank you.'

She sat at the desk and logged on to the computer. There were a surprising number of emails for the paper, ranging from letters to the editor to notices of upcoming events. There was also an email from Des, the sports reporter, which included a piece about the under-9s match that she'd seen on Saturday, in which he praised the courage and determination of the Ardbawn team and called Josh Meagher a leading light, which Sheridan thought was a bit over the top. In fact Des's entire piece, while wooden and laden with unnecessary detail, was over the top for a report about a kids' match, but she supposed that a bit of hyperbole was OK in small-town reporting. She wished she'd seen him there so that she could have introduced herself, but she hadn't spotted anyone who looked like they were taking notes on the game.

She'd work on his report later. Meantime she skimmed through the postbag for Sarah, the agony aunt, and added the letters to the folder that Myra had left her. She would have to pick the one to answer and already she was in a total quandary. She didn't know what to say to the woman who was contemplating an affair with her brother-in-law, or to the girl who didn't have a boyfriend. And as for the man who'd written in saying that he was trapped inside a woman's body – well, if she said the wrong thing, surely she'd damage his psyche for ever? Yet Myra, younger than her and with no qualifications at all, would probably have had all the answers. Or at least she'd have known what to say.

'We don't pretend to give them professional advice,' she'd told Sheridan. 'We give them places to go to. All we are is a sympathetic ear.'

But that was part of Sheridan's problem. She'd never had

to be a sympathetic ear before. Although she always tried to show the positives in her sports reporting, when it came to everyday emotional issues her parents had always told her to exploit people's weaknesses, not empathise with them.

'You OK?' asked DJ at lunchtime, while she was once again looking at a report from Des (this time on a men's soccer match). It was the dullest piece of sports writing she'd ever had to read and she was wondering how much editing she'd be allowed to do.

'Not bad,' she told him.

'Want to go for a sandwich?'

'I was going to have one at my desk.'

'Ah, leave the desk, why don't you?' He stood up. 'C'mon. I'll take you to the pub. They do a very decent lunch there.'

The Riverside Inn, on the main street, was bright and airy, with a clearly popular menu, because it was very busy when DJ and Sheridan arrived. They sat at a window seat over-looking the plaza (the pub owners had taken a bit of licence with the name, because the river itself was only visible through a high window in the ladies' loo).

As she still hadn't got to grips with cooking in her studio, Sheridan took the opportunity to order some hot food, and asked for a burger and chips while DJ opted for a steak.

She'd expected DJ to quiz her over lunch about her thoughts on Ardbawn or her expectations about the job or how she was getting on, but there was very little time to talk because they were constantly being interrupted by people coming over to speak to him. Many of them already knew who she was too, and DJ introduced her to those who didn't. She realised that the editor was a popular figure in the town and that many people seemed to think of him as their public representative.

After hearing a woman offload on him about the problems she was having in getting planning permission for an extension to her house, Sheridan said this to him and he laughed good-naturedly.

'Nobody in Ardbawn has much time for the local councillors or politicians any more,' he said. 'Not that all of them are a bad bunch, but there's too much infighting for them to be really effective. No matter how idealistic they are at the start, it all goes horribly wrong for them in the end. So people use the newspaper as a way of expressing how they feel. Which is what all newspapers should be about.'

'And getting the facts right,' she added. Martyn Powell had always told her to write with passion but to get her facts straight too.

'Sure,' agreed DJ and then turned away from her. 'How'ya, Robbie? What's the news?'

The pinched-faced man with straggling hair who'd come up to DJ chatted for a while about cattle (a conversation that went totally over Sheridan's head) and then said that he had to go because he had a flight to London later that day.

'He's our resident celebrity,' DJ told her as Robbie left. 'Used to be in a rock band, Dunston Death Stars, sold a few albums that went platinum, did the drink-and-drugs thing but now embraces healthy living and the country life. He lives in a big house off the Carlow road. Owns a prize-winning herd of Charolais cattle.'

'I didn't recognise him,' said Sheridan. 'Is he famous?'

'A bit before your time, pet. And he looks nothing like he did back in the day. The recreational drugs take a bit of a toll. But he's all cleaned up and into the whole organic lifestyle now.'

'You're joking.'

'Not at all.' DJ grinned. 'All life comes to Ardbawn, you know.'

He was distracted again, this time by a woman who stood for a moment in the doorway and then walked over to them and sat down. She was stunningly beautiful, with long blond hair, wide baby-blue eyes and flawless skin.

'This is Ritz Boland.' DJ introduced her. 'She's the manager of the hotel spa, and every so often she invites me in to lose a few pounds on some mad personalised programme that I never stick to. Ritz, this is Sheridan, our new ace reporter.'

'Pleased to meet you.' Ritz nodded at Sheridan.

'So what's new, Ritzy?' asked DJ. 'D'you want anything to eat?'

Ritz shook her head and then told DJ that she was interested in doing an advertorial in the paper for some new treatments in the spa but that she wanted a better rate than the last time.

'Why?' asked DJ.

'Because times are tough.'

'For me too,' said DJ.

'Ah, go on.' Ritz fluttered her long lashes at him. 'We're old friends, aren't we?'

'You always do your best to twist me round your little finger. But it's Shimmy you need to talk to,' said DJ. 'At least as far as the rates go. Sheridan here will look after the text for you.'

Ritz turned an appraising look towards her. 'Maybe we could do it as a before-and-after piece on you,' she said thoughtfully, and Sheridan spluttered into her water. 'The aromatherapy wrap would be ideal,' Ritz said. 'It takes inches off your thighs.'

'Why would she want to do that?' demanded DJ. 'Women these days are obsessed with looking like sticks. She's fine the way she is.'

'Thanks, DJ, but Ritz is right about my thighs.' Sheridan knew there was no point in being offended. The spa manager was making a professional observation, after all. 'I've always thought they were a bit on the bulky side.'

'I prefer women with a bit of meat on them,' said DJ. 'That's why me and Ritzy didn't last the pace, eh, Ritz?'

Sheridan's eyes widened but Ritz laughed.

'That and the fact that you had too *much* meat on you. And ate too much of the damn stuff too,' she said equably. She stood up again. 'Have a think about the ad, DJ. Give me a call.'

'Did you really date her?' asked Sheridan as Ritz left the pub.

'For three glorious months,' said DJ. 'I was the envy of the town because, let's face it, she's a cracker. But we have very different views on life.'

'I can imagine.' Sheridan looked at his almost empty plate.

'Ah, it was a bit of fun for both of us. But she has her sights set on bigger and better things and I'm free and single.' He winked at her.

'Are you hitting on me?' she asked.

'I'm being friendly,' said DJ. 'That's all. I hate this bloody PC life where you can't make jokes to women without them thinking you're trying to—'

'I wasn't thinking anything,' said Sheridan. 'Just trying to set boundaries. You're my boss, after all.'

'You could probably buy and sell me,' he said in amusement. 'Give you a few more weeks and you'll be running the *Central News*.'

'I'd be a shockingly bad editor,' she said. 'I don't know enough about the town or the people or how things work. But I do want to do my best while I'm here.'

'You've a good heart,' he told her. 'I'm glad you're with us.'

She felt unaccountably pleased at his words, although she was perfectly sure that he would've said the same to whoever had joined the paper.

'And who knows, maybe you'll break a big story for us and get us national recognition,' he joked.

He probably wouldn't like the fact that she hoped her big story would be about Paudie O'Malley, even if it was a story that would never get printed in the *Central News*. She said nothing while DJ finished his steak and chips and ordered some peach pie and ice cream. Sheridan, who hadn't planned on dessert, felt her resolve weaken when the plate was put in front of DJ and she ordered some too.

When both of them had finished, she decided to ask DJ a few casual questions about the owner of the *Central News*. She said that she was interested in knowing about the man who was ultimately paying her salary, and she was also curious to see if DJ's account of him would be the same as Nina's.

It didn't differ very much, though DJ added a few extra snippets. He told her the story of Paudie's most recent renovation of his house, and added that keeping cattle was an occupational hazard among the rich and famous of Ardbawn, because, like the rock star, Paudie also had a herd, although in his case they were Limousins.

'Does he look after them himself?' asked Sheridan.

'Not at all. He has a stockman. But he could, I'm sure. Paudie comes from a farming family. He knows his cattle.'

Sheridan couldn't help laughing. 'I'm sorry,' she said. 'I just never thought that I'd be in a position in my life where I'd be talking about cattle.'

'There you go,' said DJ. 'Ardbawn is broadening your horizons already.'

'How about Paudie?' she asked, returning to the topic of the businessman. 'Is there anyone in his life?'

Nina might not think so, but maybe DJ would have a better idea.

'He has a very busy life,' said DJ. 'There's a lot of people in it.'

'I meant romantically.'

'Oh. There was someone briefly, shortly after his wife died. But not at the moment, not that I know of.'

'I heard all about Elva.'

DJ's smile was knowing. 'I thought you'd check up on him,' he said.

'Excuse me?'

'Paudie is Ardbawn's best-known resident. I'd have been surprised if you didn't do a bit of digging.'

Sheridan shrugged. 'Naturally I looked him up.'

'It was big news when Elva died,' said DJ. 'She fell out of a window.'

Everyone was very keen to emphasise that Elva fell out of the window, thought Sheridan. She told DJ she'd already heard about that. 'Although there isn't much material on the web. Too long ago, I guess.'

'He threw himself into his businesses afterwards,' said DJ.

'His way of getting over it. He did a lot for the town. So we're very supportive of him here.'

'I know,' said Sheridan.

DJ looked at her curiously.

'Nina told me.'

'Ah.'

'It seemed to me that there was some kind of history there,' said Sheridan. 'She wasn't entirely comfortable talking about him.'

'Nina isn't a gossip,' DJ told her. 'She respects Paudie and so should you. After all, he owns the paper you work for, no matter what might have happened before. C'mon, ace reporter, we'd better get back. You have some horoscopes to write.'

Sheridan wished he hadn't reminded her of the horoscopes. She was dreading them. And she still hadn't a clue what she was going to do about the Ask Sarah agony column either. She followed him out of the pub. He told her that he wasn't going directly back to the office, that he had to call in and see the local councillor first (a piece we're doing about car parking charges, he said) but that he'd catch up with her later.

Sheridan headed towards the *Central News*, realising that she was starting to recognise more and more people in the town, even though she didn't yet know all of them by name. By the end of my stint here, she thought, I'll be practically a native. And maybe I won't want to upset the Paudie O'Malley apple cart either. So I'd better get a move on with it.

There was a silver Audi convertible parked in front of the entrance to the *Central News*. Sheridan's first thought was

210

that it might belong to Paudie, that Mr Slash-and-Burn himself had come to check up on the temporary reporter on his newspaper. But she dismissed the idea as being ludicrous – Paudie probably didn't even know that Myra was on maternity leave. And then she saw the man walking out of the deli and she recognised him straight away.

Immediately she felt as if she were in a high-speed lift shooting upwards, leaving her stomach behind. It was unlike anything she'd ever experienced before. She told herself that she was being beyond silly by allowing herself to be attracted to Josh Meagher's father. But she simply couldn't help the way her heart was fluttering and the sense of expectation that enveloped her. She looked away as he opened the car door, but it was he who said hello to her.

'Hi.' She gave him a friendly smile and took out the office door key. She put it into the lock and opened it.

'Do you work here?' The man sounded surprised.

'Yes. With the *Central News*. I'm a temp,' she added.

'Oh, right. I didn't know they had one. Well, nice to meet you again.'

'You too. Hope Josh enjoyed his lunch after the match.'

'He sure did. That child could pack away an entire buffet and not even notice.' There was a note of admiration in his father's voice.

'A growing boy.'

'Indeed.'

'He's a good footballer.'

'He's good at anything that works off energy, which is just as well, because he's got so much of it. Totally exhausting. I don't know how his mum puts up with it.'

'In a few years he'll be a moody teenager who doesn't get

out of bed,' Sheridan said. 'And you'll be complaining about that too.'

The man laughed. 'I guess you're right. His energy should be embraced and we should make the most of it.'

'You should. Well, good talking to you, but I've got to go.'

'Good talking to you too. The name's Joe, by the way.'

'Sheridan.' She gave him a quick smile and then let herself into the office. She couldn't quite believe that she was trembling. She didn't know why she was feeling what she was feeling. But she knew she was head over heels in lust with a man named Joe who had a son who was a good footballer.

She hoped she'd never see either of them again.

Chapter 17

During her time at the *City Scope*, Sheridan had always met her deadlines with considerable ease. But near the end of the week she was panicking as she typed, glancing between the notes on her desk and some open web pages on the screen in front of her and hoping desperately that she'd get everything done in time. She'd managed to lick Des Browne's sports reports into shape, had written two pieces about local events from notes that DJ had emailed her, plus a column on the latest in winter fashions (having asked Talia for some hints), and was now struggling through the last of the horoscopes. She'd finished the Ask Sarah advice piece the day before, telling the writer that having an affair with her husband's brother probably wasn't going to work out well in the long run. She'd become quite animated as she wrote the advice and had ended up cutting half of it when she realised that she'd gone way over the word count necessary.

By the time she got as far as the horoscopes, she was exhausted. I suppose I should have something nice happen for me, she thought, as she contemplated her own sign, Leo. Like a lottery win. Only that would mean buying a ticket, which I always forget to do. Besides, nobody ever forecasts lottery wins. That's the thing about astrologers. I'd believe in them if someone accurately predicted a lottery win!

Meeting someone new. Horoscopes were always talking about meeting new people. A stranger to bring love into your life. She closed her eyes and saw Josh's dad again. A classic tall, dark and handsome stranger. She felt her stomach flutter in the disconcerting way it had done on the two occasions she'd met him. She was at a complete loss to understand why a man she'd barely spoken to was having such a profound effect on her. It was bizarre. And strangely pleasurable. She opened her eyes again and looked at the blank screen in front of her. No strange men bringing love into her life. Especially, she reminded herself, strange married men. That wasn't what she was here for. She needed to focus. She needed to remember that her job was to churn out words, not get involved in feelings.

A win of some sort, she decided eventually. She needed to be a winner as far as her job was concerned, and that was what Pat and Alice wanted for her too. Maybe telling herself that she was one would make it happen. So she typed that Leos were back to winning ways, and she hoped that her own prediction would come true.

When she'd finally finished, she leaned back in her chair and sighed deeply.

'What's the matter with you?' asked DJ.

'I'm knackered,' she told him. 'I've never had a more stressful week at a paper. Except maybe last week.'

'Get used to it,' Shimmy warned her, although his tone was cheerful. 'You cosseted Dublin hacks haven't a clue when it comes to real pressure.'

'You'll be grand once you've got another few days under

your belt,' said DJ. 'And I have some more things in mind for you next week. The drama society are starting rehearsals for their latest play, and I thought it'd be good to interview the chairwoman to get a sense of where they're at. It's a good group, and talented too.'

'That's how Sean Fallon got his break,' remarked Shimmy. 'He stepped in at the last minute after a panicked call from Hayley Goodwin and got them out of a hole. It was all total chance, but I bet half of Ardbawn are hoping to be as lucky!'

It took Sheridan a minute to place the name and then remember that she was Talia's aunt. The woman who'd launched Sean Fallon on to the set of *Chandler's Park* and catapulted him into the arms of another woman had also been indirectly responsible for her own job! It would be interesting to meet her.

'Also,' said DJ, 'there's a bit of a barney going on between the golf club and a local business. They're both claiming ownership of a strip of land that the club wants to develop. I want you to talk to both sides.'

'Really?' That sounded like proper journalism to Sheridan.

DJ smiled at her. 'You're very enthusiastic all of a sudden.'

'Why wouldn't I be when you're allowing me to do actual reporting on something interesting instead of making up nonsense about the future?'

'The horoscopes are very popular,' DJ reminded her. 'And as far as reporting goes, I'm not allowing you, I'm assigning you.'

'Allowing, assigning, whatever.' Sheridan grinned. 'I have ideas already.'

'But just to bring you back to earth, ace reporter, don't

forget you're meeting Ritz today at the Riverview to do the advertorial for the Ard Spa.'

'I know.' Sheridan glanced at her watch. 'So I'd better get on with tidying up the report on the plans to clean up the Bawnee River.'

She began typing rapidly again. When she sent the completed piece to DJ, he gave her a satisfied thumbs-up that made her feel as though her winning ways had already started.

The hotel was about a kilometre outside the town, and like the guesthouse it was situated close to the river. It was also right beside the Ardbawn Golf Club, which was one of the reasons why it was very popular for short breaks. Sheridan had looked up its website before leaving the office and saw that the spa was a major draw too.

The Riverview was built around a paved courtyard containing a large fountain in a granite setting. The building itself was a modern smoked-glass and steel construction that seemed out of place in laid-back Ardbawn, but the brightly coloured flowers and carefully tended plants also lent an air of quiet luxury.

Sheridan drove into the underground car park and took the lift to reception. This was another modern design, with glossy cream marble tiles and a matching reception desk. The receptionist, a man in his twenties, was wearing a well-cut suit and a red tie. Sheridan said that she was here to see Ritz and he told her to make her way to the spa area, which was accessed by a private lift. It was a far cry from Nina's homely guesthouse, she thought, as the lift descended smoothly to the basement, and I bet the owners would never ask me to have dinner with them and talk about their lives like Nina did.

Ritz was waiting to greet her as she pushed open the opaque glass doors that led to the spa. Once again Sheridan was struck by how beautiful the manager was, carrying herself with the same effortless grace as Talia and with a sheen of glamour about her that made her seem glossy and airbrushed.

How come I seem to spend so much time with gorgeous, skinny people? she asked herself as she glanced at her own reflection in the mirror in front of her and noticed that her hair was looking as wild as ever. Is it some kind of masochism on my part?

'Hi,' said Ritz. 'Good to see you. Let me give you the tour.'

Sheridan followed her down a subtly lit corridor. The air was warm and scented with sandalwood and the mood music soft and gentle. Sheridan, who'd done quite a few spa freebies with Talia in the past, thought that the Riverview was hitting all the right spots so far. Ritz stopped outside a row of closed doors and began talking about the different treatments on offer and how the Ard Spa had some of the best therapists in the country.

'It's important to let everyone know how good we are,' she told Sheridan. 'Now what treatment would you like? Our signature massage? Or would you rather have something more specific?'

'I wasn't expecting to have a treatment,' said Sheridan, who was worried that Ritz would remember her suggestion of a before-and-after piece and was determined not to let that happen. 'I'm just here to get information.'

'Of course you have to have a treatment!' exclaimed Ritz. 'How can you write about it otherwise?'

'I suppose . . .'

'You have to do your research properly,' the spa manager added. 'Besides, I bet working for DJ is stressful. You need some time off for relaxation!'

Sheridan nodded. Being truthful, she was finding the restful ambience and subtle scents of the spa very enticing.

'So, what would you like? Something to help you lose a few pounds, cellulite, anything like that?'

Sheridan tried not to mind Ritz suggesting weight-loss and cellulite treatments. She could hardly blame her when she was constantly trying to drop a dress size and bemoaning the state of her thighs herself.

'The aromatherapy massage and the facial,' Ritz decided when Sheridan didn't reply. 'I'll get Katya to do it. She's our best therapist and she's free in ten minutes. Before that, let me show you the pool. I love it.'

Sheridan could see why. It was like a fairy grotto, with twinkling lights set into both the ceiling above it and the bottom of the pool.

'I guess you don't let kids use it.'

'No, we don't. We had a big discussion about that because we do get families down here. But the feedback was that we get even more people coming for spa breaks who wouldn't be too keen on kids, so the spa is an adult-only area.'

Sheridan knew she'd have to describe that so that it sounded like a potential guest-pleaser and didn't put people off.

'Right,' said Ritz. 'Let's get you into a treatment room and a gown, and see what you think once we've pampered you till you can take no more.'

*   *   *

Nearly two hours later Sheridan emerged from the spa feeling suitably cleansed and relaxed and thinking that spa treatments could probably trump tickets to football matches, particularly when it was damp and miserable outside. Ritz was waiting for her in the reception area and asked her if she'd enjoyed herself.

'How could I not?' Sheridan replied. 'I feel better than I have in ages.' Which was perfectly true. For the first time since she'd been made redundant, she hadn't been thinking that she was teetering on the edge. She'd allowed herself to drift so that the only thing in her head was the gentle sound of the music (music she usually dismissed as plinky-plonky earth-mother stuff but which had been very soothing).

'Glad to hear it,' said Ritz. 'Would you like something to eat? We have a lovely café upstairs that does a nice line in healthy-option food. The restaurant itself doesn't open till this evening, though you should check it out sometime. It's brilliant.'

'Do many people go for the healthy options?' asked Sheridan.

'After the spa treatments they do,' replied Ritz. 'Dunno if they stick to them afterwards though.'

The two of them went into the café and Sheridan, feeling virtuous, chose a smoked chicken salad. She only felt as though she were overdoing it when Ritz asked for an apple and hot water with a slice of lemon.

They sat at one of the high bistro tables with views towards the river.

'So, how are you enjoying your time in Ardbawn?' Ritz stirred her lemon water as she spoke.

'So far so good,' replied Sheridan. 'Although obviously

working with DJ and Shimmy is quite different to what I did before.'

'DJ is a darling,' said Ritz. 'I love him to bits.'

'But you broke up with him?'

'Love him to bits like a brother,' she amended. 'We get on famously but there wasn't that thing between us. That special electricity, you know?'

Not really, thought Sheridan. There hadn't been a special electricity between her and any of her boyfriends, even Griff. They'd been more about companionship, getting on with each other, and occasionally enjoyable (if not mind-blowing) sex. She'd never seen a man and fancied him like crazy, thought about him all the time and drawn up fantasies of how things would be if they were together. (At least not until she'd been made redundant and Talia had suggested that Griff move in with her. She'd wondered what living with him would be like then and it had turned out to be complete fantasy in the end anyway.) She'd never stayed awake hoping that someone would call, frantic at the thought of never seeing him again. Nor had she ever wished her life away, living from date to date, thinking that every second away from a boyfriend was a wasted second as she knew some of her friends occasionally did. It wasn't her. It never had been. The only time she'd felt the frisson Ritz spoke about (and it hadn't been a frisson then, it had been an intense bolt of lightning) had been when she'd met Josh Meagher's father, Joe. And that didn't count.

'DJ and I could've stayed together,' Ritz continued, not noticing that Sheridan's attention had wavered. 'But the truth is it wouldn't have gone anywhere.'

'Are you going out with anyone now?' asked Sheridan,

thinking that Ritz could probably have anyone in the town she liked.

'Not yet,' replied the spa manager. She gave a philosophical shrug. 'There isn't what you'd call a vast array of men to choose from in Ardbawn. The ones who are eligible are well in demand. Which is why I thought long and hard about breaking up with DJ. Then I realised I wanted to stay with him because I wasn't keen on being on my own, which, let's face it, is a ridiculous reason for being with anyone.'

'Although a reason that lots of women use,' observed Sheridan.

'True. But not me. Besides,' Ritz looked confidingly at Sheridan, 'he's a fair bit older than me and a bit of a stick-in-the-mud for all of his good humour. He likes things the way they are, whereas I like change.'

'DJ campaigns for change,' Sheridan pointed out. 'He writes a lot in the paper about the need for reform.'

'But the focus is all Ardbawn. I do understand that the community is important, but I can't imagine my entire life revolving around it.'

'So do you plan to move away?' asked Sheridan.

'Perhaps,' said Ritz. 'Although that depends on how things pan out with . . .' Her voice trailed off as she broke into a smile and raised her hand to wave at someone across the room.

Sheridan caught her breath as the man she'd waved at came over to them. It was Joe, dressed in jeans and a fine-knit jumper, his dark hair tousled and a little unkempt. The tingling of electricity that Ritz had spoken about suddenly jangled every nerve end in her body and she dropped the fork she'd been holding, only just managing to catch it before it hit the ground.

'Well, look who it is,' said Ritz as Joe approached. 'How're you doing?' She kissed him on the cheek and turned to Sheridan. 'Do you know . . .'

'Joe. Yes, we've met.' Sheridan, keeping her hands clenched to hide her trembling fingers, gave him her most professional smile.

'Sheridan, isn't it?' He held out his hand and she took it. His handshake was firm, but not bone-crushing like DJ's.

'What are you doing here, sweetheart?' Ritz's voice was like syrup. 'Not that it isn't always lovely to see you.'

Sweetheart? Sheridan's glance flickered between them.

'I was up in Dublin and I haven't had anything to eat,' said Joe. 'I thought that stopping off here might be nicer than having something at home.'

His comment seemed totally out of character to Sheridan. Ever since she'd met him, she'd thought of him as a family man, sitting down to dinner every night with his wife who did the home cooking and Josh who appreciated it.

'Well it's nice to see you again,' said Ritz. 'I was beginning to think I'd offended you somehow.'

It was clear that Ritz felt proprietorial towards Joe. Sheridan could hear it in the sweetening of the other girl's voice, in the way her gaze lingered on him and the way she'd said 'sweetheart', careless, yet with an underlying sense of ownership. But how did he feel about her? And what about the home-cooking wife and the adorable boy?

'You? Offend me? Never,' said Joe. 'I've just been very busy. Which is good, of course, but at the moment it's all about keeping the customer satisfied. Not that you need reminding of that.' He grinned at her.

'Oh, we do our best,' she said. 'That's why Sheridan's

222

here. I'm running an advertorial in the *News*. Got to remind the people of Ardbawn that no matter what's going on in their lives, it's good to have some pamper time, as she's hopefully discovered.'

'Did you have a nice pampering?' Joe turned to Sheridan.

'Absolutely.'

'I'm trying to persuade her to come in for some targeted treatments,' said Ritz.

Sheridan held her breath. If the spa manager came up with a list of her beauty failings in front of Joe, she'd clock her.

'You look fine to me the way you are,' Joe told her. 'Treatments are all very well, but it's what's inside that counts.'

'You're such a charmer!' Ritz looked at him indulgently and then made an exclamation of annoyance as her mobile shrilled. 'What?' she said into it. 'You've got to be kidding me. No. No. I'll be right there.' She stood up. 'I'm sorry,' she said. 'Small crisis downstairs. They can't manage without me.' She smiled at Sheridan. 'I hope you have everything you need, but feel free to call me if there's anything else.'

'I should be OK,' said Sheridan. 'I have all your brochures and, of course, my very own sublime experience to talk about. I'll send you the copy for approval tomorrow afternoon.'

'Great, thanks.' Then she turned a mega-watt beam towards Joe. 'Don't be a stranger,' she said. 'Call in more often.'

'I'll try,' said Joe. 'I promise.'

Sheridan wasn't sure what she should do next. She still had more than half the chicken salad on her plate, but she was totally unable to eat it with Joe standing beside the table sending shivers up and down her spine. She wanted him to stay. But she knew it would be better if he went.

'D'you want to join me?' she heard herself asking when she realised he wasn't leaving.

'That'd be good,' said Joe. 'I hate eating on my own. I was going to go to the bar and have their cottage pie and chips, but looking at you with the salad, I'd feel too guilty.'

'Oh, listen, I would've loved the cottage pie and chips too.' Sheridan realised that she was speaking like a normal person even though every nerve end still tingled. 'But after having the treatments, I thought the least I could do was make an effort.'

Joe laughed. 'I'll keep you company in your misery,' he said. 'They do a nice goat's-cheese tart thingy here, and although I wouldn't put it down as a decent meal for a starving man, it does have a lot of flavour. Perhaps I could persuade them to add some chips to it, which would help.'

I want to run away with him, she thought, but I'm talking to him about goat's cheese. Which is probably telling me something, only I don't know what.

While she stayed silent, totally unsure of what to say next, Joe called the waitress over and gave his order.

'So,' he said, after she'd gone, 'how are you enjoying the *Central News* and Ardbawn?'

'More and more as time goes by.' The nerve-jangling had eased off a little and she felt able to reply. 'It's not like I'll stay here, of course, but it's a good experience.'

'I'm glad you're enjoying it.'

'And it's giving me lots of ideas for the future.'

'Really?'

'Yes. All I have to do is act on them. Easier said than done, but hopefully my plans will work out.'

She was proud of the way she'd got herself under control and was having a conversation with him now. Even though all her senses seemed to be on high alert in his company, she was also feeling herself begin to relax. He told her that he hoped her ideas would pan out too, and that she'd continue to enjoy her time in Ardbawn, which, he said, was one of the nicest towns in Ireland.

The waitress arrived with his food. The sight of the chips made Sheridan's mouth water despite the fact that she hadn't truly regained her appetite. She recalled friends who said that they'd lost weight when they were in love because they couldn't eat. She'd been unable to imagine such a scenario before. But she was unexpectedly living it now.

I'm not in love, she reminded herself sharply. I'm just . . . just . . . it's some weird physical thing. Pheromones or something. Because it's not possible to love someone you don't know. Love doesn't come at you as a physical force. It's part and parcel of being caught up with a person, not just looking at them and being very grateful they can't read your mind because you're having disgracefully erotic thoughts about them. And yet, she thought, there's something about this man . . . something that . . .

And then she remembered that the something about him was the fact that he was married and therefore not available to her. That even contemplating a relationship of any sort with him was ridiculous. And very, very wrong.

But how is it, she asked herself, that the one time I find what it is that everyone talks about, the one time I'm totally overwhelmed by feelings for someone, I end up with the married man who has a home-cooking wife and cute kid? Why don't I find the gorgeous single guy who's overwhelmed by me too?

Because I'm a loser. She answered her own question. Because I'm the kind of person who has a great job and loses it. And a boyfriend who might've turned out OK if I hadn't got it all wrong and lost him too.

Loser.

'Are you OK?' he asked.

'Of course.' She pushed her hair out of her eyes and wondered if she was trying to look sexy doing it. She let her hands drop again. 'Thinking random thoughts . . . nothing.'

His dark blue eyes regarded her studiously.

'I thought you might be looking down on me,' he said. 'Thinking I was a country bumpkin.'

'Absolutely not.' Her response was too vehement, she thought. She needed to tone it down a bit. Get back on track. She poked at her salad.

'So tell me about yourself,' said Joe.

Why did he want to know? Was he just being Ardbawn-friendly or did he want to know about her because he was someone who would happily cheat on the stay-at-home wife and football-mad son and wanted to find out if she was the sort of person who wouldn't mind? Of course she was being a bit presumptuous in thinking that if he was a cheating bastard he'd want to cheat with her! The reality was that Ritz Boland was a far more attractive proposition for a bit of offside action, if that was what he wanted.

But she didn't want him to be that sort of person. She wanted him to be a kind, decent, happily married man. Even if the idea was breaking her heart. (Don't be idiotic, she said to herself when she thought about her heart being broken. You've never had a broken heart before. Even Griff didn't break it. He just bruised it. And that was probably your ego

226

as much as your heart. So stop being melodramatic and turning this encounter into some weird impossible love thing. Be sensible.)

'I don't have an exciting life.' And yet she wanted to keep talking to him. So she told him about her brothers instead. Most men liked to hear about her brothers. Most of them knew enough about sport to admire them.

Joe was no different. His eyes lit up when she mentioned them.

'I've heard of Con and Mattie Gray, of course,' he said. 'Both of them were hugely talented. Wow, it's an honour to meet their sister.'

It wasn't the first time someone had said that to her. But it was the first time she wished she hadn't mentioned them. She didn't want him to like her because of her brothers.

'I enjoy Gaelic football, but I was never any good at it. Rugby either, although I was on the school team for a while. But to be totally honest with you, I was always afraid of getting killed.'

Sheridan's laugh was genuine, but she couldn't help thinking that it was too loud. It would be better, she thought, to have a dainty, girlish laugh instead of a big guffaw.

'Truly,' he said. 'My school was very much into rugby, and we had some fearless players. It's just that I wasn't one of them.'

'You went to school here, in Ardbawn?' She looked at him curiously, because she'd covered schools rugby for the paper and she'd never heard of one in Ardbawn competing at a high level.

'No,' said Joe. 'My parents thought it would be a good idea to send me to boarding school.'

'Oh.' Sheridan was surprised. There wasn't a big tradition

of boarding schools in Ireland, although many families considered them to be academically superior. But many of them did indeed have strong rugby teams.

'I went to primary school here,' said Joe. 'I think my folks thought I'd do better as a boarder for secondary.'

'What was it like?' she asked. 'When I was a kid, I read all those Enid Blyton stories about boarding school and it sounded brilliant. Looking back, though, I'm not sure how brilliant it really would be.'

'I hated it,' said Joe in a matter-of-fact voice. 'I hated being away from home and away from my family. But the truth is that it was as much for my mother's sake as mine. She found it hard to cope sometimes, so it was a good idea to reduce the numbers at home.'

Sheridan wasn't sure what to say. Alice would have been horrified at the idea of sending any of her children away. But then by no stretch of the imagination could anyone imagine Alice being unable to cope with anything.

'However . . .' Joe smiled. 'It didn't do me any harm, and I probably needed to be toughened up.'

'My parents frequently tell me I need to be tougher,' remarked Sheridan. 'I don't know if it's a good thing or not, to be honest.'

The two of them sat in silence for a moment.

'Sorry,' said Joe. 'I seem to have turned our conversation into a ramble down a particularly thorny memory lane.'

'Not at all,' said Sheridan. She realised that she'd stopped trembling. And that she was feeling more relaxed in his company. Nevertheless, she didn't think it would be a good idea to stay. She looked at her watch and realised that she couldn't stay anyway.

'I have to go,' she told him. 'I've to see Hayley Goodwin from the drama society shortly, and then I need to write the piece for Ritz.'

'I know Hayley.' Joe nodded. 'Nice lady. Does some fantastic work in the community.'

'Everyone here seems to do something for the community, if all the stuff we get in to the *Central News* is anything to go by.'

'We're a nice bunch here in the sticks.' Joe's eyes were full of merriment.

Sheridan felt the frisson again.

'Perhaps you'd like to meet me for coffee sometime?' he asked. 'I can tell you more about how fantastic life in Ardbawn can be.'

She caught her breath.

'Not if you don't want to,' said Joe. 'I just thought that maybe you'd like to . . . Well, it would be nice to see you. That's all.'

She desperately wanted to say yes to a cup of coffee with him. After all, having coffee with a man, even a married man, was a perfectly innocent thing to do. But how could she regard it as innocent when her feelings for Joe were nothing of the sort?

'I'm really sorry,' she said. 'I don't think it would be a good idea.'

'Oh.' He looked disappointed. 'I apologise. I totally misinterpreted . . . I thought . . .'

'Thought what?' Sheridan couldn't stop herself from speaking.

'I thought we had a connection,' said Joe.

She was suddenly angry with him. A man like him, with

a home-cooking wife and a gorgeous son, shouldn't be looking for connections with single women.

'I think you're connected enough already,' she said.

'Excuse me?' This time he looked puzzled.

'You're married, with a gorgeous boy,' she said. 'And while I've no problem about bumping into you in a hotel or café, I don't think that you should be trying to set up intimate cups of coffee with me.'

His eyes opened wide as she spoke. Sheridan was proud of herself for putting him on the spot, pleased that she'd done the right thing. She stood up and pulled on her jacket.

'I'll be off,' she said. 'I'm sure I'll see you around, because Ardbawn is a small town, but I guess I'll steer clear of you and your absolutely adorable and talented son. Who, quite frankly, deserves better from his dad.'

'I think you've got the wrong end of the stick,' Joe told her. 'I'm not Josh's father.'

Sheridan stared at him.

'He's my godson,' said Joe. 'I bring him to all his Gaelic matches. His football and rugby games too. I'm the current president of the soccer club, so I like going to as many games as I can. Besides, I love watching him play.'

'Oh.'

'And I'm not married,' he added with a grin. 'I wouldn't have asked you if you'd like to meet for coffee if I was. Besides, like you said, this is a small town. It'd be back to my poor wife in an instant if I was seen having cups of coffee with flame-haired reporters from Dublin.'

'Stop,' said Sheridan as she sat down again abruptly. 'You're making me feel like a total idiot.'

'I wasn't trying to do that,' Joe said.

'I thought . . . Well, it was the way you and Josh talked about going home for something to eat . . . I thought there was someone . . .' She held up her hand as he started to speak. 'Don't say anything. I'm absolutely mortified.'

He laughed. 'No need to be. And I'm delighted you have such strong principles.'

'I doubt that.'

'I mean it. It's sweet that you'd jump on to a moral high horse and give out to me for not being a good enough dad. I like it.'

She sighed. He was laughing at her and she couldn't blame him.

'So the only other thing we need to deal with is the coffee.' He looked at her hopefully. 'Now that you're not compromising, would that be OK? Or maybe we could move straight on to dinner? Unless, of course, you're seeing someone yourself? My principles might allow me to have a go at convincing you I'm a better bet than whoever is in your life right now, but I won't try to mess it up.'

As Sheridan listened, she realised that he'd moved on from asking her for coffee to suggesting dinner. That actually sounded like a proper date to her. Which meant that the most attractive – and thankfully single – man she'd ever met in her life, the man who made her heart beat faster and butterflies dance in her stomach, was asking her out! And it wasn't one bit like being asked by any of the other men she'd ever known. It wasn't like just being friends and going out together seeming like a good idea. It was sort of romantic.

The thought of spending a romantic evening with him was turning her legs to jelly.

'I'm not seeing anyone right now,' she said, hoping her

voice didn't betray the excitement she was feeling. 'Dinner would be great.'

'Excellent.' Joe looked pleased. 'I'm glad we've got that sorted. So now the question is, when suits you? Much as I'd love to meet you later tonight, I know you're busy with your interviews and stuff and I'm a bit tied up too. After that I'm away on business for a couple of days so I can't, but how does next week suit you?'

'Perfectly.' Sheridan took a card out of her bag and handed it to him. It was an old *City Scope* business card, but she'd scribbled over the paper's logo and landline numbers, leaving only her mobile number and email address. 'It's not like I have a hectic social life right now.' She was suddenly afraid that she'd sounded too eager, that she'd handed him her card too quickly. Maybe she shouldn't have told him that she wasn't seeing anyone. Maybe she should've just said that her evenings were totally booked up with loads of important interviews. Or she could have told him that she was working on a major investigative story.

But that would've been stupid. He was single. She was single and she fancied him like mad. Besides, there was a limit to how busy she could be. What was the point in playing games?

'Well, let's say next Wednesday back here,' said Joe as he looked up from her card. 'I'll book the restaurant for seven thirty. It's a lovely place to eat – Ardbawn's best. Which for a Dub like you might not mean much, but it matters to us.'

Sheridan didn't need to be brought to the best restaurant in the town. She would've been just as happy with pizza and beer. But Joe was looking at her expectantly.

'Sounds good,' she said.

'You'll like it,' he promised. 'The food is great.'

'I'll see you here, so.'

'Wonderful.'

She slung her bag on to her shoulder. She didn't want to go but she thought that this was a good time. Leave him feeling keen – it was something that Talia believed in and which Sheridan used to laugh about, protesting that it wasn't a game. But right now she was going to follow her best friend's advice.

'Better get back to the office.' She gave him a brief smile and then turned away.

'Don't work too hard.'

She looked over her shoulder. 'I'll try not to.'

He waved and she walked out of the room, conscious that he was still watching her. Her smile was much wider when she had her back to him. In fact, she was beaming.

OK, she said to herself as she got into her Beetle. Let's just recap. I thought I was a loser, but in fact this has turned into a winning situation. Which means that I've managed to fulfil my destiny already. Even if it's one I made up for myself. Of course, I would've been right with my prediction even if I'd gone for the stranger in my life. Because I've met one. A gorgeous, handsome, available man who's asked me on a date. A man who makes me feel like nobody else in the world.

Ardbawn is a lovely place, she thought, as she started the engine. I was right to come here. And who would've thought there'd be such great opportunities for me in a one-horse town!

Chapter 18

Ever since Sheridan had asked her about Elva O'Malley's accident, Nina hadn't been able to stop thinking about it. For the last sixteen years the day had been buried deep in her consciousness, but it astonished her how she could recall it so clearly now. When she closed her eyes, it was as though she'd stepped back in time. She could feel the warmth of the sun pouring through the French windows of the breakfast room as she served the guests. She could hear herself chatting with them about things they could do later in the day. She remembered thinking, as she cleared up afterwards, that this had been one of their best seasons ever so far.

The guesthouse had been booked solid for weeks and she'd been run off her feet tending to the visitors as well as looking after the children. Alan, due to start school the following September, had been a total handful all summer. He was an adventurous child who got into everything and who loved being outdoors. She was always terrified that one day he'd manage to escape the confines of the fenced area of the garden and find his way down to the riverbank. The Bawnee was fast moving, with plenty of eddies and pools in which someone could come to grief. Nina never quite got over worrying about Alan and his love of danger, even when he was older and it was perfectly allowable for him to go down to the river. (Then he would construct bridges and rope ladders as a means to cross it, telling her that he was Indiana Jones, searching for treasure.)

The day that Elva fell out of the window, Nina had been worrying about Alan falling into the river. She hadn't had to worry about Chrissie. Her daughter was far more placid than her older brother and had been happily occupied playing with her dolls.

Sean had been out earlier in the day, having told her that he'd a number of things to do, one of which was dropping some leaflets up to March Manor so that Paudie could look at them and give him a quote for printing up a glossy brochure. Nina would've preferred him to be around the guesthouse because it was so busy, but he promised to help her catch up with anything that needed doing as soon as he got back.

After he'd left, she'd spent the morning in a flurry of multitasking – which included spending nearly half an hour trying to find a pair of earrings that one of the guests was convinced she'd left in the residents' lounge and which were now missing. Nina's stomach had turned when she heard this, because the last thing she wanted was for people to think there was a thief in the house. Philly Purcell told her that the earrings were very valuable and worth over a thousand pounds, and Nina had almost been sick on the spot, even though she wasn't sure whether to believe Philly's valuation or not. In the end it hadn't mattered, because eventually she'd discovered the earrings carefully placed on the window ledge of an upstairs bathroom. Philly had apologised and said that she simply couldn't recall leaving them there, but Nina still remembered the feeling of absolute relief that had washed over her when she'd seen the diamonds glittering in the midday sun. She remembered feeling lucky too, that nobody else had seen them and been tempted by them, or simply picked them up and put them somewhere else.

The other thing she remembered was the lemon scent of the burning bush plants in the garden, mingling with that of the mown grass. She remembered thinking how beautiful it was and how fortunate she was to live where she did. In fact her overriding memory of the morning of Elva's death was one of happiness and satisfaction and feeling very, very blessed.

It had been wonderfully peaceful, and then Sean had come home in an absolutely foul mood and with a small, but deep, cut on the side of his face. Nina had fussed around him asking him what on earth had happened, which made Sean touch his face and then look at his bloodstained fingers.

'Stupid accident,' he said. 'I'd better stick a plaster on it.'

He strode into the house, leaving her looking after him, a concerned expression on her face. His bad-tempered return had ruined her sense of contentment and serenity. A few minutes later he came downstairs again, a small plaster on his cheek, and muttered something about clearing ivy from the end of the garden.

She'd tried not to be annoyed with Sean for being in bad humour and spoiling her feeling of well-being. She asked him if Paudie had agreed to do the printing, and he'd said that the businessman hadn't been there – obviously he had bigger fish to fry these days than work for local people. Then he'd taken a hoe and garden shears out of the shed and set to clearing the ivy with a vengeance. Nina had left him to it and gone indoors, where she whipped egg whites for pavlovas and sang along to Roberta Flack's version of 'Killing Me Softly', which she had on loud enough to hear over the electric beater. Later, when the pavlovas were in the oven, she starting preparing fruit for that evening's dessert, and continued to sing along to the radio. She remembered getting strawberry juice on her white cotton top and going upstairs to change. And when she came down, Sean was standing in the kitchen, a frozen look on his face.

'What's wrong?' Her immediate, visceral concern was that something had happened to one of the children. But then, from the corner of her eye, she saw both of them playing outside and she allowed herself a sigh of relief. 'What is it?' she asked.

'Elva O'Malley,' said Sean blankly. 'Ellie. She's dead.'

'She's what?' Nina was absolutely stunned. She'd spoken to Elva only the previous day, when she'd met her in the delicatessen on Main Street. 'How? What happened?'

She listened as Sean told her about Elva's fall. PJ Dalton had been the one to phone him and tell him. PJ was Sean's closest friend in Ardbawn and was the foreman at Paudie's printing works.

'But how did she fall?' asked Nina. 'Was she leaning out of the window or what?'

'How the hell do I know?' demanded Sean. 'I wasn't there.'

'You were there earlier,' said Nina. 'Did you see her? Was she unwell? Did she maybe have a dizzy spell or something?'

'I don't know,' replied Sean. 'She was . . . she was fine when I saw her. A bit . . . No . . . she was fine.'

'Poor Paudie.' Nina felt a tear roll down her cheek. 'He must be devastated.'

Sean said nothing.

'Was it Paudie who found her?'

'I don't bloody know!' cried Sean. 'All I know is that she's dead. OK?'

Nina stared at him. There was no reason for Sean to snap at her like that.

'Sorry,' he said. 'It was a shock, that's all.'

Nina put her arms around him. Sean was easily affected by people and events. He felt things more deeply than anyone ever imagined. She thought that perhaps it was part of his artistic nature. He leaned his head on hers for a moment and then moved away from her.

'I'm OK,' he said. 'I don't know why I'm so . . . so . . .'

'She was an old girlfriend,' said Nina. 'Of course you're upset.'

Sean and Nina had only once discussed the fact that Elva was an old flame of his. It had been shortly before their marriage, and she'd teased him about the number of hearts in Ardbawn that he'd broken in the past, and the ones that were about to be broken by his marriage. Sean had laughed and said that his exploits had been totally overhyped and that he was happy to be settling down with her. He'd told her he'd already forgotten every other woman he'd ever dated.

Nina only vaguely remembered Sean and Elva as a couple, although they'd made a striking pair walking along the main street together at the time; Sean dark and brooding and Elva blonde and graceful.

Sean's words brought her back to the present. 'We were only kids back then. Jeez, she's been married to Paudie for, what, fifteen, sixteen years now, you can hardly call her an old girlfriend.'

'Sixteen years sounds like for ever when you're young, but it isn't that long really.'

'Yeah, right.'

'Why did you break it off with her?'

It was a question she'd never asked him about any of his previous relationships. It had never been something she either needed or wanted to know.

'It was a mutual decision,' said Sean.

Nina raised an eyebrow. Everyone knew that Elva had been heartbroken when Sean had dumped her. It certainly hadn't been a mutual decision.

'We were too young,' he said impatiently. 'Although maybe it was me who was too young for her at the time. After all, she married Paudie soon after.'

'But she threw herself into the river after you two split up, didn't she?'

'That old chestnut!' He snorted. 'She tripped and fell.'

'How d'you know?'

'I . . . Look, Ellie didn't . . . Oh, this is ridiculous! It was years ago.'

'Sorry.' Nina realised she was probably being insensitive.

'She's . . . she was the sort of person who could get under your skin. She could overdramatise things sometimes. But I never thought there was any truth in that story.' He swallowed hard. 'Never.'

'She wasn't pregnant when she married Paudie, was she?'

'Why on earth would you think that?'

'It's surprising, that's all. You break it off with her, she's devastated, and the next thing she's waltzing up the aisle with him.'

'She couldn't have been pregnant when she married him. JJ was born much later. Look, Nina, I don't want to talk about her any more. I'm going out to the ivy again. I need to do something physical.'

'OK,' she said.

She watched him as he strode down the garden, his shoulders hunched. The news about Elva had clearly shaken him. Which was understandable, it had shaken her too. She remembered her mother talking about her once. Dolores had remarked that Ellie Slater was a girl who thought too much of herself. She believed she was made for better things. Which, Nina supposed, in her marriage to Paudie O'Malley, she'd certainly got.

And she would have got even more if she'd lived, Nina thought now as the ringing phone brought her abruptly back to the present. She would have been part of the rich and glamorous set that wanted to welcome Paudie into its midst. After Elva's death, Paudie had maintained a dignified silence despite innuendo in some of the less reputable newspapers that there had been something untoward about it. That thirty-eight-year-old women didn't just fall from bedroom windows. That the gardai weren't happy about the circumstances. No matter what was printed, Paudie said nothing. Until the day he sued one of the papers and got a substantial settlement as a result.

A clever man, Paudie, thought Nina as she picked up the phone.

Always was. Always would be. But sometimes being clever just wasn't enough.

Sheridan was enjoying her conversation with Hayley Goodwin. Talia's aunt was younger than she'd expected, and as elegantly groomed as her niece. Sheridan thanked her for telling Talia about the job, and told her that she was enjoying her stay in Ardbawn.

'A bit quiet for you, I'm sure.' Hayley's blue eyes twinkled.

'Different,' said Sheridan.

'Getting to know people yet?'

Sheridan thought of all the people she'd met over the last couple of weeks, but mostly about her upcoming date with Joe, and she couldn't help smiling.

'A bit,' she told Hayley. 'I'm staying with Nina Fallon.'

'I know.' Hayley grinned at her. 'The younger people in the town like to think that Ardbawn has grown into more than a village, but the truth is that most of the time everyone always has a good idea about what's going on. We only have a few deep, dark secrets.'

'You hardly need a newspaper, so,' said Sheridan while wondering about the deep, dark secrets.

'The bush telegraph can be quicker,' agreed Hayley. 'But it's nice to have your name in the paper. Well, depending on the circumstances, I guess.'

'In your case, definitely,' said Sheridan. 'We're doing a piece about your next play.'

Hayley chatted happily about *Blithe Spirit*, the play they were putting on for the Ardbawn Festival, and how the dramatic society hoped it would be their best performance yet.

'A pity you don't have your famous leading man for it,' said Sheridan. 'Or will Sean Fallon return to Ardbawn?'

'I doubt that very much,' said Hayley. 'He hasn't been here to rehearse with us. Besides, we wouldn't dream of insulting Nina by asking him.'

I'm turning into a desperate gossip, thought Sheridan as she listened to Hayley talk about Sean and Nina, and how upset most people were for the guesthouse owner. I never used to care about people's personal lives before. But since coming here, all I want to know is personal stuff about guys like Paudie and Sean!

'But you must know it all already,' finished Hayley, who'd repeated the story Nina had told with lots more embellishment about Sean's appearances in Dublin nightclubs with Lulu Adams and other female members of the *Chandler's Park* cast.

'Is he a complete pig, then?' asked Sheridan.

'It's a funny thing,' said Hayley slowly. 'He and Nina seemed an almost perfect couple. Which surprised everyone in the town, because she's not at all the sort of woman he usually went for. There was a bit of talk at the time they got married that it was old man Fallon who pushed his son into it. The doc seemed to think that there was money in the Doherty family. Certainly the house and land was worth a lot.'

'Hardly seems a reason for marriage, though.'

'I'd be the last person to know.' Hayley chuckled. 'I'm an old spinster.'

'Hayley!'

'I know. Doesn't it sound sad and lonesome and awful? But I'm forty-five and unmarried, so I'm not sure what else you could call me. Except I love living on my own. I'd hate to be married. Hate to go through what Nina's going through. I like my life far too much for that.'

'Nina said she threw Sean out.'

'She may well have done. In which case, I wouldn't bet on him staying out.'

'Why?'

'Oh, there was gossip before about Sean Fallon having a bit on the side. The bush telegraph didn't work as well as it might have, though, or else he was incredibly discreet, because it never came out one way or the other. But if he did, Nina forgave him, and I can't help thinking she'll forgive him now too, if that's what he wants.'

'And is it?'

'Maybe not right now, when he's behaving like a child in a sweet shop. But d'you seriously expect a girl in her twenties to keep someone like Sean Fallon interested? He may be a flirt and he might like a bit of extramarital sex, but he's an intelligent man and she's a total airhead.'

'You know that because . . .?'

'I saw her being interviewed. All smiles and giggles and simpering. She's not a proper actress. She's a silly tart.'

'So no part for her in *Blithe Spirit*, then?' joked Sheridan.

'Absolutely not.' Hayley looked wistful. 'I wish that Sean had kept it in his pants. Then he'd be with us again this year, *Chandler's Park* or not.'

'Can't have everything, I suppose,' said Sheridan. She got up to leave. 'I'll be along for the first night.'

'Of course you will,' said Hayley. 'We always have front-row seats reserved for the local press.'

* * *

On her way back to the guesthouse, Sheridan phoned Nina to say she was going to spend some time in the lounge that evening so that she could access the internet. Alo Brady, her ex-colleague on the *City Scope*, had emailed her wanting to know if she was still working on something about Paudie O'Malley and his business empire. Sheridan replied that she was still getting her research together but that she was hoping to interview him shortly (she didn't say that she'd still no idea how to go about that, although she was hopeful that one of her increasing number of contacts in the town would eventually make it happen). Alo had then mailed her back to say that he was leaving the *City Scope* for a position with an online business news site. The way of the future, he'd said, and Business Today was becoming more and more influential. The news site was very interested in Paudie's empire. If Sheridan thought she could put a good story with a personal interview together, it could be a potential winner to submit to the site's editor.

When she read Alo's email, Sheridan's immediate thought was that, once again, she'd been beaten by an ex-colleague in the new jobs stakes. She was trying very hard not to brood on the fact that since everyone else was getting jobs, she must be the worst journalist in the world. It was like being home again, with Con and Matt taking all the glory and her in the background wondering why she didn't succeed like them. But there are new opportunities on the horizon for me, she reminded herself. My horoscope says so, and it's been right so far, even if I did write it myself.

One way or another she was determined to get an interview with Paudie O'Malley and reveal something about him that nobody knew. And when she did that, she would surprise all those people who seemed to think that she could only write about a dismal League of Ireland match on a wet Friday in the back of beyond.

Sheridan was pleased when Nina suggested that she have dinner in the house before doing whatever she needed to do on the computer. Her appetite had returned (so much for love robbing me of a desire to eat, she thought, and looking more sylph-like when I meet Joe) and she was ravenous; the only food she'd eaten all day being the emergency Kit Kat she kept in her desk drawer. The thought of Nina's cooking made her mouth water, and she remembered the half-eaten packet of fruit pastilles in her bag. She popped one into her mouth, not caring that it was green and therefore not one of her favourite flavours.

She stopped off at the deli before going to the house and picked up a bottle of wine. Although she'd come to an arrangement with Nina about paying for any dinners (because she didn't think it was right to sponge off the other woman's generous nature), the price Nina had suggested didn't reflect the fact that last time they'd guzzled a bottle between them.

The guesthouse was, as ever, warm and cosy, but Sheridan thought that Nina was distracted as she served up an aromatic shepherd's pie.

'Is everything OK?' she asked eventually.

'Sure,' said Nina, who then retreated into silence again while Sheridan studied her covertly. She thought the older woman looked stressed, and eventually said so.

'Ah, I was just reminiscing,' said Nina. 'Thinking about life here a long time ago.'

'It must be strange to have lived in the same small town for your whole life,' remarked Sheridan.

'Not for me,' Nina said. 'But maybe for Sean.'

'Did he go away?'

Nina told her about Sean's years in Dublin, of his struggle to be an actor and of how he eventually returned to Ardbawn.

'So that's why you think he's living the dream now? And why you're prepared to forgive him for Lulu Adams?'

'I've always felt . . . that I held him back,' admitted Nina. 'I trapped him into the sort of life that he wasn't really suited to.'

'Hardly trapped,' said Sheridan.

Nina looked pensive.

'Sean's failings are his, not yours,' Sheridan said. 'You shouldn't feel that him having an affair is your fault. That's ridiculous.'

'I wish I was as strong as you,' said Nina.

'You are,' Sheridan reminded her. 'You threw him out in the first place.'

'Yes, I did.'

Sheridan desperately wanted to tell Nina not to take him back. But, she told herself, she knew nothing about their relationship. It wasn't up to her to tell Nina anything at all.

After dinner, Sheridan sat in the residents' lounge with her laptop and a cup of coffee. Nina said that she had things to do in the kitchen and left her alone. Sheridan had found out the name of the police sergeant who'd investigated Elva O'Malley's accidental death, and she was planning to set up a meeting with him to ask him about it. Vinnie Murray was now a superintendent based in Kilkenny. Sheridan hadn't yet decided how she'd explain her interest in the old tragedy, but she was good at getting people to talk to her, and she hoped the policeman would have snippets of information that weren't already public knowledge. She was now absolutely convinced there was something worth writing about when it came to Paudie O'Malley's private life. The only thing that surprised her was that nobody else seemed to have beaten her to it.

After a while she stopped looking at her laptop and gazed into space instead. Without even meaning to, she was thinking of Joe again. She had to keep reminding herself that the most attractive man she'd ever met in her life had asked her on a date. A proper date, in the posh restaurant of the Riverview Hotel. She didn't usually do posh restaurants. She frowned slightly as she considered her wardrobe, which was certainly not posh-restaurant friendly. But you don't have to get tarted up, she reminded herself. People don't, these days. Not unless it's a seriously glam affair. You're only going to dinner. With a man you want to impress. She realised, with a shock, that impressing men wasn't something she'd tried to do much of before.

Now you're being silly, she said, under her breath. He's a man, not some kind of being you have to dazzle. Cop on to yourself, woman. You can wear jeans and a nice top and you'll be fine.

She turned to her laptop again, but she was still thinking about Joe. The trouble was, she wanted to be more than fine for him. She wanted to be special. She wanted him to be pleased that he'd asked her out. Proud to be with her. She didn't care if that made her seem shallow. It wasn't shallow to want to look your best. Was it?

She twirled a strand of her hair between her fingers. It could do with a cut, she thought. Maybe a conditioning treatment too. Perhaps . . . No, she told herself firmly. No way am I getting a full body treatment at the spa before meeting him. No matter how soft and smooth Ritz promises I'll be afterwards. I can't afford it. And I'm not going to turn into the sort of woman who thinks she has to spend hours primping and preening herself before going out. I'm not. Absolutely. I'm fine the way I am.

I still need a new dress, though, she murmured. Maybe I'll check out the shops at the weekend. After all, I haven't bought anything but fleeces in ages.

Chapter 19

Sheridan picked up a copy of the *Central News* on her way to Kilkenny the following Saturday morning. She scanned her piece on the land dispute, which she thought was very even handed (it had been a major challenge to explain the opposing points of view of both parties because they were both reasonable yet mutually exclusive); she also saw that DJ hadn't changed her amendments to Des's sports reports, which pleased her (she wondered if Des himself noticed them; they were even more radical than the previous week). Her Ask Sarah column, which advised an angst-ridden girl against stalking a previous boyfriend, sounded both calm and sympathetic and she hoped that the girl herself would think so too. She finished up with a look at the horoscopes, hoping that Nina would take her advice about putting the past behind her. As for her own – her life had improved immeasurably since telling herself that she was back to winning ways. She totally was. Absolutely. Even if her winning ways were entirely related to having a date with the sexiest man in Ardbawn.

Despite the fact that the main reason for her trip to Kilkenny was to talk to the garda superintendent who'd been involved in the investigation into Elva O'Malley's death, she also planned to see if she could find a suitable dress for her night out – though without Talia to advise her she wasn't entirely sure she'd succeed in achieving the wow factor she aspired to. All the same, she was hopeful of finding something a little more upmarket than her wardrobe currently contained.

I've got to stop thinking about clothes and make-up, she told herself as she swung into the grounds of the garda station, at least until I've interviewed Superintendent Vinnie Murray and got the low-down from him on Elva's death. After that I can embrace my inner feminine side. If I can find it.

She got out of the car, locked it and went inside. The superintendent, a genial man who looked to be in his late fifties, was ready for her. Sheridan had been slightly surprised, but also relieved, when he'd readily agreed to talk to her. She'd told him – without mentioning Paudie or Elva – that she was just looking for background information on a past case he'd been involved in. Vinnie Murray had reminded her that there was a press office that could help her with whatever she was writing about, and Sheridan had replied that she was just trying to get a feel for the subject and that her piece wasn't about the case as such but it would be great to talk to him all the same.

Martyn Powell had always said that one of Sheridan's greatest assets as a sports reporter was in persuading even the most reluctant athlete or manager to open up to her. When Vinnie Murray told her he could spare her half an hour, she was relieved she hadn't lost her touch.

'We'll go out for a cup of tea,' he said. 'My office is a mess.'

They walked as far as the Hibernian Hotel, where Sheridan

ordered a cappuccino for herself and a tea for the garda and explained that she was interested in the Elva O'Malley case.

'I thought as much,' he said. 'Every so often someone with an interest in Paudie asks about it. It was a tragedy for him, of course.'

'There's very little concrete information. I wondered if there was more to it than came out at the time.'

'Like what?'

'I don't know,' confessed Sheridan. 'I suppose I was hoping for a juicy murder mystery.'

The superintendent laughed. 'I've only investigated one murder in my life and this wasn't it. Ardbawn isn't Midsomer, you know.'

Sheridan chuckled. 'I'm glad to hear it. I wouldn't have liked to think I could be struck down at any moment by a member of the church choir or something.'

'Hopefully there are no homicidal maniacs in the stalls waiting to hit you over the head with a candlestick. You said you're working with the *Central News*. A bit of conflict, don't you think, in investigating Paudie?'

'I'm not investigating him,' protested Sheridan. 'I'm trying to put a story together. It's not for the *Central News*. It's just a profile piece on him and his life.'

'Have you spoken to him at all yet?'

'Not yet,' admitted Sheridan. 'I wanted to know as much as possible about him before I did.'

'Have you spoken to anybody in Ardbawn?'

'Only Nina Fallon. She's the owner of the guesthouse where I'm staying.'

Vinnie Murray nodded and added a heaped spoonful of sugar to his tea.

'Look, I'm curious, that's all. He's such a successful man and there's so little about him. The whole thing about his wife is interesting. Defining, maybe.'

'Defining?' The garda looked thoughtful. 'Probably. It certainly changed his outlook on life.'

'So what exactly happened?' asked Sheridan.

'Elva O'Malley fell out of an upstairs window, hit the ground below and died instantly,' said Superintendent Murray.

'How did she fall?' asked Sheridan.

'We could never say for sure what caused it.'

'Was it an accident?'

The garda spooned more sugar into his cup.

'There was no one else involved.'

'Was she drunk? Or on drugs?'

'There was alcohol in her blood, and we found a half-empty bottle of wine on the kitchen table.'

'Oh. I didn't see anything about that in the stuff I read.' Vinnie shrugged.

'So it's possible that alcohol contributed to it.'

'Possible.'

'Was it suicide?' asked Sheridan.

'There was no note. Suicides, tragically, are something I've seen a few times. And every time there was a note.'

'So you think it was simply an accident?'

'Yes. I do.'

'You're very sure about that.'

'There was nothing to make us believe otherwise. There was no break-in and no burglary, so we had no reason to think that she surprised an intruder. Her husband – and you know how it is in the best detective novels, we always suspect the husband – was at a meeting with three other people when

252

she died. Cast-iron alibi.' The superintendent looked intently at her. 'In real life when people have cast-iron alibis it usually means they're in the clear. It's not like the movies, where they're involved in some elaborate and frankly implausible plot.'

'Oh, I don't know.' Sheridan shook her head. 'There's plenty of unsolved cases around. Or ones where years later you find out that someone's got away with what seemed the perfect crime.'

'Not this time.' Vinnie Murray was definite.

'All the same, there was big, big insurance payout afterwards.'

'That's why we investigated it thoroughly. We might be in the sticks but we're not morons, you know.'

'Had she been upset or worried in the days leading up to the accident?'

The garda smiled. 'You're a right little Miss Marple, aren't you?'

'Not really,' said Sheridan. 'I'm not trying to solve anything here. Apparently you know what happened. But it's a sad story.'

'It was sad for everyone.'

'Could Paudie have hit her?' asked Sheridan, after a moment where neither of them spoke. 'Maybe earlier in the day or something? And she could have had concussion, which led to her falling out of the window.'

'There were no signs of injury on Elva O'Malley that weren't consistent with a fall.'

Sheridan sighed. 'OK. OK. So maybe she was simply drunk . . . Did she have an alcohol problem?'

'Not that I'm aware of.'

'So why the wine in the middle of the day?'

'It wasn't that much,' the garda said. 'A couple of glasses. Perhaps she'd drunk them in the garden earlier, relaxing. It was a glorious weather.'

'All the same . . .' Sheridan considered things a bit more. 'Any chance Paudie was having an affair?'

'If he was, the woman didn't turn up in his life afterwards,' Vinnie pointed out.

'I heard that there *was* a woman.' Sheridan looked suddenly hopeful. 'I even saw her picture in the paper.'

But the superintendent shook his head. 'Rose O'Reilly, from Castlecomer. More than three years later. And it didn't last.'

'Perhaps they were playing a waiting game. Maybe Paudie knew that Elva was a bit flaky and was trying to drive her to it.'

Vinnie Murray laughed. 'You've definitely been watching too much TV,' he told her.

Sheridan looked dejected. 'You're making it very difficult.'

'I'm just saying that perhaps you're barking up the wrong tree,' said the garda. 'Elva's death was a tragic accident and Paudie had to work hard to get over it.'

'It's the money part that makes it interesting,' Sheridan confessed. 'Mid-level businessman becomes multimillionaire after his wife dies. So it's not surprising people were suspicious.'

'Of course they were,' said the superintendent. 'We were too. We'd have been negligent not to have been. But I can tell you here and now that Paudie would've preferred to have his wife than the insurance money. He loved her, and he was truly devastated when she died.'

'He could've been a great actor.'

'No,' said the garda. 'His grief was genuine.'

'Fair enough.' Sheridan slumped in the seat. 'I guess I wanted it to be dramatic and exciting, but things don't always work out the way you want. I should bloody well know that by now.'

'Sorry to disappoint you.'

'Ah, you know, it's probably a good thing.' Sheridan smiled at him. 'I'm trying too hard to find mysteries where there aren't any.'

'We did a thorough investigation,' said Vinnie Murray. 'Paudie wasn't the big businessman that he is now, but he was still a well-known figure in the town. If there'd been something untoward, we would have uncovered it. We're not stupid.'

'I didn't think you were.'

'Go on!' Vinnie grinned. 'You were looking for incompetent country bumpkins floundering around.'

'I wasn't,' she protested.

'Sometimes a tragedy is just a tragedy,' said the garda. 'And the truth is that Paudie really had to pick himself up afterwards. It was hard for him. But, like you said, defining in the end.'

'D'you like him?' she asked.

'I haven't seen him in years,' replied Vinnie. 'But I liked him back then. I still like him now. He's done a lot for this area of the country. He deserves his success.'

'Fair enough.' Sheridan stood up. 'Thanks for your time and for the information.'

'Maybe not the information you wanted. But the truth,' said the garda. 'However,' he added, 'I can tell you something that you seem to have missed.'

'What?' She looked at him hopefully.

'He sued a local paper over suggestions that he had something to do with it. He won. That paper doesn't exist any more.'

'He bankrupted them!' Sheridan was astounded.

'I don't think it was entirely due to him. But having to make a payment to him certainly didn't help. So if you were thinking of saying anything scurrilous about him, you'd want to be very sure of your facts first.'

Sheridan nodded glumly. Then she picked up the bill and went to the cash desk to pay it. When she turned around again, the superintendent had gone.

The boutique just off the main street wasn't the sort of place Sheridan normally shopped, but she'd caught sight of the jade-green dress as she and the garda superintendent were walking to the hotel, and the image had stuck with her. However, she felt a little awkward when she walked inside and realised that she was the only customer, and that the sales assistant was already asking if she could help. Sheridan's preferred method of buying clothes was to go into a chain store and rummage through the racks with no clear ideas of what she wanted. Which was why she usually ended up in T-shirts and jeans.

'It's a lovely dress,' said the sales assistant when Sheridan mumbled that she was sort of interested in it. 'Very flattering because of its wrap-around styling. Why don't you try it on? What size are you?'

'Fourteen.' Sheridan always felt fat when she had to confess to being a fourteen, no matter how often she was told that she was just well built (a term she nevertheless felt made her sound like a horse). In any event, it freaked her out when she went through the rails and saw dresses starting at size eight. Or sometimes even six. They couldn't be for real people, she often thought, while sometimes wishing she could fit into one.

The assistant, though, didn't look at her as though she was a freak, but simply selected a dress and handed it to her. Sheridan went into the changing room and pulled her jumper over her head. She hoped the assistant wasn't the sort who rapped at the door, poked her head around and asked how you were getting on when you were still standing around in your knickers and trying to suck in your stomach. But she didn't need to worry. The assistant left her alone.

She was a completely different person in the dress. So different that she couldn't quite believe it. The gentle folds of the material fell loosely around her, the wrap-around effect smoothing her shape so that her thighs didn't seem to signal their presence straight away, as was usually the case on the rare occasions she tried on dresses. The colour, a few shades darker than she normally chose when wearing green, enhanced the flame of her hair and the tawny brown of her eyes. She stared at her reflection in shock, then looked for her mobile, took a photo and sent it to Talia asking for her opinion, because she couldn't trust herself to think that she was wearing a dress and looking good.

A few seconds later the mobile rang.

'Where are you?' demanded Talia.

'A shop in Kilkenny.' Sheridan's voice was low because she didn't want the assistant to hear her.

'Who's that dress for?'

'Me, of course.'

'I know that!' Talia said impatiently. 'But you're buying it because of someone. Who?'

'Can't I just buy a dress?'

'It's me you're talking to,' said Talia. 'Who?'

'I met a guy,' confessed Sheridan. 'He asked me out.'

'Way to go, girl! You're holed up in the country and you've met someone. Fair play to you. I wasn't expecting that!'

'We're just having dinner,' protested Sheridan. 'It doesn't mean anything.'

'Come on, Sheridan. You never bought a dress for Griff. And you thought you loved him.'

'This is different,' Sheridan said. 'He's bringing me to a nice restaurant and I have to look good.'

'And that *certainly* never bothered you before,' said Talia. 'Didn't Griff bring you to L'Ecrivain once? You wore Levis.'

'They were my very best Levis,' Sheridan reminded her.

'You had three days to buy a dress but you didn't. As I recall, Ms Gray, you said that you weren't going to be shoehorned into the whole stupidness of feeling you had to be someone other than yourself just because you were going to one of Dublin's finest eateries.'

'Yeah, well, Dublin's different too,' said Sheridan.

'Tell me about this man,' demanded Talia.

'He's just someone I met. He's nice but it's not a big deal.' Sheridan tried to sound casual.

'Don't talk rubbish, it's a massive deal!' cried Talia. 'You've been keeping secrets from me. Whenever you email, you just say it's going well and you're enjoying Ardbawn more than you thought but that you'll be glad when that girl comes back from her maternity leave and you can high tail back to

Dublin. You never said anything about hunky men who might keep you there.'

'You're reading way more into this than you should,' said Sheridan. 'OK, he's nice and I . . . I have to admit that I fancy the pants off him. I've never really felt like this before. But I'm sure I'll get over it.'

'Sheridan! You've never felt this way before? Not even with Griff? Who is this guy?'

'I'm probably exaggerating,' said Sheridan, even though she could still feel shivers up her spine every time she thought of Joe.

'You sound excited. Different.'

'Oh, I'm sure it's just because there isn't much going on here,' said Sheridan. 'Perhaps if I'd met him in Dublin I wouldn't even have noticed him.'

'You think?'

'He's very attractive,' Sheridan conceded. 'I suppose I would've noticed at least.'

'You're in love!' exclaimed Talia. 'I've never heard you sound so thrilled about a guy before.'

'I'm not in love! I hardly know him.'

'Love at first sight! Even better.'

'Stop it!' cried Sheridan, although she was laughing. 'It's just . . . Oh, I don't know. Anyway, I didn't intend for us to have a big discussion about him. All I wanted to know is what you thought of the dress.'

'You know perfectly well already what I think,' said Talia. 'You must have known when you sent the pic. He'll be thinking about getting you out of it from the moment he sees you.'

'I don't want that sort of dress,' Sheridan protested. 'I want to look gorgeous and elegant, not slutty.'

'And you do,' Talia told her. 'You look incredible, Sheridan. All I'm saying is that any red-blooded man will want to have sex with you.'

'I don't want to have sex with him,' Sheridan said. 'At least . . . not on a first date.'

'I'm so excited for you!' Talia's enthusiasm for the dress and for the new man in Sheridan's life was very evident. 'You went through a rotten time and you're coming out of it with a replacement job and a replacement man too.'

'Both could be equally temporary,' Sheridan reminded her.

'So what!' cried Talia. 'You're back in the saddle, Sheridan Gray. And I'm delighted for you.'

Sheridan smiled as she closed her phone. She realised that she'd only sent the picture to Talia because she wanted to let her friend know about Joe. And because she wanted to show off in her dress. Maybe she wasn't so different from every other girl in the world after all.

The sales assistant tapped at the door and Sheridan opened it.

'Stunning,' was all the assistant said.

'It is, isn't it?' Sheridan twirled slowly in front of the mirror and looked anxiously at the other girl. 'I didn't check the price, though.'

The dress was expensive. But not outrageous. Sheridan handed over her credit card. Even if it all went pear shaped with Joe later, the dress was an investment. But the truth was, she hoped it would be more than that.

Sheridan took a more winding route back from Kilkenny so that she could drive past March Manor. Although she now accepted Superintendent Vinnie Murray's insistence that

Elva's death had been a tragedy, the story was still going round in her head. She stopped a few yards short of the house, on the opposite side of the road, just outside the entrance gates to the Ardbawn Riding School. There was little to see from her position, as the house was sheltered by the high trees that were planted either side of the driveway, but Sheridan could make out the structure of the building, its slate roof and tall chimney stacks. She could also see cows in the field behind it, and assumed that this was Paudie's famed Limousin herd.

Perhaps there was no point in thinking about him as a potential route back into a full-time job. Her original intention had been to find out and reveal something untoward about his business dealings, simply to get her own back on him for the staffing policies that had made her redundant. Learning about Elva had made her more interested in the man himself. The whiff of intrigue about her death had made it seem all the more fascinating. But looking at his house now simply made her feel like a snoop. The man had suffered a tragedy in his life, had picked himself up, ruined a newspaper and made a fortune afterwards. Most people would think of that as success.

But Alo had said that the site would be interested if she did a profile. It didn't have to be sensational, just revealing. She could write something thoughtful and positive about his recovery from personal grief, and show that she was more than just a sports writer. She could persuade him that the time was right to be more open about himself. Being here in Ardbawn was a massive advantage. She could get him to talk to her because she was a local now. He wouldn't think of her as being a hostile interviewer. He'd see her as the girl who was working on the *Central News*. His very own news-paper. His tame reporter. He'd be well disposed towards her. Why wouldn't he?

She'd talk to DJ about it. Explain how important it was to her future career. Maybe he could set it up. After all, she thought he liked her. He'd surely want to help her get a proper job.

She put her car into gear and was about to move off again when the gates opened and a big Range Rover turned on to the road in front her. She peered through the windscreen of the Beetle, wondering if Paudie was driving it. But the only part of the driver she could see was a red baseball cap pulled low over his (or her) eyes to protect them from the glare of the setting sun.

She waited for the gates to close. They didn't. She edged the car forward, craning her neck to see if someone else was coming down the driveway, but it was empty. She hesitated for a moment, took a deep breath, glanced in her rear-view mirror to make sure there was no traffic on the road, then swung her car across it and powered her way through the still open gates.

Chapter 20

It wasn't possible to see the entrance to the riding school from the stables, which was where Nina was talking to Peggy Merchant, the owner. The two of them had trusted and respected each other ever since Nina had come to Peggy with her idea about running joint promotions for the guesthouse and the riding school over twenty years earlier. Peggy had been impressed with Nina's determination then, thinking that the young girl had a smart head on her shoulders. She'd revised her opinion somewhat when Nina had married Sean Fallon. In Peggy's view, Sean was a shallow man who didn't deserve someone like Nina Doherty. But, like everyone else in Ardbawn, she'd re-evaluated her opinions about him over the years, particularly the last decade or so, when he seemed to have become far more settled and content with his place in the community. Peggy put a lot of value on the community – she believed in people working hard and helping each other for the common good, which was why she regularly protested about developments that would change the character of the town. Although the councillors thought she was a pain in the butt, most of the residents supported her, and she'd managed to stop or change some of the worst proposals.

Nina often suggested that perhaps Peggy should run for a seat on the council herself, but her friend always said that she was an issues-based woman and would be hopeless with the day-to-day stuff that went on.

She was doing day-to-day stuff now, brushing the horses as Nina watched, pleased to see her friend, who'd called around to chat about the Spring Festival. Until her break-up with Sean, Nina had dropped by Peggy's at least once a week, but over the last while she had been reluctant to talk even to her closest friends. So Peggy was pleased to see her now, even though her face was still far too pale and her eyes were like dark smudges on parchment.

Nina was relaxed in Peggy's company, soothed by her rhythmic brushing of the horses and the familiar conversation about the festival. She knew that Peggy wouldn't ask about Sean until she herself was ready. She was a wise woman, Nina thought, tall and rangy with iron-grey hair and a long face that some of the less kind people in the town said was very similar to those of the horses she loved so much. Nina had to agree that Peggy wasn't attractive in the way the word was normally used to describe beauty, but there was a certain purpose about her that held your attention. Her clear grey eyes were firm and determined and she walked with a confident stride. Nina had never seen Peggy anything other than positive. And she wanted some of that positivity now.

'I need some advice,' she said as Peggy finished with the last horse, an amiable mare called Lucy who was good with first-time riders. 'My head is in a whirl.'

'Come in for tea,' said Peggy. 'These things are easier to discuss over tea.'

She led the way to the house, scraping her boots at the door.

'It's good to be here with you,' said Nina when they were sitting at the pine table, which was covered by an old-fashioned oilskin. 'I'm sorry I haven't been around, but I haven't felt like talking. Or, to be honest, listening to other people's advice. But since I've been forced into conversation with the girl who's staying with me, I felt the time had come to chat to people who are really my friends.'

'The journalist.' Peggy poured the tea. 'Sheridan Gray. What's she like?'

'Friendly, if a bit too curious and gossipy,' said Nina. 'I think she's in shock at being in Ardbawn, to be honest. I'm sure the *Central News* is a bit on the quiet side for her.'

'Oh, people always think country towns are quiet,' Peggy said. 'But all life goes on here.'

'She's stressed about having lost her job,' Nina continued. 'And of course she's only at the *Central News* as cover for Myra.'

'Speaking of whom, she had her baby last night.' Peggy shared the latest news, knowing that they'd eventually start talking about Sean but aware that it was difficult for Nina to launch into what she wanted to say. 'I was in the newsagent's today and Eleanor told me. A girl. Seven pounds two. A little early, but I'm sure Myra won't mind that, better than being overdue.'

'That's great news.' Nina knew and liked Myra. 'I must send her a card.'

'And your journalist can do an interview with her about being a new mum.' Peggy grinned.

'She keeps asking me about Paudie O'Malley,' said Nina, tapping her finger on the rim of her cup.

Peggy looked at her friend enquiringly.

'She thinks he's hiding a dark secret.'

'Does she indeed?'

'I'm not sure how convinced she is about that,' admitted Nina. 'But she was talking about his desire to keep himself to himself. She thinks there's a reason for it.'

'We don't need reasons not to want to be public people,' said Peggy.

'Hmm.' Nina sighed. 'I understand how Sheridan's mind is working. Paudie has a fearsome reputation for being ruthless in business and inaccessible in private. It's not usual. Those hard-core businessmen are usually all over the finance pages in the papers. And often on the social pages too with their trophy wives.' Her voice hardened.

'And are you worried about what she'll uncover? Is Paudie?'

'I haven't spoken to Paudie in years,' said Nina. 'It's not that I'm worried, or that there's anything to be worried about in that context. It's just . . . she knows nothing about us and it's weird having someone nosy and gossipy around the place asking questions that nobody else thinks to ask any more. Though I guess it's just an occupational hazard with all journalists.'

Peggy smiled. 'You could hardly call DJ gossipy.'

'No,' agreed Nina. 'God love him, but he's far too sweet to be running a paper. If Sheridan was in charge, she'd be investigating all sorts of stuff going on in this town that we try to pretend isn't happening. Like Donie Ferriter taking backhanders for re-zoning decisions, which was an absolute disgrace.'

'Sometimes it's easier to let things slide,' said Peggy. 'I don't have the energy to fight those battles any more.'

266

'Nonsense. You're fit as a fiddle,' said Nina.

'Maybe for some things,' conceded Peggy. 'But there's times you think you've argued the toss before and you just can't summon up the will to do it again. We did the re-zoning thing ten years ago. I can't face a repeat of it.'

'That's how I feel about Sean,' said Nina. She pressed her fingers to her eyes. 'Here we are all over again. A mess.'

'All over again?'

'You know there was a . . . lapse before.'

'I've never asked about it and you don't have to tell me.'

'Which I'm grateful for. For your unconditional support. I can always depend on you, Peggy.'

'I'm your friend,' said Peggy simply.

'Anyway, that's all water under the bridge, but he swore on my mother's grave he'd never do anything like it again. If we were in a horror movie – which sometimes I feel I am – she'd come back to haunt him.'

Peggy laughed and then apologised. 'I know it's not funny. But the image of Dolores haunting Sean is a very powerful one.'

'Isn't it,' agreed Nina. She told her friend about the letter from Sean's solicitor.

'D'you think he's serious about selling the house?' Peggy sounded shocked for the first time.

'I don't know.'

'It's the family home,' said Peggy.

'And the family business. God knows, Peggy, if I had to sell the house because of Sean, my mother would probably come back to haunt *me*!'

'Is there much of a mortgage on it now?' asked Peggy.

'It's manageable,' replied Nina. 'We've repaid most of what

we took out for the renovations. It was something my mother drilled into me, and I'm glad she did. It meant that when the bad times came, we weren't struggling with mountains of debt like some other people. But still, it hasn't been easy the last few years.'

'Who are you telling?' Peggy shook her head. 'We've never had such a bad time here. Larry is demented every time he looks at the accounts.'

Larry and Peggy had been married for over thirty years. He was a man who was happy to stay in the background, but Peggy always said she'd be lost without him.

'For the first time ever he talked about selling up, but Tina threw a fit at the idea,' she told Nina.

Nina wasn't surprised. Larry and Peggy's only daughter had worked at the riding school all her life.

'I suppose it's her inheritance,' said Peggy. 'But I can't help thinking we're bequeathing her a millstone.'

Nina suddenly wondered what would happen when she was too old to run the guesthouse herself. Neither Alan nor Chrissie had any interest in it as a business. She supposed they'd sell it. The idea of the house passing out of the family hurt, yet she wouldn't blame her children for letting it go. They had their own lives to lead. It took her a moment or two to realise that she hadn't thought of Sean as part of this picture. Even after she realised it, she still couldn't quite figure out where he was in the grand scheme of things.

'I guess it's fortunate for me that Tina wants to take over,' continued Peggy. 'Just like you did from your mam. But times change. Our kids aren't always interested in the same things as us.'

'I know,' said Nina. 'I've always known that about mine. I just never thought about it before.'

'But you've got a good few years in you yet, woman!' Peggy guffawed. 'You're only a young one yourself.'

'Nearly fifty,' said Nina. 'In mam's day, that was old.'

'And these days it's not.'

'Not when the government doesn't want us to retire until we're seventy plus,' observed Nina. She frowned. 'I've always thought that the guesthouse was my life, but now I'm imagining another twenty-odd years dishing up a full Irish to people every morning, and suddenly it seems less appealing. All the same,' she added, 'I don't want to be forced into selling it yet. Not because of Sean.'

'D'you think he genuinely wants a reconciliation?' Peggy glanced at the solicitor's letter, which Nina had brought to show her.

'They probably have to say that,' said Nina. 'To make it seem like he's the wronged party.'

'If it was just a fling . . .' Peggy looked at her thoughtfully. 'You know what men are like, Nina. They're so damn easy to flatter. A young girl, a few drinks . . . they think they're young and virile and handsome again.'

'I'm quite sure it's just a fling, no matter what Lulu Adams might think. What I don't know is whether I should forgive him for it just because he's decided he wants to be forgiven.'

'D'you *want* to forgive him?'

'Almost from the moment I told him to go. And yet now that he's asked to come back, I'm not so sure.'

'Maybe you should go for counselling or something,' suggested Peggy.

'Ah, no.' Nina shook her head. 'I'm not into that, really I'm not.'

'It could be useful.'

'I don't want to sit and talk about my problems,' said Nina. 'I know exactly what they are.'

Peggy grinned. 'Which is a start.'

'And I suppose the question I need to ask myself is . . . how many chances should someone get before you realise that you're the fool after all?'

Peggy looked at Nina in silence. Then she poured them both another cup of tea.

The driveway that led to March Manor was long, with a gentle curve. Sheridan was almost certain that another car would come hurtling down from the house to the open gates, and she was ready to swerve out of the way, but nothing appeared in front of her and soon she was gliding to a halt in front of Paudie O'Malley's home.

It was a beautiful building, Georgian in its styling, with wide steps leading up to a glossy white-painted door with an overhead fanlight window. There were two sash windows either side of the door and five across the top on the upper storey. In front of each of the upper-floor windows was a narrow wrought-iron balcony, painted black. Sheridan stared at them for a moment, wondering from which, if any of them, Elva had fallen to her death. The thought made her look at the gravel outside the car, as though she might have stopped in a pool of blood. It was an uncomfortable feeling.

Just as uncomfortable, from Sheridan's point of view, was what she intended to do now that she was here. She'd acted impulsively, without a plan, and she was beginning to regret it.

Normally, when she was interviewing somebody, she'd already done buckets of research and worked out her questions in advance. She would also have made an appointment to see them. She didn't know what had triggered the sudden impulse to turn in to Paudie O'Malley's driveway. And now that she was here, she had no idea what to do next.

The best thing, without a doubt, would be to turn around and drive out again. Which was exactly what she was going to do. Right now. Before she got into a situation she couldn't retrieve.

And then the front door was suddenly opened. The woman standing at the top of the steps was tall and slender, wearing an elegant black dress and black heels, her dark hair pinned back from her face, a short string of pearls around her neck. She reminded Sheridan of photos she'd seen of Jackie O, although without Jackie's signature sunglasses. She gestured to Sheridan, who slowly got out of the car.

'You're early,' said the woman. 'How did you get in?'

'The gates were open.' Sheridan looked at her in confusion. 'Someone was leaving as I drove in.'

'Peter should've closed them behind him. He's dreadful like that.' The woman sighed.

Sheridan recalled that Peter O'Malley was the younger of the two O'Malley sons. This woman, she thought, must be the elder daughter. Sinead. Who seemed to have mistaken her for someone else entirely.

'I think you've made a mistake . . .' she began, when there was the sound of a phone trilling.

'I've got to answer that,' said Sinead. 'Come in and wait for me.'

Sheridan thought of getting back into the car and speeding

down the driveway again, but an inexorable force was drawing her to the house despite her better judgement. So she followed Sinead up the steps and into March Manor.

Paudie's daughter opened the door to a room off the hallway. Sheridan remained just outside.

It was an impressive hallway. The parquet floor was gleaming. The walls were painted in a deep maroon above a dado rail, and a buttermilk white beneath. They were hung with a number of paintings in gold frames, most of which seemed to be of the local area. Sheridan recognised one of the bridge over the Bawnee River. An enormous chandelier hung from the ceiling.

'Swarovski.' Sinead had come out of the room again and seen Sheridan staring at it. 'Personally I think it's a bit vulgar, but it's lovely when it's lit.' She smiled warmly. 'Sorry about that. I'm trying to organise about a million things all at the same time, and I'm the world's worst planner.'

Sheridan was relieved that the other woman didn't seem to be as chilly as she'd first imagined, although the chill might reappear when she found out that she was making a mistake about Sheridan's reason for being here.

'You're still a bit early,' Sinead said. 'Peter will only be gone for a few minutes, but I have to wait till he comes back before we go. Would you like to sit in the drawing room?'

'I'm sorry, Sinead, isn't it?' Sheridan knew she had to come clean straight away, although she was aching to check out more of the house. 'I'm not your taxi driver, if that's what you thought.'

'Oh.' Sinead looked startled. 'In that case, why on earth are you here?'

'I'm an employee of the *Central News*.' Even as she said

the words, she couldn't help thinking it might have been better to have lied. To have said that she was a tourist who'd got lost or something and was looking for directions. Although why a lost tourist would turn up the driveway of a private house would be almost as difficult to explain as her real reasons for being here.

What were you thinking? she asked herself again.

'Is there a problem at the paper?' asked Sinead. 'DJ didn't call.'

'Does he usually?'

'I don't know,' said Sinead. She frowned. 'Who are you? I don't remember seeing you before.'

'Sheridan Gray. I'm Myra's maternity cover.'

'Of course.' Sinead nodded slowly. 'DJ told me he'd got someone in. Pleased to meet you.'

'You too.'

'My father isn't here,' said Sinead. 'Did you want to talk to him about something? I'd offer you coffee, but, like I said, I'm going out shortly and—'

'No. No.' Sheridan shook her head. 'I . . . Well, truthfully I didn't entirely intend to come here, it was a bit of a mistake on my part.'

'Oh?' Sinead was looking at her curiously.

'I . . .' Sheridan wanted to phrase her intentions carefully. Sinead was still being polite and reasonably friendly, and she didn't want to alienate her. 'I'd been thinking of talking to your father about his business success.'

'But what's that got to do with the *Central News*?' asked Sinead.

'Nothing really,' conceded Sheridan. 'I just thought it would be interesting to talk to him.'

273

Sinead still looked puzzled. 'I don't understand . . .'

Her words were interrupted by the sound of a car pulling up outside the house and beeping the horn. If this is Paudie, thought Sheridan, I'm totally doomed. She wondered if there was any way she could just make a run for it, but then Sinead opened the door and there was a flurry of motion before she was enveloped by a small boy and a big dog.

'Josh, for heaven's sake, control him!' she cried. 'He'll ruin my dress!'

The boy tugged on the dog's leash. It was a grey and white Old English sheepdog, and Sheridan, who loved animals, immediately wanted to pet him.

'Sit, Bobby!' commanded Josh, and the dog obeyed him immediately.

The boy looked at Sinead, and then at Sheridan.

'Hey, Mum! It's her,' he said.

'Excuse me, Josh,' said Sinead. 'What have I told you about pointing?'

Josh dropped the arm he'd extended in Sheridan's direction.

'It's her. The woman at the football.'

'We got back quicker than we thought.'

Before either Sinead or Sheridan had time to speak, a man walked into the hallway and pulled the baseball cap from his head. Sheridan exhaled sharply. He was the image of Joe. Younger, certainly, and with a less angular face, but still very like him. She felt her head begin to pound.

'Hello,' he said, looking at Sheridan. 'We haven't met before, have we?'

'It's her, Uncle Pete,' said Josh again. 'She thinks I'm a good footballer. She was at my match.'

'Was she?' asked Josh's uncle.

'She works for the *Central News*,' said Sinead.

Sheridan was finding it difficult to process the information that was assailing her. She didn't know what order to place it in. Josh, Joe's godson, was also his nephew. Sinead was Josh's mum. Sinead was Joe's sister. She was also Paudie O'Malley's daughter. Which meant that Joe was Paudie's son. Joe was, therefore, JJ O'Malley, the elder son. The man who'd asked her on a date was the son of the man she'd wanted to believe had got away with murdering his wife.

She felt faint.

'And your name is?' Peter looked at her curiously.

'Sheridan Gray,' she croaked.

She was also finding it difficult to accept that the glamorous woman in front of her was the woman who apparently dished up home-cooked meals to Josh and Joe. She couldn't imagine Sinead even knowing where the kitchen was, let alone peeling potatoes and flipping burgers. Why was she here in Paudie's house, looking so glamorous, when she was supposed to be at home being the perfect mother?

'She wants to talk to Dad,' Sinead said.

'So why are we all standing in the hall?' asked Peter. 'Nice to meet you, Sheridan.'

'Because she just turned up,' Sinead said. 'She drove in after you left the gates open. I thought she was my taxi.'

Peter laughed.

'You know the gate's been giving trouble,' Sinead said. 'I told you to check it had closed behind you.'

'Nag, nag, nag,' teased Peter. 'I was only gone five minutes. It's not like it's far to the dog-training school.'

'That's not the point.' Sinead made a tutting sound. 'Not

that it matters. The issue is why you need to see my father about his business interests, Sheridan.'

'I . . . Well . . . I was interested in how successful he's become,' she said.

'I still don't understand what that has to do with the *Central News*?'

'It's got nothing to do with the paper,' explained Sheridan. 'It's more of a . . . a professional interest.'

Both Peter and Sheridan were looking at her in puzzlement. And then Josh spoke again.

'Uncle Joe fancies her.'

'Josh!' Both his mother and his uncle spoke at the same time.

'Well he does. He said she was a—'

'You can go out now,' said Sinead quickly.

Josh and the dog rushed along the hallway and through a door, leaving Sheridan facing Sinead and Peter alone.

'Did you want to write something about Dad?' asked Peter.

'Yes,' confessed Sheridan.

'In the *Central News*?' Sinead was puzzled. 'What could DJ possibly want to write about my father that would cause him to send you here?'

'This wasn't DJ's idea,' admitted Sheridan.

'You're doing a piece yourself?' Realisation began to dawn on Peter's face.

'And you simply barged in?' Sinead's voice was a lot cooler now.

'Not barged,' said Sheridan. 'The gate was open.'

'You must have known it wasn't open for you,' said Sinead.

'Well, yes, but . . .'

'I think you've an awful cheek,' said the other woman.

'Hey, sis, she's working on the newspaper.' Peter grinned. 'I believe they all have necks like a jockey's—'

'That's fine, Peter.' Sinead stopped him and Peter winked at Sheridan. She smiled tentatively in return.

'OK,' said Sinead. 'You forced your way into the house under false pretences—'

'Ah, Sinead, give her a break,' said Peter. 'She didn't force her way in. She took an opportunity.'

'Which she shouldn't have,' said Sinead.

'I'm sorry.' Sheridan looked contrite.

'But you want to talk to Dad, yes?'

'Yes.'

'My father doesn't give interviews,' said Sinead.

'I know. But I thought . . .'

'That being on the *Central News* gave you an advantage?' finished Peter.

'Yes.'

'It doesn't,' said Sinead. 'And personally I think you've breached the paper's trust.'

'I'm sorry if that's what you think.' Sheridan had regained a little of her composure. 'It's not the case, though. I'm only working as a temp on the paper. I thought there might be something interesting in your father's life . . . work . . . business . . .'

This time both Peter and Sinead were looking at her sceptically.

'I'm a reporter!' she cried. 'I do sports mostly, but I'm not getting much work with that. I thought a profile on Mr Sl— someone so reclusive with his harsh reputation would be worthwhile.'

'Harsh reputation?' said Sinead.

'You must know about that.'

'If that's how you're thinking of him, I can't imagine you were going to write anything very flattering,' said Sinead.

'I was going to write an accurate portrayal,' Sheridan told her. 'Whatever that is.'

'Well you're not going to write anything at all now,' said Sinead. 'And I think you should leave.'

'Sure. Fine.' Sheridan knew there was no point in talking to them any more. 'I'm sorry it all got a bit mixed up. I didn't mean . . .' She shrugged helplessly.

'Goodbye,' said Sinead. 'Drive slowly to the gates. I'll open them for you.'

'And I'll make sure they close behind you,' said Peter. But he gave her a sympathetic smile as he spoke.

Sheridan was shaking as she left the house by the front door. There was no way she was ever going to get an interview with Paudie O'Malley now. His son and daughter would be on the alert for her and would block any opportunity she might have to meet him. Both Sinead and Peter were clearly protective of their father. Sinead had also been annoyed with herself for mistaking who Sheridan was, which would have antagonised her further. Peter had shown a certain amount of sympathy – even pride – for her ambition, but he didn't seem like the kind of person who'd rock the family boat.

And Joe . . . She knew, as she drove out of the front gate and saw it closing behind her, that she'd deliberately pushed Joe to the very back of her mind because she didn't want to think what this might have done to her relationship with him. Not that she actually had a relationship at this point. And it seemed highly likely that there wouldn't be one in the future either. Because Joe would find out that she'd been at the house earlier, and Peter and Sinead would tell him why. He might assume (and she wouldn't blame him) that her reason for having dinner with him was more to do with trying to meet his father than anything else. And even if he thought that there was another reason – that she liked him – he surely wasn't going to spend an evening with someone who held his father in such low esteem.

'You idiot!' she said out loud. 'You total and utter idiot.'

Why oh why hadn't she suspected that Joe was JJ O'Malley, the businessman son of Paudie? Now that she thought about it, Joe resembled his father in many ways. He had the same high forehead, the same frown and the same thick head of hair. She'd even seen a photograph of them, side by side at his mother's funeral. Admittedly grainy and sixteen years earlier, but she should've recognised him. She searched her memory banks, because she couldn't help feeling sure she would have remembered the name of Sinead's husband and maybe put two and two together and saved herself a certain amount of grief. It took a while before she recalled the piece about their wedding, and then she realised why she hadn't associated them. In the piece, Mike, Sinead's husband, had been referred to as Michael Maher. His actual surname, Meagher, as she'd seen in Des's report on Josh's match, was pronounced the same way, even though the spelling was different. If someone had read the pieces aloud to her she would have cottoned on. But seeing the names written down hadn't triggered the connection because of the different spelling.

I should've caught it all the same, she thought, annoyed with herself. And I don't know what I'm going to do about my story now. Seems to me that Paudie O'Malley manages to mess up my life at every turn, whether he means to or not.

She wondered when Peter and Sinead would tell Joe that she'd been at the house. And what his reaction would be. Would he be as disgusted with her as his sister, or amused like his brother? Would he call her to cancel their date? Or would he just assume that she knew dinner was off? She glanced at the speedometer and realised that in her anxiety to get away from March Manor, she was breaking the speed limit. She eased off on the accelerator. It would cap a great day to get done for speeding.

Damn, she thought, if only I'd asked for his card instead of giving him mine I would've seen his surname and I'd have twigged straight away who he was. And even I, the stupidest journalist in the world, wouldn't have made such a fool of myself. I'd've steered clear of March Manor and the O'Malleys and I'd have had a great meal with him, and who knows what might have happened next? Maybe he'd have introduced me to his dad. Paudie might even have liked me, enough perhaps to give me a story, anyhow. But no, I had to go barging around like the proverbial bull in a china shop, like the total idiot I am.

She was uncomfortably aware that Peter and Sinead would also tell Paudie that she'd been at his house. She swallowed hard. Mr Slash-and-Burn would hardly be pleased to hear that his temporary employee had been sniffing around his personal life. He might even fire her. Again. Her fingers tightened around the steering wheel. If she lost this job, she could definitely kiss her journalistic career goodbye. Paudie O'Malley had enough influence to prevent her ever getting another job in the industry. The man had closed down a paper, for heaven's sake! The potential fallout from her moment of madness was getting worse by the second.

She continued to call herself names all through the rest of her journey back to the guesthouse. She was pretty sure she'd blown everything. But what upset her the most, she realised, wasn't the potential end to her time at the *Central News*, or even the idea that Paudie O'Malley could bad-mouth her to other people in the industry; the worst thing of all was that she'd torpedoed her possible relationship with Joe. And so, when she reached the studio and took the bag containing her newly bought dress out of her car, she couldn't help wondering if she'd ever have the opportunity to wear it.

Chapter 21

Nina arrived back at the guesthouse just as Sheridan was getting out of the car. She saw her lift the bag with the dress from the back seat and she recognised the logo of the boutique in Kilkenny. Not a cheap shop, she thought, as she recalled the glow that she'd noticed in Sheridan previously. So who's she buying posh clothes for? Someone in Ardbawn? Or does she have a man waiting for her in Dublin?

She slowed her Qashqai and rolled down the window.

'Shopping-spree day?' she called. 'Off anywhere nice tonight?'

She was surprised when Sheridan shook her head. Surely Saturday night would be the most appropriate night for dressing up and going out. And then she saw that Sheridan's expression was grim.

'In that case, would you like to come to the house for dinner?' she asked. She realised that she was curious about Sheridan. She'd never really been curious about her before, about her job in Dublin or what she wanted from her stay in Ardbawn.

'That's nice of you, but . . .' Sheridan wasn't in the mood for small talk. Nor did she think she could do justice to

Nina's food. Then her stomach rumbled. For God's sake, she reminded herself, I'm miserable. I shouldn't be hungry and I should be able to face a night on my own, playing Wii football again. She thanked the older woman and said that she had work to do that evening.

'No problem.' Nina raised the window again and drove towards the house, while Sheridan unlocked the studio door. She dropped her handbag and the bag containing her gorgeous dress on to the sofa and then lay across the bed and stared at the ceiling.

The day had been a total disaster and she couldn't help thinking that things could only get worse. Getting a bee in her bonnet about Paudie O'Malley's businesses, and his tragic personal story, had led her completely astray. She'd lost focus on what she should have been doing, which was keeping her head down at the *Central News* while continuing to look for work elsewhere. And she shouldn't have let herself get distracted either by falling for random strangers who – even if they weren't the sons of business moguls – would be way out of her league in any event. As it was, she dreaded to think what Joe would say when he found out that she'd turned up uninvited at his family home. She shivered and felt tears brim up in her eyes.

She allowed a couple to trickle down her cheeks before sniffing hard and then sitting up. She wasn't a bloody crybaby, for heaven's sake. There was nothing to cry about. There wasn't. Other than the fact that she'd blown a ridiculous amount of money she couldn't really afford on a dress that she was never going to wear. After all, she reminded herself as she wiped her eyes, it's not like I was Joe's long-term girlfriend and he broke it off with me over something. I've only spoken to him a couple of times. We didn't have a relationship. Getting upset about this is daft. I need to get things in perspective. What would my parents say? They'd tell me to buck up and bounce back, she told herself. To stop snivelling. And I will. It's just . . . I thought the last few days were me bouncing back. That things were coming right. But they've gone pear shaped again. And I'm fed up with it.

She continued to lie on the bed until, despite her misery, the hollow feeling in her stomach finally sent her into the galley kitchen in search of something to eat. There was a half-finished packet of Hobnobs in the cupboard and a past-its-sell-by-date yoghurt in the fridge. She looked at her food options with dismay and wondered once again why misery seemed to make her hungrier.

She glanced at her watch. Six thirty. She remembered Nina's invitation and her own dismissal of it. Right now, the idea of the guesthouse owner's cooking was immensely tempting. But she couldn't change her mind at this stage. Nina would think she was a complete flake, and besides, she was probably already sitting down to a delicious and nutritious meal made from the ingredients of a properly stocked fridge.

Sheridan put the kettle on and shook the biscuits on to a plate.

Nina was feeling unexpectedly cheerful. She realised that she'd been keeping herself to herself for far too long. Retreating into herself had been her way of dealing with things in the past, in the days when she'd been the only one living at home with Dolores and it was easier to say nothing than to risk the sharp end of her mother's tongue on whatever the current issue might be. There were lots of issues with Dolores. She'd been a nit-picking sort of woman. Nina had got used to bottling things up so that Dolores couldn't criticise her, but the truth was that it had been a welcome release to share her worries with Peggy.

I'm too damn sensitive about what other people think, she told herself as she seared a tuna steak in the pan. I wasn't like that after Mam died. I was tough then. I need to find my inner toughness again now.

She added some chopped peppers to the pan and allowed them to cook alongside the tuna. She was sorry that Sheridan hadn't taken up her invitation to dinner. She was feeling in an expansive mood, ready to chat. Not ready, obviously, to fill her guest tenant in on all of Ardbawn's gossip, but prepared to talk a bit more about the town and the people who lived there. She missed talking, she realised suddenly. She missed the idle chatter that she and Sean had shared. There had been very few guests over recent weeks and most of them had been simply overnighters, not looking for information or chat, simply staying in Ardbawn for a particular event without paying the premium prices of the Riverview Hotel. In other years, during the quiet times, there had been Sean and the children to talk to. But now there was nobody, and although she wasn't feeling as starkly alone as she had in the first weeks after his departure, she was missing the company.

Put the past behind you. That was what Phaedra had instructed Cancerians to do. And that was what she would do. Although, she murmured to herself as she transferred her meal to a plate, the jury was still out on which part of the past needed to be forgotten most.

*   *   *

Sheridan was hungry and bored. The Hobnobs had been soft and unappetising and she hadn't been able to take the edge off her hunger by starting a Wii soccer game in which, inexplicably, Xabi Alonso was playing like a total muppet.

It's Saturday night and I'm a single woman, she told herself. I should be out on the town, not sitting in eating stale biscuits and yelling at a computer game. She got up and starting moving around the studio, tidying away bits and pieces that didn't need to be tidied at all, feeling restless and discontent.

She realised that in the time she'd so far spent in Ardbawn, she'd been trying desperately to keep busy and convince herself that she was becoming an investigative journalist and adding to her CV, when the truth was that she was just a temp filling in for someone else. The whole thing with Joe O'Malley was something she'd built up out of all proportion simply because she was lonely and wanted someone – anyone – to care about her. The knees-turning-to-jelly stuff was nonsense. And getting into a tizzy about the fact that he was the son of the man who'd chopped her job was silly. She was giving her feelings for Joe way too much importance and she was only doing that because she was substituting a sudden obsession with a man she hardly knew for real love. It was far more likely that what she'd felt for Griff (even if he hadn't reduced her to a trembling wreck) was love. Maybe it was love *because* it hadn't reduced her to a trembling wreck. When she'd realised he wasn't interested in marrying her, she'd been devastated. She wouldn't have felt like that if she hadn't had genuine feelings for him. And those feelings had been nurtured over a long time. Whereas with Joe O'Malley it had all been based on some kind of ridiculous rush of the electricity that Ritz had talked about. Which wasn't anything to do with real feelings at all.

She sighed. She needed to centre herself again and remember what was important in her life. Although, being honest with herself, she wasn't quite sure what that was right now. But sitting in the studio, feeling sorry for herself, wasn't going to help.

She changed out of her slouch jeans and sweatshirt into her favourite Levi 505s and a chocolate-coloured top with embroidered detail around the neckline and cuffs. Then she put on her only boots with a heel. She was going out for something to eat. She wasn't going to wallow in gloom any longer.

She got into the Beetle and drove slowly down the driveway, stopping before she reached the gates because another car had turned in and there wasn't enough room for them both to pass through. She waited while the other driver accelerated quickly and passed her by without acknowledging the fact that she'd allowed him the right of way.

Tosser, she thought, as she glanced in her rear-view mirror and saw the car stop in front of the house. Just as well I didn't call up to Nina if she has a new arrival. And I'm glad for her that she has, even if he's an ignorant pig of a driver and probably just as ignorant a guest.

She parked in the designated spaces surrounding the plaza and walked to the Riverside pub. She knew from her lunch with DJ that it also had an evening bar-food menu, and she wanted to eat somewhere warm and friendly. She'd brought

Andre Agassi's autobiography with her, a book she'd been meaning to read for ages, and she was prepared to sit on her own, eat a meal and read. But she was equally prepared to chat to people if anyone started up a conversation with her. Sheridan didn't mind being in pubs on her own, although she knew it was something a lot of women felt uncomfortable about. Men on their own in pubs usually looked perfectly at ease. Women always looked as though they were waiting for someone (and usually were).

The Riverside was half full and showing a round-up of the day's soccer matches on TV. Sheridan sat at a corner table that had a good view of the screen, glanced at the menu, then ordered chicken goujons and chips as well as a bottle of non-alcoholic beer. She sat back in her seat and felt herself relax. She was perfectly fine with her own company. But she liked the buzz of conversation going on around her.

'Sheridan Gray!'

She hadn't spotted Shimmy when she'd first walked into the pub because he was in the centre of a group of people, but he'd seen her and he came over to her.

'What are you doing here all on your own?' he asked.

'Waiting for dinner,' she told him. 'I'm starving and the fridge at home is totally empty.'

'Is anyone joining you?' he asked.

'Only Andre,' she replied as she picked up the biography. 'But I believe he's good company.'

'You're a weird person, you know that,' said Shimmy.

'No weirder than you.'

'There's no need to sit here by yourself. Come and join us.' He gestured towards the group, who were clustered around a number of tables at the other end of the lounge.

'I'll be in the way,' she protested. 'And none of you are eating.'

'A couple of the girls have ordered food. It's fine.'

'OK, so.' She nodded and followed him, asking the waitress to bring the food to her new table.

Shimmy introduced her to the group, which was a mixture of men and women in their late twenties and early thirties who'd all been watching the live soccer earlier.

'I enjoy the footie,' said one of the girls, a pretty brunette wearing a short tartan skirt and a red jumper over opaque black tights and black boots. 'Though it's just an excuse to come to the pub, isn't it? You must be a true fan, though, Sheridan. What's the best match you've ever seen?'

'I was in the Nou Camp for a Barcelona cup tie,' said Sheridan. 'That was very exciting.'

'Great team. Great stadium,' agreed the man sitting beside Shimmy, a glass of beer in front of him.

'Wonderful,' she agreed.

The group of friends was welcoming and chatty, drawing Sheridan in to their conversation so that she was soon exchanging stories of her time on the *City Scope*, comparing it with the *Central News* and telling them that the *News* was a far more exciting place to work, which caused them to laugh.

'It's more diverse,' she explained.

'I bet you miss interviewing famous sports stars, though,' said the brunette, whose name was Jasmine.

'I didn't get to interview that many famous people,' Sheridan said. 'But I once had my photo taken with Cristiano Ronaldo.' She took out her phone and showed it to them.

'He's so fit,' said Jasmine, who turned to the man beside her and poked him in the ribs. 'You need to get on the treadmill, Terry! Otherwise I'm trading you in.'

There was more good-natured banter between the group. Sheridan realised that this was what she'd missed since losing her job. The last time she'd been out like this was the night she'd ended up drinking whiskey with her ex-colleagues and woken with a hangover in Griff's bed the following morning. At least there was no chance of her having a hangover this time, she thought as she ordered another alcohol-free beer. Which meant that tonight was already a better night than that one had been.

As the conversation ebbed and flowed, Sheridan found herself chatting to Jasmine and two other girls, Laura and Roisin, while the men watched more football highlights.

'I'm glad to meet you at last,' said Laura. 'My sister said you were very nice.'

'That's good of her. Who *is* your sister?' asked Sheridan.

'Myra.'

'Oh.' Sheridan was surprised. Laura, who wore her dark hair loose around her shoulders and was dressed conservatively if fashionably in jeans and a T-shirt, didn't look in the slightest bit like Myra.

'She's the mad one and I'm the sensible one.' Laura laughed at Sheridan's expression. 'Anyway, you and I have been in touch already, so it's about time we met face to face. I send you the knitting patterns for the paper.'

'You're Laura Kennedy!' Sheridan was shocked. She'd pictured an elderly, grey-haired woman poring over patterns every week before sending them in to the *Central News*. Myra hadn't mentioned that Laura was her sister or that she was in her twenties. But then they hadn't discussed the knitting patterns in any great detail.

Laura grinned. 'My mother owns the wool and fabric shop in the town. I love wool. Love knitting. Always have. I sew and crochet too, but knitting is my favourite thing. Sending patterns in to the paper was Myra's idea. People like them, plus, of course, it advertises the fact that we have a great website so you can buy stuff online as well as in the shop.'

'I was sent out of my knitting class in school for being hopeless,' confessed Sheridan. 'I'm totally uncoordinated when it comes to crafts.'

'Don't be silly,' said Laura. 'You could do it if you put your mind to it. I run knitting classes in the community centre on Thursday nights. You should come. It's mainly younger people, you'd be surprised.'

'I'm sure I absolutely would be surprised,' said Sheridan. 'But to be honest, it's not me.'

'We'll get you yet,' said Laura.

'What about you?' Sheridan turned to Roisin. 'Are you a contributor to the paper too?'

Roisin shook her head. 'Until the recession kicked in a few years ago, I was working in a technology company in Galway. Then it went wallop and so I ended up coming back here. I was very lucky, because a job came up in Paudie O'Malley's printing works in Carlow and I got it.'

'Oh,' said Sheridan. For probably the first time since she'd come to Ardbawn, she hadn't been thinking, even subliminally, about Paudie O'Malley.

'It's a great job and the people there are fantastic,' said Roisin.

'Paudie does seem to have his fingers in a lot of pies,'

remarked Sheridan, 'particularly around this neck of the woods.'

'He's done well for himself,' agreed Roisin. 'He's lovely to work for, though.'

'Mr Slash-and-Burn?' Sheridan looked sceptical.

'That's such an inappropriate name for him. He comes in to ailing businesses and fixes them up,' said Roisin.

'I know.' Sheridan looked wryly at her. 'He came in to my previous newspaper and decimated the staff numbers.'

There was an awkward silence as it dawned on the other girls that Sheridan had been one of those decimated.

'But you're here now,' Jasmine said brightly after a moment or two. 'How are you liking Ardbawn?'

Sheridan decided not to allow her resentment over her situation ruin an enjoyable evening. She told the girls that she liked Ardbawn very much, that DJ and Shimmy were great to work with and that staying with Nina was perfect for her.

'How's she doing?' enquired Roisin. 'It was a bit of a shock when all that stuff happened with Sean, the feckin' eejit.'

'OK-ish.' Sheridan felt good about being asked about someone else in Ardbawn for a change. Almost as if she belonged. 'I'm sure it's been hard for her, but she seems to be coping.'

'In some ways I'm surprised it didn't happen sooner,' said Jasmine. 'Sean Fallon is sex on legs.'

'He looks good on the telly,' agreed Sheridan.

'A million times better in real life,' Laura assured her. 'There'd be times when he'd be walking down the street and you'd stop to look at him.'

'Wow.'

'Of course back in the day he's supposed to have slept with half the town.'

'You're kidding.'

'So I've heard. There was talk of a bit of offside action after he was married, too. There's a fair few men in Ardbawn who probably wouldn't be fans of our Seanie. But all the women love him.'

'I'd hate that,' said Roisin. 'Going with someone so gorgeous that everyone else fancies him too. It'd be very stressful.'

'We don't have to worry about it too much, though!' Laura roared with laughter. 'There aren't any men around here with that level of sex appeal.'

'Too true.' Roisin agreed. 'If you were coming here for the quality of our men, Sheridan, you'd be sorely disappointed.'

Sheridan smiled, although she was thinking of Joe O'Malley again. As far as she was concerned, he was devastatingly attractive. But maybe the town didn't have a good track record with its devastatingly attractive men. In which case she might have done herself a favour after all.

The girls allowed themselves to be drawn back into the main conversation of the group, which was continuing on a sporting theme, although this time locally. Every so often Sheridan made a comment or asked a question, but she was happy mainly to listen, filing away the names of the teams and the players, knowing that she'd be able to recall them again if she needed to.

It was great to feel part of the group. And lovely to chat and to gossip. She was very glad that she hadn't gone to

Nina's for another quiet night in the guesthouse or stayed in the studio yelling at Xabi Alonso's avatar. She'd taken some positive steps to be part of Ardbawn tonight, and she was pleased with herself.

It was almost eleven by the time she got up to leave. She was feeling tired and hopeful that for the first time since coming to the town she'd fall asleep without spending an age listening to the silence outside, missing the comforting sound of passing cars and trucks. It had never been silent in Kilmainham. If she had to pick one thing in Ardbawn that freaked her out more than anything else, it was the silence of the night.

She said goodbye to everyone, telling Shimmy she'd see him in the office on Monday and the others that it had been great to meet them. Laura said not to forget about the knitting classes, Roisin and Jasmine suggested they get together again soon and Sheridan told them to text her with any plans.

She got into her car and drove back to the guesthouse. When she pulled up in front of the studio she saw that the car that she'd encountered earlier was still parked outside the house itself. The guest hadn't, she noted, moved it to one of the bays to the side. Which was very inconsiderate.

Earlier that evening, when Nina had heard the front door of the guesthouse open, she'd frozen in the act of washing the pan she'd cooked the tuna in. Guests had keys to the door, but there was no one staying overnight, which was partly why she'd asked Sheridan to join her. Sheridan, because she was staying in the studio, didn't have a key and always rang the bell when she arrived. Nina left the pan in the sink and

294

sat at the table, uncertain what she should do as she listened to the footsteps in the hallway.

'Hello.' He pushed open the kitchen door and looked tentatively at her.

At some level she'd known it would be Sean. She'd processed information about guests and keys and who could be opening her front door, and the only possible answer was her husband. He stood in the doorway, as tall and as handsome as ever, his hands thrust deep into the pockets of his fleecy jacket.

'What are you doing here?' she asked.

'I thought I should come home,' said Sean.

'Tonight? To stay?' Her voice was a squeak.

'Is that what you want?'

That was the question she'd been asking herself for weeks. And now that *he* was asking her, she still didn't know the answer.

'I told you to leave.'

'But did you mean for ever?'

'I'm not sure,' she said.

'I guess that's better than a straight no.' Sean smiled at her and she felt the shell of ice around her heart crack. He always got her when he smiled.

'It's not a yes, either.' She stood up. 'I was going to make coffee. D'you want some?'

'Yes please.'

It was good to have something to do. She moved around the kitchen, filling the kettle, spooning coffee into cups, taking some Mr Kipling cakes out of a box.

'Shop cake?' He raised his eyebrow as she placed a cherry Bakewell in front of him.

'No visitors this week.'

He nodded. 'I guess it's quiet enough right now.'

'Yes.'

'So . . . struggling a bit?'

'Same as this time every year. But the new season is getting under way and the festival will bring people into the town. Hopefully we . . . I'll be busy.'

'Do you miss me?' he asked.

She sat down opposite him but didn't look at him while she stirred her coffee and composed herself.

'Of course I miss you,' she said eventually. 'But I'm getting used to it.'

She was glad she'd been to Peggy's earlier in the day. Glad that she had the strength of her friend's support behind her.

'It's not the same, though, is it? Being without each other.'

'No.'

'I miss you,' he told her.

She thought of him with Lulu Adams and the crack in the ice closed over again.

'I got your letter. Your *solicitor's* letter.'

'I tried to contact you myself. You know I did. But you never replied. I thought that if you heard from Gerard it might help focus your thoughts.'

'My thoughts don't need focusing,' she said, although she knew that was exactly what they did need. She cleared her throat. 'What I got from that letter, Sean, was that you either want to move back into the house or you want me to sell it.'

'That's a bit stark,' he said.

'The truth, though.'

'For God's sake, Nina, I never wanted to go in the first place,' said Sean. 'You made me leave. You. Alone.'

How was it, she asked herself, that he always managed to make her feel as though she was in the wrong even when she wasn't? It was a trick of his and she didn't know how it worked. He was the one who'd cheated. He was the one who'd messed up. Not her. She took a deep breath.

'I asked you to leave because you were having an affair with one of your co-stars. It wasn't my choice that you did that.'

'I've already told you it was nothing.'

'She didn't seem to think so,' said Nina.

'She's young and foolish and headstrong.'

'That's her excuse. So what's yours?'

'I admit I was bowled over.' Sean kept his eyes fixed firmly on her. 'I let myself get carried away. She's pretty and smart and, oh, outgoing, you know? And it was so much more exciting than being here in Ardbawn.'

'Here in Ardbawn with me, who's none of those things.'

'You're an attractive woman, Nina. I've always said that.'

'But not pretty and smart. Or outgoing. And not young any more either.'

'By outgoing I mean – well, fun.'

'Great. I'm no fun either. It's hard to understand why you'd want to come back.'

'This is my home,' said Sean.

'You should have thought about that before you slept with her.' Nina was surprised at how firm her voice was. 'You should have known better. And you promised me.'

'I know. I'm so sorry I didn't keep that promise. It was a lapse. But it'll never happen again, Nina. I swear.'

'You hurt me, Sean. Not just having the affair with her, but the fact that it was so damn public.'

'I know you'll find this hard to believe,' said Sean, 'but we weren't together that much.'

'You were everywhere with her,' protested Nina. 'If you google your name, you get loads of hits of you in pictures with her. And there's reams and reams about the pair of you. Hardly anything about you and me!'

'Bloody internet. I bet you'll just see the same old stories over and over. I swear to you, Nina, it was a fling. Yes, it was intense for a while. But it's over.'

'And that stuff is going to be there for ever!' cried Nina. 'It's not like years ago when yesterday's news was tomorrow's fish-and-chip paper. Now yesterday's news is permanently on the web for anyone to see. Your children, for example. *Their* children!'

'I've said I'm sorry.'

'And you think that makes it all right? That because you're sorry, I should tell you to come on home? How deep do you suppose the well of my forgiveness is, Sean?'

'I know you're a forgiving woman. I know you've seen my side of things before.'

Nina said nothing.

'Look, sweetheart, I'm not seeing Lulu Adams any more. I accept that the effects of my . . . my moment of madness have been hard on you. I understand how you feel. But I'm here, saying I'm sorry and meaning it. I want to come home. I want to make things right.'

'What about *Chandler's Park*?' she asked. 'How would you work on *Chandler's Park* if you were back here again?'

'There's going to be a break for my character,' said Sean. 'They're planning a special in which there's a massive gas explosion. Not everyone survives.'

'They're killing you off?' Nina looked shocked. 'Just as we said they might.'

'I'm not being killed off. The whole thing is being left open. I'll be in hospital in a coma while they decide where to go with the storyline. That's confidential, by the way,' he added.

'And when does this happen?' asked Nina.

'The end of next month.'

'So in fact you want to come home because you'll be out of work.' She was feeling angry now. Angry was good, she thought. Angry was better than broken hearted.

'I knew you'd think that, but it's not the case at all. I've been offered other work. The same company that does *Chandler's Park* wants me to front a special about great Irish love affairs, and I've already got loads of voice-over offers. It's absolutely not about being out of work.'

Nina looked at him sceptically.

'You can talk to them if you like.' He took his mobile out of his pocket and handed it to her. 'Here, phone the commissioning editor. Ronan Fleming. He'll confirm it.'

'I'm not phoning anyone. You coming back here has nothing to do with where you work. It's about us.'

'Exactly.'

'You swore,' she said fiercely. 'You swore on my mother's grave. I didn't want you to do anything as dramatic as that, but you insisted. You told her that you loved me and that you'd always love me and that you'd never do anything to hurt me again. But you did, Sean. That's the truth of it.'

Sean sighed. 'And I'm paying for it every single day,' he said. 'In how I feel when I go back to the apartment at night. Alone. Like you.'

299

'But you're not alone every single night. I am.'

'I swear to you, I've been alone for weeks.'

'I trusted you before.' Nina got up and stood in front of the sink, her back to him. 'I trusted you then and I believed in you.'

'And you were right to believe in me,' said Sean. 'Nina, listen, you can't let everything we have disappear just because I had a bit of a midlife crisis. That's what it was. But I'm over it now. I swear to you. I'm ready to come home.'

She turned to face him.

'I wanted you to come home. I have to admit that. Living on my own and running the guesthouse by myself wasn't where I saw myself at this point in my life. I hate the children calling up and asking me how I am as though I could top myself at any moment. I don't like people worrying about me. Talking about me. Knowing that you made a fool out of me.'

'I understand.'

'It's been hard for me,' she said. 'I've had lots of time to think and wonder and worry . . . too much time. And I know that I haven't finished with all that yet.'

'You just said it, Nina. Too much time. You don't need to mope around wondering when is a good moment to forgive me. You don't have to come up with a time frame for letting me back.'

'That's exactly what I have to do. If I think that getting back with you is the right thing to do.'

'Of course it is.' His tone was persuasive. 'You know that. You just haven't admitted it to yourself. We're good together, Nina. We always were and we always will be.'

Was he right? wondered Nina. Should she have talked to

300

him before now, instead of making the grand gesture of throwing him out and ignoring his emails and calls? Had she made things worse by doing what she'd done?

'I need time to think,' she told him. 'I'm not going to let you pick up our lives from where they were before just as if nothing's happened.'

'Absolutely,' he said. 'You're right. How about I come back next week?'

'I . . . That's too soon. I have to . . .'

'We need to decide. To move on.'

'That's what I've been trying to do. Without you.'

He looked at her contritely. 'I'm sorry I put you in that position, but it doesn't have to be that way now.'

'Doesn't it?'

'I'll give you time, Nina. To realise that we can still work things out.'

'How much time were you thinking of?'

'A week?'

'Are you nuts? I can't make important decisions like this in a week!' cried Nina.

'OK, OK.' Sean looked at her placatingly. 'A month. And after that we put the past behind us.'

'A month, and then I decide about what I want,' she amended.

'Of course,' said Sean. 'It's your decision.'

But why, Nina wondered, do I feel as though you've already made it for me? She twirled her wedding ring around on her finger. Even though she'd asked Sean to leave, she still hadn't taken it off.

'Can I stay the night?' He looked at his watch. 'It's late.'

'It's not a bit late.' Nina glanced at the kitchen clock.

'You're being very hard,' he said.

'You made me hard,' she told him.

'Nina . . . I can't say sorry enough.' He got up and went over to her. He put his arms around her and drew her close. His smell was comforting and familiar. She wanted him to leave but she wanted him to stay even more. She knew she did. Even though it might be a terrible mistake.

Chapter 22

DJ was already in the office when Sheridan arrived on Monday morning, which surprised her. DJ was flexible about his working hours, sometimes not coming in until after ten but then staying late into the evening. Not a morning person, he often said, but damn good after midday. Which was true.

His expression, when she walked into the office, was grim, and she knew straight away that it was because of her. He nodded at her before she'd even put her takeaway coffee on her desk and told her that he wanted to see her in the conference room straight away.

The conference room wasn't anything of the sort. It was just a small office off the open-plan area, with a table and six chairs around it. Shimmy had told her it was where they had strategy meetings, but since Sheridan had started work there had never been a strategy meeting. There hadn't been formal meetings of any sort, just chats around DJ's desk. She sat on one of the high-backed chairs. The table, she noticed, was marked by the rings of hot cups that had been placed directly on to the polished wood. There had been a table just like it at the *City Scope*.

'What the hell is all this about?' DJ didn't bother with niceties, and although his voice was low, it was angry.

Sheridan said nothing.

'I get a call from Paudie O'Malley last night,' said DJ, 'while I'm stretched out on the sofa watching the telly, enjoying my Sunday evening at home. And he tells me that my temporary employee is investigating him. Investigating him! What in God's name are you playing at?'

'I'm not investigating him,' lied Sheridan. 'I just . . . I wanted to find out more about him.'

'Why?'

'He's a very interesting man.'

'So you turned up at his house and pretended to be a taxi driver?' DJ looked at her in bemusement. 'What on earth were you thinking?'

'I didn't pretend to be anyone,' protested Sheridan. 'Sinead made a mistake. I tried to correct her, but she was busy and—'

'But why go there in the first place? If you weren't planning to "investigate" him?'

'I was driving past. The gates were open. It seemed like a good idea to go in.'

'How could it possibly . . . ?' DJ looked truly bewildered. 'I don't understand your apparent obsession with the man.'

'It's not an obsession. It's simply that he's mega-rich and mega-reclusive and he owns this paper, so I'm interested in him.'

'In that case, why not ask me whatever you wanted to know?'

Sheridan looked uncomfortable. 'I'm not sure.'

'You've put me in an extremely awkward position,' said DJ.

'Paudie wasn't one bit happy with what happened. Nor am I. I don't see why you felt the need to sneak around spying on him. You already checked him out before you came here – you said so.'

'Yes, but it's not the same as meeting a person.'

'You want to meet him?' DJ's eyes glinted. 'That can be arranged!'

'I'm sorry if I caused trouble for you . . .'

'He wants to know why I employed you. If you're a spy.'

'A spy!' She laughed and then stopped herself. 'What sort of spy could I possibly be?'

'When you're a man in Paudie's position, there could be any number of reasons for people wanting to know more about your life. He's a private person.'

'A private person who's very wealthy and who controls a chunk of the media industry. Which means he's able to stay private.'

'That's not a bad thing.'

'But where are the checks and balances on his businesses?' asked Sheridan. 'Most of them aren't publicly quoted companies, so he can do what he likes.'

'That's his prerogative.'

'It shouldn't be,' she said. 'That's how we ended up in recession before. Businessmen doing whatever they liked and thinking they shouldn't be questioned about their decisions.'

'And is there a decision you want to question him about?' asked DJ. 'Your position on the *City Scope*, for example?'

'You know I was gutted when I lost my job,' said Sheridan. 'I wasn't planning to quiz him about it, though. I wasn't planning to ask him to give it back to me.'

305

'Just as well. I'm not sure how he feels about having you on the payroll here, either.'

Sheridan said nothing.

'This is a small town,' said DJ. 'You can't go around upsetting people.'

'Hey, I haven't upset anyone in the town!' she cried. 'I've pissed off the owner of the paper, which, I agree, is probably not a good move on my part. I knew that even when I was there. It was a mistake. But that doesn't mean he should fire me. Does it?' She looked anxiously at DJ.

'If you'd prowled around the home of the editor of the *City Scope*, I'm pretty sure he wouldn't have been too happy with you either,' said DJ.

'I know. I know.'

'Paudie wanted to know more about you. So I told him.'

'Told him what?'

'That you'd been a great reporter on the *City Scope*. He was surprised to hear that you'd worked there.'

'Did you say that it was all his fault I was given the boot?'

'I said you weren't happy about it.'

'Thanks.' She made a face. 'Now he probably thinks I'm some nutter hell-bent on retribution.'

'A bit,' agreed DJ.

'Can't blame him, I suppose. Can't blame him for wanting to get rid of me again, either.'

'Paudie doesn't hire and fire on the *Central News*,' said DJ. 'I do.'

'Are you going to fire me?' asked Sheridan.

'I was very tempted to last night,' replied DJ.

'And this morning?'

He sighed. 'I like you. You're a good writer. You've improved Des's match reports no end.'

She looked at him hopefully.

'Don't do that,' he said.

'What?'

'Turn those big puppy-dog eyes on me.'

'Sorry.' She looked away.

'I don't want to fire you. And I'm sure Paudie doesn't want me to throw you out of another job either. Fan the flames of your rage against him and all that. Turn you into some psycho killer stalking the streets of Ardbawn.'

She tried not to smile.

'But you can't carry on some kind of personal crusade against him.'

'I'm not,' she said. 'Honestly. I'm curious by nature, that's all.'

'There's nothing to be curious about as far as Paudie's concerned.'

'There's loads.'

'Leave it,' said DJ. 'Please.'

'Oh, all right.'

On one level she was relieved. Meeting Paudie's family had made her feel guilty for thinking that he had, in some way, been responsible for the death of his wife. Sinead and Peter were nice people and she couldn't blame them for being annoyed with her (even though Peter had also seemed amused). Josh, of course, was a total treasure. It was hard to believe that his grandfather was a murderer. Or that he'd driven his wife to suicide. But even as she was thinking these things, she still wanted to know why Elva had died.

'This is a friendly newspaper,' said DJ. 'Sure we talk about bad things that happen, but we're not here to be doom-mongering and scandal driven. So whatever ideas you had from your previous employer, you can just forget them.'

'All right.'

'Now get outside and start doing something useful,' said DJ. 'There's a dog show in the community centre next Friday. I want interviews and pictures and human-interest stories on dogs. I want dogs that look like their owners and owners who look like their dogs. I want heart-warming stories about dogs who've saved the day. I want celebrity dogs and celebrity dog owners. I want warm and fuzzy and happy reading. OK?'

'OK,' said Sheridan.

'And spend a bit more time on the horoscopes this week,' said DJ. 'I thought the last lot were a bit vague.'

'They're meant to be.'

'Yeah, but not quite so airy-fairy. A few general pointers.'

'Like what?

'Like how my sign can keep calm in stressful situations.'

She grinned at him.

'It's not funny,' he said.

'Sorry.'

'Ah, it's all right.' He grinned too. 'It'd be boring if life was simple for me, now wouldn't it?'

'I guess it was easier with Myra around.'

'Ah, Myra.' DJ's face lit up. 'Did you hear she's had her baby? So that's another thing for this week's edition. A little piece on the new mum and the new arrival. Lots of love from all of us. Give her a call and ask her for some of the gory details.'

'I heard about the baby. You're sure she won't mind me calling her?'

'Not at all. She knows how we do things.'

And I don't, thought Sheridan as she made her way to her desk. I probably never will, either.

Nina was baking cookies while her part-time housekeeper, Anais, was vacuuming and polishing. Nina was quite happy to leave the cleaning to Anais while she concentrated on cutting the dough into different shapes and placing them carefully on the baking tray. Even when Sean had taken over the cooking for a while, Nina had always done the baking. It was soothing, and the warm aromas that wafted from the oven never failed to comfort her.

She didn't know if she needed to be soothed or comforted following Sean's visit. She couldn't help feeling pleased that he wanted to come home, but there was a corner of her that continued to worry that it had more to do with his investment in the guesthouse than his love for her. Yet if that was the case, surely he'd be happy to stay away and then force her to sell it?

He'd been chivalrous enough on Saturday night, retreating to the deserted residents' lounge to watch the TV while she stayed in the kitchen. She'd brought tea into the lounge later and they'd sat in two armchairs, the coffee table between them, as they drank it. Sean had asked her about the number of visitors she had, and she'd explained about Sheridan, and then said that there was a group coming the next week as part of one of her riding-lesson packages with Peggy. Par for the course, she'd told him, and he'd asked her about the dramatic society's contribution to the festival. She told him that Brian Carton was going to star in *Blithe Spirit* this year and that Hayley had expressly forbidden him to climb down riverbanks looking for stray sheep. Sean had laughed at that, which caused her to laugh too, leading her to feel as though things between them could be retrievable and that she'd be totally wrong not to forgive him, because they were good together no matter what.

At midnight he'd said that he was tired and needed to get some sleep, and she'd told him that the Buttercup bedroom was freshly made up. He'd hesitated for a moment, then nodded and gone upstairs, but she'd stayed in the residents' lounge for another thirty minutes, staring at the images on the TV without taking any of them in.

She'd locked her bedroom door even though there hadn't been any need, because Sean didn't come to the room. She'd have known if he had, because she hadn't slept a wink.

He'd left on Sunday morning, dropping a swift kiss on her head before he opened the door. She wondered if he wanted her to ask him to stay, but she was silent as she watched the car disappear down the driveway and turn on to the road.

She'd felt unsettled for the rest of the day, but less so than after she'd first told him to leave. It was as though his temporary return had allowed certain segments of her life to find their place. A place from which she would move on eventually, only, as yet, she didn't know where she would move on to.

Sean Fallon hadn't bothered to cook since he'd moved into the apartment off Morehampton Road but had lived on ready meals, pub grub and takeaways. After seeing Nina and spending the night at home again, however, the urge had come upon him to cook for himself. It was something he'd had to learn when Nina was pregnant with Alan, when the smell of meat on the grill or in the oven had made her feel sick. Given that most of the people who came to the guesthouse expected a full fry-up for their breakfasts, Sean had to take on the duties of chef, at least for the first few months of Nina's pregnancy. But even after she'd got over her nausea, he occasionally did a stint in the kitchen. It wasn't that he particularly liked to cook, but he liked the logistics of planning a meal and he found the chopping, the blending and the stirring therapeutic.

In the small apartment kitchen he was trying to re-create the aroma that had met him when he'd walked into the kitchen at Ardbawn. But it wasn't just the lingering hint of cooking in the air that had suddenly made him feel homesick – it had been every scent of the Bawnee River Guesthouse. The fresh flowers in the hallway. The lingering beeswax of the furniture polish. The cotton fragrance of the lighted candle in the living room. The scent of home.

He liked living in the apartment, but he missed home. He missed the comfort of it, the warmth and the security. He missed knowing that Nina was there, ready to laugh with him at something a guest had said or to share the anxieties of the weeks when there were no guests. He hadn't thought he'd miss it, but he did.

Lulu Adams wouldn't have had the faintest idea how to cook a tuna steak, or bake an apple pie, or do any of the domesticated things that Nina could do without even thinking. Of course that was what had first attracted him to her – her overt sensuality, her aura of being above mundane things like making shopping lists or scrubbing baths. The image of Lulu with a bottle of Cif and a cloth in her hand was one he couldn't even attempt to conjure up. No, when he thought of Lulu, he thought of wantonness and sex and pleasure without limits. When he thought of Nina, he thought of practicalities and comfort and someone to look after him.

Which was what his father had said she would do when they had their one and only man-to-man conversation. Anthony had wanted to know what Sean's intentions towards Nina were. Not, he said, because he cared if Sean bedded her and then left her – times were changing, after all. But Nina was becoming an attractive woman and there were other men in Ardbawn who'd be interested in a good-looking girl with a house of her own. Anthony had pointed out that Sean's acting career had come to nothing and that he wasn't getting any younger. The time had come, he said, to choose the sort of life he wanted to lead.

Sean's dream had been to lead an exciting, glamorous life. Coming back to Ardbawn had never been part of his plan. But he cared for Nina. She was witty and clever and good in bed. So who – or what – he asked himself, was he holding out for? He'd sat down one night and made a list of pros and cons about marrying her. The pros outweighed the cons. It was a no-brainer in the end.

Of course he'd never entirely settled into the role of guest-house owner. Sometimes the grind of looking after other people and the pettiness of some of the guests drove him to distraction. Yet he was good with them, playing the role of concerned host no matter how trivial or annoying their problems might be. But he couldn't be expected to be totally immune to other possibilities. Other lives. Other people.

His affair – the disastrous affair before Lulu – had been entirely different. And afterwards, shocked though Nina had been, she'd forgiven him. Sean, stunned at how things had turned out, had allowed her practical nature to take over. They had a family, she'd said. That was more important than anything. And perhaps, she conceded, she'd been partly responsible, because she'd thrown herself into her mission of turning the Bawnee River Guesthouse into the best in Ireland. She'd taken him for granted. She'd made a mistake.

Sean was happy to allow Nina to shoulder some of the blame for what had happened. And, he'd reasoned, he wouldn't have looked at another woman if he'd been perfectly happy at home. So it wasn't all his fault. Nevertheless, he'd sworn it wouldn't happen again. At the time, he'd meant it.

He knew that he'd let Nina down by having a fling (he didn't even want to use the word affair this time) with Lulu Adams. But that was all it was. Caught up in the excitement of *Chandler's Park* and his new life, he'd hardly have been human if he hadn't been attracted to the voluptuous actress. And he knew that on set he'd regained a lot of the arrogance and attitude that had made him such a desirable date in his younger years too. OK, it wasn't right, exactly. But that was the way it was. And he'd been sure that Nina would understand and forgive him, even if he'd let her down again.

Instead she'd been so bloody angry that he'd decided it would be better to stay away from the house for a while. Nina had thought she was telling him to go. From Sean's point of view, he was removing himself from the line of fire until things had cooled down a bit. Now that they had, he wanted to come back. The thing with Lulu had run its course. He'd got Lulu, and the idea of being a man about town again, out of his system. It was time for him to come home. He hadn't believed that Nina would be able to ignore the barrage of calls and emails that he'd sent her, but he knew she wouldn't ignore a missive from his solicitor. Even though she'd tried to be distant to him when he'd turned up at the guesthouse, he knew that the idea of selling it had shocked her. Not that it would come to that. Nina was his wife. She always would be.

Sheridan still didn't know what to do about her date with Joe. So far he hadn't called or texted to say that he didn't want to see her, and yet she couldn't for a second imagine that he'd want to have dinner with her now. Nor could she imagine that he didn't know about her turning up at March Manor – she was sure it had been a hot topic of gossip at the house over the rest of the weekend. Of course he had said that he was going to be away for a few days, so he might not have immediately been aware of it, but surely by now they'd have said something to him. Mistaking journalists for taxi drivers wasn't an everyday occurrence, after all.

She took out her phone and checked it for messages again. But there weren't any. She knew that she was being silly and that she should just call him herself, but she couldn't bring herself to do that. Besides, if he was away on business, he wouldn't necessarily welcome a call from her saying that she was sorry she'd impersonated a cab driver and stalked his father. Best wait, she thought, until the last possible moment. And then . . . well, she hadn't decided yet.

To distract herself, she phoned Myra to tell her about the congratulatory baby piece that DJ wanted to do.

'I'll send you a picture of her,' said Myra. 'She's an absolute dote. I'm over the pain of it now. I tell you something, nobody ever admits to the total agony that childbirth is. I mean, you see it in all those historical movies where women are sweating and screaming and biting on rags and stuff and you think that it's moved on, but I swear to God it hasn't. The air around me was totally blue from the things I was shouting. But then the little darling was in my arms and, oh, I dunno, you do sort of forget.'

'D'you want me to say all that in the piece?' asked Sheridan in amusement.

'Ah, no. I don't want to be scaring any other poor pregnant woman out there. All I'm saying is that it'll be a long time before Barney Clarke gets next or near me again.'

Sheridan laughed. 'Are you looking forward to coming back to work, or will you want to stay with your baby? I'm sure the readers of the *Central News* will want to know.'

'She's only a couple of days old,' said Myra. 'Right now, I don't want to let her out of my sight. But I'm sure that'll change slightly over time. How's it going for you? Keeping my chair warm OK?'

'I think they'd prefer it if you were still here,' Sheridan told her.

'I didn't get a chance to look at the paper this weekend, what with being so busy pushing Genevieve out of a body that truly needs a better design for the job,' said Myra. 'But I'm sure it's great.'

'It's OK,' said Sheridan. 'I'm not entirely up to speed yet, but the good news is that I'm on top of the accounts stuff so far; that's what I was most scared of.'

'How're the horror-scopes going?'

'Not too bad. I feel a bit guilty about people believing in them, though. It ends up being a kind of responsibility, doesn't it? Nina Fallon reads hers religiously.'

'You'd be surprised how many people do. But, hey, you're just giving thoughts that can apply to anyone. And if they help . . .'

'I hope so, but I'm not convinced.'

'And I believe you were sampling more of Ardbawn's glittering social life on Saturday night.'

Sheridan smiled and said that she'd been totally taken aback to discover that Laura was Myra's sister.

'Sure we're all related down here in Ardbawn,' quipped Myra. 'My sister is genuinely talented, though. Part of me thinks she could be the next Lainey Keogh or Orla Kiely, but she's far too modest.'

'Maybe I should do a piece about reviving old crafts,' mused Sheridan. 'I know knitting clubs have become very popular again. It might be interesting to find out if any well-known people knit or sew or crochet or whatever. Maybe get Laura to do a special pattern for them.'

'Sports people,' suggested Myra. 'You must know some of them. It's a good idea.'

'Glad you think so,' said Sheridan. 'I need something to keep DJ happy right now. I'm not entirely flavour of the month with him today.'

'Why?'

Sheridan told her about calling to Paudie O'Malley's house.

'What on earth made you do that?' asked Myra in absolute astonishment.

'I thought there might be a story.'

'Paudie's a total darling,' said Myra. 'He's a great family man. When Michael's away, Sinead and Josh often spend a few days with him. I guess that's a side to him that people don't see.'

316

Sheridan didn't say that wasn't the story she'd planned to write.

'I like Josh,' she said.

'He's a good kid,' agreed Myra. 'Involved in every sport there is. Just like his dad. I went out with him myself, you know.'

'Josh's dad! Michael? You're kidding me! When?'

'Ah, years ago. I was mad about him. All big and manly and outdoorsy.'

'Why did you split up?'

'I was too much of a dipstick for him,' said Myra cheerfully. 'Sinead suits him much better.'

'Do you know her well?'

'We're not really in the same social set.' Myra shrugged. 'Not that she gives herself airs or graces or anything like that, but her life is way different to mine. I went out with Peter for a few weeks too,' she added casually.

'What!' Sheridan supposed it wasn't unusual that in a small town people's relationships would be entangled, but it was freaking her out that Myra (and everyone else in the town) seemed to be involved in some way or another with the O'Malleys.

'It wasn't anything much. He was into motorbikes and so was I. But there was no spark there. I never slept with him.'

'Too much information,' said Sheridan.

Myra chortled. 'DJ says there's no such thing as too much information when it comes to being a reporter.'

'He's probably right,' acknowledged Sheridan. 'But I'm not doing a piece on the hearts you broke in Ardbawn!'

'Oh, we're only scratching the surface here,' Myra assured her. 'Not that it matters, because despite what I told you

317

earlier, my heart belongs to Barney Clarke, and no matter how I feel now, sooner or later I'll let him peck me chastely on the cheek again.'

'That's a relief. And how about the other two O'Malleys? How well do you know them?'

'I occasionally babysat Cushla,' said Myra. 'She's the sweetest of them all, and when Peter went off to boarding school, she was home on her own a lot of the time. It was the year that Elva died. I was fifteen or sixteen and she was about ten. I felt so sorry for her.'

'What do you think about Elva's death?' It had never occurred to Sheridan that the greatest font of information on the O'Malleys had worked at the *Central News* herself.

'I was only a kid at the time, but the general consensus was that drink had something to do with it,' said Myra. 'I'd only met her a couple of times myself back then, but she was a strange woman. Really friendly one minute and distant the next. I never felt entirely comfortable with her.'

'Had she mental problems, d'you think?'

'Not that I know of – hey, are you interviewing *me* now?'

'God, no,' said Sheridan. 'It's fascinating stuff, that's all.'

'Only because you weren't living here at the time,' said Myra. 'In Ardbawn it was just a tragedy.'

'I guess so.'

'Don't waste your time with the O'Malleys,' advised Myra. 'They're decent people.'

For the first time since the idea of investigating Paudie O'Malley had come to her, Sheridan thought that perhaps the statement was true. He was a decent man who'd had a tragedy in his life. So had his children. Who the hell was she to think that it could have been anything more?

'Oops, gotta go,' said Myra. 'My bundle of joy is making some mewing noises, which I think means she's hungry again. I'm nothing but a mobile feeding station as far as she's concerned. I'll send you the photo by tomorrow.'

'Thanks.'

'You're welcome,' said Myra, and hung up.

Sheridan looked at the doodles she'd made on the page in front of her as she'd been talking to Myra. Myra and Mike. Myra and Peter. But not Myra and Joe. They hadn't got round to talking about Joe. Sheridan was sure that all the other girl would have said was that he was a decent man. Like the rest of his family.

Chapter 23

By the end of the following evening Joe still hadn't phoned or texted and Sheridan was in a complete quandary. Did he know about her intrusion into the family home or not? And if he did, did he plan to meet her simply to tear strips off her like DJ had? (To be fair, Sheridan allowed, DJ had been nice about it in the end. She wasn't entirely sure that Joe O'Malley would take the same relaxed approach.) She didn't know what he'd think of her. But she cared about that, and that was the problem. She'd be able to take whatever he threw at her and deal with it if it didn't matter to her personally. Leaving aside (if that was remotely possible) the way he made her feel, she liked Joe O'Malley. She wanted him to like her too. Because of the buzz and the electricity, it mattered a lot.

She let out her breath slowly. She felt as though she was no longer in control of her own life, that she didn't really know why she was making the choices she did. She wished she had a fairy godmother who would wave a wand and make everything turn out all right. Knowing it was all up to herself was hard.

Her phone rang and her heart thudded. Maybe it was Joe

at last. Even if he'd ducked out of their date, it would be a relief to know for sure.

However, the caller was Talia, asking if she'd like to come to Belfast the following weekend for the launch of a new nightclub. It would be full of hip and happening people, Talia told her and might be a bit of a laugh. She was going along to check out the style and write about it. Like old times, she added, so I hope you can come.

Sheridan agreed straight away. 'I can't wait to see you,' she said. 'I miss being able to talk to you every day.'

'You can talk to me any time,' said Talia. 'What's texting for?'

'It's not the same.'

'You OK?' asked Talia, concerned that Sheridan's bleak tone was so untypical of her.

'Sure. Yes. I'm fine.'

'All set up for your big date tomorrow night?'

Sheridan hesitated, then brought her friend up to speed on the latest developments.

'Lordy, lordy,' said Talia. 'You've muddied the waters a bit, haven't you?'

'I thought this was a bigger town than it is,' said Sheridan. 'Everybody knows everybody else and they're all pals or related or something! It never occurred to me that Joe was Paudie's son. Of course if the original reporter had spelled Mike's surname right when they were writing about the wedding, I might have made the connection. Or maybe not. Who knows? My mind isn't as sharp as it used to be, that's for sure. Maybe I have sheep-brain or something.'

'He might think it's funny,' said Talia.

'Or perhaps he'll just think I'm a crazy psycho.'

'You'll never know till you see him.'

'I can't.' Sheridan sounded suddenly panicked. 'It's too embarrassing.'

'Are you planning to be the one who cancels, so?'

'Right now, I don't know what I'm planning to do.'

'Listen to me, Sheridan Gray. Once you're wearing that sexy dress, it doesn't matter what you've done. He'll be smitten.'

'I think it'll take more than a dress.'

'Don't underestimate the power of good clothes,' said Talia. 'Think about Liz Hurley. An entire career built around a dress held together by safety pins. Even if they were Versace safety pins.'

'After the fool I made of myself in gatecrashing March Manor, I'm lucky to have a job, let alone a date,' observed Sheridan.

'It'll all work out,' Talia told her. 'The job and the date. And if he does cancel, no harm done.'

'I guess not.'

But after she hung up from Talia, she knew that she didn't want him to cancel. Even though she was terrified at the thought of meeting him again.

She spent the following day with her mobile on the desk in front of her, jittery with anxiety over its silent state and equally anxious any time it beeped or rang. DJ asked her a number of times what the matter was. He'd never seen her so jumpy, he said; was she now working on some secret exposé about the dog show or something?

'Don't be silly.'

'You're not planning another stakeout at March Manor, are you?'

'Of course not.'

'Well then chill, for heaven's sake.'

'Sorry.'

None of the messages that came in that day were from Joe. She couldn't chill. She was strung out with tension. And even more strung out because she kept telling herself there was nothing to be tense about.

She was logging out of her computer before going home when DJ's phone rang, and she knew from the tone of his voice that it was something out of the ordinary. Her first thought (how self-centred can you be, she asked herself afterwards; you need to keep a sense of perspective) was that Joe had rung DJ to complain about her, just as Paudie had done. But the editor of the paper hung up and looked at her.

'There's an incident developing at the school on the Kilkenny road,' he said. 'Some sort of protest. I need you to go there. Find out as much as you can. Get photos.'

Another night she would have jumped at the chance to cover something even vaguely newsworthy, but she'd planned to wash her hair before meeting Joe and it always took ages to dry. She didn't want to waste time on some non-story at the local school.

'Don't you want to do it yourself?' she asked DJ.

'I've things to do here. Besides, you're perfectly capable. I want you to get the details back to Shimmy and me so that we can update the website. OK?'

'OK,' she said. A few pupils staging a protest about too much homework or whatever else was going on at the school wouldn't delay her that much, after all. She'd still have time to wash her hair and do her make-up the way Talia had taught her. If she was going to have to face the wrath of Joe O'Malley, she'd do it looking her very best!

She pulled on her jacket and hurried out of the office building. The school was about three kilometres outside the town, so she hopped into her car and turned on to the main street. A soft drizzle had begun to fall, misting the windows and slowing traffic. However, it didn't take her long to reach the school, where a small knot of people had already gathered and were looking at the building. The flashing blue lights of a police car illuminated the bystanders.

She got out of the Beetle and looked at the building too. The original two-storey flat-roof structure had been built in the seventies. A further single-storey extension had been added to the side of it, making an L-shape. The large windows were currently in darkness, and it took Sheridan a few seconds to realise that people weren't trying to peer into the building itself – they were staring at the figure standing on the two-storey roof.

'Who is it?' she asked a woman in a red coat and blue scarf.

'Conall Brophy,' she said. 'He's from the Bawnbeg Estate. I don't know what he's doing up there.'

Sheridan circled the onlookers and stood beside a young garda. She introduced herself and asked what was going on.

'He's protesting because the bank is repossessing his house,' said the garda.

'Why is he doing it on the school roof?' asked Sheridan.

'The bank manager is married to the school principal,' explained the garda. 'They recently moved to a bigger house on the other side of Ardbawn. He's upset that they're trading up while he's being turfed out.'

'Right.' Sheridan nodded. 'So what's—'

As she spoke, Conall started shouting from the rooftop.

'They're all thieving bastards!' he cried. 'Them and their swanky cars and their big salaries. And what happens to the likes of me? What? I'm shafted because I miss a couple of payments.'

'He also lost his job recently,' the garda said.

Sheridan's sympathies were entirely with Conall Brophy. She knew how he felt.

'He has an industrial gas canister up there,' continued the garda. 'He's threatening to blow up the school.'

'You're joking!' Sheridan took her phone out of her pocket, ready to call DJ.

'My sergeant is going to try to reason with him,' said the garda.

'I hope he's successful.'

'We've called for the fire brigade all the same,' the garda added, just as his sergeant beckoned to him to join him.

Sheridan called the *Central News* and brought DJ up to speed.

'Conall Brophy?' DJ paused, and Sheridan imagined him trawling his brain and maybe also his computer for information. 'I don't know him. Get as much info on him as you can, OK? I can put together something about the bank manager and the teacher. It must be the IRB. Clinton O'Grady is the manager there. Jude Delaney manages the other one. She's grand, but Clinton can be a bit of a pompous arse sometimes. I'll do some background checking on the bank. See what other dastardly deeds I can pin on them. It's a while since we've done a bastard bankers story.' He sounded cheerful now. 'This is great.'

'Not if he lights that canister and blows us all to hell,' remarked Sheridan.

'There's no chance of that, surely?'

'I don't know.' She was watching the agitated man on the rooftop. 'He seems pretty strung out to me.'

'Any likelihood he'll jump?' This time DJ sounded concerned.

'It's a possibility, I guess.'

'Ask people about him,' said DJ urgently. 'Don't waste any time.'

'I'm on it.' Sheridan ended the call and put her phone back in her pocket. It was raining more heavily now. Which might be a good thing, she told herself, if he really does try to burn the school down.

She spoke to more people in the ever-increasing crowd, and then the tender from the local voluntary fire crew arrived. Conall Brophy was getting more and more voluble and she couldn't help thinking the likelihood of the whole thing ending without some sort of disaster was decreasing by the minute.

She phoned DJ back, giving him additional details. As well as losing his job and having a repossession order for his house, Mr Brophy had been turned down for the caretaker job at the school the previous week. He'd come back earlier that day to talk to the principal, but she'd refused to see him. Somehow he'd managed to secrete himself in an office and stay there until the school had closed. Nobody was sure whether he'd brought the gas canister with him (difficult, they reckoned; it was big and heavy) or if he'd found one on the premises, but it seemed that he'd managed to manoeuvre it up the stairs, climbed out of a window on to the roof of the extension and dragged it up a fire escape to the higher roof.

'Ironic him using a fire escape,' said DJ, 'if the place goes up in flames.'

'Absolutely,' she said. 'Has the national media got hold of it yet?'

'Oh yes. I'm sure they have people on the way. It's all over Twitter now and I'm keeping the website updated. Stay in touch.'

'Of course. I've emailed you a couple of photos, but the phone isn't good enough in the dark.'

'That's OK,' he said. 'Anything will do. Get one or two of the locals rubbernecking too.'

The gardai and the firemen were now talking to Conall's wife, Lorraine, who'd been brought to the scene to plead with her husband. He was ignoring her, continuing to shout from the roof, berating the bank and the school and shouting about how they'd let him down. Sheridan still felt sorry for him. So did many of the crowd. But she knew that if he succeeded in causing a fireball, their sympathies would evaporate very quickly.

She detached herself from the group and walked around the side of the extension. It was quiet there, all the activity taking place at the front of the school. She continued to walk around the building, not entirely sure what she was doing but covering all the bases.

She was at the back of the school when she saw it. An enormous oak tree as tall as the second storey, with wide branches well spaced. An easy climb, she thought. One she could do herself. She gripped the lowest branch and tested it. Strong enough for someone twice her weight, she reckoned. She began to pull herself up, then stopped. It wasn't her job to climb the tree and try to reach Conall Brophy. If things went wrong, she might not be able to prevent him either throwing himself from the roof or igniting the gas. She wanted to be a hero but she also had to be sensible. Adding her own presence to the mix might make things worse. She wrestled with her conscience and her desire to be part of the action for another minute, before walking back to the front of the building and speaking to the chief firefighter instead. She knew him. She'd met him with Shimmy in the pub on Saturday night.

She told him about the tree, and he spoke to the garda sergeant, who'd taken a few minutes out from negotiating with the man on the roof. The sergeant looked at the younger garda, who nodded.

'A rescue attempt.' Sheridan phoned DJ. 'Hope it works.'

The garda sergeant continued to talk to Conall Brophy while the junior officer walked around to the tree. Sheridan hoped that she'd been right about it as a potential way on to the roof. And that the garda would be able to climb it. It might be easy enough in the daylight and when the weather was dry, she thought. But in the dark, and with falling rain . . . maybe she'd been stupid in suggesting it.

The young officer (Charlie Sweetman, she told DJ, who was waiting on the phone to hear the outcome; he's single and lives with his parents on the Dublin road) was almost beside the man on the roof before the onlookers spotted him and took a collective breath. And then, suddenly, he'd caught Conall Brophy and in one fluid movement had him face down on the roof and handcuffed.

Almost at once the firemen raised their ladder, and a couple of minutes later Conall was being brought to the ground amid a mixture of applause and jeers from the assembled crowd.

His wife rushed over to him and put her arms around him. The police led him to the squad car and arrested him. Sheridan wasn't sure what she should do next. She didn't think she'd be able to talk to him at the police station, and she wasn't sure that the gardai would answer questions there.

'I'll give you a call later,' said the sergeant when she spoke to him just as he was about to get into the squad car. 'I'll let you know what's happening. We might keep him in overnight but we may have to release him. Can't tell you now. But . . . good idea on the tree.'

'Thanks,' she said. She looked around her. Lorraine Brophy, a pale-faced woman in her mid-twenties, was being comforted by one of her neighbours. Sheridan explained that she was with the *Central News* and told Lorraine she was sorry about what had happened.

'My husband is a good person,' said Lorraine as she wiped tears from her eyes. 'He's had a hard time. This wasn't his fault. You can't make him out to be a criminal.'

'Do you want to tell me about it?' Sheridan looked at her anxiously. She didn't want to upset Lorraine any more than she was already. Yet she knew that she had to ask.

'I have to get to the station to be with him,' said Lorraine. 'It's in Kilkenny.'

'I'll drive you,' Sheridan told her. 'You can talk as we go.'

By the time they got to Kilkenny, she knew everything there was to know about Conall and Lorraine – his frustration at losing three different jobs when the companies where he'd worked closed down, his concern about their financial state and his attempts to resolve the situation. He was a forklift operator, Lorraine said, and there just wasn't the work any more. He thought he'd be good at the caretaking job in the school because he was a useful handyman, but it had gone to a man in his late fifties who, according to Lorraine, was a friend of the principal and who didn't need the money.

'If he gets prosecuted he'll have a criminal record,' she said miserably. 'That won't help with the job hunt either. Or getting another loan for a house. Not that we'll ever get that. We're going to end up living with his mother again, the aul' wagon. She'll blame me for how things have turned out. She always does.' She blew her nose in the tissue that Sheridan handed her before going on to say, in reply to Sheridan's question, that they'd no children. When they'd first married, the fact that babies hadn't come along straight away had been something that had upset her. But now she was glad. An unemployed criminal for a dad, she sniffed.

'He's not a criminal,' Sheridan told her. 'He's just someone who snapped. We all do from time to time.'

'Yeah, but the rest of us do it quietly, behind closed doors.'

'Maybe we shouldn't,' said Sheridan. 'Maybe it's good to make a fuss sometimes.'

'You're very nice,' Lorraine said. 'I know he shouldn't have done what he did, but please don't trash him in the newspaper.'

'DJ is a good man too,' said Sheridan. 'He'll give your side of the story, don't worry.'

'Thanks.'

She followed Lorraine into the station, where Vinnie Murray was standing in the hallway. He greeted her cordially but told her, as the sergeant had done earlier, that there would be no news on Conall for a while.

'I see you're following trouble,' he said to her while Lorraine went in search of water.

'Ah, not really,' she told him. 'I feel sorry for Mr Brophy.'

'Idiot,' said the superintendent.

She grinned at him.

'That was off the record,' said Vinnie Murray hastily.

'Absolutely,' she assured him. 'You'll let me know how he gets on.'

'I said I'd call you and I will.'

'Thanks,' she said. 'And the truth is, I only came to the station because his wife needed a lift.'

'Managed to get yourself in the right place at the right time all the same, didn't you?'

'Not really,' she said. 'I was quite prepared to go home and— Oh!' The right place at the right time! She looked at her watch. Unbelievably, she'd forgotten about Joe O'Malley. And she was supposed to be meeting him in twenty minutes. 'Bloody hell,' she said. 'I'd better go. Promise you'll ring?'

'Absolutely.'

Sheridan saw Lorraine returning with a plastic glass of water and asked her if she'd be OK on her own.

'Yes.' The other woman nodded. 'I'll ring one of my friends when I know what's happening.'

'All right then.' Sheridan gave her a tentative hug.

'Thanks,' said Lorraine. 'Thanks for listening.'

'You're welcome,' said Sheridan as she hurried back to her car.

* * *

She didn't have time to go home and change. She drove straight to the hotel and immediately went to the ladies' room. She rummaged in her bag and wished she was more like Talia, who seemed to carry a mini beauty bar around with her and was therefore equipped for every appearance emergency. Talia would've had serum to deal with the rain-soaked hair, as well as foundation and eyeshadow to hide the blotchy face and panda eyes of her reflection. Sheridan's bag, in contrast, contained two mismatched hair bobbles, a Boots No. 7 tinted lip gloss and a bottle of Jo Malone Pomegranate Noir (which Talia had given her the previous Christmas).

She dried her hair by crouching beneath the hand-dryer and continuously hitting the silver button for hot air. The effort left her looking like Albert Einstein on a particularly bad-hair day. She pulled a brush through her tangled locks and tied them back with the bobbles. Slightly less scary, she thought, but still very far from the sleek look she'd intended. She then moistened a tissue and wiped some specks of mud from her forehead before slicking on the lip gloss. Finally she sprayed herself with the perfume. Not my finest hour, she thought as she inspected the face staring back from the mirror. There's no way I look as though I've made even the faintest of efforts.

She reminded herself, as she pushed the door opened and headed towards the restaurant, that it wasn't just about looks. It was about personality too. Though it was hard to see how Joe could be impressed by the personality of someone who had more or less been stalking his father.

There was a part of her that still believed he wouldn't be there. She hadn't yet decided how she'd react to that eventuality – if the thing to do would be to act dismissive and say to the restaurant staff that she'd got the day wrong or something like that. She'd practised various lines to use, but as she stood at the entrance to the softly lit room, she realised she didn't need any of them. Because Joe *was* there, sitting at a table near the wall, reading a menu.

He looked up as she walked towards him, and then stood to greet her. He was wearing navy trousers, a white open-necked shirt and a casual jacket. His dark hair was lightly gelled, and despite a tiny nick on his cheek from what had obviously been a recent shave, he looked great.

'Hello,' he said.

'Hi.'

She looked at him uncertainly as she sat down and apologised for being late. She explained about Conall Brophy and his protest, all the time expecting him to tell her to shut up about some man he'd never heard of and explain instead why she'd turned up uninvited at his father's house.

Instead, his expression was concerned, and after she'd finished, he said he hoped that things would turn out all right for him.

'To be honest, I can't see how,' said Sheridan. 'He's going to lose his house, he hasn't got a job . . .' She thought again of how panicked she'd felt when she'd lost her own job. And how devastated she'd been to have to leave the apartment, even though it was only a rental.

'There are people who can give him advice,' Joe said.

'Hmm. Like retrain and learn new skills and all that sort of guff.' Sheridan had temporarily forgotten her concern about her dinner with Joe as she thought of Conall's situation. 'Easy to say, not alway so easy to do. And when he did try to do something else, the job went to a friend of a friend instead.'

'I can see how that would upset him,' agreed Joe.

'He was very distressed,' Sheridan said. 'And now his wife is worried that he'll have a criminal record, which will prevent him from getting work in the future. It's terrible,' she added, 'how one simple mistake can wreck your life . . .' Her voice trailed off as she thought of her own mistake. Joe hadn't referred to it yet. It was impossible that he didn't know. Surely.

She glanced around the room and felt even more uncomfortable as she realised just how inappropriate her current garb of jeans (still a bit damp from the rain) and sweatshirt was. Almost all the other female diners had dressed up and were looking subtly sophisticated, while the men wore suits, or a least a jacket, like Joe. Nobody else looked like they'd just come in from a tramp around the hillside. She'd known the right thing to wear. Her sexy green dress would have been perfect. But right now she stuck out like a sore thumb.

'Everything OK?' asked Joe.

'Just wishing I'd had time to go home and change first,' she replied.

'You're fine the way you are,' said Joe.

She smiled nervously. If he was trying to put her at her ease by telling her she looked OK when she knew that she absolutely didn't, did that mean he was still unaware of her visit to his father's house? She felt as though she were sitting on an unexploded bomb, expecting it to go off at any moment but not knowing when. Neither did she know if the bomb was ticking. Right now, he seemed far too relaxed to have a go at her, but how could she know what he was really thinking?

'It's good to see you,' he added.

'Have you been busy yourself?' she asked. 'You were away on business, weren't you?'

'Nightmare.' He poured iced water from a jug already on the table into her glass. 'Problems at the company I manage, issues with some overseas investors. Got it sorted eventually, but it's not my favourite way of spending time.'

'Were you abroad?'

'Dubai,' he said. 'My father has some business interests there.'

Perhaps they hadn't wanted to bother him while he was away, she thought, even as the mention of his father made her stomach churn. She took a sip of her water and steeled herself to confess.

Before she could speak, a waiter came over and asked if they were ready to order. Sheridan, who hadn't managed to take in what was on the menu, looked at him blankly and Joe asked him to give them another few minutes.

'Of course, Mr O'Malley,' said the waiter. 'Take as much time as you like.'

'I think before we eat . . .' She took another sip of the water. 'Before we eat, we need to just . . . um . . . there's something we need to talk about first.'

He leaned forward. 'This isn't anything to do with you thinking I'm married, is it?' he asked.

'No. No. Of course not.'

'Whew.' He relaxed again. 'I was worried there for a moment.'

'It's nothing about you,' she said hesitantly. 'It's . . . it's . . .'

'What? What's the matter?'

'I think . . . I think you might have a problem being here with me,' she said. 'You might decide that this is a big mistake.'

He continued to look at her, a puzzled expression on his face.

Then she told him, the words tumbling from her lips in a rush. About losing her job in Dublin and blaming Paudie, about her plans to write an in-depth piece about him, about going to March Manor and being mistaken for a taxi driver. As she spoke, his expression grew from puzzled to surprised, to slightly amused and finally grim.

'So dinner with me tonight was what for you?' he asked. 'An opportunity to pump me for details about my family?'

'No,' she replied. 'Of course not. You asked me and I came because I . . . I wanted to.'

'But you knew I was Paudie's son.'

'Not when you asked me,' Sheridan reminded him. 'I thought you were Josh's dad then. It was only when I went to the house that I realised who everyone was.'

'What were you expecting when you did that?' he asked. 'That my dad would simply say yes to an interview? That he'd tell you all sorts of things he's never told anyone else so that you could – what – make a name for yourself?'

'I went to the house on impulse. I really had no idea what I planned to ask him.'

'And how did you intend to publish whatever you finally wrote?'

'I hadn't decided. I just saw it as a way to get back into the mainstream press or perhaps build up a reputation as a freelance journalist. It's bloody hard, you know, to get a foot in the door, even for someone like me who should know exactly how to open those doors. Everything I did before was sports related. I wanted to show that I could do something different. That I wasn't a loser just because I was turfed out of the *City Scope* when your dad invested in it.'

The waiter returned, but Joe waved him away again.

'Are you blaming my father for the fact that you lost your job?' Joe sounded incredulous.

'Well, he has this reputation, you know. Mr Slash-and-Burn, that's what he's called.'

'Not by anyone close to him.'

'He takes over businesses and gets rid of people,' said Sheridan. 'You can't deny that.'

'He invests in ailing businesses and turns them around, preserving jobs for most of the employees,' Joe said.

'But what about the jobs that aren't saved? What about the people who're thrown on the street? The ones he calls dead wood?'

'It's hard to lose your job, of course' said Joe. 'But everyone would lose their job in a failing company if it wasn't for people like my father.'

'Yet people like your dad make loads of money out of it,' Sheridan reminded him. 'You see it all the time, these so-called saviours coming in, firing people and then rewarding themselves with huge bonuses. Those bonuses could've kept staff working.'

'You're a right little socialist, aren't you?'

'Oh, please!' She looked at him, suddenly annoyed. 'I'm stating a fact. And it's not that I think we should have a communist state set-up, but there are people who take too much on the back of the work of others, and they live great lives and don't have a clue, not a clue, how bloody demoralising it is to send out a million CVs without even a reply, because they're already cocooned in their luxury offices with jobs that pay them far too much in the first place.'

'If that's how you think about my father, I'm guessing you weren't planning on writing anything very flattering about him,' observed Joe.

'I would have done a balanced piece.'

'Nothing you've said to me has been very balanced.'

'You don't understand!' she cried. 'I've seen your father's house. I've seen how you live. Your family has it all. But tonight I met someone who was driven to total despair over his unemployment situation. He nearly burned down the school, for heaven's sake.'

'Are you trying to blame my dad for that too?' asked Joe.

'No. No. And I know he's not exactly responsible for me ending up in a place like Ardbawn either . . .'

'A place like Ardbawn?' Joe looked at her wryly. 'You mean a backwater like Ardbawn? Somewhere that doesn't value your investigative skills? Your passion for a story?'

'I didn't mean it like that,' said Sheridan. 'I meant . . . Oh, look, it's just I had plans, you know? Dreams about what I wanted from my life, from my career. And somehow your father has scuppered them.'

'So you're out to scupper him, is that it?' asked Joe when she lapsed into silence.

'I thought I could . . . oh, I don't know, upset him a bit. Let him know how it feels.' Sheridan pushed a stray lock of hair from her face. 'I realise that makes me sound completely bonkers. I'm sorry. And I'm sorry I didn't know who you were and that I agreed to meet you for dinner. I'm particularly sorry I barged into your home last Saturday. But I'm not sorry I was thinking of doing a story, because that's my job and that's what I do, and even though I prefer my stuff to be about sports stars not businessmen, I'm proud of it.'

'Fair enough,' said Joe.

'And I'm sorry I didn't get in touch with you and tell you about what happened. I thought you would've heard from your brother and sister already about me. I didn't honestly believe you'd be here tonight. I should've texted you and cancelled. It would have been better. As it is . . .' she stood up, 'I think I should go.'

'Sheridan . . .' He didn't finish the sentence.

She had to go before she burst into tears. It was one thing having a private sniffle, but she never, ever cried in front of other people. Least of all men. That was a total sign of weakness. She picked up her bag and took a deep breath.

'Goodbye,' she said.

He looked at her thoughtfully and then spoke in a calm, measured voice.

'Goodbye,' he said.

She was sure she could hear a trace of anger behind the calm. She couldn't blame him for being angry with her. She was angry with herself too.

He hadn't stopped her. Sheridan realised, after she'd left the hotel, that a part of her had half hoped that he would come running after her and tell her that everything was fine, that he understood how she felt, that it didn't matter, he loved her anyway. Which might have worked well in the romantic movies she enjoyed watching from time to time, but it never actually happened in real life. In real life what happened was that you got outside and realised that it was now bucketing down with rain, and that in the few seconds it took to get to your car, your hair was getting plastered to your head and your trainers weren't heavy enough to keep out the deluge.

She was aware, as she sat in the Beetle, that she hadn't handled events particularly well. She leaned her head on the steering wheel and asked herself why things never turned out the way she wanted, what it was that seemed to mess up her best-laid plans and left her feeling hopelessly inadequate. When she'd first got the job at the *City Scope*, she'd thought that she was travelling a new path; a successful one that would make her parents proud of her. Now she realised that it had only been a diversion, that getting things wrong was her default mode and that Pat and Alice would always regard her as the child they had to worry about.

It took nearly ten minutes before she felt composed enough to start the engine and pull out on to the road. There was very little traffic moving through the town now, the rain clearly having persuaded people to stay indoors. She wondered if it would be worthwhile driving to Kilkenny again to see how things were turning out for Conall and Lorraine Brophy, but she didn't want to piss off Vinnie Murray. She supposed that proper journalists never cared about pissing people off, but she did. Whenever she interviewed sports stars, she was always polite and understanding, even when she was asking them questions they didn't especially want to answer. (Matt had once told her that she lacked a killer instinct, that she didn't go for the jugular or kick a man when he was down. Sheridan couldn't understand why anyone would want to.)

Her phone rang just as she pulled up outside the studio. For the briefest of moments she hoped it was Joe, but in fact it was Vinnie Murray, who told her that Conall had been released on bail and that he and his wife had gone home.

'How is he?' asked Sheridan.

'A bit calmer,' Vinnie replied. 'I think he realises that he hasn't made things any easier by his actions.'

'I'm glad he's out of prison, though.'

The superintendent sounded amused. 'He was never in prison, love. Just in the station. He'll probably get probation anyway. Don't worry about him.'

'I'm not worried,' said Sheridan. 'I just . . . Oh, well, thanks for ringing.'

She changed out of her jeans and tidied her hair before putting on her jacket again and picking up her laptop. She wanted to go up to the house and check the *Central News* website for the story. Given that she'd messed up her personal life, she might as well devote all her energies to her career, no matter how far down the toilet it appeared to be. Besides, she was sure that Nina would be interested in first-hand gossip too!

Nina was surprised to see her and even more surprised when she heard about the incident at the school.

'I don't know Conall,' she said as she led Sheridan into the lounge. 'I don't know many people from the Bawnbeg Estate. In my mind they're all newcomers, which is silly, because the estate was built more than ten years ago. But you know what it's like, you remember places how they were when you were younger. New houses, new buildings are always new to you.'

341

'You certainly can't say that about your house,' said Sheridan. 'It must be fifty years old.'

'More than that,' said Nina. 'My grandparents built it.'

'The stories these walls could tell, eh?'

'Yes.' Nina's eyes had a faraway expression and it was a moment or two before she realised Sheridan was standing looking at her.

'Would you like some tea while you're working?' she asked.

Sheridan was suddenly starving. Maybe I'm the sort of person who eats when they're miserable, she thought. She wanted to ask Nina for some biscuits to go with the tea, but decided the other woman might think she was being rude. So she just said yes to the hot drink.

After Nina had gone into the kitchen, Sheridan opened the laptop. The *Central News* was her browser's home screen now, and the front-page story had one of the grainy photos she'd taken with her phone and the caption 'Stand off at St Raphaela's' as the headline.

DJ had done a good job, she thought, noting that he'd put in every bit of the information she'd given him, spelling the names of people she'd talked to correctly, giving snippets of information about them. He'd also discovered the names of Conall's previous employers and had got quotes from two of them, both saying that Conall was a hard-working man and easy to get on with, and that they'd been sorry to let him go. There was some background information on the bank manager and his wife as well, although DJ hadn't said anything about bastard bankers.

Sheridan surfed the websites of the national media and read their versions of the event, some of which were clearly just cut-and-paste jobs. She remembered that there had been a reporter from the TV news at the school and she hoped that Nina would allow her to stay in the lounge and wait for the late-night news bulletin to see if they covered it.

'No problem at all,' said Nina a few minutes later when she returned with a tray, which she set down on the coffee table. 'I know it's prurient interest, but I want to see it too.' She poured a cup of tea and handed it to Sheridan. 'Would you like a cupcake? I baked a lot today because I've got guests arriving tomorrow.'

'I can't eat your guests' cake,' protested Sheridan, even as she hungrily eyed the selection of delicate cupcakes on the tray.

'I made plenty. Don't worry.'

'I should stay away from cake, though. A minute on the lips and all that sort of thing.'

'Don't be silly,' said Nina. 'You've a great figure.'

Sheridan looked startled.

'Seriously,' said Nina. 'You have. When Chrissie was younger she went through a phase of being totally self-conscious about her body shape. Thankfully it didn't evolve into full-blown anorexia, but she went on diet after ridiculous diet where she spent her time measuring out the quantities of food she could put on her plate and knew the calorie count of just about every morsel that went into her mouth. She lost nearly two stone in weight and it wasn't one bit good for her. This obsession girls have with looking skinny and boyish is ridiculous. Curves are so much nicer.'

'I'm sure that's not what most people think,' said Sheridan. 'But thank you for saying so.'

'We all want to be something we aren't,' observed Nina. 'We all think someone else's body is more desirable than our own.'

Sheridan nodded slowly. Nina was right.

'I've always wanted to be tall and willowy,' said Nina. 'Or maybe blonde and fragile.' There was a sudden cynicism in her tone that startled Sheridan.

'I don't see you as blonde and fragile,' she said. 'It's not you.'

Nina shrugged. 'Do we act a certain way because of how we look? Or do we try to fit our looks to the way we are?'

'Interesting question.' Sheridan bit into a melt-in-the-mouth cupcake. 'Truth is, even if I was willowy and fragile to begin with, it'd all go horribly wrong for me. Because I can't resist my food.'

'Good,' said Nina. 'You must have dinner with me again soon.'

'That'd be nice,' agreed Sheridan. 'Oh – the news!'

They turned up the volume of the TV. The story about the school siege came midway through, with a piece to camera in front of the school from the station's reporter.

'The eventual capture of the man happened when garda Charlie Sweetman daringly climbed a tree to get to the roof of the building,' said the reporter.

'It wasn't that daring,' said Sheridan. She was about to tell Nina that it had been her suggestion, but she didn't want to sound as though she was looking for glory.

'What d'you think will happen to him?' asked Nina.

'I don't know.' Sheridan shook her head. 'I spoke to the superintendent at the station and he seemed to think that Conall might get probation or something. Regardless of how things turned out, there was the potential for disaster.'

'I'm glad that didn't happen,' said Nina.

'Me too.'

'So it was an all's-well-that-ends-well kind of night.'

For Conall Brophy and his wife, thought Sheridan. But not for her. She reached for another cupcake. She didn't care if she was comfort-eating. Besides, being an ace reporter – even a broken-hearted ace reporter – was hungry work.

She was still feeling a glow from Nina's comments when she went back to the studio to go to bed. As she opened the wardrobe door to hang up her jeans, the first thing she saw was the green dress. She'd managed to keep the disaster that had been her date with Joe O'Malley out of her mind for the last couple of hours, but it came back to her now and her cheeks burned with embarrassment. She'd allowed her emotions to run away with her and she'd implied his father was some fat-cat uncaring capitalist who'd ruined her life. Who would blame Joe for not liking her after that!

She took the dress from the hanger and slipped into it. Damn and blast, she muttered, I do look good wearing it. Maybe Nina's right about my figure. Maybe it is good. She couldn't help wondering when the opportunity for anyone else to notice would ever arise.

Chapter 24

The hall was crowded with people and their dogs. Sheridan couldn't believe there were so many of both in Ardbawn. The noise of animals and owners together was deafening, and quite unlike the TV footage she'd once seen of Crufts, where cute canines were looked at by earnest judges in apparent silence. The Ardbawn show was a far more relaxed affair. Most of the dogs were mongrels and most of the owners excited children.

'It's a fun day out,' DJ had told her. 'Keeps us going until the festival and gives a bit of a buzz to the town. There's always a few serious entrants, but most people take it light-heartedly. So report on it that way. Unless, of course, there's a massive fight between a shih-tzu and a Great Dane, which would be hard news.' He chuckled.

Mindful of DJ's previous instructions that he wanted quirky shots and stories, she kept her eyes peeled for unusual dogs and equally unusual owners as she walked around the hall. Her collection so far included eighty-year-old Myrtle Mullens and her two enormous German shepherds, Fairy and Buttercup; beefy gym instructor Lance Comiskey and his cute-as-pie white poodle, Barbra; hairdresser Grainne Yates

346

and her American hairless terrier, Fluffy; and the glamorous manager of the spa, Ritz Boland, with her grey schnauzer.

'He's my mum's dog,' said Ritz, when Sheridan asked if she could take a photograph. 'God help us, he's not the best-looking mutt in the world.'

'He's sort of ugly,' agreed Sheridan as she wrote Boxie's name into her notebook. 'But he's got lots of character.'

Con had once said that about her, she remembered suddenly. He'd been on the phone to one of his friends, who'd been dumped by his girlfriend the night before a charity ball. Con had suggested that Sheridan might be a good substitute. 'She's not beautiful but she's got a great personality,' she'd heard him tell his friend earnestly. Which had apparently been enough to swing the deal, because Hector Lannigan had asked her to come with him; she'd said yes and it had been a good night, though he hadn't asked her out again. She thought that he might have got back with the previous girlfriend. Who'd been a stunner, whatever her personality.

I should stop having random associations with my past and concentrate on what I'm supposed to be doing today, she told herself, as she threaded her way between more people and their pets. *I've got the mismatched pairs, now I need people who look like their dogs.*

As she scanned the crowd for likely candidates, she instead saw the dark head of Josh Meagher bending down towards the Old English sheepdog whose name she couldn't remember. Her heart skipped a beat as she looked for Joe too. Not that she'd know what to say if she saw him. On a competence scale of one to ten, her handling of the Joe situation had been minus eleven.

He hadn't been in touch with her since their disastrous dinner date (or rather non-dinner date). Not that she'd expected him to call – she'd walked out, after all – but she would have liked the opportunity to try to explain herself to him again, this time more eloquently. Calling him herself, however, seemed too pushy. The whole episode had been entirely unsatisfactory and had left her feeling both inadequate and embarrassed.

There was no sign of Joe. But then she spotted his brother, Peter, who was flicking through the stapled sheets of paper that were the programme. He looked up and caught her eye, then waved enthusiastically.

She walked over to them, remembering that Peter had been friendly even when he'd learned why she was at the house.

'Hi, Peter. Hi, Josh.'

'Hello.' Josh looked at her happily. 'It's good here, isn't it? Bobby isn't keen on all these other dogs, but he's going to win a prize.'

'For the best Old English sheepdog, definitely,' agreed Sheridan.

'I haven't seen any others,' Peter said.

'Because Bobby is so much nicer than them,' she told him. 'They're afraid to show their faces.'

'Exactly.' Josh beamed. 'Plus, now that we're going to classes, he's very, very obedient. He always does what he's told.'

'Just like you,' said Sheridan.

'If only,' said Peter.

'I have to apologise again,' Sheridan said to Peter while Josh – having had his photo taken – brought Bobby for a

348

walk around the big hall. 'I was so out of order coming to your house like that.'

'I didn't think you were the boring sort of person who feels the need to keep saying sorry for their actions.' Peter frowned at her. 'I see no reason why you shouldn't have grasped the opportunity to give us the once-over.'

'I should've rung up and asked to see your father.'

'And why didn't you?' asked Peter.

'Well, because . . .'

'Because you knew he'd tell you to eff off.'

She gave him a crooked smile.

'Of course that's what he'd have said and of course that's why you were right to do what you did.'

'Your sister was upset.'

'Not as much as she made out,' said Peter. 'She hates being made a fool of and she felt really silly mistaking you for a taxi driver. Especially as you were driving a Beetle! Don't worry about Sinead.'

'Your father wasn't best pleased either,' said Sheridan.

'We weren't going to tell him. But Josh blurted something out and so we had to clear things up.' Peter grinned suddenly. 'Josh has a bit of a crush on you.'

Sheridan laughed. 'I doubt that.'

'You praised his footballing skills. That's more than enough to wriggle your way into my nephew's affections. And then, of course, you caught the eye of my brother, too.'

'Oh, look . . .'

'But maybe I should get there ahead of him. Are you doing anything tonight? Fancy going for a drink? Or dinner, perhaps?'

She looked at him wordlessly. She couldn't quite believe that another O'Malley was asking her on a date.

'That's really nice of you, but—' she began, before Peter interrupted her.

'Don't be boring again and say no,' he told her. 'You'll ruin my image of you as a free spirit. Besides, I desperately need someone else in this town to talk to.'

'I'm sure there are plenty of people . . .'

'I don't live here any more,' he said. 'I feel like a fish out of water whenever I come back. It would be great to go out with someone who isn't from Ardbawn.'

'It's just . . .'

'I'm not asking you on a big romantic date,' he said. 'I'll be leaving again soon. So it's just a drink and something to eat. Nothing more. No pressure.'

'It's not that,' she said. 'It's . . . well . . .'

She took a deep breath and told him about Joe. His eyes opened wide.

'Well, isn't he the dark horse. He never said a word.'

'So you can see why I can't go out with you.'

'Don't be silly. Of course you can. My brother let you walk and didn't try to get you back. Foolish man. Though typical of him, I have to say. He's not good with women. Probably because of the whole boarding-school thing – he never got to meet many of them in his formative dating years. Makes him uptight. So does being the eldest and having an inbuilt sense of responsibility, which happily passed me by. But he's a decent guy.'

A decent guy. That phrase again. She seemed to be coming off worst in all her entanglements with decent guys these days.

'I'm sure he is. But it would be weird to meet you instead of him for dinner.'

'I'm not asking you on an extravagant dinner date to the poshest restaurant in Ardbawn. Which, quite frankly, is so not you. There's no need to feel weird about it. We can do pub grub if you like.' Peter made a face at her and then smiled wickedly. 'C'mon, Sheridan Gray. I'll give you the low-down on all my father's business dealings. I'll be your inside source.'

'No you won't,' she said. 'And I wouldn't expect you to either.'

'Maybe I can give you some family information that will make you see there's nothing for you to write about.'

'There's always something to write about,' Sheridan told him. 'The flimsiest of things can be turned into a major story if you play it right.'

'And is that what you want to do?' asked Peter.

'I'd love to have a major story,' she said. 'But not about your dad any more.'

'Because of Joe?'

'Because of me,' said Sheridan. 'I wanted to do an all-guns-blazing story, but even if there is one it would hurt your family. I didn't think of them before.'

'You're more like Joe than I thought.'

'I'm not a bit like him.'

'Yes you are. All fair minded and conscience stricken.'

'Depends on the circumstances,' said Sheridan.

'You could write something warm and wonderful,' said Peter. 'And I'll give you the right info if you come to the pub.'

He was insistent. And charming too, although in a different way to Joe.

What the hell, she thought. I might as well talk to all the O'Malleys!

'OK.'

'Excellent.' Peter looked pleased. 'The Riverside Inn?'

'Sure.'

He was easier to talk to than Joe. He didn't make her stomach flip and her legs shake. He was like all the other men she'd gone out with just for fun. That was what she was good at. Being fun and being friends. Not being some kind of sex-bomb in a slinky dress. And not being a hot shot investigative reporter either.

She arranged a time to meet Peter and then went off in search of more owners who looked like their dogs to add to her report for the *Central News.*

She had plenty of time to go home and change before meeting Peter at the pub. There was no need for sexy green dresses, but she wore her most flattering jeans, teaming them with an amber top worn over a white blouse, a combination that always looked well on her. She left her hair loose.

Peter was already there when she walked into the pub, and his face lit up as she approached.

'I see now why my brother rushed into asking you out,' he said. 'You look great.'

Sheridan felt herself blush. She was hopeless with compliments.

'I love redheads,' Peter continued. 'I love their fiery tempers and unbridled impatience.'

'I'm not your stereotypical redhead,' said Sheridan as she sat down beside him. 'I don't lose my temper easily. Though I'll admit to the impatience.'

'It was the red-headed blood that got you sneaking around March Manor trying to find the dirt on Dad,' he said.

'No, that was my desire to be a news-hound,' she said.

'Ah, well, can't have everything. What would you like to drink?'

She asked for a non-alcoholic beer, because she'd driven into the town.

Peter ordered it for her, and a pint of Guinness for himself.

'I hardly ever drink it,' he confessed as he waited for it to settle. 'But the Riverside does a lovely pint.'

'It's a nice pub.'

'I don't come here that often,' said Peter. 'It was a different sort of place when I was younger. Darker. Dingier.' He looked around him. 'Better now, though.'

'Tell me about the motorbike racing,' she said.

Peter talked animatedly about his short-lived bike-racing career and said that he was now working with a motor-sports team in the UK.

'I'm lucky,' he said. 'I'm doing what I always wanted to do.'

'Did your father ever put pressure on you to join the family business?' asked Sheridan.

'No. He knew I'd be hopeless at it. Besides, he had JJ.'

'How d'you decide whether to call him Joe or JJ?' she asked.

Peter grinned. 'Usually Joe at home, JJ for business.' He looked at her curiously. 'So now that we know that he fancies you, the question is, how much do you fancy him in return?'

'Peter!'

'Well, he asked you to dinner and you said yes, so you can't find him repellent, despite being an O'Malley boy.'

'You asked me to dinner too,' she pointed out. 'And here I am.'

'I had to twist your arm to get you here. Are we going to eat, by the way? I'm starving.'

'Me too,' she admitted.

'I'm going for steak and chips, what about you?'

'Pasta,' she said.

They ordered the food and settled back in their seats.

'Ask me,' said Peter.

'What?'

'About my dad. About the business. Any question at all.'

'No.'

'Why not? You want to know, don't you?'

'Yes, but . . .'

'But nothing. I can give you the whole, unadulterated truth and save you having to skulk around March Manor ever again. Although the truth is boring beyond belief. Our family is boring beyond belief. The only interesting thing about us is that we're sort of wealthy because my dad is the hardest-working man on the planet. OK, he isn't great with strangers, he's wary of them and far too abrupt, but he's a pussycat at home. He loves his work, loves his businesses and yes, has a ruthless streak, which, if I'm being totally honest, Joe has probably inherited, despite the occasional uptightness. I'm not saying that to put you off him, just to warn you. He's a stubborn sonofabitch too.'

'I see.'

'So if you've upset him, he's not going to come running back to you.'

'I wasn't expecting him to, said Sheridan.

'Which means you *did* only meet him to learn about Dad.'

'Oh, look, I don't know why I met him,' said Sheridan, while still remembering the devastating effect he'd had on her – the whole butterflies-in-the-stomach, trembling-knees sort of thing that had been so new to her. 'Anyway, he's not important.'

'Pity,' said Peter. 'The more I get to know you, the more I think you'd be good for him.'

'Good for him? Why?' Sheridan couldn't help asking the question even though she knew it was pointless.

'Joe's very serious, very focused,' Peter said. 'Maybe it comes with being the eldest. You . . . well, I get the impression you take a more scattergun approach. Even though I accept you're focused on your job. Also, you're more fun than Joe.'

'You make me sound like therapy for him.'

'You could be that too.' Peter winked at her and Sheridan felt her face flame, which caused him to remark that it was now the colour of her hair.

'Give me a break,' she said, but she smiled too, because Peter's laughter hadn't been cruel, just amused.

'We're an OK bunch of people, us O'Malleys,' he told her. 'I promise we are. I'm sorry that my dad's investment in your paper meant you ended up losing your job, but I'm pretty sure he didn't mark you out personally for the chop. He doesn't get that involved.'

'I wanted someone to blame and your dad was an easy target,' admitted Sheridan. 'But when I looked him up, I became interested in him.' She paused. 'Especially when I read about your mother too. That was a tragedy.'

Peter's eyes clouded over and she saw his jaw tighten.

'Yes,' he said, and his voice was filled with sorrow. 'Yes, it was. Mum's accident changed our lives for ever.'

*   *   *

Nina took the big box of photographs from its storage place in the spare room and brought it downstairs. It was a long time since she'd looked through it. She rarely bothered taking photos any more, and those she did were with her mobile phone and consequently never printed, but when she was younger, she'd enjoyed using a camera. Shortly after they'd married, Sean had bought her an expensive Olympus and she'd used it to record their lives together. She'd taken lots of shots of the guesthouse as they'd continued to improve it, and there were plenty of Sean, wielding a drill or a hammer, handsome even with the bad haircuts of the early nineties. Then came Alan and Chrissie's baby photos, hundreds of them; she hadn't been able to help herself taking them every single day. Both of her children had been beautiful babies, she thought as she looked at the colour prints. They'd inherited her so-called smouldering eyes, but also Sean's chiselled features. There were snaps of them as toddlers too, trying to get the attention of the guests, usually succeeding and usual charming them just as Sean did.

Then there were the photos of the Sunday lunches and afternoon teas, the venture she and Sean had offered for a couple of years. It had been a popular thing to do and had raised the profile of the business significantly, although as the children grew older it had become too much trouble. But during the years they'd done it, she'd taken occasional pictures of Sean with the guests, some of which she'd framed and hung in the hallway of the guesthouse.

Now she was looking for a specific photograph. One she'd never framed and hung. She remembered the day clearly, a perfect summer's day with azure skies and warm breezes. She'd opened the French doors to the patio and set up tables outside, and every single one had been occupied. Most people had lingered in the garden, soaking up the sun and, in the case of those with an Irish complexion, going a rosy shade of pink. She hadn't sat out much herself, because she was pregnant with Chrissie and finding any heat exhausting. But later, as the temperatures subsided and the sun slid behind the surrounding trees, she'd joined Sean and the only remaining guests, Paudie O'Malley, his wife Elva and their four children, John-Joe, Sinead, Peter and Cushla. Cushla, the youngest and by far the most stunning in a quartet of attractive children, had spent most of the afternoon playing with baby Alan, while the other three had variously tucked into the additional scones and sandwiches she'd brought out to them and played down by the river.

They were all nice kids. Peter had been a bit of a handful, she remembered, a bundle of energy, struggling to be kept under control. Sinead was friendly and outgoing, while Joe was quiet and watchful. He'd spent a lot of time in the shade of the big apple tree, reading adventure stories while keeping an eye on his brother and sisters. Nina had photographed him and later given the result (a thoughtful, contemplative picture) to Elva. She'd taken other photos of the group too, that day. At one point, when all the children, Joe included, had been messing about on the riverbank, she'd used the camera's automatic timer to take one of the adults.

She finally found it. There had been two attempts at the photo because she'd made a mistake in the timing of the first one and the shutter had activated before she'd got back to the others. So the photograph in her hand was of Elva, sitting between Paudie and Sean, looking serene and beautiful as she smiled at the camera. The photo in which Nina herself featured wasn't as posed because she'd only just made it back to the seat and hadn't managed to smile. It was still a good picture, though, the four of them framed by the background of greenery and blue skies. Friends and neighbours. Supporting each other as people always did in Ardbawn.

She realised that her fingers were trembling. She had a sudden urge to rip up both photographs. She even started to tear them. But then she stopped. Photos weren't important. Despite what people said, she knew the camera lied easily. That was why she took so few photographs these days.

The pub had filled up. Several of Shimmy's friends had arrived, including Roisin and Laura, who stopped beside Peter and Sheridan.

'Peter O'Malley!' Roisin hugged him. 'How're you? I didn't know you were back in town.'

'Only for a couple of weeks,' he said.

'Are you staying with your dad?'

Peter nodded.

'Well tell him he's looking a bit peaky,' said Roisin. 'He was in the office the other day and I thought he needed a bit of TLC.'

Sheridan spluttered. No matter how much his sons would like to paint him as a caring, decent soul, the last man on earth who needed TLC was Slash-and-Burn O'Malley.

'It's probably the strain of having me back in the house.' Peter grinned. 'But I'll tell him the staff are concerned. How're you keeping yourself?'

This is such a village, thought Sheridan as Peter and Roisin chatted for a while. They all bloody well know each other.

'We were in the same class at school,' Peter told her after

Roisin and Laura left them to join Shimmy at the back of the bar (the girls had asked Sheridan and Peter to join them, and Peter said that they'd do that after their food). 'I love Roisin. She's an angel.'

'Everybody in Ardbawn seems to love everyone else. Aren't there any bitter feuds or petty rivalries?' asked Sheridan. 'I thought small towns were supposed to be hotbeds of both.'

'Plenty,' Peter acknowledged. 'Kitty Shanahan hasn't spoken to Lena O'Leary for over fifty years. Something to do with missing cattle, I don't know the gory details. Jem Baker will never forgive Laurie Kenny for pipping him to the captaincy of the hurling team back in the seventies and then getting him dropped for the final. Stewart Langrishe and Tessa Marks have been living together for forty years but haven't married, even though they insist that they are husband and wife. I'm sure there's plenty of more recent stuff too, but I headed off when I was just twenty so I didn't get the chance to sink into the gossipy morass.'

'Why did you leave?'

'For the bike racing, of course,' said Peter. 'Besides, I needed to leave home. To be honest, I didn't like rattling around in March Manor after my mother died. It was never the same.'

'I guess not,' said Sheridan.

'I was afraid of her ghost.' Peter looked shamefaced.

'You're kidding me.'

'No. And I've never admitted this to another soul, not even Joe, so don't you go blabbing about it either in print or in person.'

'I won't, don't worry,' she assured him. 'But . . . did you actually *see* her ghost?'

'Of course not.' He laughed. 'But I was terrified I might. It's ridiculous of me, I know. I was only a kid then, and Mum was the first person I knew who'd died. It made a deep impression on me.'

'Poor you.' She sympathised. 'All the same, I'm sure you had no need to be afraid of your mother, even if she was a ghost.'

'She was a lovely person,' Peter told her. 'But troubled. I was afraid that if she came back, she'd be a wailing sort of ghost, and I didn't want that.'

'In what way was she troubled?' asked Sheridan.

'My father used to call her highly strung,' replied Peter. 'She was very intense. Things mattered to her. The sort of stuff that most of us ignore or get over used to rattle her. She couldn't let it go.'

Sheridan nodded in understanding.

'It used to cause a lot of tension between them. At the same time, she was great fun as a mother,' Peter recalled. 'She never seemed to mind us doing mad things. She allowed me to drive Dad's car when I was about seven. She pushed the seat forward as far as it would go, and I could only barely reach the pedals, but she encouraged me. Dad nearly freaked when he found out.'

'Did you drive on the roads?' Sheridan was slightly shocked at the idea.

'There wasn't much traffic around here back then,' said Peter. 'It was probably a crazy thing to do all the same. Mum used to say that you have to live on the edge from time to time. I think she was sorry that she didn't do more of it herself. She used to paint . . .'

'Landscapes, portraits, that sort of thing?'

'A bit of everything,' said Peter. 'Modern stuff too. Bright swathes of colour. Or sometimes dark swathes of colour depending on her mood.'

'Did she have . . . well, not mental problems, but . . .'

'She suffered from depression in her teens,' said Peter. 'She told me once that having a family saved her . . .' His voice trailed off as both he and Sheridan remembered that Elva had died before she was forty and so hadn't been saved at all.

'I'm so sorry,' Sheridan said. 'I don't want to upset you by asking you about things you'd rather forget.'

He smiled. 'I'm not really upset. It was a long time ago, even though I remember it clearly. At least, I think I do. You know how it is, you think you've got total recall and then someone else tells you something completely different. We all remember things in different ways. But I do remember the day she died.'

'That must have been awful.'

Peter nodded, a distant expression in his eyes. 'We – me and Joe and Sinead and Cushla – were at a party. It was quite odd all of us being out together. After all, Joe was nearly seventeen at the time and Cushla was only ten. It wasn't as though we generally hung around with the same people. But it was – oh, someone's birthday, someone that the whole family knew.' His brow furrowed with the effort of remembering. 'You'd think I'd remember who exactly, but it's fuzzy. Bottom line, though, nobody was in the house when Mum fell out of the window. They told us she'd been killed instantly, but I didn't believe them; I always wondered whether she could've been saved if she hadn't been alone. I remember Mrs Merchant was the one to come and tell us.'

361

'Peggy Merchant? The riding-school woman?'

'Yes. She told us there'd been an accident at home and we needed to come with her.'

Sheridan looked at him sympathetically.

'We thought she was bringing us back to March Manor. But she brought us to the riding school instead. We wanted to go home. Joe got very het up about it. The house was a crime scene, you see. We didn't go back there for a few weeks. Dad took us to Dublin, then, to stay with family.'

'A crime scene?'

'They weren't sure how she fell,' explained Peter. 'It had to be investigated.'

'It must have been awful,' said Sheridan.

'Yes and no,' said Peter. 'I think we all blanked a lot of it out. That's what I mean about it being a blur. But it was on the TV and radio. We heard the news. Dad hated it when they started talking about it. And then the papers – well, it was all over them too. I guess we were lucky that the tabloids weren't as big a force back then. One of the regional papers ran a disgusting piece about the lord and lady of the manor, which was unbelievably offensive and implied that Dad had something to do with Mum's death.' Peter looked grim. 'He sued them in the end. Got an apology. Gave the money to charity.'

Sheridan was startled. She'd assumed that Paudie had ploughed the money into his own businesses after bankrupting the paper.

'When we were finally allowed back into the house,' continued Peter, a hint of embarrassment in his voice, 'I went looking for blood.'

'What!'

362

'On the ground outside the window. I think I couldn't quite believe it had happened. I wanted real proof. I started raking the gravel, looking for bloodstained stones. Dad went nuts.'

'I don't blame him.'

'He was furious when I came home and told him that someone at school had said Mum was murdered,' said Peter. 'He got us all together and said that some people, nasty people, wanted to believe that he'd had something to do with it. He explained that this was how the news worked. That people made guesses that weren't true but wrote about them anyway.'

Sheridan looked uncomfortable.

'I don't mean you,' he said. 'I mean generally. That's why he got into it, in the end. I think he thought he could make papers more . . . more . . . oh, I don't know, ethical maybe?'

'The *City Scope* was a very ethical paper to work for.' Once again, Sheridan couldn't help springing to the defence of her former employers.

'Maybe that's why he bought into it. Anyway, that was the start of him branching into media. And that's what made him a bit more high profile for a time. His other businesses, the packaging companies, had always done well, but packaging isn't as exciting as TV or radio. Nobody noticed him very much back then.'

'I guess not.'

'So that's the story of Paudie O'Malley, my dad,' said Peter. 'It's hardly going to launch you into a career of business journalism. Nor will rehashing Mum's death do anything for you on the investigative side.'

'I'm honoured you told me,' said Sheridan. 'And I'm sorry if I offended you all. I was thoughtless and insensitive.'

'Nothing offends me,' Peter told her cheerfully. 'And no need to worry about the rest of the family. Eventually I managed to persuade Dad that the idea of you masquerading as a taxi driver was funny.'

'I didn't . . .' Sheridan was going to say, once again, that she hadn't masqueraded as a taxi driver. But her attention had been distracted by the woman who had just walked into the bar. Ritz Boland had left her ugly schnauzer at home. She was accompanied by a man instead.

And that man was Peter's brother, Joe.

Chapter 25

Joe saw Sheridan straight away. She was unmissable with her cloud of vibrant red hair framing her face, and his heart skipped a beat as she glanced in his direction. He wasn't exactly sure why his heart should be skipping beats because of her. She wasn't glamorous or elegant like Ritz. Nor was she model-thin like so many girls he'd dated – although that was a point in her favour, really, because Joe disliked excessively skinny women. She didn't fawn over him, an occupational hazard he sometimes encountered when a woman he met realised he was part of the O'Malley family. Well, no chance of her fawning, he supposed, since Sheridan Gray despised everything to do with the O'Malley family, thanks to his father's investment in the *City Scope*. When she'd told him how she felt, Joe had some sympathy for her point of view, but he couldn't help thinking that she was being irrational about it. However, after she'd abandoned him in the restaurant, he'd conceded that he too would have harboured irrational feelings of anger and resentment if he'd lost his job in similar circumstances.

Perhaps, he thought, it would be good to go and speak to her. Clear the air between them. Perhaps even start again.

Surely it would be possible to put the whole job issue behind them? After all, it was partly thanks to his father's support of the *Central News* that she had a job now!

But even as he was preparing what he might say to her, he felt Ritz Boland take his arm. He couldn't abandon Ritz. And then he realised that there would be no point in abandoning her anyway. Because Sheridan Gray was sitting opposite his younger brother and smiling at something he'd just said.

'Anyway, if all else fails, you can still become a taxi driver,' Peter was telling Sheridan. 'Is everything OK?' he added, realising she wasn't listening to him.

'Oh, fine, fine.' She turned to him and smiled. 'Sorry, lost the thread of what you were saying. Or maybe it's just that I can't imagine myself as anything other than a journalist.'

'Right.' Peter looked at her curiously for a moment, but she was sipping her beer and her attention was fixed on the TV behind the bar, which was screening a Formula 1 race.

'I've never gone out with a girl who was more into sports than me,' he observed.

'I thought you'd be interested in motor racing,' she said, her eyes following the on-screen action.

'I am,' he said. 'I just never imagined you'd be too.'

What the hell was Sheridan doing with his feckless brother? wondered Joe, as he watched them covertly. How on earth had she ended up in the bar with him?

Joe always called Peter feckless, even though he knew he was being unfair. But Peter's life had been based on doing what he wanted when he wanted, and the rows that his

366

headstrong, self-centred nature caused had sometimes stressed Joe to breaking point. When he was in a forgiving mood, he put it all down to the trauma of the day their mother had died; to them being rushed to Peggy Merchant's home and shielded from what had gone on, and Peter getting more and more upset about being dragged away from the party, where he'd been having a good time and had been the centre of attention doing magic tricks for his friends. He'd demanded to know why he had to stop, saying that he wasn't leaving until she gave him a good reason. In fact they all wanted to know what was happening, but Peggy had simply said that their father would come and get them shortly and that they were to wait with her until then. Typically Peter had given in quite suddenly, shrugged his shoulders and said that he'd go if he could bring some birthday cake with him. Which had meant that Sharon Forbes, whose birthday it was, had to cut the cake before blowing out the candles. Joe had always felt sorry for Sharon, who'd had her birthday hijacked by his mother's tragedy.

When they'd got to Peggy's, Peter, Sinead and Cushla had gone to the stables with Peggy's daughter, Tina, who'd taken their minds off things by asking them to help her groom the horses. Joe had told Peggy that he'd join them shortly, but as soon as she was distracted by an incoming phone call, he'd walked out of the house, through the fields and across the road until he was back home.

There was a lot of activity outside the house. An ambulance and two garda cars, their blue lights still flashing, were parked directly outside the front door. He could see his father standing on the steps, a garda beside him. There was a huddle of people around a shape on the ground. Joe felt the metallic taste of fear in his mouth. He walked across the garden until one of the gardai saw him and stopped him.

'He's my son,' said Paudie, when they tried to turn Joe away. 'Leave him alone.'

'What's happened, Dad?' Joe remembered how difficult it was for him to speak. It must have been equally difficult for Paudie to say anything, because he just kept shaking his head, his eyes unfocused. Then he reached out and pulled his son close to him. That frightened Joe more than anything, because Paudie wasn't a demonstrative man. It had always been Elva who'd kissed them and hugged them and wiped away their tears. Paudie was gruff and dismissive and would tell them (the girls included) not to be crybabies. But he was crying now, Joe realised with shock. He could feel his father's body shaking as he told him that Elva had had an accident.

The sequence of events after that was hazy in his mind, but he knew that his mother was dead. He'd known from the moment he'd seen the broken shape on the gravel that he was looking at a dead body.

The gardai spent a lot of time at the scene. They talked to Paudie and to the gardener, who'd turned up shortly after Elva's body had been discovered. And they talked to Joe himself, although not until Paudie's solicitor had arrived. Joe worried that Ger Ruane's arrival meant his father thought he had something to do with Elva's death, but Paudie said that he was only a kid and that he wasn't going to let the guards mislead him into saying the wrong thing.

'I'm not a child,' Joe protested. 'And there's no right or wrong thing to say.'

He'd been mistaken about that. When it came to an

unexpected death, he realised that there was always a right and a wrong thing to say. The guards had questioned him about everything. About his mother's state of mind. His father's. The relationship between Elva and her children. How he personally got on with her. It had all been traumatising, and he realised then why Paudie had wanted the children kept at Peggy's and out of the way of people who claimed to be sympathetic but who seemed to regard every word he spoke as a potential lie.

But they must have believed him, because in the end, Elva's death was found to be misadventure, a tragic accident. The fact that she'd consumed alcohol that day was mentioned, but not as a contributing factor. And nothing at all was said about the monumental row that she and his father had had the previous night – the one in which Joe had heard her yelling at Paudie that one day she'd kill him, and Paudie retorting angrily, 'Not if I kill you first.'

Joe had never told the police about the row. And he'd never told his father that he'd heard it either.

Sheridan didn't let her eyes stray to the alcove where Joe and Ritz were sitting. She focused her entire attention on the Formula 1 race and Peter's current work with the motorsports team. But all the time she was listening to him talk about the excitement of the Nürburgring, she was wondering why Joe was here with Ritz and what exactly the relationship between them was. It had been evident at the hotel that Ritz was attracted to Joe. It was impossible she thought, as she allowed herself a very quick glance at the spa manager, that he wouldn't be attracted to her too. She contrasted Ritz's sleek good looks and on-trend clothes (she was wearing a

purple knitted dress that clung to her enviable figure) with
her own appearance every time Joe saw her – windswept at
Josh's football match, tousled after her freebie at the spa and
rain soaked after covering the school story – and she knew
that there was no comparison. Ritz won the glamour stakes
hands down. Then she reminded herself that there was no
point in even thinking about competition between them,
because Joe thought she was a snooping journalist and she'd
run away and left him sitting on his own in a restaurant.

So, she told herself, there's no chance of him wanting to
know me socially any more, even if I somehow found a
glamorous version of myself to turn into. Which I've never
wanted to do for a man before and I'm not going to do now
either. I'm not that kind of person. I never will be.

'Will we join Shimmy and the gang?' It occurred to her
as she asked Peter this that it would be a good way of getting
out of Joe's sight. It would also (hopefully) prevent Peter
from noticing his brother and calling him over or something
equally embarrassing.

Peter agreed, and they moved to the end of the bar, where
they could neither see nor be seen by people nearer the door.
Peter hadn't spotted Joe as they'd moved and Sheridan
allowed herself to exhale again.

She realised, as he started talking to Shimmy and his
pals, that Peter was the kind of person who got on with
everyone. He fitted right in, laughing and joking with the
men, telling them stories about bike races, listening to their
own sporting tales and arguing passionately (as the men of
Ardbawn always did) about the local hurling team. He was
easy to get to know. Easy to like. He was, in fact, her ideal
guy. Sporty. Uncomplicated. Fun. So much better for her

than someone who sent shivers up her spine and turned her legs to jelly.

Sheridan was drawn into the conversation with the girls. Laura complained that she hadn't yet dropped into the shop, and Sheridan apologised, saying that she'd been very busy.

'Of course you were there at the Great Siege of St Raphaela's, weren't you?' asked Roisin. 'In fact, according to the *Central News*, you were the one who suggested that Charlie Sweetman climb the tree and bring Conall Brophy down. The heroine of the hour!'

Sheridan laughed. 'I'm sure they would've thought of it themselves,' she said. 'It was the obvious route to the roof.'

'Perhaps, but this way DJ got the chance to say what great staff the paper has,' Roisin said.

'True.'

'And good news for Mr Brophy and his wife, too,' added Laura.

'Not entirely,' protested Sheridan. 'He was arrested.'

'That's not what I meant,' said Laura. 'Lorraine was in the shop yesterday. She said that Conall's been offered a job since the incident.'

'That's fantastic.' Sheridan was pleased for him and for Lorraine.

'Yes, apparently JJ O'Malley got in touch with him and told him that there was a temporary job in the Carlow plant if he was interested.'

'Oh.' Sheridan glanced involuntarily towards the alcove where Joe and Ritz were sitting, even though she knew she wouldn't be able to see them. When had JJ spoken to Conall? Why? Because she'd talked about it? Hardly. And yet . . .

'Nice guy, JJ,' said Roisin. 'He's around the offices quite a lot and he's always friendly. I heard . . .' she looked inquisitively at Sheridan, glanced at Peter and then lowered her voice, 'that you and he were spotted at the Riverview last week.'

'That was nothing,' said Sheridan, although she was sure that her face was a fiery red. 'Interview stuff, that's all.' She kicked herself mentally as she spoke. If her comment somehow got back to Joe, he'd think that he was right about her being with him to snoop on his father.

'Shame.' Laura's eyes twinkled wickedly. 'We were just saying earlier that you were doing a great job of playing one O'Malley boy against the other.'

'That's *so* not what's happening.' Sheridan's expression was hunted.

Roisin chuckled. 'Wouldn't be at all bad for them,' she said. 'Well, not bad for Peter, anyhow. He was desperate when he was younger. Chased everything in a skirt. But you can't help liking him.'

'Roisin!' Laura made a face at her.

'Well he did,' said Roisin. 'You. Me. Myra. Jasmine.'

'Holy Mother of God!' exclaimed Sheridan.

'He was – still is – a good-looking guy,' said Laura defensively. 'With a tragic background. Plus, of course, the family was loaded. Made him irresistible.'

'Peter more than Joe?' asked Sheridan.

'What d'you think?' asked Roisin in return. 'You've been out with both of them.'

'Not out.' Sheridan's expression was embarrassed. 'Not the way you mean.'

The two girls looked at her teasingly, and Peter glanced over at them.

'Hope you're not telling tales,' he called.

'Would we?' Laura grinned.

'Peter was way more irresistible than Joe when we were younger,' she told Sheridan. 'He was nearer our ages for starters. I know it doesn't matter now, but four years is a lot when you're a teenager. Plus he was always a bit of a rebel. Made him all the more interesting. He went the Goth route for a while – though that's when he was seeing Myra, so not entirely surprising. She embraces her inner Goth on a regular basis. He had an earring before anyone else too.'

'He's not wearing it now,' observed Sheridan.

'I guess some men grow out of earrings. It looked good on him, though.'

'And Joe wasn't a rebel?'

'Not really,' said Laura. 'He was a nice enough guy, but there wasn't the same whiff of danger about him as there was about Peter. And, like I said, he was that bit older. He sort of looked down on us.'

'He was kind of stand-offish,' Roisin agreed. 'Though some people said that he was shy. Can't see that myself; he's pretty successful now, and you don't get that way by hiding your light.'

'Successful in his dad's company,' Laura reminded her.

'Sure, but he still has to know what he's doing, doesn't he. And he did give the job to Conall.'

Sheridan decided to meet Lorraine Brophy again and ask her about Conall's job. It would be a good-news story for the paper, and DJ liked good news. Especially, she reckoned, when it was courtesy of the O'Malley empire.

An hour later, Sheridan decided it was time for her to leave. On one level she'd had a good time with Peter, especially after meeting Shimmy and his friends again too, but ever since Joe and Ritz had walked in, she'd felt on edge. She'd kept sneaking looks in their direction, even though they were hidden from her view. She couldn't help thinking that she was behaving like a sixteen year old with a crush. She hadn't had a crush on anyone when she was sixteen, but she remembered how giggly and silly the girls in school had been over boys they fancied, and she was feeling, if not giggly, certainly a bit silly now. She reminded herself that a crush was a short-lived, intense sort of thing and that she'd get over it. Although she remembered that one of her school friends, Karen Matthews, had spend an entire year swooning over Pierce Mooney, a boy in the year ahead of them, who'd never even noticed she existed.

I won't spend a year obsessing about Joe O'Malley, she told herself. I won't be in Ardbawn long enough for that. Besides, Joe isn't around all the time either, what with his trips to Dubai and looking after different parts of the great Paudie O'Malley conglomerate.

'You surely don't want to leave now?' Peter was saying. 'It's just getting interesting.'

Sheridan told him that she was sorry, she was really tired and wanted to go home, but that he was perfectly free to stay until closing time if he wanted.

'Ah, no. I'll head off with you. I could probably do with an early night.'

It wasn't all that early, thought Sheridan, but it was the weekend, and she supposed she was being a bit of a party-pooper. However, she just couldn't stay in the pub, worrying about being spotted by Joe, any longer. She hoped that Peter would remain unaware of his brother's presence as she ushered him out, keeping her face averted from the corner where she knew he and Ritz were sitting, but Peter spotted them immediately and waved at them.

'Hi, bro!'

'Hello.' Joe raised a hand in greeting, and Ritz Boland smiled in acknowledgement.

'Didn't see you here earlier,' said Peter as he walked over to them.

'We arrived after you,' Joe told him.

'You mean you saw me and didn't bother to say hello?' There was an amused undercurrent to Peter's voice.

'I saw Sheridan,' said Joe.

'You never said.' Peter turned accusingly towards Sheridan, though his eyes were twinkling.

'I didn't notice them,' she lied, knowing that her face was flaming red again.

'Ritz, you're looking great as always,' Peter said. 'You get hotter every year.'

'Flattery will get you everywhere,' she told him with a grin. 'How's things? I heard you were back in town.'

'Flying visit.'

Ritz glanced at Sheridan. 'Is he introducing you to anyone who's anyone in the town?'

'Oh, I think I've met all the important people already,' Sheridan replied, hoping her face had calmed down. 'How did the advertorial work for you? Were you happy with it?'

'Business is booming,' said Ritz. 'So I guess it was worth it.'

'I'm glad to hear it.' Sheridan turned to Peter. 'I've got to go.'

'Off to cover another major scoop?' asked Ritz. 'I believe

you were in the thick of it when that loony tried to burn down St Raphaela's.'

'I was there,' said Sheridan, who noticed that Joe's jaw had tightened at Ritz's words. 'He was just a very distressed man.'

'I get very distressed from time to time, but I don't stand on rooftops and threaten to blow the world to hell,' said Ritz.

'It ended up OK,' Sheridan said. 'Which is the main thing. And –' she turned to Joe – 'I believe he's got a job in one of your father's plants. That was really good of you . . . of him.'

Ritz turned to look at Joe too.

'Are you being a bit of a bleeding heart again?' she asked.

'Of course not,' said Joe. 'The man needed a job, and we needed someone to do it.'

'C'mon, Sheridan,' said Peter. 'Given that you were foolish enough to drive, you can drop me home.' He put his arm around her shoulder. 'See you later, bro. Ritz.'

'My car's over here,' said Sheridan.

She unlocked the Beetle, and Peter got into the passenger seat.

'So,' he said as she put it into gear. 'What's the real story with you and Joe?'

'I told you.'

'You told me you'd left him sitting alone in a restaurant. You didn't say anything about the electricity.'

'What electricity?'

'Between the two of you,' said Peter. 'Definite electricity.'

'Don't be silly.'

'I'm a man!' he cried. 'And even I felt it. Both of you crackling at each other. Communicating without saying a word.'

She shook her head. 'We weren't communicating at all.'

'My brother is one of the good guys,' Peter told her, his voice suddenly serious. 'Don't mess with him.'

'I promise you, there's no chance of that.'

Less than five minutes later, she pulled up outside the big double gates of March Manor.

'I don't have my zapper,' said Peter. 'But if you wait, I can key in the number and you can drive up. Come in for coffee.'

'I don't think I'd be very welcome in your house,' said Sheridan.

'Sinead isn't home,' Peter told her. 'She was only here the day you called because Josh was having a sleepover while she went to a fund-raiser. So she's back in her own house tonight. Dad isn't around either. Cushla is in London. And you know where Joe is.'

'I'm not coming in, thank you all the same,' said Sheridan.

'Sorry, you're probably getting the wrong impression because I'm pointing out we'd be alone together,' said Peter. 'I'm not going to try anything on with you, honestly. There wouldn't be any point anyway. Not now that I know about you and Joe.'

'There's nothing . . .'

'In that case, what are the chances of you and me?' asked Peter.

She stared at him and he grinned.

'I had hopes,' he said. 'You seemed to be my sort of girl. But you're not. You're Joe's.'

'I really don't think so.'

'D'you want to be?' asked Peter.

Sheridan said nothing.

'I hope it works out,' Peter said. 'And you don't have to worry about me. I'm heading back to the UK next week – just as well, otherwise I'd have to nurse my broken heart when my brother does something about you.'

'That's not going to happen.'

'He's difficult, is Joe,' Peter said. 'But worth it.'

'Look . . .'

'I'm absolutely certain he's not going out with Ritz Boland, in case that's what you think. Lovely girl, but definitely not Joe's type. Far too high maintenance for him. They've worked together once or twice on things for the Spring Festival and stuff like that. But there's no romantic entanglement.'

Maybe not as far as Joe's concerned, thought Sheridan. But it's different for Ritz.

'Your brother is a lovely man,' she told Peter. 'I like him. But I'm not going to be staying in Ardbawn for long myself either. When I met him for dinner, it was just for socialising. Like with you.'

'If you say so,' said Peter. 'Though I think it's very unfair of you to come down here from Dublin and try to win the hearts of two country boys.'

'Get over yourself.' Sheridan poked him gently in the side.

'Good night, Sheridan Gray,' said Peter. 'May all your dreams come true.'

'Good night, Peter O'Malley,' she said. 'See you around.'

Chapter 26

Joe liked his apartment in Dublin. It was in a block that had been built in the early seventies and looked dull from the outside, but the apartment itself was much bigger and brighter than many modern ones. It had a large living room, small kitchen, two generously sized bedrooms and a more than adequate bathroom. It was located on the Rock Road, convenient for the city centre but also close to the chi-chi towns of Blackrock and Dun Laoghaire. Although Joe had grown up in land-locked Ardbawn, he loved being near the sea in Dublin. It meant that he didn't feel as claustrophobic as he sometimes did in other cities, because being near the water allowed him a sense of space.

The only thing he'd change about the apartment, he thought, as he sat in the living room a few days after his evening in the Riverside Inn with Ritz Boland, was the fact that the Rock Road was always busy and the steady drone of traffic sometimes irritated him. He was more used to the stillness of Ardbawn, although it was fair to say that the silence of the countryside could just as easily be broken by the roar of a tractor as the sound of a songbird. And these days, of course, there was always traffic on the road past March Manor, because it led directly to the M9 motorway.

Everything about Ardbawn had changed hugely since his teenage years, not just the fact that he could get from March Manor to the apartment in less than an hour and a half. Ardbawn itself had evolved from a sleepy town where everyone knew each other to a thriving community with an influx of new residents, thanks to the new housing that had been built in the last ten years. Not everybody liked the housing estates, but most of the people who'd moved into them had settled well into the area and had brought new skills and a new outlook to the town. Some people mourned the passing of a place where nobody was a stranger, but it didn't bother Joe. He'd never entirely been comfortable with the fact that most of the people in the town knew as much about his family as he did.

Or at least they thought they did. Ardbawn had been a gossipy place sixteen years ago. It was still a gossipy place, but the conversations about people were far more superficial now than they'd been when he was younger. He remembered going into the local newsagent's with his mother as a child and the woman behind the counter wishing him a happy birthday even though he hadn't been wearing the 'I am 10' badge that had been attached to the card his parents had given him. He remembered too that the woman (Mrs Clancy, Mrs Clooney?) had looked outside and remarked that it was a great day for a wedding, and his mother nodding, while Mrs Clancy or Clooney had said that she never would have thought that Bernadine Doherty would've managed to nab Sean Fallon, God help her. He'd heard the sharp intake of breath from his mother before she'd replied that it took all sorts, and the woman behind the counter had nodded and said yes, and that Bernadine was a nice girl and she hoped she'd be happy with Sean. It was about time he settled down, she'd said; sure, hadn't he broken the hearts of half the town . . . and then she'd looked at his mother, narrowed her eyes and said, 'Sorry.' Elva had said that there was nothing for the woman to be sorry about, that it was a long, long time since she'd gone out with Sean Fallon. She'd been a foolish kid back then, she'd told her, and then laughed a brittle laugh that Joe had never heard before.

She'd bought him an ice cream in the newsagent's, even though before they'd gone in she'd said that he wasn't getting anything at all because he was having a party tea afterwards and she didn't want him to spoil his appetite. They'd walked back to March Manor, the ice cream melting over his hand in the warmth of the sun.

He hadn't thought about that in years. But now he remembered the party, where he'd had a fight with Peter, Sinead had taken his Biggles book to read and Cushla had nearly choked on a tube of Smarties. He shook his head. Normally when he remembered scenes from his childhood they were softened by the passage of time and he recalled them as happy and contented. But his memories of that day included Elva slapping him across the leg for punching Peter in the face (a provoked attack; Peter had broken the toy robot he'd been given), and yelling that being chained to four spoiled brats wasn't what she'd expected when she'd married his father. Marriage was a trap, she'd cried, designed to enslave women who were seduced by one day of looking like a princess and thinking that they'd be happy.

He'd been shocked at her words, and at the raw anger

381

and pain in her voice. He'd been frightened, too, frightened that she didn't love him any more, didn't love any of them. He'd wanted to fling his arms around her and tell her that he was sorry, but he'd been too scared to do anything other than sit down in the big armchair in the corner of the room.

She'd come up to him a moment later, her eyes bright, her voice soft.

'I'm sorry, love,' she'd said. 'I lost my temper. That was very wrong of me.'

'I shouldn't have been fighting.' It had been all he could do not to cry. He was the eldest, a big boy. Big boys didn't cry, everyone knew that.

'I'm sure your brother was driving you mad.'

'Like we drive you mad?'

She'd smiled then, although he couldn't help thinking it was a sad smile.

'Sooner or later everyone drives everyone else a bit mad,' she'd said. 'But we get over it.'

'Are you over it?'

'Of course I am.'

She'd put her arms around him and hugged him, and he'd stayed longer than was absolutely necessary in the comfort of her embrace. And then she'd told him that she'd better get on with things before his dad came home and she'd headed off to the kitchen, her high heels clicking on the tiled floor.

How had all this stayed stuck in his mind, unremembered for so long? he asked himself. Where had it been buried? Why hadn't he remembered before now?

He stared unseeingly out of the window as the images of his beautiful mother flickered through his mind. He hadn't remembered because it wasn't important any more, he decided. The past wasn't important. The only thing that mattered was the future.

Paudie said that. And his father was always right.

It was like old times, thought Sheridan, as she and Talia inspected themselves in the mirror before heading off for the nightclub. Both of them had glammed up for the night, and the pretty brooch that Talia had lent her for the lapel of her jacket was glittering beneath the ceiling light. It was ages since she'd looked as good as this. Clearly she missed Talia's influence. She vowed to take a bit more care over her appearance when she went back to Ardbawn. Just because she was living in the heart of the country didn't mean she had to let every single fashion trick she'd ever learned pass her by.

The party that Talia had invited her to was being sponsored by a new restaurant and nightclub in the city, and the owners wanted to get as much publicity as possible. The venue was being marketed as funky yet sophisticated, ideal for the modern, independent woman. Talia had told Sheridan that the magazine was using it as the backdrop to a piece about fashion in the city, and that the club was taking a chunk of advertising in an arrangement that suited everybody.

'The mag is very commercially focused,' she said. 'A bit of an eye-opener really, I thought it would be more laid-back But I guess the current environment has made everyone up their game.'

'They won't go the route of the *City Scope*, will they?'

'Hopefully not.' Talia sounded relaxed. 'It's a good team. I'm sorry that we're a fashion and beauty magazine and there isn't room for sports. You'd like working on it.'

'I'm sure I'll get something permanent soon.' Sheridan didn't want to talk about her precarious job situation at the start of a night out. 'Tell me about the club.'

'It's a converted courthouse,' said Talia. 'So the theme is very much legal-eagle sort of stuff. I think it's lovely, though.'

'Hey, I don't care what it is, I'm just glad to be out and about and away from Ardbawn.'

'Poor Sheridan.' Talia made a face at her. 'A city girl stuck in the sticks. Is it absolutely awful?'

'It's OK in small doses,' admitted Sheridan. 'There's parts of it that I like. But I don't think it's for me, to be honest.'

'You haven't fallen in love with village life and decided that the city is a horrible place and that everything is so much nicer when you know your neighbours?'

Sheridan laughed. 'I'm not a stressed-out executive who needs to embrace a slower pace to find the meaning of life,' she said. 'I like cities. And I like not knowing everything about everybody. Not that I do in Ardbawn – at least not yet – but you know what I mean.'

'Aunt Hayley said that you went to see her,' Talia remarked as she adjusted the brooch and then rearranged some loose strands of Sheridan's hair (which she'd put up for the night). 'She told me you were a nice girl who was fitting in well. She liked you.'

'Everyone in Ardbawn likes everyone else,' Sheridan said. 'It's all one big love-fest.'

'Not a hotbed of intrigue and mystery?' asked Talia.

'Apparently they all lead lives that are nearly as boring as mine,' said Sheridan drily.

'What about your complicated love life? Any more developments?'

Sheridan had rung Talia after the dinner with Joe had gone horribly wrong, and had called her too to tell her about seeing him with Ritz in the pub. Talia had been taken aback to hear that Sheridan herself had been there with Peter, and hadn't entirely believed her when she'd insisted that they were just friends, even though Sheridan had reminded her that she had more 'just friends' who were male than any woman she knew.

Now she shuddered. 'I'm staying away from anyone with the surname O'Malley.'

'Maybe you just have to pick the right O'Malley brother.'

'There *is* no right O'Malley brother.'

'All the same . . . I thought you and this Joe guy . . . When you talked about him, you sounded different.'

'How?'

'Excited.'

'Truth? I was excited about him when I didn't know who he was. Now that I do . . . let's face it, I'm never going to be a fan of the family, and they're certainly not fans of mine.'

'He could still be, though.'

'No. He couldn't. As far as he's concerned, I'm just a nosy journalist who'll print anything about his father and his family.'

'That's not true.'

'What if I suddenly found out that there was something dark and sinister about Elva's death, d'you think I'd be obliged to write it?'

'But you said there wasn't.'

'That's not the point. If there was, as a journalist, I think I would have to.'

'However since there isn't – you won't!'

'He doesn't know that.'

'Tell him.'

Sheridan shook her head.

'You're crazy,' said Talia. 'Can I remind you again that you went out and bought a dress for this guy.'

'I bought the dress for me.'

'You're impossible,' said Talia.

'I'm being realistic,' Sheridan told her. 'So can we drop it now? Please?'

'Fair enough.' Talia stood back and looked at her friend's appearance critically. 'Perfect, Cinders, you shall go to the ball. Although – given that you bought it for yourself – you should have worn the green dress tonight, it was stunning on you.'

'I didn't bring it with me. I was afraid I'd be overdressed.'

'We're going to a nightclub,' Talia reminded her. 'Overdressing is impossible.'

'Perhaps I've been embracing the countryside too much.'

'Hmm. Well, it might have affected your dress sense, but I have to say, Mizz Gray, there's a certain glow about you.'

'God knows why,' said Sheridan.

'Nothing like fresh air,' teased Talia. 'And maybe you're still in love with the country man.'

'Give it a rest,' said Sheridan.

'Whatever you say.' But Talia winked as she picked up the VIP passes and ushered her friend out of the door.

The nightclub was fun. They drank cocktails, chatted to a variety of people and then danced until Talia confessed that her stylish skyscraper shoes weren't built for anything other than sitting on a bar stool looking fabulous, and that her feet were killing her. It was exactly like old times, thought Sheridan, even if the times in the clubs had been few and far between. But it was good to be out with her friend, and good to feel that she was still part of something bigger and brighter than Ardbawn town and the *Central News*.

Her head was throbbing the next morning, although she thought it was more from the noise of the club than alcohol – she'd only had three glasses of champagne, after all. Her eyes were gritty, too, as she made enough tea and toast for her and her friend. She stood at the window of the apartment with its view across the city while she waited for the tea to brew. She'd enjoyed herself the previous night and she knew that no matter what happened with her career, she wouldn't be staying in Ardbawn longer than was strictly necessary. A place where the only decent social outlets were the Riverside Inn and the Riverview Hotel just didn't have enough long-term appeal for her.

Not, of course, that she'd have the opportunity to stay longer. Although she hadn't given an exact date for her return, Myra was very definitely coming back to the *Central News* before the summer.

Which means, Sheridan told herself as she switched her gaze to the mountains that ringed the city, I need to get my act together on the job front again. She was wondering if there was any newspaper in the country that she hadn't already contacted about work when Talia padded sleepily into the room.

'Ooh, buttery toast. Lovely.' She yawned as she picked up a slice. 'I miss having you around, Sher. Enya's great, but it's not the same.'

Enya was Talia's new flatmate. She was originally from Mayo, and went home most weekends.

'I miss Kilmainham,' said Sheridan. 'We had such good times there. And I miss the *City Scope* too.'

'I believe things aren't going great there at the moment,' said Talia as she poured herself some tea from the big red pot. 'There's talk of letting more people go.'

'Oh no. What about Mr Slash-and-Burn's success rate in rescuing failing businesses?'

'I don't think he can save the paper,' Talia said. 'You know yourself it wasn't the world's most efficient place to work.'

'The journalists were efficient,' Sheridan protested. 'Whatever other problems they had weren't our fault. I was thinking about it earlier,' she added. 'When I was wondering who I could apply to for a job. I was thinking that maybe I should become a blogger instead.'

'But you wouldn't make any money out of it.'

'It would just be for something to do. And if it became really successful, I might pick up some ads. It's better than nothing. Anyway, I've been looking at the sports blogs. I know I could do better.'

'I guess it would keep your name out there at least.' Talia nodded her approval. 'Especially if you were tweeting and Facebooking as well.'

'Right now the *Central News* is keeping me occupied,' said Sheridan. 'But sports is what I love doing and what I ultimately want to concentrate on. So this would be a good way of staying involved.'

'Go for it.' Talia spoke positively. 'Start off with the tweeting; you can get up and running with that really quickly.

I'm glad you're looking at different options. You just have to have an open mind.'

Sheridan stared at her friend.

'What?' asked Talia.

'That's what I wrote for my horoscope this week,' she said. 'That I needed an open mind.'

Talia laughed. 'Maybe you're sending yourself subliminal messages.'

'Maybe.'

'In which case, keep that mind wide open. To job opportunities and other opportunities too.'

'Blogger heaven,' said Sheridan.

'I was thinking of *romantic* opportunities,' Talia said. 'Given that you didn't meet Mr Right last night, perhaps you'll have to give Paudie's son another chance.'

'He'd be the one giving me another chance, but I can't see it somehow,' said Sheridan.

Talia grinned at her. 'Maybe he's keeping an open mind too.'

'I shouldn't have said anything to you about it,' groaned Sheridan.

'What did you predict for Virgos?' asked Talia. 'Given that you seem to have a talent for this.'

'That everything you do will turn out exactly as you hope.'

'Crikey. I'd better get my act together this week.'

'You won't need to,' Sheridan assured her. 'Phaedra, the oracle, has spoken. You're tipped for the top whether you like it or not.'

'So are you,' Talia said. 'You're a winner at heart, Sheridan Gray. You know you are.'

Chapter 27

Nina was reading the *Central News* as she waited in the bar of Dublin's Shelbourne Hotel for Sean to arrive. She'd only skimmed the paper earlier in the week because, thankfully, the guesthouse was exceptionally busy, due to people arriving for a golden wedding anniversary party in the town. Pat and Stan Buchan's extended family was too big to stay in the house with them. Nina was delighted to have them stay with her, especially as they'd booked in not only for the night of the party itself but for a couple of days afterwards too.

Having every room occupied reminded her of why she enjoyed running a guesthouse. She didn't mind the fact that she was up early to make a cooked breakfast every morning, or that she was constantly stacking and unloading the dishwasher. She realised that, for the first time since he'd left, her thoughts weren't continually straying back to Sean. Nor was she agonising over what her next step should be. She was too busy grilling sausages and bacon, clearing tables and generally looking after people to think of anything else.

All in all, she was doing much better now, and certainly felt more able to deal with her cheating husband than she'd been even a few weeks earlier. But no matter how much she told herself to be strong and unyielding, she couldn't quite get over the fact that she still missed him very, very much.

'Hi, Nina.'

He walked into the bar looking as handsome and as confident as ever. She wondered how men did that. How it was that they never appeared shaken or worried or insecure, no matter how appropriate those emotions might be. She knew that if their roles had been reversed, she would have slunk into the room, her guilty expression plain for all to see.

He sat down beside her.

'Nice to see you in town for a change,' he said. 'And looking so well.'

She heard the slight tone of surprise in his voice. She knew she was looking better than the last time he'd seen her. She'd had her hair done at the weekend and had asked Danielle to update her colour and style. The more subtle shade and added highlights suited her.

'You look well yourself,' she told him.

'Thanks. Can I get you anything?'

'Another coffee,' she said.

Sean ordered two coffees and then relaxed back into the seat.

'So, when will I come back?'

She stared at him. There was no doubt in his mind that she'd forgiven him and was ready to allow him home. Why? Did he think she was so weak that she couldn't cope without him?

'I don't know,' she said.

'For heaven's sake, Nina! What's the point in us meeting if I'm not coming home?' His voice was harsh.

'I . . .' Her original reason for meeting him had been to tell him that she was ready for him to return. But when he made that assumption, when he'd already decided for her, she just couldn't. 'I needed to talk to you again,' she said. 'The last time was unexpected. I didn't know what I wanted to say.'

'What d'you need to say? You know I made a mistake, I've admitted it, I'm sorry about it. I'm sorry that I embarrassed you and our children. I know I was in the wrong.'

'It's not that. It's just . . . I don't want to be overwhelmed by you, Sean.'

'What on earth are you talking about?'

'That's what you do,' said Nina. 'You take people over. You get into their heads and their lives and you make them think that they're the most important person in the world to you. And then you move on, and they're not.'

'You're talking absolute bullshit,' said Sean. 'I didn't do that to you, Nina. You've always been a strong person, with or without me.'

'Maybe I'm stronger without you.'

He stared at her. 'You can't mean that.'

'I used not to think so. But now . . . I feel like we were living a lie before. That the only reason you were with me was because you and your dad thought it was a good idea. There was the house, after all, and—'

'Oh my God, you're not banging that old drum again, are you? It's a long, long time since you thought I married you for some bricks and mortar.'

'It felt like it when I got your solicitor's letter,' she told him. 'The one where you said you wanted to come back or you wanted your share.'

'I told you, I needed to send you something to make you think.'

'What it made me think was that the house mattered more to you than I did.'

'That's not true, Nina,' said Sean. 'It isn't. You're the constant thing in my life. The person who matters to me the most.'

'Am I?'

He looked at her warily. 'What are you up to?'

'Nothing,' she said. 'Absolutely nothing. I just want to be sure that whatever choice I make, it's for the right reason.'

'There is only one choice, Nina. You and me. We're a team. We always have been, no matter what.'

They sat in silence for a moment. A group of people came into the bar. To her surprise, Nina recognised JJ O'Malley among them. His tall frame towered over the others, reminding her of Paudie. Now there was a man with real inner strength, she thought. After Elva's death he had been a rock for his children. And he'd lived his life in a focused way ever since.

She wondered if he was happy.

She wondered how easy he found it to forgive.

Sheridan was hyperventilating. She was telling herself to stay calm, but she was finding it difficult, because the deadline for getting the paper to the printer was drawing closer and closer, and she was on her own in the office, trying to get everything done. The reason she was alone was that DJ and Shimmy had both called in unwell that day.

Shimmy had phoned first, a couple of minutes after nine, telling her that he had some kind of bug and had been sick all night. He shared some graphic descriptions of how ill he'd been, until she told him to stop, that she believed him. He said that everything was up to date and she didn't need to worry because DJ knew what needed to be done, but that he simply couldn't come in, he was as weak as a kitten and had a blinding headache. Sheridan assured him that she wasn't a bit worried and that he should look after himself. Then she'd got on with her own work and waited for DJ to arrive. It had been half an hour later when he'd called, with the exact same symptoms as Shimmy. She knew that they'd both been in Kilkenny the previous evening, meeting with an IT expert (something to do with their website hosting, the details of which had completely passed her by), and at first she thought that they must have been on the total lash and were both suffering from alcohol poisoning, but DJ assured her that he'd only had a couple of pints.

'We were a bit silly,' he conceded groggily. 'We got spice burgers on the way home. I should know better, I always get sick after spice burgers. Fortunately Shimmy has a cast-iron stomach and can eat anything.'

She didn't tell him that Shimmy hadn't come in either, and that he'd sounded even worse than DJ himself on the phone. There was no point in the editor getting stressed about the newspaper as well as being ill. So she said the same as she'd said to Shimmy, that she hoped he'd feel better soon and that he should take care of himself, then she applied herself to getting the paper ready.

She'd been quietly confident, because although she hadn't had to do it all before, she understood the processes now. It wasn't complicated. But it was all taking so much more time than she'd expected, and for some inexplicable reason the phone kept ringing, with people wanting to give information about local events or ask questions about placing small ads for the weekend's edition. Usually the small ads were all done by email, and she couldn't understand why the one day that she didn't have time to talk, so many of Ardbawn's residents seemed to want to chat instead of simply getting on with things.

She was rearranging a page layout when the buzzer sounded. She groaned softly.

'I'm here to see DJ.' The voice through the speaker was brusque.

It was easier to buzz the visitor in than try to explain over the intercom where her boss was. Besides, in the few seconds it took him to come up the stairs, she managed to drag an article to the correct place on the page and anchor it there.

She looked up as the door opened. She recognised the man immediately, even though he was older and his hair was greyer than she'd expected. But there was no mistaking the tall, well-built frame, or the blue eyes in the slightly weathered face. She felt her stomach lurch.

'Paudie O'Malley,' he said. 'Where's DJ?'

She'd often thought about how she'd feel if and when she came face to face with Mr Slash-and-Burn. Angry, she thought. Resentful. Perhaps slightly intimidated. Right now, although she felt all of those things, her overriding emotion was annoyance that he was interrupting her when she was so busy.

'Not here,' she said succinctly. 'Off sick.'

'Today?' Paudie's eyes darkened. 'When the paper is going to press?'

'Yeah, well, a dodgy spice burger holds no respect for deadlines,' said Sheridan.

'Spice burger?' Paudie looked appalled. Sheridan supposed that the millionaire businessman wouldn't be seen dead in a chipper getting a greasy burger and chips. Paudie O'Malley was more of your fine-dining sort of person.

'Him and Shimmy both,' she said.

'Seamus is off too? You're here on your own?' This time he sounded horrified.

'I can cope,' she said. 'Once I don't have to spend too much time on things that don't matter.'

'Like talking to me?' asked Paudie.

Sheridan felt her face redden. She hadn't meant to sound rude or stroppy, but she knew she must have.

'I'm sorry,' she said, suddenly nervous again. 'It's been a busy day.'

'I understand. So . . . you're Sheridan Gray?'

'Yes.'

'We meet at last.' His tone was dry, and she knew she was still blushing.

'Um . . . yes. Nice to meet you.' The lie was blatant. She would've preferred to meet Paudie O'Malley at a time of her choosing, and when she wasn't sweating buckets over meeting impossible deadlines.

'Are you sure you know what you're doing?' he asked.

'Of course.'

He drummed his fingers on the edge of the desk.

She couldn't concentrate with him standing there, his blue eyes boring into her. She wondered if he was going to lay into her about her supposed taxi-driver impersonation. She didn't have time for all that right now.

'Do you need help?' His tone was slightly less abrupt than previously.

'I think I can manage.'

'Would you prefer it if I wasn't here?'

She winced. Was she making her feelings that obvious?

'I don't know,' she replied. 'If you've been involved in getting it all together, maybe there's something you can do. But if not . . . well, I don't have the time to explain stuff.' She managed to stop herself adding that she wasn't entirely sure that she didn't need someone explaining it to her again too. She'd thought about ringing Myra, but she hadn't wanted to drag her away from Genevieve. Besides, there was a part of her that relished the challenge. Even if it was stressing her out completely.

'I'll leave you to it,' said Paudie. 'But I'll call them at the printing works. Tell them that there might be a delay on the files.'

'There won't be,' said Sheridan.

'Never make impossible promises,' advised Paudie. 'Give yourself a bit of leeway. Allow me to say that things might be a little later than usual.'

That didn't sound very Slash-and-Burn to her. She glanced at him. His eyes had softened and he was looking at her thoughtfully.

'I can manage,' she repeated.

'I don't want you just to manage,' he said. 'I want everything to be as perfect as it always is.'

'OK, then. Maybe an extra hour. Or two.'

'Sure,' said Paudie.

'Thanks.'

'I'll see you later, then,' he said.

'Today?' She couldn't help sounding appalled. She didn't want to see Paudie O'Malley again. He'd be sure to want to talk about her incursion into his home, and God only knew what else.

'Depends on how well you get on,' he said, which made her feel even more appalled. Would he throw a complete wobbler if she didn't manage to get the paper to bed in time? Was he testing her? And then the horrible thought – were they all testing her? Was the spice-burger story a complete fabrication? Were they putting her under pressure for no apparent reason . . . did they want her to fail?

I won't fail, she told herself, as she dragged and dropped another article into the right place. I absolutely won't. And this is going to be a great edition of the *Central News*. She grimaced as she turned her attention to the horoscopes. She'd finished them that morning. She'd instructed Leos not to hold back. Which meant, she thought, that she should be a bit firmer with Mr Slash-and-Burn. She looked up from the desk.

But he'd already gone.

Chapter 28

It was the strident ringing of her mobile phone that eventually woke Sheridan the following morning. It took her a few seconds to find it, underneath the bed where it had somehow ended up the previous night. Despite her optimism, the newspaper file had been over an hour late in reaching the printer, and by the time she'd left the office she was tense and drained. She'd kept an eye out for Paudie O'Malley but hadn't seen him, and so she'd hurried into her car and back to the studio as quickly as possible. She realised, as soon as she got home, that she was absolutely ravenous, so she'd called the local Chinese takeaway, which had delivered an enormous portion of kung-po chicken and rice. She ate in front of the TV, watching an episode of *CSI: Miami*, still vaguely anxious about the paper and hoping that she hadn't made some mind-blowing mistake that would only be revealed when it hit the news-stands. She'd washed the food down with a can of beer, thinking that a late-night takeaway plus beer plus telly had turned her into a clichéd sports journalist. But the most important thing, she'd told herself, was that she'd got the job done. The *Central News* would be in the shops the following day. She'd been thrown in at the deep end and she'd survived.

She spent the rest of the evening with her feet up, treating herself to another beer, which had the effect of making her so sleepy that she crawled into bed without bothering to tidy away the empty cans and dirty plates.

It had given her a bit of a hangover too, she thought as she finally answered the phone, yawning.

'Hi, Sheridan, it's me.'

'DJ, how's it going?' She hauled herself into an upright position and looked at her watch. No wonder I'm still feeling ropey she thought. It's only eight o'clock in the morning.

'I heard you were on your own yesterday,' said DJ. 'That plonker Shimmy never turned up.'

'No more a plonker than you,' she retorted. 'Honest to God, DJ. Spice burgers. Have you no bloody sense?'

'I like spice burgers,' he said defensively.

'Yeah, well, they didn't do either of you much good. Anyway, Shimmy called in first, so he was perfectly entitled to stay off. He said he was sick as a dog. Sounded it too.'

'I wasn't much better myself,' admitted DJ. 'Listen, pet, I'm sorry that you were stuck on your own like that, today of all days. I can't believe you got everything done.'

'It wasn't that hard,' she said. 'We had most of the articles ready. It was just layout.'

'You've never done that before.'

'I know how to do it, though,' she said. 'Let's face it, anyone can pull a paper together with the right computer program. I was just worried I'd make a complete hash of it. I might have yet,' she added. 'I haven't seen the finished product.'

'I have,' said DJ. 'Paudie brought it round to me this morning.'

Paudie! What had he said about her?

'He thought you did a fantastic job,' DJ told her, as though she'd spoken out loud. 'He said that when he called into the office you had your head down and were working full steam ahead.'

'Mainly because of all the small ads,' she told him. 'I know how you feel about the advertising revenue, so I had to make room for them.'

DJ laughed. 'You've become quite the corporate mogul, worrying about revenue!'

'Oh well.' She massaged the back of her neck. 'The bottom line is important.'

'Anyway, I'm just ringing to say well done, and thanks for not cracking up or walking out.'

'Why would I do that?' she asked, truly surprised. 'It's my job.'

DJ's silence reminded her that it wasn't really. She was still only a temp, no matter how well she'd done. And the truth was that Myra probably would've coped just as well, if not better. The chances were she wouldn't have missed the deadline and had the printing press working late as a result. Sheridan suddenly wondered if Paudie had had to pay overtime to the printers. And if her edition of the paper (she couldn't help thinking of it as hers) had ultimately cost more money than it would bring in.

Not my problem, she muttered to herself after DJ had congratulated her again before hanging up. I did what I had to do. And from my perspective it worked out OK.

She was a couple of minutes out of the shower when the

phone rang again. This time it was Shimmy telling her that she'd done a great job and that DJ had already been on to him singing her praises. Sheridan couldn't help smiling. She'd been silly to worry about the printers' overtime. All that mattered was that the paper was out on time. And it was.

She was feeling so energised after Shimmy's call that, after she'd tidied up, she decided to go for a run. It shocked her to think that she'd taken so little exercise since coming to Ardbawn, but the truth was her heart hadn't been in it, and anyhow she was more used to running on city streets than country roads. But this morning, her hangover washed away by her shower, she felt ready to get out there again.

She pulled on her leggings and her fleece and laced up her running shoes. Then she stepped outside into a morning that was bright and clear. She knew that the chill that was still in the air would eventually dissipate. She stretched a few times, then began to run down the driveway, her stride easy and even and her breathing calm and controlled.

She avoided the main turn for Ardbawn and continued to follow the twisty, winding road as it crossed the countryside. There was very little traffic, and the only sound she heard, apart from her own breathing, was the continual chirping of the birds.

I could get to like this, she thought. I could get to like Ardbawn. In fact I do like Ardbawn, although I'm still not sure I could live here my whole life. But there's something very relaxing about being able to run through the country all on my own.

After nearly ten kilometres she was tiring rapidly. She put it down to the beer and the Chinese food as well as being out of condition, because she'd often run that far without it taking too much of a toll. To be fair, though, she told herself, the road was on a bit of an incline, so she'd been running uphill the whole time. It also looped around the town, and she figured that it would ultimately bring her back into it, although approaching it from the north rather than the south. Which would be a good thing, she decided. She could pop into the newsagent's and pick up a copy of the *Central News*. Maybe more than a single copy. She wanted to send one to her parents to show them that she'd put an entire newspaper together.

As she drew nearer the town, she could hear the sounds of cheers coming from the playing fields. She would be running straight past them, she realised. And even as she approached, she knew she'd stop and see who was playing.

The game had just started and it was, once again, a match between the Ardbawn Under-9s and a rival team from a local town. She recognised Josh Meagher almost immediately. He was making a blistering run up the pitch, keeping control of the ball and watching for the opposition tackle that was certain to come. He managed to evade two defenders and then finally launched a shot, which the keeper tried to block. But the force of Josh's kick was too much, and the ball ended up in the back of the net.

The crowd cheered ecstatically and, louder than all the rest, Sheridan heard Joe's voice.

'Brilliant score, Josh!' he shouted. 'Way to go!'

Josh looked up at the stands and waved to his uncle, who was on his feet, punching the air, oblivious to anyone but his nephew. Sheridan couldn't help smiling. She loved the passion of sport. She loved how enthusiastic the spectators got. She couldn't help it. It was in her blood.

She stretched her legs as she continued to watch the game. By the end of the first half, the opposition had equalised thanks to a tall, gangly attacker who had managed to shoot over the bar three times for points. The excitement in Gaelic football, Sheridan always thought, was the fact that players could score points as well as goals. With three points equalling one goal, it meant that games could be fast, furious and close even if one team didn't manage to get the ball in the back of the net.

She had to wait and see how things turned out. It was work, after all. The following week she'd be editing Des's match report and turning it into something that people wanted to read. (She still hadn't met Des, and sometimes wondered if he attended any of the matches he wrote about, or if he didn't just get a rundown from someone else who'd been there.)

Early in the second half, the opposition racked up another five points and maintained their attack with a greater ferocity than before, which left the Ardbawn boys looking tired and dispirited. Then one of Josh's teammates scored a complete fluke of a goal from an improbable angle, which meant that they were only two points behind. The goal infused them with a new burst of energy and they set about attacking their opponents' half with fresh enthusiasm. Sheridan was close to the action herself now, shouting encouragement from the sidelines, urging the boys on. With less than a minute to go, Josh got control of the ball once again and raced down the pitch.

'Go for a goal, Josh!' Sheridan yelled, although she knew the boy couldn't hear her. 'A point isn't enough.'

The supporters of both teams held their breath as Josh

drew near the goal mouth. The Ardbawn supporters looked anxious because it seemed to them that Josh had totally forgotten that a single point would mean they would lose the match and he was shaping up to go for a shot over the bar. The supporters of the visiting team were shouting at him to kick it high.

Josh steadied himself. The young keeper stretched out his arms, trying to force him to go for the shot over the bar. And then, calmly and decisively, Josh sent the ball past him, where it rolled into the corner of the net.

Everyone in the stands jumped up and down, shouting with joy. Sheridan realised that she was almost in tears. She sniffed a couple of times, telling herself that she needed to get a grip when it came to games. This was just a kids' league match. Nice to win, of course, but hardly a cup final. And yet the unconfined elation of the team was impossible to ignore. The boys were racing up the pitch to Josh, arms held aloft in delight. The woman standing beside her, the mother of the Ardbawn goalie, slapped her on the back. The two of them embraced. And then the final whistle blew.

'Hey, Sheridan!' Josh ran over to her. 'I saw you there. I heard you yelling at me.'

'You did?'

'Everyone heard you.' It was Joe, who was suddenly by her side. 'I think you were single-handedly driving the team forward.'

'Really?' Even as her heart fluttered at Joe's proximity, Sheridan blushed at the thought that she'd made a show of herself at the match.

'Really.' Joe nodded. 'You've got a proper passion for it, haven't you?'

'I like to see people winning,' she said.

'Which we did.' Josh sounded satisfied. 'And I scored two goals. I'm man of the match. Definitely. I've got to talk to the coach!' He scampered away, leaving Joe and Sheridan standing together, the atmosphere between them suddenly tense.

'How've you been?' Joe spoke first.

'Oh, good. Busy. And you?'

'Busy too. Not so good, though.'

She turned to look at him. 'Why?'

'I've been wondering how it is we seem to be totally on the wrong foot with each other.'

'I guess . . . Well, you thought I was one kind of person, and I'm probably not.'

'I thought you were a nice, fun-loving girl, which I still think you are.'

Sheridan said nothing.

'I was a bit taken aback when you walked out on me,' continued Joe. 'Nothing you said to me that night was so awful that we couldn't have discussed it further. And then I saw you with Peter.' His brow furrowed.

'Ah, Peter.' She smiled slightly. 'I like Peter, he's a good guy.'

'He breaks women's hearts,' Joe told her.

She made a face. 'All men do that.'

'Nevertheless . . .'

'Are you warning me off him?' she asked.

'I wanted to,' confessed Joe. 'When I saw the two of you together, I was . . . I felt . . .'

'You were with Ritz Boland,' Sheridan pointed out. 'The most glamorous woman in Ardbawn.'

406

'She is, isn't she?' Joe said. 'Way too glam for me, though. But good company.'

'Seems like we were both out with people who were good company. And both entitled to be, because you thought I'd met you under false pretences and you were angry with me and I don't think I would've changed your mind that night no matter what you say now.'

'I was . . . Oh, look, let's not do the whole opening-up-our-hearts thing here on the side of a football pitch. It's hardly the time or the place.'

'It's a perfect place,' she said with a smile. 'But maybe not a good time.'

'How about we choose another time?' suggested Joe.

'To talk?'

'To have that dinner,' he said. 'To pick up where we allowed ourselves to get distracted.'

She was trying not to allow the smile to break into a large grin. Because she could feel it again. The fluttering stomach, the jelly legs, the feeling that Joe O'Malley was the most important person in her life.

'That's a good idea,' she said.

'Great. Well, how about we make it soon?'

'Whatever you like.'

'Tonight?'

She looked startled.

'Unless you've better things to do?' asked Joe.

'No,' she said. 'No. I don't.'

'D'you want to give the Riverview another chance?' he asked.

'To be honest,' she said, 'I'm not a Riverview kind of girl. DJ told me about a nice Italian off the main street . . .'

'Siciliana?'

She nodded.

'Great,' he said. 'I like Italian. Seven thirty?'

'Perfect.' She was astonished at how composed she was outwardly while inside she was bubbling over with excitement. 'I'm looking forward to it.'

'So am I,' said Joe, and then he looked away as Josh came scampering over to them.

'Well?' asked Joe. 'Man of the match?'

'Totally,' said Josh. 'Are we going home now? I'm absolutely starving, and Mum said she was making sausage and mash for lunch.'

'Lucky you,' observed Sheridan. 'I love sausage and mash.'

'You can come if you want,' said Josh. 'Can't she, Uncle Joe?'

'It's OK,' said Sheridan, before Joe had time to answer. 'I have other stuff to do, Josh. I can't make it for sausage and mash. But thanks for asking me.'

'That's all right.' Josh beamed at her. 'I'm trying to be helpful. Uncle Joe said he'd have to find a way to have dinner with you again, and so I thought I'd ask and make it easy for him.'

'Josh!' Joe's face was an agony of embarrassment, and Sheridan burst out laughing.

'What?' Josh looked at his uncle with injured innocence.

'Your uncle is meeting me later,' she told him. 'We've sorted that out.'

'Good,' said Josh. ''Cos he definitely fancies you.'

'Oh my God.' Joe groaned. 'C'mon, young Meagher. I'd better get you home, before you ruin my hard-man reputation completely.'

'Ah, leave him be.' Sheridan grinned. 'I think he's bringing out your softer side. And I like it.'

'I don't have a soft side,' said Joe. 'As Josh should know.' He ruffled his nephew's hair, and Josh wriggled away from him.

'Stop,' he said. 'You know I hate it when you do that.'

'I used to hate it too,' admitted Joe. Then he looked enquiringly at Sheridan. 'Would you like a lift home?'

She didn't want to let him out of her sight. But she was hot and a bit sweaty and didn't want to perspire all over his car. So she said that she was going to run home, then have a shower. Joe told her that he admired her fitness and that he'd have to take up running himself. He'd become a bit of a corporate animal over the last few years, he said. He wasn't as fit as he'd once been. Sheridan said he looked fairly fit to her, and he said that maybe she could work out a plan for him, and both of them kept looking into each other's eyes until Josh demanded that they break it up because he was absolutely starving and wanted sausage and mash right now.

Sheridan waved as the two of them walked to the car park. Then she stretched her legs again. She was feeling so full of energy and excitement she thought she could do another ten kilometres. She thought she might need to, to work her excess spirits off.

Nina had just come out of the other studio when she saw Sheridan jogging through the entrance to the guesthouse. It was the first time she'd ever seen her dressed in running gear, and she couldn't help thinking that despite Sheridan's claims that she ate like a horse and that her thighs were too big and that her shape was all wrong, she looked very fit.

She raised her hand and waved at her long-term guest. Sheridan jogged up to her and then stopped, breathing heavily.

'I'm so out of shape,' she said. 'My legs are killing me.'

'I was just thinking that you looked great,' Nina told her. 'All sort of strong and Amazonian.'

Sheridan laughed. 'I'd lose a battle with a kitten right now,' she said. 'They always tell you to work up to a run, but it was so gorgeous this morning that I set off and couldn't stop. Well,' she corrected herself, 'I did stop for a while to watch the boys' under-nines GAA match.'

'And you ran back from that?' asked Nina.

Sheridan nodded. 'Via the newsagent's to buy a Lucozade Sport and the paper,' she said. And then, because she couldn't help herself, she told Nina about being left on her own the previous day.

'You're joking! You poor thing. You must have been exhausted when you got home. You should've called up to me. I'd've made you something to eat and looked after you.'

'That's really sweet of you,' said Sheridan. 'But I flaked out in front of the telly and ordered a takeaway. Maybe that's why I felt I had to go running today. I was the world's unhealthiest woman last night.'

'You had a right to be. D'you want to come up to the house now, have a cup of coffee?'

'I'm a puddle of sweat,' said Sheridan. 'I have to shower before I do anything else.'

'Drop up to me afterwards,' said Nina.

'OK. That'd be lovely.'

Sheridan went into her studio, showered for the second time that day, and dressed in a loose T-shirt and cargo pants.

She brought her copy of the *Central News* up to the guest-house with her so that she could skim through it while they were having coffee.

When she arrived, though, she realised that there wouldn't be a chance of skimming through anything, because Nina led her into a small sitting room where a table was covered by brightly coloured cartons and boxes filled with papers, padded envelopes and various bits and pieces.

'It's for the Spring Festival,' Nina explained. 'Because it's our tenth, we're doing a retrospective exhibition in the community centre. Perry Andrews asked us to see if we had any old photos and news clippings about the town. I have loads, because my mother was a complete hoarder. My father and my grandfather both liked taking photographs. Obviously Grandad's are old and grainy and there aren't that many of them. My dad had an old Kodak, but he loved it and took plenty of snaps. So I thought I'd go through them today and see if I could pick out some good ones.'

'What a great idea,' said Sheridan. 'I love old photos. It's so interesting to see places as they were years ago. I bet Ardbawn was very different.'

'Oh, the town has changed immensely, especially over the last twenty years,' said Nina. 'You wouldn't recognise it.'

'D'you need some help?' asked Sheridan. 'I've no idea what everything is, but I have a good eye for interesting photos.'

'That'd be great,' said Nina enthusiastically. 'Perry wants them by tomorrow, and I was panicking a bit because I've got eight people staying in the house tonight, as well as a fisherman for the other studio. Some help would be wonderful, if you're sure you don't mind.'

'I'll enjoy it,' Sheridan told her.

'In that case, finish your coffee and then we can get stuck in,' said Nina. 'There's lots to go through and Perry's a stickler for the very best.'

'Then that's what he'll get,' said Sheridan as she drained her cup.

Nina had been right about Dolores hoarding stuff, Sheridan thought as she sat opposite the guesthouse owner and began going through the contents of the red carton nearest to her. It was full of yellowed newspaper cuttings from the 1940s and 1950s, with photographs of women wearing headscarves and men in gaberdine coats.

'This is fantastic,' Sheridan said as she read a report about a dance in the church hall fifty years previously. 'Are these from a local newspaper? Was the *Central News* going that long ago?'

'I think the paper back then was called the *Farmer's Friend*,' replied Nina. 'This was essentially a rural community. The only big employer outside of the farms was the local creamery.' She went on to talk about her father's job there, and his subsequent accident. 'Not that I remember much about that,' she added.

'These days he probably would've got massive compensation,' observed Sheridan as she continued to flick through the cuttings.

'I guess so,' Nina agreed. 'I'm not a big fan of the whole compensation culture thing, but the truth is that Dad loved his job in the creamery and I don't think he was all that keen about working in the guesthouse. Unlike Sean,' she added.

'What's the story on Sean, if you don't mind talking about

it?' Sheridan asked casually, remembering that her horoscope advice to Nina for the week ahead was to focus on what was important to her.

'He wants to come back. And part of me, most of me, wants it too. Yet when he suggested that he should come back now, I couldn't say yes.'

'Does that mean it's a no, then?' Sheridan couldn't help being pleased for Nina. She was convinced the older woman would be better off without her philandering husband.

'Yes. No. I don't know.' Nina sighed. 'I love him no matter what. But is that enough? I want to act with my head as much as my heart. I want to be sensible about this.'

'I think you've been very sensible so far,' said Sheridan.

'Thank you,' Nina said. 'Part of my problem is that Sean was the first guy I was ever in love with. I fell head over heels for him. He was one of the most eligible men in Ardbawn and I married him. There's a part of me that thinks I did it just because I could.'

'I wonder, is it possible to separate being in love with fancying someone like crazy?' mused Sheridan.

'Have you found someone in Ardbawn to fancy like crazy?' enquired Nina, and was rewarded by seeing confusion on Sheridan's face. She looked at her quizzically and Sheridan, whose every thought was dominated by her date with Joe, told her about him. She didn't tell the guesthouse owner the full story of her investigations at March Manor and the subsequent disaster that had been their first date, but simply said that she was looking forward to dinner at Siciliana's later.

'I don't know him well.' Nina's head was bent over a pile of photos. 'But I'm sure he's a nice man.'

'I think he is,' said Sheridan, while thinking that calling

someone 'a nice man' was damning them with faint praise. 'I know I'm biased against his father, but Joe seems great. He takes his nephew to GAA matches every weekend and he seems to work extremely hard in the company. Plus he found a job for Conall Brophy, which was amazingly kind of him.'

'And he's very good looking,' added Nina as she glanced up from the photos.

'That too,' agreed Sheridan. 'They're all good looking in that family.'

'Have you met them all?' Nina looked startled.

'I've met Sinead and Peter,' said Sheridan, although she still didn't give the details of her first meeting with them. 'Sinead was dressed up for a dinner or something, she looked classy and sophisticated. And Peter is nearly as handsome as Joe. I haven't met Cushla, though someone once said to me that she was the most attractive of all.'

'Excuse me for a moment.' Nina got up from the table and walked out of the kitchen.

Sheridan looked after her in surprise. Nina had seemed upset, but for the life of her she had no idea what she could have said to bother her. She was an odd woman, thought Sheridan. Warm and friendly one minute, distant and self-centred the next. Of course she was under stress because of her marital situation, and Sheridan supposed that this was enough to make anyone act strangely from time to time. All the same, she couldn't help thinking that Nina was one of the most complex people she'd ever met.

Nina was totally shocked to hear that Sheridan Gray was going on a date with Joe O'Malley. For starters, she'd thought that Sheridan's antipathy towards Paudie would have been enough to keep her away from his son. And she couldn't imagine Paudie being too enamoured with the fact that Joe was having dinner with a woman he'd made redundant. It seemed wrong to Nina. But then, she admitted to herself as she sat on the edge of her bed, everything to do with the O'Malleys always seemed wrong to her. Except, in many ways, Paudie himself. She knew that he was a good man. She'd always thought so. But that wasn't enough in the whole scheme of things.

She picked up the hairbrush from the dressing table and began to brush her hair. A hundred strokes, as Dolores had taught her. Not that she ever bothered with giving her hair a hundred strokes in the normal course of events. But she sometimes did it when she was stressed. It helped to soothe her. It was helping now. She felt herself drifting into a trance, not thinking of anything other than the feel of the brush through her hair. And then the doorbell rang.

She was startled back into the present and realised that it was nearly two o'clock, and that the first of her guests had probably arrived. She left the brush on the dressing table, hurried downstairs and opened the door, a welcoming smile on her face. And after that she didn't have time to think about the O'Malleys or Sheridan Gray or anyone else, because she was too busy doing her job to allow her mind to wander.

Sheridan had remained in the sitting room when Nina went upstairs, and she was still there when she heard her welcoming her new guests. She supposed she should leave, although she was enjoying going through the pictures and cuttings. It didn't matter to her that they were of and about people she didn't know. She'd always been fascinated by old stories and photographs. There were old sports reports too. She'd read some of them, thinking that while the language the reporters used might have changed (no chance of the 1958 losing football team being called muppets, despite the fact that they'd apparently played abysmally), the passion and enthusiasm for their sports hadn't.

She placed the items she'd decided would be interesting for the exhibition on one side and put the lid back on the cardboard box. She decided to move it out of the way so that Nina wouldn't bother going through it again. As she did, she tripped over another box that had been halfway under the table. The box tipped over and its contents spilled out on to the floor.

'Oh, crap,' she muttered as she started to gather them up again. 'Why am I so bloody clumsy?'

There weren't any newspaper cuttings in this one, just masses of photos and a few silly items that looked to Sheridan as though they'd come from old Christmas crackers – there was a plastic fish that was meant to gauge your mood by changing colour and curling up in your hand to indicate how you were feeling; a set of sewing needles, still pristine and gleaming; a First Holy Communion medal (inscribed *Christine Fallon* and the year 2000) and a small mirror in a jewelled frame. Sheridan couldn't imagine why on earth Nina would keep such rubbishy items (although the communion medal was clearly of sentimental value), though she knew that Alice too had often kept silly things for ridiculous reasons. Although in her mother's case her mementos were somewhat different – the programme from Con's first competitive match; a pennant that Pat had been given by a visiting soccer team; a pair of gloves that Matt had worn the day he'd scored a winning goal . . . and a lock of Sheridan's hair. When she had first discovered Alice's stash, she'd felt let down by the fact that she hadn't had anything winning to contribute to it, but now she couldn't help thinking that keeping a lock of hair was more appropriate than a pair of gloves. Mothers worked in mysterious ways, she thought, as she put things back into Nina's box. You couldn't really get inside their heads.

She looked at some of the photos too, before realising that they were all of Nina's family. She didn't know whether the other woman had wanted her to include them or not, but there were so many that she didn't have time to go through them all. Anyway, she thought, it was something Nina should do herself. She had put almost everything back into the box before noticing that the envelope she'd left until the end was bigger than the others and didn't easily fit in. She was going to fold it but was afraid that it might contain larger photos, which she didn't want to bend, and so she shook the contents on to the table, realising as she did so that there was something hard inside. Even as it fell out of the envelope she told herself that she probably didn't want to know what it was – one of Nina's children's teeth, perhaps. Or maybe Sean Fallon's gallstone (she'd no idea if Sean had ever had gallstones removed, but when the thought came into her head she couldn't shift it).

In fact, the object was a ring. A delicate hoop of silver with a single small amber stone in a simple setting. Although plain, it was dainty, and Sheridan almost automatically tried it on. It was too small to fit on to her ring finger, so she tried it on her little finger instead. An old ring of Nina's, she thought, one she kept for sentimental reasons.

As the rest of the contents of the envelope emerged, she realised that they weren't photos at all, but small watercolour paintings. Some were landscapes, but then she saw one of a man sitting on a riverbank, his shirt open. It was a sensual painting even though his pose was relaxed and casual; a painting that made you take a second look. Sheridan studied it more closely. The man seemed vaguely familiar. She looked through more of the paintings. The same man appeared in many of them, even more sensual than the first. But there were others too, hearts with daggers through them, in bold blocks of colours that were utterly different to either the peaceful landscapes or the sensual portraits. She looked for the artist's signature, but all she saw was a vague squiggle that could have been anything. And then she picked up the pink notepaper that had also fallen from the envelope.

Sean: I hate you. But I'll always love you too. I'm leaving these for you. Remember the good times. Remember me. Elva.

Sheridan sat immobile on the chair. And then she read the note again. And again.

Of course! She hit her forehead with the palm of her hand. The man in the paintings was Sean Fallon. A younger Sean, but definitely the guesthouse proprietor turned soap star. And the painter of the pictures was a woman called Elva. The only Elva in Ardbawn that Sheridan knew was Elva O'Malley. Paudie's wife. Who had been a painter, according to her son, and whose work this obviously was.

I'll always love you. Sheridan's brow furrowed. When had Elva written this note? When had she sent all these things to Sean? How much had she loved him. Or hated him?

418

Remember me. Was Elva breaking up with Sean? Or was she saying goodbye more permanently? Had she written the note just before she died?

Sheridan's heart was thumping in her chest. Sean and Elva had been lovers. Elva had died in tragic circumstances. Had anyone else known about their affair?

Did Paudie know? Did Nina know?

Well of course Nina knew! These boxes were hers, after all. But why had she kept her husband's lover's paintings, and the note? And . . . Sheridan picked it up and looked at it again . . . the ring. Which she was sure now must have belonged to Elva.

When had Nina found out? Before or after Elva had died?

Poor Nina, thought Sheridan, her husband had an affair before and he's having another one now. Why did she forgive him the first time? And is she really thinking about forgiving him again?

She heard the sound of a door closing and Nina's footsteps in the hallway. She was sure Nina would be embarrassed if she thought she had seen the contents of the envelope, and she tried to push the paintings back inside, but they caught in the flap and she dropped some of them. Panicking slightly as the footsteps approached, she picked them up and pushed all of them, including the note from Elva, into her own big canvas bag.

The door opened and Nina smiled at her apologetically.

'We'd better leave it for today,' she said. 'D'you mind dropping by again tomorrow?'

'Sure. Sure. No problem.' Sheridan knew that her voice was too bright.

'OK, then,' said Nina. She looked at Sheridan, who realised

that she was expected to leave. She slung the canvas bag awkwardly over her shoulder.

'I'll be off, so,' she said.

'Thanks. See you tomorrow.'

'See you tomorrow.'

It was only when she'd got back to the studio and taken the paintings out of her bag to smooth and fold them properly again that Sheridan realised that she was still wearing the amber ring on the little finger of her left hand.

Chapter 29

She removed the ring and placed it carefully on the table. Then she looked at the paintings again. The more she studied the ones of Sean, the more erotic they appeared. As for the others, they made uncomfortable viewing. She supposed they reflected Elva's state of mind at the time. Which, from what she could see, was very disturbed.

She studied the note again. Raw emotion leapt from the page, not only from the words but from the way that the pen had been pressed hard into the paper. Hate and love. Elva O'Malley had hated Sean Fallon. She'd loved him too. And both her love and her hate were reflected in the paintings she'd sent him.

Had Paudie found out? Had he discovered the paintings, realised they were of Sean, and guessed that they were having an affair? How would he have felt? Mr Slash and-Burn, the ruthless businessman, suddenly realising that his wife loved someone else. But he hadn't become a ruthless businessman until after she died, had he? So . . . so . . .

The thought flashed into her mind and she dismissed it again straight away. After all, Vinnie Murray had said that Paudie had a cast-iron alibi for the time his wife had died.

And cast-iron meant cast-iron as far as Vinnie was concerned. But still – a wronged husband. An angry husband. A vengeful husband. What might he have done?

It was, she supposed, a bit much to suspect Paudie of having hired a hit man to do away with his wife because he was angry with her. It would've made a great story, though, one that even DJ couldn't spin. Yet it was also very coincidental (or convenient) that Elva O'Malley had died when she did. Without her death, Paudie wouldn't have got the insurance payout, and Nina and Sean . . . well, what would've happened with Nina and Sean? Clearly Nina had forgiven Sean. But had she forgiven him before or after Elva had died? When had she learned about the affair? If she'd discovered it before, maybe she'd confronted the other woman. Maybe there'd been an argument and . . . OK, Sheridan admonished herself, you're letting your imagination run away with you here. Because the notion of Nina accidentally pushing Elva out of the window in some crazy catfight was definitely a step too far.

Martyn Powell had once told her to look at the facts as they were and not as she imagined them to be. It was when she'd been writing a story about the sudden retirement of a high-profile soccer player from the Irish international team and she'd come up with twelve different reasons why the player had decided to hang up his boots, none of which were the fact that he simply felt too worn out to continue. Speculation is fine, Martyn had said, but keep it within the bounds of possibility.

So she could speculate as much as she liked about Elva's death, but it was utterly impossible that Paudie had been involved and highly unlikely that Nina had anything to do with it either. But how about Sean himself? What if he'd grown tired of Elva and had wanted to get rid of her? What if . . .

'Oh, for heaven's sake!' she exclaimed out loud. The woman fell out of a window. Just because I didn't want it to be an accident when I heard about it first doesn't mean it wasn't. Her affair with Sean complicates things, but if anything . . . she looked at the note again . . . if anything this is a damn suicide note and Elva O'Malley killed herself. Which perhaps everyone in Ardbawn knows but nobody wants to say. Because it's a small town and they all care about each other and nobody wants to admit that one of them might have taken their own life.

But boy was it a more interesting story than appeared in the papers back then. She thought back to the reports, most of which had been dry and factual, even those that had posed questions about the tragedy. She wondered, if she'd been reporting on it back then, would she have dug any deeper? In any event, leaving aside her wild fantasies about murder, it was still a story of passions hidden in a small town. It was a human-interest story, and Sheridan knew that it was the kind of story that the *City Scope* would love.

She was so lost in her thoughts that she didn't realise how late it had become. When she looked at her watch she gasped in dismay, remembering (though she couldn't believe that she'd forgotten, even for a short time) that she was to meet Joe O'Malley in less than half an hour. She did a quick change into another, more flattering, pair of jeans, and a navy blue shirt that brought out the flame-red of her hair and the soft brown of her eyes. As she left the studio, she saw Nina standing on the steps of the guesthouse talking to one of her guests. Nina raised her arm and waved at Sheridan, who waved in return then climbed into her car, hoping that she'd get the opportunity to return the paintings and the ring before Nina noticed they were missing.

Once again Joe had arrived before her. He was sitting at a table beside the wall, and he looked up the moment she walked in. She felt the jolt that seeing him always seemed to give her, the feeling that he was the most important man in her life.

He stood up and kissed her on the cheek.

'It's great to see you,' he said.

She wanted to say something witty in return, but the touch of his lips on her cheek was sending tremors through her body and she could do nothing but smile at him.

'Have a nice day?' he asked.

Ever since I saw you at the football match my day has been monumental, she thought. Not entirely because of seeing you there, though mostly. But learning more about Elva and Sean and Nina . . . Suddenly she caught her breath. In all of her speculation about Elva's death, she'd somehow managed to push the fact that she had been Joe's mother out of her head completely. What did Joe himself know about it? Anything? Or everything? It suddenly occurred to her that she might know more about his mother than he did himself, and the idea unsettled her.

She dragged herself away from the thoughts swirling around in her head and told him that her day had been fine. 'How about yours?' she asked.

'I took Josh home to his mum,' he replied. 'It was very

relaxing for about ten minutes while he lay on the sofa and played with his Nintendo DS. Then he got his breath back and wanted to go outside again. I think he gets his energy from his dad. It certainly isn't from me or Sinead.'

'It must be hard on him to have his father away so much.' She was astonished at how calm she sounded, at how she was managing to function as a perfectly rational being when there were so many things going around in her head. Although the most important was that she wanted him to kiss her on the cheek and on the lips and in a million other places too.

She focused her attention entirely on Joe, who was saying that Michael's absences worked for him and Sinead. They were both very independent people, he told her, they needed their space and Josh accepted that.

'I'd find it tricky but they don't,' he added. 'And of course she has a lot of support from Dad when Mike's away.'

His mention of his father reminded her again of his mother and Sean and Nina. And then suddenly she wasn't able to help herself putting a question to him, even as she told herself it wasn't the time or the place.

'Did your dad have lots of support when your mum died?'

Joe said nothing for a moment.

'You don't have to answer that,' she said, annoyed at herself for allowing her mouth to run away with her. 'It's none of my business.'

'Why don't we get everything you ever wanted to know about my dad out of the way,' suggested Joe. 'Then we can forget about him and enjoy ourselves.'

'I didn't come out tonight to ask you about your dad.'

'No?'

'Sometimes asking unwanted questions is an occupational hazard with me,' she said apologetically. 'I ask things I don't even want to know the answer to.'

'In that case can I ask you something instead?'

'Of course.'

She had no secrets. Her family had no secrets. He could ask her whatever he liked.

'What would you like to eat?'

She laughed and felt herself relax. They both ordered pasta, and Joe asked for a large bottle of sparkling water, which she said she'd share with him. After the waitress had left them, Joe asked about Sheridan's life before Ardbawn. She told him about growing up in her family of massively high achievers, and of feeling the odd one out because she didn't regularly bring home gold medals or trophies and because winning at all costs didn't matter to her.

'You're too nice,' he said. 'You don't have a ruthless streak.'

'I can be ruthless when I have to be,' she said.

'And when is that?' he asked.

There was only one time in her life when she'd been utterly ruthless. Although not perhaps in the way he was expecting.

'When I started working on the *City Scope*,' she told him finally. 'I was the only female journalist in the sports department and the lads were giving me a bit of a hard time. The normal sort of hard time that guys give each other. You know, the whole alpha-male thing.'

Joe nodded.

'And they asked me to the local pub for a few pints, to kind of prove myself, I guess. We Irish are shocking like that,' she added. 'Ability to knock back alcohol is practically defining, you know.'

'We're growing out of it,' said Joe.

'Not everywhere,' she said. 'Anyhow, we went to the pub and it was all very macho and they were making lots of comments designed to make me feel girlie and stupid.'

'Wouldn't that get classed as bullying in the workplace?' asked Joe.

'Look, if I'd taken a case for bullying, that would've been the end of my career,' said Sheridan. 'Besides, sometimes you have to be able to put up with a bit of it. Not constant, abusive stuff. But the kind that's designed to make you either crack or be part of the team. It's the way life is. And what doesn't kill you makes you stronger.' She realised she was using one of Alice's phrases.

'In the end I had two pints and then they were playing pool and . . . well, I did that thing,' she said.

'What thing?'

'The thing they do in all those gunslinging buddy-buddy movies,' she told him. 'The thing where you pretend to be shit at something and sucker them in and then they discover you're really good at it. But too late because you've cleaned them out and taken the money.'

'You hustled them?' Joe sounded incredulous.

'And how,' she said, satisfaction in her voice. 'Took every last one of them down. Pretended my first win was a fluke. Played a cannon to put the black into a corner pocket and did a girlish giggle and apologised. It looked totally accidental. All of the balls seemed just by chance. And so the next guy was convinced he'd hammer me. But I stayed ahead of them. They weren't sure about me then. They were after the next game. I won it from the break.'

'You demon,' he said.

'I know.' She looked apologetic but her voice bubbled with merriment. 'Anyway, there was no more crap from them after that.'

'You weren't exactly ruthless, though,' said Joe. 'You were just putting down a marker.'

'I guess so,' she said. 'But I took them for a lot of money. And afterwards they respected me.'

'You liked your job at the *City Scope*.' It was a statement, not a question.

'Loved it,' she said. 'I was good at it. It made my parents proud.'

'I'm sorry, about what happened.'

'Not your fault.'

'You blame my dad, though, don't you?'

'I certainly tried to blame him,' she agreed. 'It was convenient to make one person a focus for how angry and upset I was, especially since that person was an outsider, not someone I'd worked for or with. But I know it wasn't specifically his decision.'

'I wish I could change things for you.'

'Like you did for Conall Brophy? Setting him up with a job?'

Joe looked a little embarrassed. 'We needed someone.'

'It was lovely of you all the same. I'm sure it meant a lot to him.'

'I'm not a soft touch,' Joe said. 'If he isn't up to scratch he'll be let go. But he needed a break.'

'Yeah, he did.'

'And so do you.'

She grinned. 'I got one. I came to Ardbawn.'

'I hardly think . . .'

428

'Don't knock it. Didn't you hear I produced the entire last edition of the *Central News* myself? I was the editor, subeditor and roving reporter all rolled into one. How many people get that opportunity?'

'My father told me about that,' said Joe. 'He said you were very determined. He was impressed.'

'A bit late to be impressing him,' she said, and then she held up her hands. 'Sorry, sorry, I don't mean to go on about him, really. Anyway, it was an interesting few hours.'

'D'you like working for the *Central News*?' he asked.

'Yes.' She hadn't intended to say yes, because no matter what, the only reason she was there was because it was the only job she'd been offered. And she wasn't enjoying the fact that nobody else seemed to want her.

'What will happen when your time at the paper is up?'

'I don't know. My CV is out there with a ton of people. I've started tweeting some comments on sports stories and I've set up a blog, though I haven't got around to writing anything for that yet because, believe it or not, I've been too busy.'

'Whoever gets you will be lucky,' said Joe.

'You think so?'

'Yes.'

'You don't know anything about me,' she said. 'Not professionally.'

'I know that you spent a lot of time on the Conall Brophy story,' he told her. 'I know that you were caught up enough in it not to care about meeting me – which was perfectly fine,' he added when she tried to interrupt him. 'It was a good thing. You were right to stick with it. Afterwards you wrote a very sensitive piece about unemployment and what it can do to you. I know that you were very concerned about the whole incident of calling to see my father and how I'd feel about that. So I know that you're a good person.'

But you don't know that I know stuff about your family that you might not even know yourself, she thought. And you don't know that ever since I saw the note and the paintings and realised that there was a whole human drama going on there, I haven't been able to put it out of my head.

'I know that I'm glad we talked again and I'm glad you came here tonight,' he said when she didn't speak.

When he smiled, she could feel the electricity again. Crackling between them, drawing them together, making her want to be near him. Then the waitress appeared with their food and spoiled the moment. Sheridan picked up her fork and pushed the pasta around the plate. She wasn't hungry. She placed the fork on the table. All she wanted to do was touch him. She was wondering if it would be totally inappropriate to take his hand when her phone rang and startled both of them.

'I'm sorry.' She fished it out of her bag and her eyes widened. It was Alo Brady. She glanced at Joe. 'Would you mind awfully if I took this call?' she asked. 'It's an old colleague of mine, and just in case he has something . . .'

'Go ahead,' said Joe.

Sheridan accepted the call and stood up from the table.

'Hi, Sher,' said Alo. 'How're you doing?'

'Not bad,' she told him. 'What's up?'

'Can you talk?'

'Sure.' She gave Joe an apologetic smile and stepped into the small vestibule of the restaurant. 'What's up?' she repeated.

'I know you were working on a story about Paudie O'Malley,' said Alo.

'Yes,' she said tentatively as she turned up the volume on her phone to counteract the noise from the restaurant. Whatever story she'd thought she might write had been completely overtaken by what she'd found out about Sean and Elva.

'Well, our site is running a piece on him next week,' said Alo. 'He's part of a consortium arranging a telecoms deal in the Middle East. There are rumours of backhanders and bribes.'

'Paudie's been bribing people?' Sheridan couldn't help feeling shocked.

'Maybe the word bribe won't be used,' said Alo. 'We don't want to be sued by him. But put it this way, the consortium seems to have had the inside track the whole way through the process, and we've seen some emails that are definitely ambiguous. It's certainly worth our while posing the question.'

A few weeks earlier, Sheridan would have happily believed that Paudie had been involved in all sorts of shady deals to get what he wanted. Now, with a certain amount of surprise, she realised that she wasn't so sure.

'What can I possibly add to a story like that?' she asked.

'Well, in your emails to me you said you were looking at the personal angle,' Alo told her. 'Background family stuff. That's what I want.'

'I doubt that anything I have would be of interest to you,' she said. Her knowledge that Paudie's wife had had an affair years ago was hardly relevant to dodgy dealings in the Middle East today.

'Paudie has a network of interlinked companies. So his

431

family members might be involved too.' She could hear the excitement in Alo's voice at the idea of a potentially great story. She knew the feeling.

'What would be beyond brilliant would be if you had stuff going back a while,' he said. 'The early years. I read all that about the wife's death. Depending on how we look at it, it could put a kind of sympathetic slant on the whole thing, because it'll make people sorry for him, though it's not an excuse, of course, for breaking the law.'

'You definitely think he's broken the law?'

'Could be, if it's proven that the deal is dodgy. Course, if he got away with pushing his wife out of a window, he's already ahead in the breaking-the-law stakes – have you looked at that? There was a bit of gossip at the time, though not as much as you'd think really, which is interesting in itself. Like it was hushed up.'

'He didn't kill her.' Sheridan realised that her voice was sharp. 'I checked it out,' she said more calmly. 'It was an accident.' But even as she spoke, she couldn't help wondering again. After all, Elva had been cheating on him. Other men had murdered cheating wives.

She glanced back inside the restaurant. Joe was still sitting at the table, staring into the distance. As much as the idea of having her name linked to a story on the *Business Today* site made her pulse quicken, being with Joe made it quicken even more. So she couldn't be involved with anything that accused his father of financial double-dealing. Just as she couldn't tell Alo about the fact that Elva O'Malley had been having an affair when she died.

But she knew that Alo's story would be big. Stories about corporate malpractice were always big, especially if they featured someone as well known as Paudie O'Malley. It could only be good for her career to have her name attached to it, couldn't it?

Good for her career, she reasoned, but what about good for her? Because if she wrote anything at all about Paudie, her relationship with Joe would be over. If, of course, there was a relationship with Joe at all. If she meant anything to him other than someone new to pass the time with. That was all she'd been to most of her exes. A girl to hang around with until someone better came along. And someone better always had. Except in the case of Griff, who hadn't even waited for anyone else but who'd bailed out at the thought of living with her. She wanted to believe that with Joe it would be different, but how likely was that, after all? The odds were stacked against her. And her mother had always told her to play the odds.

So what were the odds against her and Joe? He'd been pretty keen to have dinner with her, he'd even said that he fancied her in front of his young nephew, but perhaps it was all just a bit of fun to him. She was the one, after all, whose heart broke into a canter every time she was near him – she had no idea what effect she had on him. He was used to being in the company of women who liked him, women like Ritz Boland who were beautiful as well as intelligent and who would surely be far more welcome in his world than her. If she passed on contributing to Alo's story she could be giving up her opportunity to be part of something huge, something that would add a whole heap extra to her CV and get her name right out there again. How could she say no just because some guy she hardly knew made her feel like she'd never felt before?

Even as these thoughts raged through her head, Alo continued talking about the story and its importance and suggesting that if there was a possibility she could even get to talk to Paudie O'Malley, or, he added, his son JJ, that would be fantastic.

'JJ?' Her mouth was suddenly dry.

'Yeah, he's involved with the Middle East deal. Like his old man, he doesn't do much media stuff. But he's a shrewd operator.'

Joe had been to Dubai recently, she remembered. Maybe he'd only asked her out because he wanted to distract the out-of-town reporter from looking into Paudie's business. Maybe he was totally stringing her along. Her hand tightened around her phone. That made a lot more sense than him actually fancying her, didn't it? The O'Malleys covering all the angles.

'So, are you on, Sher? You and me, the *City Scope* old guard breaking ground again?'

'I'll see what I can do,' she said.

'It had better be a bit more than that,' Alo told her. 'I want really good extra info. A whole family-angle thing; people love gossip and it'll bring in even more readers.'

The pleasure of Joe's kisses was temporary. But her career was for ever. She recalled her parents' words about winning at all costs. About taking chances. About not finishing second.

'Yes,' she said eventually. 'I'll get something to you. And I'm sure you'll like it when I do.'

'Attagirl,' said Alo. 'Now I'm off to figure out how to bribe a sheikh.'

She walked back into the restaurant. Joe's smile marked a hint of anxiety in his look.

'Everything all right?' he asked.

'Fine,' she said. 'My friend . . . well . . . he might have some work for me.' She felt as though there was a rock in her throat.

'That's fantastic,' said Joe. 'Fantastic for you, anyway. I'm not sure how Dad will feel about it.'

'Why?' She looked warily at him. 'Why would he mind?'

'You think he wants to lose the woman who single-handedly got out the last edition?' Joe laughed. 'He wants to make you editor.'

'You're joking,' she said.

'Not a very sensitive joke,' he said apologetically. 'I'm sorry. I'm sure, though, that Dad would like to find some way of keeping you on the payroll. He loves initiative.'

Well I'm certainly using mine now, she thought, as she rubbed her temples. The whole situation was giving her a headache.

'You OK?' asked Joe.

'Yes,' she said. 'I just . . . I'm . . . Don't mind me.'

'Your pasta is going cold.' He indicated her almost untouched meal. She noticed that he'd eaten about half of his while she was on the phone.

'I'm not hungry.'

'This isn't great.' He looked at her with amused concern. 'Twice I've asked you to dinner and twice you haven't got around to eating anything. Is it me?'

'No,' she said. 'No, it isn't you.'

'Good. Because I'd hate to think it was.' He reached across the table and put his hand on hers.

The electricity surged through her again, a physical force, reaching every part of her body. She had never wanted anyone

435

as badly in her life as she wanted Joe O'Malley. Never. Damn the man and damn the feeble female emotions that were threatening to swamp her just when she needed to be cool and clinical.

'Maybe we should go,' he said.

There was no way she was going to eat anything else. She nodded.

Joe paid the bill and led her outside. She wanted to pull herself together and start firing questions about the O'Malley business empire at him. But she couldn't speak.

'Are you sure you're all right?' he asked again. 'You've gone really quiet and you're awfully pale.'

'I . . .' She didn't want to believe that his concern wasn't genuine. She didn't want to believe that she was so wrong about him. That he wasn't the person she thought he was. She thought of the first time she'd seen him, cheering Josh on on the football pitch, his honest, open enjoyment in his nephew's success. Joe O'Malley was a good man, she told herself. I have to tell him. Everything.

'I know you brought your car, but would you like me to drive you home?' asked Joe. 'You seem a bit distracted.'

'That would be great.' She would tell him about Alo's story as he drove. She would give him the chance to explain himself. And she'd believe him.

Joe put his arm around her shoulder as they walked the short distance to his car. She sank into the passenger seat, thinking that she could get to like luxury cars, with their walnut trims and leather smell. When Joe got in on the other side, she wondered for a moment if he was going to lean over and kiss her, like Matt or Con's friends had done in the early days when they'd used her to practise their seduction skills. If he kisses me here and now, he's a fake, she decided.

Joe simply started the car and drove smoothly towards the guesthouse. But she couldn't find the right words to say what she wanted. Which was ironic, she thought. She was a reporter. She wasn't supposed to be lost for words.

'D'you want to come in for coffee?'

'If you don't mind.'

OK, so that whole coffee thing is sort of naff, she told herself as she led him inside. But it's a better environment in which to tackle thorny issues.

Joe sat on the sofa and flicked through the *Central News* while she busied herself with the kettle and cups, suddenly feeling like a teenager again. Right, she said as she poured boiling water on to the granules, cards-on-the-table time. Open and honest. That's what he is, that's what I'm going to be.

She felt him standing behind her. She turned around.

And then he kissed her.

And she knew that the discussions could wait. Because this moment was more important than anything that had ever happened to her before.

She didn't realise she'd fallen asleep until she suddenly jerked awake. Joe was sliding his arm from beneath her neck.

'I'm so sorry for waking you,' he said as he flexed his wrist. 'But I've lost all feeling in it.'

She moved her head. 'It was a lovely sleep,' she told him. 'I haven't conked out like that since I came here. It's too quiet, you see.'

He kissed her and she felt herself dissolve beneath him.

Later, when she came up for air, she wondered if it would always be like this. If she would always love him. If he would always make her feel this way.

'Would you like anything to drink?' she asked as she sat up and ran her fingers through her tousled hair.

'I'm drunk on you,' he said, and then looked shamefaced. 'Sorry, that's so clichéd and awful, you probably want to hit me.'

She punched him gently on the chest and told him that she was an expert in awful clichés.

'A game of two halves, sick as a parrot, the boy done good . . .'

'Stop, stop!' he laughed. 'Water would be nice.'

She clambered out of the bed and pulled her long sweatshirt over her naked body. She went to the fridge and took out two bottles of Vittel, handing one of them to him.

'That was – amazing,' she told him.

'I know.' He drank some water. 'You make me feel . . .'

'. . . like dancing,' she finished for him with a smile.

'Not quite.' He grinned. 'I'm a hopeless dancer. Desperate sense of rhythm.'

'Your rhythm seemed damn good to me,' she told him.

He laughed and then kissed her. And kissed her again. And it was still amazing.

Later, she finished her water and left him sitting on the bed while she went to the bathroom. She hardly recognised the face that looked back at her from the mirror. There was a glow to her cheeks that she'd never seen before, a certain lift to her mouth that made her look slightly wanton and definitely sexy. She'd changed. Because of Joe.

She'd never realised that love could be like this. So intense, so deep, so absolutely perfect. She couldn't have imagined it could happen to her here, in Ardbawn, where she hadn't even wanted to be.

Chapter 30

Nina had spent most of the day working. Her guests had arrived over the course of the afternoon and early evening, not leaving her any time to get back to looking at the photos and cuttings for Perry's exhibition. She'd seen the small pile of photos that Sheridan had thought might be of interest, and she decided to look through them when the guests were settled and she had some time to herself.

But it had taken longer than she expected, especially as six of them had decided to eat in and she'd had to prepare a meal and clear up afterwards. She didn't mind that at all. She enjoyed looking after her guests, and besides, six for dinner was good money.

She left them sitting in the residents' lounge after the meal, and was about to go into the sitting room when the phone rang. It was Sean.

'Just checking in on you,' he said.

'Checking in on me? In what way? Making sure I haven't run off or something?'

'I know you'd never do that,' he said. 'Your heart is in the house.'

'You're right.'

'Have you been thinking about me?' he asked.

'I never stop thinking about you.' Her tone was dry, but he said he was glad to hear it.

'I've got to go,' she said. 'It was a busy day today, lots of guests staying, and I have things to do.'

'Of course it should all be looking up from here on in,' he said. 'The festival will bring more punters to the town. How are the preparations going for that?'

Even though she didn't really want to spend time talking to him as though everything between them was back to normal, she told him about the exhibition, and he said that was a good idea and that he'd love to come home for it. For the whole festival, he said. He missed the Ardbawn community. He missed his life there.

'You used to say we were in a backwater,' she told him.

'But *our* backwater,' he said, and despite herself, she felt her heart warm towards him. They'd shared so much, she thought. They'd come through bad times before. Perhaps she should give him another chance.

'All right,' she said. 'Come for the festival. Stay here. We'll talk then.'

'You mean it?'

'I wouldn't say it if I didn't mean it.'

'That's wonderful.'

'How's the recording for the new show you're doing coming along?'

'All right,' he said. 'Fun. Different to *Chandler's Park*, though.'

'How long are you going to be in the coma for?'

'God knows,' he said. 'Hard to tell. They're trying to save money on the production at the moment. Have you noticed that all the scenes are just the main characters, people who're still in contract? There aren't any extras.'

She hadn't noticed because she hadn't been watching. But she didn't tell him that.

'I can't wait to see you,' he told her.

'I'm looking forward to seeing you too.'

Which was sort of true. She wished she didn't feel so damn conflicted where Sean was concerned. She sat down at the kitchen table and stared into space. It was important to get it right this time, she thought. She was older now. She couldn't afford to make any wrong choices.

It was late by the time she abandoned the kitchen and went into the sitting room, bringing a glass of wine with her. She pulled up a chair and picked up the photos that Sheridan had chosen. The reporter was right, Nina thought. She had an excellent eye for a shot, and each picture that she'd put in the pile was, in some way, quirky or clever or evocative of time and place. Nina knew some of the people in the black-and-white photos because they'd been friends of Dolores or John. But many of them were strangers to her, and she wondered about them as she gazed at their faces with their fixed expressions or camera-ready smiles. She wondered if she knew their sons or their daughters, if they were still living in Ardbawn or if they'd moved on.

It's all so transient, she thought as she studied a photo of an elderly woman standing outside what had once been Meagher's Bakery but was now the Centra. In fifty years, sixty, would someone see a photograph of her and wonder who she was and what her life had been like? Or would they simply look on the internet and see that she was the ex-wife of Sean Fallon, the heart-throb actor, who'd left her for an actress called Lulu Adams? Or – the thought made her smile very faintly – would they say that he was the heart-throb actor who'd been thrown out of his home by his ex-wife?

Suddenly her eyes narrowed. She looked at one of the boxes, its lid slightly askew, and she swallowed hard. She hadn't meant to put that box out. It must have been because she'd been looking through it before. It was the personal box, filled with family photos, the children's school reports, silly tokens from Christmas crackers that she'd kept to remind her of fun times, communion and confirmation medals . . . and everything else. Her heart thudded faster as she thought of what it contained. She opened the box. The envelope was sitting on the top. And it was empty.

There was an oblong of orange light coming from the window of Sheridan's studio. Even though it was now very late, Nina pulled on a cardigan and walked towards it, trying not to make too much noise on the gravel. But when she got there, she realised that Sheridan's Beetle wasn't outside. She didn't know who the silver convertible belonged to.

She stood hesitantly beside the front door, unable to hear any sounds from within, and uncertain of her next move. As the light was on, she assumed that there was someone inside. If she rapped at the door and a stranger answered it, what on earth would she say? I'll ask them what the hell they're doing in the studio, she told herself firmly. Because only Sheridan Gray should be there.

She took a deep breath. She couldn't stand here all night

dithering. She had to act. She formed her hand into a fist and rapped loudly on the door.

Sheridan jumped in fright when she heard the knock. She came out of the bathroom and stood in the centre of the studio. Joe had already pulled on his jeans and jumper.

'It must be Nina,' said Sheridan. 'Though why she's here this late . . . Something must be wrong.'

'I'll open it,' Joe said.

'Not till I put on some more clothes.' Sheridan grabbed a pair of tracksuit bottoms to cover her naked behind and wriggled into them.

'OK,' she said. 'You can go ahead now.'

Nina blinked in the light spilling out from the open door, then blinked again in surprise at seeing Joe O'Malley standing there. When Sheridan had told her that she was meeting Paudie's son for dinner she'd been shocked, but she'd never for a moment expected that he'd come back to the studio with her.

'Is everything all right, Nina?' asked Joe.

She stared at him wordlessly.

'Has something happened at the house? Do you want me to check it out for you?'

She still couldn't speak.

'Are you all right yourself? Do you need help?'

'Hi, Nina.' Sheridan appeared behind Joe. Her expression was one of acute embarrassment. 'Is something wrong?'

'No. No.' This was turning into an even worse nightmare than she'd thought. Nina had come to accuse Sheridan of taking something that didn't belong to her. But if she started hurling allegations around now, she'd seem like a deranged, narrow-minded countrywoman throwing a strop because two grown adults were having sex in the studio. Even if they were the two unlikeliest candidates for getting it together that she could've imagined.

'Come in,' said Joe.

Nina stepped over Sheridan's carelessly abandoned shoes as she walked inside. Sheridan scooped them up and threw them into the wardrobe.

'Would you like tea?' she asked.

'I'm not here for tea,' said Nina.

'Is there a problem?' Sheridan's voice was anxious. 'It's OK for Joe to be here, isn't it? You said I could have people to stay.' Actually, Sheridan realised, Nina had told her to let her know if she was going to have guests so that she could make up the sofa bed. She hadn't mentioned anything about bringing men back to the studio for mind-blowing sex.

Nina brushed her hand through her hair as she wrestled with what she wanted to say.

'What's the matter, Nina?' asked Joe. His voice was calm and measured. 'Is it something to do with you or with us?'

The way he said 'us' startled Nina. As though he and Sheridan were more than just people having casual sex. As though there was more to their relationship than that. But there couldn't be. He was Paudie's son. Sheridan hated Paudie. She wouldn't have anything to do with his family.

Oh my God, she thought suddenly, had Sheridan had a grand plan when she'd come to Ardbawn? Get close to Paudie's son? Find out about the past? Put together an exposé of things that were better forgotten?

I thought I knew her. I thought I liked her. But she's way more devious than I could ever have imagined.

Despite Nina's comment that she wasn't there for tea, Sheridan had boiled a kettle of water and was making some anyway. She couldn't believe that the older woman was getting into a state about Joe being in the studio. How had she found out about it anyway? Had someone from the town seen Sheridan getting into Joe's car? Had they phoned Nina to say so? Was Ardbawn far more of a backwater than she'd ever believed? What business was it of anyone's that she was with Joe?

She poured tea for Nina into a brightly coloured mug and handed it to her. Nina took it automatically and wrapped her hands around it.

'So, do you want to tell us what this is all about?' asked Joe.

'You should ask her.' Nina looked at Sheridan. 'Everything's to do with her. The lying, scheming, thieving—'

'Nina!' Joe interrupted her.

Sheridan felt the blood drain from her face. It was almost inconceivable, she thought, that everything to do with Paudie, Elva and Sean had been utterly and completely driven from her mind by the time she'd just spent with Joe O'Malley. But it was true. Nothing had mattered more to her than being with him, exploring his body, talking to him, realising that the electricity was real, but more than that, discovering that she loved him . . . She put her mug on the table beside Joe's. If she hadn't, she would have dropped it.

'Sheridan?' Joe's voice was full of concern.

She felt sick. In remembering Paudie, Elva and Sean, she was also remembering her promise to Alo Brady. She'd said she'd help him because she hadn't believed that Joe could feel for her what she felt for him. But that was before. It was different now.

'It's a misunderstanding, Nina,' she said. 'I promise you.'

'I haven't misunderstood anything,' said Nina. 'At least, not today. What I did misunderstand was everything to do with you from the first time I saw you until now. I thought you were a decent, honest person. I felt sorry for you. I was so, so wrong.'

'Nina, please . . .' Sheridan knew that she was shaking. She didn't want Nina to blurt out anything about the envelope. Joe would be horrified to think she'd seen the contents, if, of course, he even knew they existed.

'What did she tell you?' Nina asked him now. 'That she was a poor redundant journalist? That she was forced to come here for a job? Did she blame your father for that?'

Joe looked from Nina to Sheridan in puzzlement. He could see real anger on Nina's face. And absolute terror on Sheridan's. Why, he asked himself, did she look so scared? What had she done?

'That's the truth,' Sheridan said. 'I lost my job. I was out of work for weeks. The *Central News* was the only job I could get.'

'Or that you wanted to get,' said Nina. 'So that you could poke around. How do we know that you didn't plan everything? That you're not employed by another paper to snoop? That you're not trying to get the inside track on me and Sean and everything to do with us? I should have guessed when you came here looking for a place to stay. No one tries to rent out rooms in a guesthouse for months on end.'

'You've got it all wrong!' cried Sheridan. 'I knew nothing about you or your guesthouse until DJ suggested it.'

'I've no idea what anyone is talking about here,' said Joe.

'Don't you?' asked Nina.

'Absolutely not.'

Nina sat down abruptly. She'd come to challenge Sheridan, not to reveal secrets to Joe O'Malley. She didn't know what Joe already knew about his mother and father's relationship, or Elva's relationship with Sean. She didn't know what Paudie had told him. If anything.

'Nina thinks I took something belonging to her.' Sheridan's voice was shaking.

'Did you?' Joe sounded both astonished and appalled.

'Yes,' said Sheridan. 'But it was a mistake. I didn't mean to. I got flustered and—'

'Flustered? I don't think you were flustered at all!' cried Nina. 'I think you planned it.'

'I didn't. How could I have? I'd no idea you'd ask me to look at photos.'

'What photos?' asked Joe.

Nina and Sheridan stared at each other, neither entirely sure what to do next. Eventually Sheridan got up and retrieved the paintings, the note and the ring from the drawer she'd put them in before she'd left the studio to meet Joe.

He watched her curiously. Then his eyes widened as he recognised the paintings and he gasped when he saw the ring.

'How the hell . . . ?' He looked at Nina, who put the ring and the paintings on the table in front of him. 'You had these? She took them from *you*?'

'Yes,' said Sheridan.

'That's my mother's ring,' he said in absolute bewilderment. 'I recognise it. And these paintings, of course. I remember her working on them.'

448

Nina's grip tightened on the note, which she still held. 'You watched her paint them?'

'Not all of them.' He was looking at the ones of the heart with the dagger through it. 'Not these. Not the ones of the man, either. But the landscapes, yes.'

Nina took a deep breath and then released it.

'Why do you have them?' asked Joe. 'And my mother's ring?' Then he turned to Sheridan. 'How could you possibly have taken them by mistake?'

'I was helping Nina look through photos for the festival exhibition,' explained Sheridan. 'I came across these when she was out of the room. I realised that I shouldn't have seen them. I thought I heard Nina coming back and I . . . I panicked.'

'Why should you panic?'

'Because I didn't want to have to talk to her about them. I knew . . . there was something . . . and the note . . .' Her glance shifted to the sheet of pink writing paper in Nina's hand.

'What note?'

'Maybe Nina should tell you,' she said helplessly.

'It's . . . Oh, Joe, I don't know what you know already.' Nina's voice trembled.

'Know about what? My mother? Her painting?'

'In a way, yes.'

'I don't know why you have my mother's ring,' said Joe. 'So an answer to that would be a good start. Perhaps I should read the note.'

'Maybe it would be better if I tell you first,' said Nina.

'I'm listening.' This time Joe sounded grim. He pulled a chair from the table and sat down. 'So go on, tell me.'

Chapter 31

Even though it was late, Sean Fallon was awake and sitting in front of the TV in his rented apartment. He'd been watching recorded episodes of *Chandler's Park*, but now he switched off the set and poured a measure of whiskey into the glass beside him. Sean wasn't a big whiskey drinker, but he found that a glass before bed relaxed him these days and helped him to sleep.

He hadn't been sleeping well lately. His mind had been buzzing with concern over his future role in *Chandler's Park* (he had the horrible feeling that his character would stay in the coma for months), but also with excitement over the new project, which was fun but now nearly completed. If he didn't have anything to do in Dublin, there was no reason for him to remain. His relationship with Lulu Adams was over. But Nina was being very stubborn about the chances of his return to Ardbawn.

He didn't blame her. She was entitled to be mad as hell with him. And, in retrospect, sending her the solicitor's letter had been stupid. It had understandably antagonised her when he should have been appeasing her. But then he didn't always get it right with Nina. He'd imagined, back when he'd first asked her to go out with him, that it would be a short-lived thing. He hadn't planned to marry her. The truth was that if he hadn't been encouraged by his father, he probably never would have asked her. Yet their lives together had been more stable and more fulfilling than he'd ever expected. It would have always been that way if it hadn't been for Elva Slater.

He'd first noticed Elva in his teens. She was by far the most beautiful girl in Ardbawn. Tall and slender, with long flaxen hair and the bluest eyes he'd ever seen, she was two years older than him, and despite the fact that he'd already chalked up quite a few conquests of his own, he considered her almost beyond his reach. But then, late one summer's evening, he'd met her walking along the road from the old creamery to the town. She was wearing a white cotton dress printed with blue and yellow flowers. Her hair hung loosely down her back, and to Sean she was like a fairy princess appearing though the dusk. A fairy princess who was limping because, as she told him, she'd tripped over a stone in the road and turned her ankle and it was absolute agony.

He'd supported her back to the town and to the house where she lived with her elderly parents, and then, seizing the moment, he asked her if she'd like to meet him again. She'd smiled and said yes, and the next thing he knew, he, Sean Fallon, was her official boyfriend.

Their relationship was deep and intense and lasted for nearly a year. But the problem was that much as Sean loved going out with the most beautiful girl in town, he found her unending neediness wearing. He hadn't realised that someone as lovely and as apparently confident as Elva would be needy. But she was. She constantly asked him if he loved her, constantly worried that she wasn't beautiful enough, constantly fretted about the littlest of things. Eventually Sean told her that he couldn't take it any more. He was tired of being the one who seemed to give all the time and received nothing in return. The undoubted pleasure he got from her was more than offset by the irritation he felt at always having to tell her how much he loved her. He longed for the days when he'd gone out with someone and it was just a bit of fun. So he broke it off with her and applied himself to seeking out less demanding female company, which he found perfectly easy to do.

At first Elva didn't seem to care. But then she started sending him notes, on pink scented notepaper, telling him that she still loved him. She said that she understood why a boy as immature as him might find it difficult to go out with an older woman. She realised that he'd been under stress. She forgave him for dumping her. He didn't reply to the notes, and when they stopped, he thought that she'd finally come to her senses. Then he heard that she wasn't eating. That didn't bother him too much – Elva talked a lot about how she needed to diet to keep her elegantly slender figure. So he ignored that too. What he couldn't ignore, though, was the day she was fished out of the Bawnee River and rushed to Kilkenny hospital. The official line was that she'd fainted at the riverside, but almost immediately rumours began to circulate that she'd thrown herself in because she was broken hearted at the end of their relationship. He thought about going to see her but dismissed it as a bad idea. Better to just let her get over it all, he thought. Better to stay away. His father, who was the Slaters' family doctor, told him that she was a type-A personality. Highly strung.

Difficult to live with. Not a good long-term prospect, no matter how beautiful she was.

Sean agreed. He was both relieved and surprised when he heard, a few months later, that Elva was engaged to Paudie O'Malley. Sean had never had much to do with the man, who was eight years older than him, and who he regarded as vintage Ardbawn – home loving and uninspiring. But the O'Malleys had a lot of land in the area and Paudie's parents had never been short of money. Elva liked the good things in life. Perhaps, Sean thought, she believed that Paudie could give them to her. And perhaps he was the sort of man who was so overawed by having snared such a beautiful woman that he wouldn't mind having to tell her how happy he was every second of every day. Elva marrying Paudie certainly lifted the vague sense of responsibility that Sean had constantly felt towards her, and he went off in search of his new life in Dublin and new girlfriends with renewed vigour.

She was married by the time he came back to Ardbawn again, and he was astonished to hear that she was pregnant. He was even more astonished when she had more children in quick succession. Elva had always seemed to him far too self-centred to be the sort of person who'd rush into motherhood. He counted himself lucky that he'd split up with her when he had, because the idea of being trapped into a marriage resulting in a brood of children made him shiver.

The day that he first spoke to her following their break-up and her subsequent marriage and family, they met by chance in St Stephen's Green. He was living in Dublin by then and the Green was one of his favourite places to relax. He was sitting on the grass enjoying some late summer sun when she walked by. He recognised her straight away, even though her long hair was shorter now and she was wearing a skirt and jacket instead of a wispy cotton dress. She was still enchantingly beautiful. When she turned and saw him, her blue eyes widened in surprise. For a moment he thought she would continue walking without acknowledging him, but then she came over and sat down on the dry grass beside him.

'How is it I never see you in Ardbawn any more but here I am on a rare trip to Dublin and one of the first people I see is you?' she asked.

'I'm hardly ever *in* Ardbawn,' he said, and went on to tell her about his acting career, making it sound like he was perpetually in demand for parts.

'I'd love to be doing that,' said Elva.

'Acting?' He looked surprised. 'I never thought it interested you.'

'Not acting. Just something that I loved.'

'Don't you love being Mrs Paudie O'Malley?' asked Sean. 'I hear the farm's doing well and that Paudie is developing outside business interests. And you're a mother, of course.'

'Can you believe it?' she said, in a tone that clearly showed she didn't believe it herself. 'I'm not even thirty and I have three kids already.' She looked at him from beneath her surprisingly dark lashes. 'You and I were lucky not to get caught out, Sean. I seem to be the most fertile woman on the planet. The man only has to turn back the bedcovers and I get pregnant.'

'Ellie!' Sean wasn't comfortable with the conversation.

She laughed. 'Oh, chill out. It's a fact, though. Maybe it's him. Maybe he just has strong swimmers.'

'Elva!'

'You lose a sense of something when you get married and have kids,' said Elva. 'You don't care what you say quite so much. You don't get so embarrassed either. That's because the kids will always do things to embarrass you first.'

'I'm sure they're great children,' said Sean.

'JJ's bright as a button. Sinead's lovely. Peter, the youngest, is mad as a hatter.'

'They're lucky to have you for a mother,' said Sean.

'You think?'

'Oh yes,' he said. 'They have the sexiest mother in Ardbawn.'

It was as though the earth tilted with his words. She looked at him enquiringly. And he remembered why he'd once thought he was in love with her.

It was a moment of madness, Sean often thought afterwards, his asking her if she was in a rush back to Ardbawn and her reply that she wasn't, and his suggestion that she might like to see his flat and her amused 'Why not?'

And then they were together in his bed and he was running his fingers along her silky-smooth body, thinking that childbirth hadn't changed it at all. Afterwards, as they lay side by side, she told him that it had been wonderful but that she was a married woman and couldn't see him again. He thought perhaps it was a kind of revenge – dumping him as he'd dumped her. But he was relieved, too. Great though the sex had been, he knew that it was also a mistake. He didn't want to get entangled with Elva again. He couldn't afford the grief it might bring.

The next time he met her, he was married himself. Their meeting was in Ardbawn, at a hurling match. Paudie, whose businesses were doing well, was now a sponsor of the local club and he went to lots of matches. The team had been doing well that year, and everyone had turned up to the game, which was against local rivals. Sean and Nina had bumped into Paudie and Elva after it had ended in a victory for the Ardbawn team. Paudie was polite and courteous, while Elva greeted Nina with a certain reserved diffidence. Afterwards, Nina said that while Paudie was always a real gentleman, she couldn't really take to Elva. She'd asked Sean what she'd been like when they'd gone out together, and he'd replied cheerily that he'd had a lucky escape. Because no way would his life with Elva have been half as good as it was with her. Nina laughed. And right then, Sean knew that she was and always would be more important to him than Elva Slater.

Even after Alan was born, Nina continued to find ways to improve the guesthouse. She was the one to decide that Sunday lunches and afternoon teas would be a draw, and Sean agreed that they could be good money-spinners. She was right. Bawnee River Sundays attracted not only the residents of Ardbawn but people from outside the town too.

They had two Sunday-lunch specials under their belts when Paudie made the booking. It was Elva's birthday, he told Nina, who took the call. Did she think she could provide a small cake too? They'd be coming with their children, so there'd be six of them.

Nina was excited when she told Sean about the booking. Paudie had become the town's most prominent businessman. He employed a lot of local people in his two printing companies and he'd recently been interviewed by RTÉ radio for a business programme, discussing opportunities for development outside of major cities. He'd been articulate and passionate, although a little brusque and impatient with the reporter, who wasn't as quick as Paudie himself. But think, she said to Sean, he could give us a mention next time. We're a successful business after all!

Sean realised that he was apprehensive about having Elva in his home, although he told himself that nerves were ridiculous. He was a bit anxious about seeing Paudie, too. After all, he'd had sex with the other man's wife. It could certainly make the occasion a little awkward.

They were an attractive family, he thought, as they walked through the door. Paudie was tall and broad and strong. Elva was pale and slender and ethereal. The three oldest children had inherited Paudie's dark good looks, but Cushla, the latest addition, was far more like Elva in appearance. Her hair was fair and curly and she had the same aquamarine eyes as her mother.

Sean welcomed them and showed them to their table. He didn't know if the brush of Elva's hand against his was deliberate or not. He felt a quiver of desire run through his body and he stepped away from her. She looked at him with the faintest hint of amusement and pushed her fingers through her still flaxen hair. The sun glinted off the warm amber of the ring she wore on her right hand, while the diamond on her left glittered hotly.

He'd given her the amber ring for her birthday when they'd first gone out together years before. He was both flattered and amused that she still had it and had worn it today.

The birthday lunch was a success. The cake that Nina had baked was devoured after Elva had blown out the single candle. The O'Malleys stayed long after the other guests had left, and Paudie chatted to Nina about how well the guest-house was doing and how proud her mother would be of her. He told Sean to come to him if there was any help he could give, and offered a discount on any printing they might need. No job too big or too small for a fellow Ardbawn man, he said warmly. We've got to help each other out whenever we can.

The O'Malleys came again the following Sunday. But the Sunday after that Elva came alone. Paudie had taken the children to see their great-uncle in hospital in Dublin, she said. They were going to stay overnight. She'd had a terrible headache that morning and had decided not to go with them. But it had lifted now. She felt a lot better.

She ate her lunch at a corner table, reading the newspaper and ignoring everyone else in the dining room. Afterwards she sat in the garden, smoking a cigarette and drinking a glass of white wine, her soft white cardigan wrapped around her shoulders against the chill of the breeze.

'She's a strange woman,' Nina observed as Sean loaded the dishwasher. 'She looks so fragile and yet I bet she's a tough cookie.'

'She's different,' agreed Sean.

Elva drank another two glasses of wine before deciding it was time to go. She stood up and wobbled on her high heels.

'I don't think you should drive home,' said Sean, who'd been watching her from the kitchen.

'I need my car at the house,' said Elva. 'I have to go out early in the morning.'

'It's still not safe for you to drive. Wait there.'

He called to Nina and told her that he was going to drive Elva home in her own car.

'Best thing,' agreed Nina. 'You don't want her wrapping herself around a tree. We shouldn't have allowed her to drink the guts of a bottle of wine. I didn't realise she was having so much.'

Sean brought Elva to the car, a bright red Honda Civic, and helped her into the passenger seat. It didn't take long to reach March Manor.

'Come in,' she said, her words more slurred than they'd been back at the guesthouse. 'Come in for a drink with me.'

'I can't,' said Sean.

'You're walking home,' she pointed out. 'It won't matter.'

'I can't,' said Sean again.

She walked over to him and rested her head on his shoulder. 'Please?' she said.

Sean thought about Nina and the various chores that awaited him back at the guesthouse.

'Oh, all right,' he said. 'But I won't stay long.'

He hadn't intended it to be the start of an affair, but it was. There was something about Elva that drew him to her as it had before. She was so different to Nina, cool and edgy, and able to do things with her body that his wife had long forgotten. She'd lost the neediness, too. She never asked him if he loved her.

He told himself that he deserved a short fling; he'd been working really hard lately. Maybe Elva deserved one too, married to someone like Paudie and with her brood of kids. He'd end it before it went too far and before anyone got hurt. In any event he knew it would have to finish before someone saw his car at March Manor when he was supposed to be somewhere else, or before Nina began to realise that he spent a lot of time nipping out to do some trivial chore that took far too long. Besides, this was Ardbawn. It was practically impossible to keep a secret. Sean couldn't decide whether it would be worse to have it discovered by Paudie, who would destroy him, or Nina, who would be devastated by his betrayal. He didn't want to be destroyed by Paudie and he didn't want to hurt Nina, but he couldn't yet give up the thrill he got from being with Elva. Besides, Nina was pregnant again, and embracing the kind of earth-mother persona she'd adopted when she was expecting Alan. Elva never made him think that she was a mother at all. She was still unbelievably, thrillingly sensual. Nevertheless, it was a dangerous road to travel. And he knew that he had to pick the right time to stop.

But he was still waiting for that time to come.

During the affair between Sean and Elva, the O'Malleys continued to be regular visitors for the Sunday lunches at the guesthouse. Sean thought these visits were entirely due to Elva, who would always behave so demurely in front of her husband that Sean himself sometimes found it hard to believe that he had slept with this woman and that she would cry out with the excitement of making love to him.

Elva never seemed to mind the fact that their meetings were sporadic, sometimes at short notice and always now away from Ardbawn, no longer at the riverbank spot that she called their own and where she'd started to paint pictures of him. 'Good cover,' she'd told him one day as she'd set up her easel. 'Paudie thinks it's important for me to have an interest of my own. I show him ones without you in them.' Sean thought that she rather liked the cloak-and-dagger nature of their affair. As he did too, even though, after Chrissie was born, he found it more difficult to justify leaving Nina at irregular intervals to look after things on her own. Anyway, it was getting too dangerous. They'd nearly been spotted in Kilkenny the previous week by TJ Meagher. There was no way they could keep it secret for much longer.

When he told Elva that it was over, she looked at him and laughed.

'You can't leave me,' she said. 'We're tied to each other. We always will be.'

He didn't want to have a row with her that night, but he knew that she was wrong. The only woman he was tied to was Nina. He could and he would break up with Elva. He didn't love her, no matter how much he desired her. Yet making a clean break was more difficult than he'd imagined. There was always some reason to see her again, some reason not to finish it straight away. But the day was drawing closer. He had his own family to think about, and he hated the idea of his children one day finding out that he'd been seeing someone else. It seemed wrong to him.

He said this one night to Elva, who nodded.

'I've been thinking about that too,' she said. 'I hate being dishonest with my children.'

Sean was surprised at how relieved he felt at her words.

'It's not right for them to think that I love their father,' she continued. 'It's not right for them to be totally unaware of the fact that the only man I've ever loved is you.'

He hadn't expected that. He didn't know what to say.

'I was stupid to marry him,' said Elva.

'Why did you?'

'Why d'you think?' She looked at Sean as though he was crazy. 'You'd dumped me. You didn't care about me. I nearly died and you didn't care. I needed to find someone who did. Paudie is crazy about me, the old fool.'

'Of course I cared,' said Sean. 'I just didn't see . . . Well, it was over. There was no point in pretending . . .'

'But it wasn't over,' said Elva. 'You came back to me. You've been with me ever since.'

Sean didn't quite see it that way.

'We've known each other for years, Sean Fallon,' Elva continued. 'We were meant to be together.'

'Oh well.' He tried to joke about it. 'Life had other plans.'

'No,' said Elva. 'We have to do something about our situation. We have to make our own plans.'

'What plans?' he asked cautiously.

'It's time for us to leave Paudie and Nina,' she said. 'I've been thinking about it a lot. They don't deserve us. We deserve each other. We descrve happiness.'

'It's not that simple.' Sean felt a chill at her words.

'It is,' said Elva. 'The time is right.'

'You can't leave Paudie,' he told her. 'It would be a terrible scandal.'

'You think I care about scandal?' She looked incredulous.

'Your children will care,' he said.

'And what about *our* child?' she asked.

He looked at her in bewilderment.

'You think Cushla is Paudie's?' She snorted. 'Oh Sean, you're so naive. Can't you see that she's yours?'

She had to be wrong about that. For Cushla to be his daughter, Elva would've had to get pregnant when they'd made love the one time six years previously, when he'd seen her in Dublin. He didn't think so. They'd used protection. Elva was deliberately winding him up. But if she started saying things, dropping hints . . . He wouldn't put it past her. And that could make things very messy indeed.

So for Sean Fallon, the overwhelming emotion the day Elva died was relief. But he was shocked too. Shocked that it had happened and shocked that she had gone for ever. And worried, because he knew he'd been one of the last people to see her alive.

When he'd driven to March Manor that morning, using the excuse that he needed to see Paudie, he hadn't known what to expect. His priority was to talk to Elva, because she'd phoned the guesthouse. She'd never done that before. They usually got in touch with each other by mobile phone, a service that was relatively new at the time, though from their point of view brilliantly convenient. It had been lucky that he was the one who'd answered the home phone, because Elva was brittle and nervous, saying that Paudie was angry with her and that they had to talk. Sean didn't want to go anywhere near March Manor, but after Elva insisted that Paudie would be out all morning, he'd relented.

She was alone in the house when he arrived.

She was wearing a gingham blouse tied under her breasts, and a short denim skirt. Her hair fell carelessly around her shoulders. She looked about twenty.

'Hello,' she said. 'I wondered if you'd come. I wonder will you come later too.' She smiled.

'I'm not here to—'

'Oh, don't be boring.' She walked into the house and he followed her.

She closed the front door and untied her blouse. She moved closer to him, and he could smell the floral scent of her perfume.

'Elva, please.'

'What?' There was a sharpness in her voice that he'd never heard before. 'What is it now?'

'I thought you wanted to end it. I thought you were worried about Paudie. What does he know?'

She shook her head. 'I don't want to end anything. I want to make love to you.'

'Come on, Ellie. This is serious.'

'I *am* serious.' She removed the blouse to reveal a lacy figure-enhancing bra underneath.

'I can't do this.' He picked up the blouse and handed it to her.

'Of course you can. *We* can. We always can.'

'Not this time.'

'Fuck you.' She'd never sworn at him before, and the words sounded harsh from her lips. 'You think you're some great man, don't you? Happy to screw me and then go home to your dumpling wife.'

'I never felt that way or thought that way, Elva. We've been having an affair. But now it's over.'

She stared at him.

'I'm sorry. I love my children and I can't keep lying to Nina. We've had a good time, haven't we, but it always had to end sooner or later.'

'No,' she said.

'We can't have an affair all of our lives.'

'That's why we have to run away.' She smiled at him. 'Today. Now.'

'You're crazy.' He stared at her. 'Are you drunk?'

'No,' she said. 'Though champagne would be nice, don't you think? To celebrate our love for each other.'

'Elva!' He caught her by the wrist. 'We don't love each other. We . . . It's something else, you and me.'

'I love you,' she said, and her voice was pettish. 'I always have.'

'I care about you,' he said. 'But it's over. We both have families. People who could get hurt.'

'You don't usually think of them when we're in the bedroom together.'

'No. I don't. But I should.'

'You're such a bastard, Sean Fallon. You've broken my heart. Again.'

'Elva . . .'

She twisted her wrist from his hold, raised her hand and hit him across the face. He felt the sting as the amber ring he'd once given her caught his cheek.

'Holy shit!' He touched it with his fingers and wiped away blood. 'Get hold of yourself, you crazy bitch!'

'How dare you call me names. You – you who're treating me like a whore!'

She was yelling now, and he looked around anxiously, as though someone might hear.

'Please, Elva.'

'Don't please Elva me,' she cried. 'It's please Sean, isn't it? Always please Sean. You come to me when you want and you leave me when you want and you don't care. You never cared. You didn't care the first time you dumped me and if I'd died you still wouldn't have cared.'

He said nothing.

'I didn't eat for weeks and I threw myself into the Bawnee and did you ask about me? No you bloody didn't.'

'Elva, for God's sake . . .'

'You waited, didn't you? Until I was married. And then you came after me again.'

He was getting seriously worried now. He had never seen her so hysterical.

'Well you'll get your comeuppance when Paudie comes home. Yes you will. Because he knows everything. But not yet the fact that his precious, darling youngest daughter is yours. When he finds out, that'll be the end of your picture-perfect marriage with your cow-eyed stupid wife.'

'That's not true,' he said. 'You're upset, I can see that. But you don't want to do this.'

'You don't know what I want to do.'

'Ah, Elva. You'll be better off without me.'

'But will you be better off without me?' she asked. 'Will you?'

'Yes,' he said as she sank to her knees and started to cry. 'Yes, I will.'

He waited for a moment but she didn't look up. So he left the house, jumped into the car and drove away.

He'd worried, at least fleetingly when he first heard the news, that she'd told Paudie about Cushla and that he'd killed her in a rage. He knew that he was being melodramatic and overemotional about it, but these things happened no matter how much you thought they never happened to people you knew. So he wondered and worried and fretted, too, that somehow he'd be dragged into it all. Then the stories had started to leak out. That perhaps she'd been drinking. That she may have leaned out of the window and lost her footing. That it was all a terrible accident.

He was still concerned that the police would want to

interview him. If they found out he'd been at the house and was probably the last person to see her alive, he'd be a suspect straight away. Sean liked watching detective series on TV. He knew how it worked. If they learned about the affair and his desire to end it, the police could decide he had a motive for killing her, and God only knew what would happen next. Just because you were innocent didn't mean mistakes couldn't be made. Or that your life couldn't be destroyed.

His relief when he heard that she'd been seen in Ardbawn early in the afternoon, and that subsequently she'd dropped the children off at a birthday party, was beyond words. Whatever had happened, however it had happened, it had been nothing to do with him.

Then the note arrived in the post, along with the paintings and the ring.

It wasn't addressed to him. Just to the guesthouse. And Nina opened it.

Chapter 32

'. . . That's how I found out. After that, he told me everything.'

Nina handed the note to Joe as she finished telling the story. The two of them had sat silently as she spoke, not interrupting her, allowing her words to flow.

'So what did you do then?' asked Sheridan while he read it.

'The way Sean tells it, Elva practically stalked him. I could believe that, you know, because she was a very intense sort of woman.'

Joe's body tensed.

'She was lovely, Joe, I know she was, but she was also . . . difficult. Sean said that he'd loved her when they were younger but that her neediness and her intensity scared him off. He always felt guilty about the whole Bawnee River thing and not going to see her afterwards. He thought that maybe if he'd done that, things might have been different. He thought she obsessed about him.'

'He thought an awful lot of himself,' Joe said, and his tone was harsh.

'Yes,' agreed Nina. 'He still does.'

'Poor Elva was clearly very disturbed,' said Sheridan, who immediately wished she'd kept her mouth shut because she saw the dart of pain in Joe's eyes.

'You're blaming her,' said Joe. 'Both of you. For the fact that she had an affair. For the fact that he kept coming back. And my sister . . . Cushla *is* my full sister. I know she is.'

'I think she is too,' said Nina, although the truth was she'd never been certain. Any time she saw Cushla O'Malley in Ardbawn she searched her features for similarities to Sean. She'd never found any. But nor had she found any real likeness to Paudie. Cushla was the image of Elva.

'I'm not blaming your mother,' said Sheridan. 'I'm just trying to put things into perspective.'

'*You* clearly blame her,' Joe told Nina. 'Otherwise why would you have forgiven your cheating, philandering husband so damn quickly?'

Nina winced. When she'd been telling the story of Sean and Elva she'd been thinking about that herself. Had forgiving him been the right thing to do? Or had it, in the end, been a long-term mistake?

'There was a second letter,' she said awkwardly. 'I don't have it,' she added as Joe held out his hand. 'I . . . It was . . . long and rambling and incoherent. She said that she loved Sean. That she hated Paudie. And then she said that she loved Paudie and hated Sean. She said she needed to be somewhere else for a while. She needed people to look after her . . .' Her words faltered as she saw the expression on Joe's face. 'She was clearly very distressed,' said Nina. 'I'm so sorry, Joe. I don't think she meant to kill herself, but I do think that somehow she made a terrible mistake.'

* * *

Joe was remembering the day she died, the day of the party, which he'd said he wouldn't bother going to. She'd been edgy and distracted and he hadn't wanted to leave her alone. But she'd insisted.

'I need time for myself,' she'd told him. 'I have things to do.'

Afterwards, he'd been devastated to think that one of those things had been to fall out of a bedroom window.

'If she wrote a suicide note, why didn't you give it to the police?' he asked Nina as he came back to the present. 'And why didn't you give the first one to the police too?'

'I was in a complete state,' said Nina. 'The first note was sort of inconclusive. It could've meant anything – that she was running away, or . . .' She broke off as Joe looked sceptically at her. 'The second one came a week later. I don't know why, because it was postmarked the same day as the first. When I read it, I felt . . . I think I wanted to protect everyone. For it all to be a mistake. For her and Sean never to have happened. Because he made her unhappy, you see. I didn't want to think that he'd made her so unhappy she'd take her own life. If I produced either note there would have been even more questions and gossip, and I didn't think any of us deserved it.'

'Sean did,' said Joe grimly.

'Sean was beyond shocked,' Nina told him. 'He really was. He blamed himself. He knew she was irrational and he said he should have stayed with her until someone came home, no matter what trouble it caused. But then I reminded him that she'd brought you all to the birthday party and had been seen in the town after that, and I said that whatever had happened it couldn't have been to do with him. I wanted

that to be the case. So I just put everything away and eventually it all died down and things went back to normal and
I thought I'd done the right thing.'

'But things didn't go back to normal for us,' said Joe. 'Because
nothing can fill the gap when you lose someone. Nothing.'

'I'm sorry,' said Nina.

'Where's the second note now?' asked Sheridan, who'd
listened to Nina's story with an increasing sense of wonder
about what went on beneath the surface of people's lives.

'I didn't know what to do with it,' said Nina. 'I kept it
for two years. And then I sent it to Paudie.'

Joe looked at her in astonishment. 'You sent it to my
father?'

'I felt he should know,' said Nina.

A few days after she'd sent the letter to Paudie O'Malley
(she hadn't told Sean what she was doing; as far as he knew,
she'd destroyed everything that Elva had sent), the businessman called around to the guesthouse. Nina nearly
collapsed when she saw him outside and her hands trembled
as she opened the door.

'I got what you sent me,' Paudie told her after she'd invited
him into the kitchen.

'I thought you should have it,' she said. 'I realise I might
have made a mistake, but I kept thinking that perhaps you
blamed yourself somehow for what happened.'

'It *was* an accident,' said Paudie. 'She might have been
distraught, but she wouldn't have deliberately . . . She loved
the children too much.'

'Perhaps she thought that if she fell from the balcony she'd
injure herself and you'd love her again.'

Sheila O'Flanagan

'I always loved her,' said Paudie fiercely. 'Always. Even though I knew . . .'

Nina released her breath slowly. If Paudie had known about Elva's affair, why hadn't he done anything about it?

'I thought it would blow over,' he said as though she'd spoken out loud. 'I knew she always had a thing for Sean Fallon. It was a bit of a joke between us. I never thought it would come to this.'

'I'm sorry,' said Nina.

'It's not your fault.' Paudie closed his eyes and then seemed to gather himself together. 'What's done is done. I want to make a life for me and for my children. I've burned the letter. I don't want to talk about this ever again.'

'That's OK,' said Nina, who had been going to give him the paintings and the ring but now decided it might be better not to. 'I want to put it behind me too.'

'So why didn't you get rid of them?' asked Sheridan.

'I was going to. But it didn't seem right somehow. I tucked them away again in the same box as I kept all our family stuff. I was the only one who ever went near it. Hidden in plain view, I thought. Because if they were somewhere else, I was afraid I'd keep looking at them. Afraid what it would do to me and Sean.'

'And so you forgave him and you just got on with your lives,' said Joe.

'Yes,' said Nina. 'We did.'

Nina didn't truly know why she'd decided to forgive him. She only knew that at the time she wanted it all to be over and done with, to forget it had ever happened, and for

472

everything to get back to the way it was before. Except this time without Elva O'Malley. Besides, her husband was utterly penitent. She'd seen a totally different side to him then. A side where he didn't know what was best, where he wasn't the one totally in control, where he was asking her advice and grateful to her for being there. It was the first time in her life that she'd felt superior to anyone, but she certainly felt superior to Sean back then. She'd felt that her role in the marriage was the important one. She'd felt suddenly and unexpectedly strong. And she had to be, because she had the business and the children to consider.

They'd rebuilt their marriage afterwards. More equally, she always thought. They'd put the past behind them and so, it seemed, had Paudie O'Malley. Neither she nor Sean had ever spoken more than a couple of words to him since.

Sheridan was totally wrapped up in the story, but she was also busy examining Nina's narrative and the effect it was having on Joe, who was now turning his mother's ring over and over in his hands. She was acutely aware that the reason he was hearing all this now was because of her. Because she'd panicked and taken Elva's paintings and ring from Nina's house.

'I guess it was lucky you're the person you are,' she said to Nina slowly. 'Because if you'd given Elva's letters to the police . . .'

'I wouldn't have done that.'

'I know. But if that second one in particular had become public knowledge—'

'What?' interrupted Joe. 'What are you trying to say?'

'Nothing.' Sheridan wished she hadn't tried to make Nina

feel better by saying it was a good thing she hadn't given the letters to the police. But as Joe continued to stare at her she said, 'If the insurance company had seen that letter, maybe they wouldn't have—'

'How dare you!' Joe was suddenly furiously angry. 'How dare you suggest that my father benefited from information being withheld about my mother's death.'

'I didn't mean . . .' Sheridan realised how callous she must have sounded. 'It was just . . .'

'My father loved my mother and he was devastated by her death and he would've given any money to have her back!' cried Joe. 'I know that! And for you to think any differently is just plain wrong.'

'I'm not saying he didn't love her,' said Sheridan helplessly. 'I'm saying—'

'I know what you're saying and I can't believe it.' His voice was hard and uncompromising.

'Joe, please.'

'Stop. Stop now. I don't want to hear anything you have to say. How do I know Nina isn't right?' He looked at Sheridan angrily. 'How do I know that this isn't all some insane ploy by you to investigate my family? To try to destroy us because you still blame my father for you losing your job? How do I know you didn't plan every single detail?'

'Joe, for heaven's sake, how could I possibly have known Nina had all this stuff?' asked Sheridan. 'And even if I wanted some kind of revenge on your dad – and I admit that I harboured some dark thoughts about him after I was made redundant – I would never have come up with this.'

But she couldn't help thinking that it was knowledge that Alo Brady would absolutely kill for.

'I'm not staying here any longer.' Joe stood up abruptly. He thrust the ring into the pocket of his jeans and held on to the paintings. 'Give me the note, Nina,' he said.

She handed it to him.

'I have to go home, talk to my father.'

'I'm sorry, Joe,' said Nina.

'It's a bit late for that,' he said. 'I don't know how to feel about all this. About knowing it was kept from me and about knowing that somehow it's all come to light. And that one of the people who's brought it to light is a journalist who . . .' He stopped and looked at Sheridan.

'Why are you thinking the worst of me?' she asked.

'You took things you shouldn't have,' he told her. 'Even if it was a mistake and you panicked, you should have brought them straight back to Nina. You came out with me tonight and you never said a word, even when we . . . You kept quiet about it and you must have known how I . . .' He shook his head.

'I thought you might have known already. And we were on a date. I didn't want to bring up stories from the past.'

The sudden sound of Sheridan's phone ringing, from inside her handbag, startled them all.

'Go ahead and answer it,' said Joe.

But by the time she picked it out of her bag it had stopped. The caller ID showed her that Alo Brady had been looking for her. She winced and put it on the table in front of her. There was no way she could talk to Alo right now. The phone started to ring again. She stared at it.

'Oh for heaven's sake, answer the damn thing,' Joe said.

But Sheridan didn't pick it up. Once again it stopped, but then beeped to indicate that Alo had left a message.

'It's not important, really.' She could hardly breathe.

'It obviously is. Check your messages,' said Joe.

She dialled her voicemail. And then, because the volume was still at maximum from when she'd been talking to Alo at the restaurant, everyone heard what he had to say.

'Hey, Sher, just wondering, can you get your hands on any of O'Malley's emails? They might lead to the Sneaky Sheikh. Looking forward to getting your stuff.'

Nina and Joe were staring at her, their expressions horrified.

'It's not what you think.' Sheridan was aghast. 'Really it's not.'

'*You're* not what I think.' Joe looked defeated. 'I never wanted to believe—'

'Joe, please, listen to me,' said Sheridan rapidly. 'That was Alo, he's an ex-colleague, he's the guy who rang me earlier. He wanted me to give him some background information on a piece he's working on—'

'Please stop,' said Joe. 'You've done enough already.'

'No, no, you're getting it all wrong.'

'He's looking forward to getting your stuff,' said Joe. 'My father's emails. I don't think I've got anything wrong there.'

'You have. You . . .' Suddenly it was all too much for her. She started to cry.

'Oh, not tears!' Joe's voice was disgusted.

'I said I'd give him information because I wanted so badly to have my name attached to a story. But Joe, I don't think I would have done it. Not after tonight. Not after . . . us.'

'Us?' His voice was scathing. 'Us?'

'OK, I know you don't trust me and you'll never believe

a word I say, but . . . but they're doing a story about corruption. And the trail leads to your dad. And maybe you. And I don't know if you've done anything wrong or not, but it's all going to come out. So . . . so . . . do whatever you have to do.'

Joe looked at her in utter astonishment.

'How long have you known about this?' He demanded.

'Only since tonight, when Alo rang. And I didn't know what to do.'

'Oh, I think you knew exactly what you were going to do,' said Joe. 'I'm out of here.'

And with that he walked out and slammed the door behind him.

Chapter 33

Sheridan looked blearily at the clock. It was past eight and she couldn't believe that she'd slept at all. After Joe and then Nina had left, she'd sat shaking in the studio, not knowing what to do, feeling as though her life had collapsed around her. She had managed to destroy something more wonderful than she'd ever imagined with Joe O'Malley. Nina Fallon was disgusted with her. And the worst of it all was, she had made up her mind not to give Alo Brady the information he was looking for. Neither Nina nor Joe had believed her, and she couldn't really blame them.

That being the case, she thought, maybe she should just give Alo what he wanted. Because the one thing she was pretty sure of was that she wouldn't have a job with the *Central News* any longer. Paudie might have forgiven her impromptu staking-out of his house, but this was entirely different. This was really personal. So with no job and no prospects, why shouldn't she get totally behind Alo? Besides, despite everything, his story might be true. Just because Joe made her feel the way she did didn't mean he couldn't be involved in anything dodgy. Just because she didn't believe it didn't mean it hadn't happened. She'd written about corruption in sport before. She violently opposed corrupt clubs, managers, players and organisations. It was no different in business. If Paudie was corrupt, he deserved what was coming to him. And if Joe was corrupt, so did he.

She went into the shower and spent a long time allowing the water to massage the back of her neck. When she got out, she made herself a coffee, took a couple of Nurofen and started to write. Her fingers flew over the keyboard, tapping as furiously as they ever had when she'd been at the *City Scope* and writing match reports or interviews with sports stars. A further hour and she was finished. Now all she had to do was send it to Alo. He'd be very, very pleased with her. And her name would be up in media lights again.

Sean Fallon came to Ardbawn the minute he got Nina's phone call. When he'd first seen her name appear on his phone he'd thought that she was ringing him to say that it was time for him to move back home. When she started gabbling on about Sheridan Gray finding the envelope with Elva O'Malley's note in it, he nearly had a fit.

He made it to Ardbawn in record time and clattered into the kitchen, where Nina was sitting at the table, the coloured box of family mementos in front of her. She was looking at Alan's first tooth. Sean had thought it was grisly to keep it, but when they'd taken it from beneath their sleeping son's pillow and substituted money instead, Nina hadn't wanted to throw it out. (Fortunately, he thought, she hadn't been quite as nostalgic about their children's subsequent dental losses.)

'I can't believe you kept all that shit,' he said angrily. 'What were you thinking?'

'They were wonderful paintings. It seemed wrong to destroy them.'

'They were a demented woman's daubs,' snapped Sean. He exhaled sharply. 'So this reporter is involved in some big story about the O'Malleys and she was actually working on his paper while she was researching it?'

'I'm not sure exactly,' said Nina. 'But the bottom line is that it's all sure to come out. You, Elva, everything.'

'What is it with people and their prurient interest in other people's personal lives!' Sean was outraged. 'Anything about Elva and me is just gossip, nothing to do with O'Malley and his damn empire.'

'I know. But people prefer gossip to news.'

'She'll ruin my career!' cried Sean.

'I doubt that.' Nina looked rueful. 'Isn't all publicity supposed to be good when you're a celebrity? You're doing OK, aren't you, even if you're currently in a coma. What with the documentary and everything.'

'Yes, but—'

'And your affair with Lulu didn't hurt it, did it?'

'I'll have to talk to my publicist,' said Sean. 'We need be spinning any story that's out there to our advantage.'

'There's an advantage in you having had an affair with a woman who died in tragic circumstances and happened to be married to the town's most influential businessman, who's being investigated for unethical dealings?'

'We can definitely make it one.' Sean looked thoughtful. 'Paint Elva as a victim too.'

'Sean!' Nina was scandalised.

'All right, all right. Sorry. But the thing is, we'll emerge from this as a strong couple,' he said firmly. 'Committed to our marriage.'

'Will we?'

'They'll think you're a saint.'

'They'll think I'm a doormat.'

'Not at all. You did the right thing before. You're doing the right thing now. We're happy together, Nina. Our marriage works.' Sean sounded self-satisfied.

'Because I forgave you.'

'Look, that thing with Elva . . . we talked about it. She was a deranged bunny-boiler and that's what I'll get the publicist to say.'

'Deranged?' Nina shook her head. 'She was very distressed. But you can't call her deranged. Think about Paudie and his family.'

'If Paudie's up the creek for giving bribes or whatever, he has more to worry about than having his dead wife called names. I'm thinking about us. And I'm thinking that we should be able to get that reporter to write something favourable to us. You know her, Nina. You can make her do the right thing.'

Nina sighed deeply, then shrugged. 'As far as I'm concerned, she can write what she likes.'

'Nina!'

'I don't care any more, Sean. I don't care about Paudie or Elva or you.'

'You don't mean that. Look, I know I hurt you. I know I made a mess of things. But it won't happen again.'

'You said that after Elva. You swore,' she reminded him. 'But Lulu still happened.'

481

'If there's sixteen years between all my affairs, then you should feel OK about it,' he said. 'I'll be too old then to care.'

'That's not the point,' said Nina. 'I can't help loving you, Sean, but I don't trust you any more. And that's not enough for a marriage.'

'Nina, darling.' His tone was persuasive. 'I know it's been a bit of a shock having all this rehashed, but I know you don't mean that. Love has always been enough for us. It always will be.'

'Not any more,' she said firmly.

'You're being silly.'

'No, I'm not.'

His eyes hardened. 'Remember the solicitor's letter?' he asked. 'We have joint assets.'

'I know.'

'You'll lose out.'

'Oh, Sean.' She looked at him regretfully. 'I think I already have.'

Chapter 34

The sound of birdsong woke Sheridan early the following morning, but she'd slept fitfully anyway. She got up and dressed in her jogging clothes. She'd always gone for a run when she needed to clear her head, and she very definitely needed to clear her head now.

She'd spent a lot of time the previous evening reading what she'd written for Alo Brady. She knew that it was good, insightful journalism. She knew it was well written and concise. Possibly one of the best things she'd ever done. Definitely something to make her name with.

She closed the door of the studio behind her and ran slowly down the driveway before turning on to the road. She ran the route she'd run before, the one that would bring her past the sports pitches. She was sure that there'd be a match later that morning, but she knew that they wouldn't have started by the time she passed by. She kept her pace steady and even, listening to her own breath as she ran, allowing the rhythm to take over.

It would be a nice day, she thought. The dreariness of winter had almost imperceptibly slid into spring. There was heat in the sun at last. She felt it on her shoulders as she put more effort into maintaining her pace because she'd reached the part of the road that was a steady incline. She liked the feeling of stretching her legs, she liked feeling her heart working harder.

The car passed her and then stopped. She stopped too, jogging on the spot as she waited to see what the driver would do next.

The roof of the convertible was down and he turned in the seat to look back at her.

'Get in.' It was an invitation, not a command.

'I'm hot and sweaty again,' she said. 'You probably don't want me in your car.'

'Please,' said Joe.

She took a deep breath and opened the passenger door.

Joe put the car into gear and eased up the road.

'Where are we going?' she asked.

'A place I know.'

He drove for about fifteen minutes, then turned down a narrow byway and stopped. They were beside the Bawnee River. It rippled past them, the clear water sparkling beneath the morning sun.

'This was my favourite place after my mother died,' said Joe. 'I used to come here when I wanted to be on my own. It's not that far from the house when you cut through the fields.'

Sheridan recognised it. Elva had painted this place, the winding river and the canopy of trees. She stood in silence, thinking about the other woman meeting Nina's husband here. In love, perhaps, but on the road to destruction.

The silence between them grew. Sheridan waited for Joe

to speak. Waiting was something she was good at. When she'd interviewed people for the *City Scope*, she'd often allowed periods of silence, during which the interviewee nearly always spoke, usually volunteering information that she never would have got if she'd kept asking questions.

'I spoke to my father.'

Sheridan tensed. She'd known he would tell Paudie about Alo's investigation. She'd known that would have implications for her too.

'He hasn't been involved in any corrupt deals.'

She said nothing.

'He admits that there was a lot – maybe an inordinate amount – of corporate hospitality and entertainment.'

She raised an eyebrow.

'Which,' Joe said, 'we don't normally do. But it seemed appropriate at the time.'

She nodded.

'So we'll be rebutting everything in that story except some grandiose dinner bills that maybe shouldn't have happened.'

'Fair enough,' she said.

'But your part in it . . . the background stuff . . . the personal stuff that you can add . . .' He looked at her pleadingly. 'You can write whatever you like about the business and it'll be up to us to make our case, but I'm begging you – whatever you say about my mother, can you please, please not make her out to be a selfish, uncaring bitch? Because she wasn't.'

'Did you talk to your father about her too?' asked Sheridan.

'How could I not? It was so much to take in. I couldn't

believe that he'd kept it from me. I couldn't believe I hadn't guessed either.'

'We never think of our parents as people with complicated lives,' said Sheridan.

'Oh, I've always thought my dad's life was complicated. I just never realised how complicated my mother's was. Dad told me everything he could about it. He was tolerant of her because he loved her so much. I know you've only heard about the unhappy side of her, and the fact that she was cheating on Dad, yet when she was with us we always seemed to be the most important people in her life. She was the kind of person who lived it to the full, you know. She could get excited about the littlest of things and turn them into great adventures. She wasn't easy to be with all the time, but she wasn't the kind of uncaring woman that you'd like her to be.'

'Joe—'

'Nevertheless . . .' He continued as though she hadn't spoken. 'Dad argued with her the night before she died. He told her that she was making a fool of herself over Sean Fallon and that people would start to talk.' He closed his eyes briefly as he remembered, then turned to look at Sheridan. 'I overheard them. I didn't know what they were fighting about at the time, though, I only knew that it was scary. She was shouting at him, and eventually he shouted back. He told her he'd kill her.'

'Joe!'

'Afterwards, when she was found . . . I was afraid he had.'

Sheridan looked at him in shock.

'I knew he wouldn't have done it deliberately,' said Joe quickly. 'But I was terrified there'd been an accident. That they'd had another row and she'd backed away from him or something . . .'

'Oh, Joe.'

'But then I found out that he wasn't near the house that day, that he'd been at a meeting, I was so relieved. It must have been an accident after all. Later the papers started with their horrible insinuations and it was incredibly difficult. Dad felt he had to do something, and when he sued, oh, the *County News*, I think it was, well, that was that. The insinuations died down pretty damn quickly. When you mentioned the life-assurance payout, I thought I was hearing them all over again.'

'I shouldn't have said anything.'

'It was a reasonable question.'

'But not a very sensitive one.'

'I was angry. It wouldn't have mattered what you said. But since then . . .'

She waited for him to compose himself.

'When Mum died, it was as though she'd never existed. Dad did his best, but it was hard for him. He didn't want to talk about it any more. He wasn't – isn't – a demonstrative man. Nor is he the kind of man who believes in talking about your feelings. Hell, I'm not that sort of man myself, but from time to time you need to . . . to say something. And what I want to say to you, Sheridan, despite everything, is thank you.'

She looked at him in astonishment.

'Thank you? For what?'

'I always felt guilty,' he said. 'At first for thinking that my dad had anything to do with it. But then – I think all of us, me, Sinead, Peter and Cushla, were all burdened with it. We weren't there when Mum died, that was one thing. And the other . . . well, we'd given her a lot of grief that day. We argued about going to the party. There was lots of bickering. We were all behaving quite badly. She was pissed off with us, told us we'd be the death of her. So when she was found, when I knew it wasn't Dad . . . I thought she'd done it because of us.'

'Oh my God.' Sheridan's eyes welled with tears. 'Oh, Joe, what a horrible thing for you to live with.'

He grimaced. 'I'm sure she would've hated for us for believing in any way that it was our fault. But knowing that her demons weren't because of us makes a huge difference. It's like . . . it's like a burden's been lifted from me.'

Sheridan was unable to speak.

'I know you need to write what you have to write,' he said. 'I don't like it, but I respect it. All I ask is that it's balanced, at least as far as my mother is concerned. She might have done some very silly things, but she was a good mother to us, no matter how hard you find that to believe.'

Sheridan took a few steps away from him so that she was standing beside the swirling waters of the Bawnee River.

'I wrote it last night,' she said.

'Oh.'

She could see defeat in his eyes as his shoulders slumped. 'But I didn't send it to Alo.'

'When will you send it?'

'I'm not going to,' she said.

He looked at her in surprise. 'Why not?'

'It's not what I do,' she said. 'I'm a sports writer. That's what I love. And yes, I like to bring people to account if they've done something wrong. But what I've never done, and what I'm not going to do now, is write about a situation where I'm personally involved. Nor do I want to hurt people I know. Nina, for example, who's gone through enough already with that husband of hers. And Josh – I don't want to be the one to call his grandfather a crook.'

'My father isn't a crook,' said Joe.

'A few months ago I would've liked to believe anything about your father,' she said. 'But I don't want to think he's a crook either. That's not why I'm staying out of it, though. Like I said, I'm personally involved. I know you all. I like your family. I . . .' She shrugged. 'I couldn't do it. Truthfully – even if I wasn't involved, I wouldn't do it. It's just wrong for me.'

'Are you absolutely sure about this?' Joe's eyes held hers and she returned his gaze confidently.

'Positive. Even though Alo is pissed off at me.'

'What about getting a job at another paper? Wasn't this your passport in?'

'In to what? More of the same sort of thing? I told you, I'm not interested. Something will come up and it'll be right for me. This isn't.'

'Are you really doing this because of us?' He was standing beside her now, his eyes searching her face.

'I care about your family,' she said.

'Not them.' He cupped her face with his hands. 'Us. Me, you and the way we are together. The way you make me feel. The way I hope I make you feel.'

'I'm not doing it because of us,' she said. 'I'm doing it because of me. Because of who I am. As for us . . .' Suddenly her smile was wide. 'I'm glad there's still an us. I've never felt as right with a person in my whole life as I feel with you.'

He smiled too. 'That's good,' he said, and as he pulled her towards him, she'd never felt more sure of herself in her life.

Chapter 35

The town was thronged with people celebrating the Spring Festival. The farmers' market stalls were set up in the plaza, there were bouncy castles and other attractions at the schools and playing fields, and there was a steady stream of visitors to Perry Andrews' Ardbawn Through the Ages exhibition of photos and newspaper cuttings.

The festival had been officially opened a few hours earlier by Paudie O'Malley, who said that he was proud of coming from such a vibrant town, and proud of counting most of the people in it as neighbours and friends. He said that he was glad to announce that the consortium his company was part of had won the Middle East telecoms bid, and that although they had been criticised for their lavish expenditure during the process, there was no evidence of any unethical dealings, as had recently been suggested in certain elements of the media. However, he added, they'd be revising their standards regarding entertainment in the future. He'd announced the company's increased sponsorship of the football and hurling teams, as well as additional sponsorship for all of Ardbawn's sporting organisations. He said that it was good to see so many young people, including his grandson, involved in sports, and that it had been great to see a big write-up about their success in the *Irish Journal* recently. He looked down at the crowd when he said this and his eyes met Sheridan's. She grinned at him and gave him a thumbs-up sign.

She'd written the piece as part of her assignment with her new employer. The day after she'd spoken to Joe at the riverbank, while she'd been sitting in the offices of the *Central News,* her mobile had rung. It was Jimmy Ahearne, the sports editor of the *City Scope*'s biggest rival, and he was asking her if she'd be interested in a position on their sports desk. He'd said that he'd been reading her tweets and her recent blog post about preparations for the next Olympic Games and he'd been very impressed by them. She'd had to remain very calm as she said yes and then agreed to meet him for a chat, but DJ had seen the beaming smile split her face and guessed that he was about to lose his temporary reporter.

She'd experienced a certain regret at leaving the *Central News,* but when she walked into her new office in Dublin's East Point Business Park, with its views over the glittering waters of the bay, she felt as though she was coming home. The buzz hit her as soon as she sat down at her desk, and she already knew what she wanted to write about: the upcoming tour by the Irish cricket team as well as the continued success of an exceptional young swimmer. She planned to keep up her tweets and her blog too, and she'd also pitched the idea to Jimmy of giving more space to junior sports reporting, to high-lighting promising talent and what was happening to support it in local communities.

Her first piece had been about the Ardbawn teams and had received good feedback, not only from Ardbawn (where the *Journal*'s circulation had quadrupled on the day the piece was published, which caused DJ to phone her and warn her that too many stories about Ardbawn would ruin him), but also nationwide. Talia had texted, reminding her that she'd always said Sheridan would find the right job (and telling her that finding the right man had been more than an added bonus); Alice and Pat were full of praise and congratulations for her dogged determination over the last few months, while her two brothers (who were big into social networking because of their sporting backgrounds) sent complimentary messages and re-tweeted links to her pieces. She'd basked in their good wishes as she settled into the new job she absolutely loved.

But, she thought, as she stood looking at the photos in the exhibition, it was nice to be back in Ardbawn, nice to see Nina and DJ and Shimmy and Myra, who had returned to the *Central News*, though having struck a deal with DJ so that she could work from home too. She'd even met Des Browne for the first time. He wasn't slow about telling her that although she was a good writer, her reports needed more factual information. Statistics, he suggested, would give them an additional authority. She'd nodded gravely while he lectured her, and only managed to get away from him eventually by pretending she'd seen someone she desperately needed to talk to.

'I hear you're going to Paudie O'Malley's tonight.'

She jumped and turned around. Ritz Boland was behind her, looking as stunning as ever, her long hair gleaming in the shaft of sunlight coming through the window.

'Hi, Ritz,' she said. 'Yes, I'll be there. How about you?'

Ritz nodded. 'Everyone from the organising committee was invited. It's very good of him.'

'Indeed it is.'

'And you're invited because . . . ?' Ritz arched an impeccably shaped eyebrow.

'Because I've got to know Paudie over the last few weeks,' she said. 'Because I used to work for the *Central News*. And because I'm going out with Joe.' She smiled as she said this, and Ritz suddenly smiled too.

'I heard about that all right,' she said. 'You Dublin girls. Coming down and robbing us of all our good men.'

'Sorry,' said Sheridan unapologetically.

'Oh look, from the moment I saw the two of you together I knew,' said Ritz. 'There was a chemistry . . .'

'There was, wasn't there,' agreed Sheridan. 'It knocked me sideways. Still does.'

'I think you'll be good for him,' Ritz told her. 'You're different to the rest of us. You're so confident. You breezed in, totally disarmed DJ, wrote some great stories – including the school siege – and now you've even got Ardbawn on the national pages. You're amazing. It's like no matter what you do you succeed.'

'Gosh.' Sheridan looked bemused. 'I don't think of it like that at all.'

'You should,' said Ritz. 'You're just a natural-born winner.'

Sheridan laughed. 'I'm not, but thank you.'

'You're welcome,' said Ritz. 'See you later.'

Sheridan watched her walk away and then turned her attention back to the photos. She saw the ones she'd chosen from Nina's collection. They were a mixture of black-and-white photos from the 1950s showing young women in printed blouses and long shorts and men in shirts and equally long shorts standing beside heavy bicycles, their hair blowing in the breeze and a look of excitement on their faces. The photos had been taken at various locations around the town and the surrounding area and they were all labelled 'Ardbawn Cycling Club'. Sheridan had chosen them because the town was so easily identifiable, but also because the people in the photographs looked so eager and excited about their futures. And because although their clothes and hairstyles (and make-up in the case of the women) were different now, people were generally still the same. They still had hopes and dreams, and although they knew that not everything they wanted would come to pass, there was still a whole world of adventure stretching out ahead of them. At the time she'd picked them she hadn't thought much about her own dreams. But, she thought, sometimes we end up living dreams that we didn't even know we had.

Paudie had organised a meal in March Manor for the festival committee. This included Hayley Goodwin, Peggy Merchant and Nina Fallon, as well as Ritz, DJ, Perry Andrews and the young garda, Charlie Sweetman. Robbie Dunston, the platinum-selling rock star, had also come along and had promised to sing a few of his greatest hits for them. Paudie's family were there too. Sheridan had been nervous about meeting them – she hadn't seen any of them since finding out about Elva and Sean. She had, though, seen Paudie, who'd dropped into the newspaper offices before she left and thanked her for all her hard work. Then he'd spoken to her about his family's history.

'JJ tells me that you trashed what you'd written about us,' he said.

'Like I said to him, it's not what I do.'

'Thank you,' said Paudie.

'Maybe someone else will write about it some day,' Sheridan warned him. 'After all, Sean is very much in the public eye still. And I hear he's been signed up for more episodes of *Chandler's Park*, so he's bound to be in the news again.'

'I'm not sure that Sean wants his involvement to come out either,' said Paudie. 'It's not a story that shows him in a particularly good light, no matter how much his publicist might try to turn it around. It was a sad time in all our lives. Sometimes you just have to move on.'

Sheridan nodded. She felt she knew a lot about moving on. She was getting good at it herself.

'I'm sorry about your job at the *City Scope*,' Paudie said. 'It wasn't my decision to get rid of you.'

'I know.'

'It turned out to be a very bad decision on the editor's part,' he said. 'Making you available to our competitors!'

'It didn't seem like that at first,' Sheridan confessed. 'None of them wanted to hire me.'

'But you've got a great job now,' Paudie said. 'So things have worked out well all round.'

'I know.' She grinned. 'The last few horoscopes I wrote for the *Central News* talked about not holding back and then reaching for the stars. I don't know what made me write them. But next thing I knew I was offered the job. I was thinking to myself then that maybe I should stay as the resident astrologer.'

Paudie laughed. 'Perhaps we can call on your talents again in the future.'

'Myra is way better than me,' said Sheridan. 'She's so patient with the contributors. I was a bit too demanding sometimes.'

'You were fine,' said Paudie. 'You're a good person, Sheridan Gray. And a great competitor.'

'Thank you.'

'And I'm delighted you're going out with my son.'

She blushed. 'It's early days . . .'

'True.' His eyes twinkled.

'. . . and I'm living in Dublin again.'

'I like that about you,' said Paudie. 'No giving it all up for love.'

'I do love Joe,' said Sheridan. 'I've never loved anyone the way I love him. But I need something for myself too, and that's my job. Besides, he spends a lot of time in Dublin. So it's working out well for us.'

'Good,' said Paudie. 'He deserves to be happy. So do you.'

'I am,' Sheridan told him. 'I really am.'

It had been a long time since March Manor had been used for a function, and the festival committee walked around the house with interest, commenting on the ornate plasterwork, the elegant drapes, the crystal chandeliers and the variety of paintings that hung on the walls. It was all tastefully done, they agreed. Paudie had an eye for style and beauty.

Nina Fallon thought so too as she stood in one of the drawing rooms that looked out over the fields behind the house. She'd been reluctant to come to the dinner, feeling uncomfortable about seeing Paudie now that their past was shared. But he'd simply welcomed her as part of the group and hadn't said anything to her to make her feel ill at ease.

'It's a lovely view.'

She whirled around and was, for the first time in years, face to face with him alone.

'Yes.' Her voice was croaky. 'Stunning.'

'You have a nice view from the guesthouse too.'

'Hopefully that will help it sell,' said Nina.

Paudie looked at her sympathetically. 'You're still going through with that?'

'I have to,' she said. 'Sean wants his share, and he's entitled to it.'

'Seems harsh.'

'Life can be harsh.'

'True. But that house has been in your family for years.'

'It's only a building when all's said and done,' said Nina. 'And maybe it's a good thing.'

'How?'

'I was getting tired of it,' she admitted. 'It's tough work in difficult times. Even in good times. I don't want to look after people all my life. There are other things I can do.'

'Oh.' Paudie looked surprised.

'I don't know what yet,' said Nina. 'I haven't decided. But there should be enough money left over after the house is sold and the mortgage repaid for me to spend a little time doing something else. Travelling, maybe. I always wanted to travel but it was never really possible when I was running the Bawnee River. I might study too,' she added. 'I was thinking of taking a course in behavioural science.'

'Really?'

She nodded. 'There are so many things I haven't done.

Selling up gives me a chance to do them.' She took a deep breath. 'Paudie, I have to tell you that I didn't realise what was going on between Sean and Elva. When it all came out, the only thing I thought about was how to keep things as they were supposed to be. I let Sean manipulate me into forgiving him. I wanted to pretend that it had never happened. Only you can't do that, can you? Sooner or later you have to face up to it.'

'There's no chance of you and Sean getting back together?'

She shook her head. 'I've moved on from Sean. Maybe I should have done it before, but the circumstances were different then. The kids are upset, but they're grown up, they have their own lives to worry about. Sean's going from strength to strength in his TV career. I don't begrudge him that. I'm glad for him. But I'm glad for me too.'

'Did you tell Alan and Chrissie about Sean and Elva?'

'No. I couldn't see the point.'

'You're one of the most philosophical people I've ever met,' said Paudie. 'I thought you'd be bitter about everything.'

'At first I was, but then I realised there was no point,' Nina said. 'It doesn't change what happens, and all it does is eat away at your insides.'

Paudie nodded slowly. 'I was bitter too,' he said. 'Bitter that Elva needed Sean more than me. Bitter that she was prepared to live a lie because even though she loved him she wanted what I could give her.'

'And do you still feel that way?'

'Strangely, no,' said Paudie. 'It's quite weird, I suppose, because it's been with me for ever, but ever since JJ came home and we talked about it, I've felt differently.'

'Maybe sharing helped.'

'Maybe.' Paudie sounded doubtful.

'You were hiding it from them,' Nina said. 'That probably wasn't a good thing in the long run.'

'Probably not,' agreed Paudie. 'I guess I wasn't great as a father.'

'Don't be silly,' said Nina. 'You did your best.'

'My best wasn't quite good enough.'

'Oh, look, when it comes to being parents, we're all muddling our way through,' Nina told him. 'We think we're doing the right thing, but sometimes we make mistakes. They get over it, though. I've got two great children. And yours have all turned out OK.'

'I have four wonderful children,' he said, his eyes fixed firmly on her.

'Yes,' she agreed. 'Each one of them deserves you as a dad.'

'I wish I'd talked to you like this before,' said Paudie. 'These few minutes, this conversation . . . it's made such a difference to me.'

'You can talk to me any time you like,' said Nina. 'Though I could be in South America or somewhere equally exotic by the time you want to chat again.'

'Come to dinner some evening,' he suggested. 'When the house isn't full of other people.'

She looked at him quizzically.

'Just dinner,' he said quickly.

'I'd love to.'

'Excellent,' said Paudie. 'I'll look forward to it. Now I'd better join the rest of the guests. Robbie is going to start belting them out in a few minutes, and he doesn't like to have his audience arriving late.'

* * *

The music could be heard outside of the house and across the huge swathe of meadow behind it.

'It's kind of bearable at this distance,' said Sheridan. 'I can't imagine what damage he's doing to the committee's collective eardrums inside.'

Joe chuckled. 'Most of them were fans. They would've worshipped at Robbie Dunston's altar.'

'It's not my thing,' said Sheridan. 'But he's a nice man. It's hard to imagine him snorting coke and smashing guitars and doing all those rock-star things.'

'Maybe we all settle down eventually,' said Joe.

'Maybe.' She walked barefoot through the grass and then turned to him. 'I was going to suggest that this was my rock-star moment, but it's more of a sixties hippy thing, isn't it? Barefoot in the grass.'

'You make a beautiful hippy,' said Joe.

She smiled at him. She was wearing the green dress. It was the first time he'd got to see it, and his eyes had opened wide. She'd explained that she'd bought it for the date that had been interrupted by the school siege, and he'd looked at her ruefully and said that if she'd been wearing that dress, he'd never have let her walk out of the restaurant.

'That makes you sound very shallow,' she teased.

'That's men for you,' he said. 'Truly, Sheridan, I've never seen you look so lovely.'

He repeated his words now as he looked at her standing in the moonlight, her fiery red hair cascading around her shoulders, the green dress enhancing all the good things about her body.

'You look fairly all right yourself,' she told him.

He walked over to her and kissed her. She was getting

501

used to being kissed by him in the open air. But she hoped she'd never get tired of it. She didn't think she would. She knew she'd found exactly what she'd been looking for. Love. Happiness. And the right person to share it with. Which, she thought to herself as she leaned her head on his shoulder, was something that could only be described as a totally win-win situation.

SHEILA O'FLANAGAN

All For You

Lainey Ryan's life is set to hit a stormy patch. After a string of failed relationships, is history about to repeat itself with the boyfriend she really thought was The One?

To add fuel to the fire, her estranged mother is returning to Dublin. A high-profile feminist, Deanna has always been dismissive of Lainey's choices – particularly in men. Her stern lectures are the last thing Lainey needs now.

There's more to her mother than Lainey knows, however. As she uncovers long-concealed family secrets, Lainey realises that everyone wants a happy-ever-after. But sometimes you need to let go of old dreams to find it.

Praise for Sheila O'Flanagan's bestsellers:

'A big, touching book sure to delight O'Flanagan fans' *Daily Mail*

'Her lightness of touch and gentle characterisations have produced another fine read' *Sunday Express*

978 0 7553 4387 4

headline
review

SHEILA O'FLANAGAN

The Perfect Man

A luxury Caribbean cruise. Warm, tropical days. Hot, sultry nights.

It's ideal for romance but for sisters Britt and Mia McDonagh it's something else entirely. Because Britt is the *Aphrodite*'s guest speaker, on board to talk about her bestselling novel *The Perfect Man*. She's billed as the expert on love, but since the break-up of her ill-fated marriage she's certain that the perfect man is just a myth.

Single mum Mia does believe in soul mates. Still secretly in love with her old flame, she's barely aware of other men, no matter how perfect they might be. As the two very different sisters spend more time together than they have in years, there's a danger that interfering in each other's lives will push them apart for ever. Or can the Caribbean work its magic even on families?

Back home, the last thing either woman expects is to encounter that elusive perfect man at last. Yet the time has come to put the past where it belongs, and finally risk everything to change the future . . .

Praise for Sheila O'Flanagan:

'Will, no doubt, once again race up the bestseller lists. Her lightness of touch and gentle characterisations have produced another fine read' *Sunday Express*

'Touching and funny' *Woman's Way*

'Hugely enjoyable' *Best*

978 0 7553 4381 2

headline
review

You can buy any of these other bestselling books by
Sheila O'Flanagan from your bookshop
or *direct from her publisher*.

FREE P&P AND UK DELIVERY
(Overseas and Ireland £3.50 per book)

Suddenly Single	£8.99
Far From Over	£7.99
My Favourite Goodbye	£7.99
He's Got To Go	£8.99
Isobel's Wedding	£7.99
Caroline's Sister	£8.99
Too Good To Be True	£7.99
Dreaming Of A Stranger	£8.99
Destinations	£7.99
Anyone But Him	£7.99
How Will I Know?	£8.99
Connections	£7.99
Yours, Faithfully	£7.99
Bad Behaviour	£7.99
Someone Special	£7.99
The Perfect Man	£7.99
Stand By Me	£7.99
A Season To Remember	£7.99
All For You	£7.99

TO ORDER SIMPLY CALL THIS NUMBER

01235 400 414

or visit our website: www.headline.co.uk

Prices and availability subject to change without notice.